FRACK!

A James Stack novel

A ruthless foreign conspiracy, corruption at the heart of government, violent anti-fracking protests and just 25 days to stop a deadly earth-shaking sabotage

Mark Wesley

For the family.
For letting me go missing in action for almost a year.

Published 2017 by Hornet Books

Paperback ISBN: 978-0-9957658-1-8

Hornet Books
www.hornetbooks.com
info@hornetbooks.com

Printed by CPI

Acknowledgements

You might think that drilling and hydraulic fracturing is all about brute force. It's true in part, but it also involves a lot of science and technical skill.

This story couldn't have been written without the patient advice of drilling supervisors Gary Taylor and Robert Chadwick - *in the face of what must have seemed remarkably dumb questions.* The technical detail about drilling, directional drilling and hydraulic fracturing they supplied are the bedrock upon which the action takes place.

Without hesitation, I take full responsibility for how that knowledge is used. To their peers I say, please don't blame them if you spot any errors.

All the characters within these pages are of my invention and don't exist in real life – with one exception. A journalist appears later in the novel. I was going to loosely base this character on one I had the good fortune to work with in my earlier radio career. I had to give him a name anyway so I ask if he wouldn't mind if I used his. I promised I'd be kind. And in particular, I promised I'd write him as I remembered him - several pounds' slimmer than he is today. Thanks David, hope you enjoy the story.

Introduction

FRACK! is a sequel to Mark Wesley's highly-rated first novel *BANGK!*. It's a hugely entertaining action thriller with a truly original plot and a mind-boggling con.

JAMES STACK: Ex-Captain Special Forces is broke again. Someone has emptied his Cayman Island bank account and he needs money, fast. Salvation lies in a bag containing a high value asset and a life-threatening chase across the Caribbean to find a villain willing to buy it for cash – no questions asked.

That's the easy part.

To recover his stolen fortune, Stack must infiltrate the UK fracking business. Nothing must halt the success of the drilling in Derbyshire if he is to ever see his money again. But sabotage deep underground is steering the drill bit towards a massive geological fault. Dormant for hundreds of years, it's about to get a catastrophic wake-up call.

In 25 days, they start to frack!

The Geology

The ground below us has many faults caused by the UK's turbulent geological past. Many are hidden deep below the surface. Most will remain quiet if left undisturbed.

These faults are places where earthquakes can occur.

Research suggests that the largest possible earthquake in the UK is around 6.5.

The British Geological Survey

Prologue: Fast Forward

Kingston, Jamaica: Night

'Put your gun down,' Stack told the driver. 'This side. Drop it on the floor, over here,' he said pushing his gun hard into the temple of the man sitting next to him on the back seat of the Mercedes.

The driver did as he was told and the gun fell to the floor at Stack's feet. He reached down and picked it up with his right hand. Gave it a quick and appreciative once over. Not as old as the relic in his left hand. It was a Browning Hi Power semi. Easy to spot even in low light. If the mag was full it had 14 nine mil parabellum's that kicked like a chorus girl.

He swapped it for the .38 pig-iron special and felt better for it.

As Stack pulled the backpack on to his shoulder once again, he gave the driver a simple instruction. 'Stay!'

He grabbed the businessman and dragged him roughly out into the street holding him in front like a shield, the Browning drilling into his temple. He'd got this far. The next bit was harder.

Both gangsters on either side of the car froze, their hands stalled over their weapons. The one sitting on the steps of the old wooden veranda back in the shadows began to grasp how things had switched. He went for his semi-automatic, but Stack turned the businessman around to show him the gun at his boss's head.

With the car door still wide open, Stack ordered the man to reach in for the briefcase. The guy hesitated for a second, but felt the muzzle pressing hard and painful and did as he was told. As he came back out with the case, Stack grabbed his collar and pulled him away from the limo, beyond the trunk and into the red glow of the tail lights.

That's when the driver suddenly popped up on the other side holding the old .38 relic. The businessman must have found it on the floor and tossed it over the seat while he was hidden from Stack. Clever move.

There were now four pissed-off Jamaicans waiting for the slightest opportunity to turn Stack into Swiss cheese.

'OK. Open the case.'

'What?'

'Pop the lid of the case open. Let's see what's inside.' Stack hit the back of the man's head with the barrel to emphasise, 'Now!'

Cowed, the businessman flipped the catches, and opened the lid, holding the contents out like a cigarette concession in a clip joint. Stack leaned round a little to take a look. The case was packed with wads of cash.

What happened next came straight out of the James Stack book of surprises. He gave the briefcase a hard kick, sending it tumbling upward, scattering a cloud of one, five and ten dollar bills into the air that came floating down like giant confetti in a Mexican carnival. Stack noticed there weren't many fifties or hundreds. Just as he'd suspected.

Out of the darkness people poured into the street grabbing handfuls of bills and ignoring the guns being pulled out of belts and shoulder holsters as the heavies turned their attention away from the money and back to Stack.

In the confusion Stack had legged it. He didn't look back. He just turned off at the first junction into another of Tivoli Garden's dangerous, un-lit back-streets. His foot hurt from the kick. He was only wearing running shoes, but that was what he needed right now - speed.

Day One

The ear-splitting noise of the heavy summer thunderstorm filled the sky from horizon to cloud covered horizon. It was as though Thor himself had slammed his hammer down sending gigantic pillars of granite rolling across the heavens.

Occasionally though, sunlight broke through wind-torn breaches in the boiling anvil-heads throwing fleeting shafts of yellow spotlights racing across the monochrome, rain drenched land below.

Sometimes a pool of sunlight would pass just right and you could make out the tall steel structure of the drilling derrick almost hidden behind Rebellion Hill, way across Hope Valley. But even then, you had to be high up on Shivering Mountain to see it.

***

Why was it always the two roustabouts who were late? They mooched onto the drilling deck still half asleep. Hands deep in pockets. Collars of their waterproofs up and shoulders hunched against the wind and driving rain. Like everyone else this morning, you could barely see their rain soaked faces under their hard-hats, tilted against the weather.

Their boss, the toolpusher, tapped his watch as they arrived. Not a good start to the day with the nightshift crew complaining bitterly about the delay – they'd already done their twelve hours.

The crew had been prepping the rig for weeks. They'd built the access road from Brough, driven it along a gully up to Donnybrook Hollow and then laid a wide pad of tarmac over the shallow bowl of the narrow valley floor. To one side, a square hole had been dug through the tarmac into the boggy ground beneath. This chamber sat directly under the steel drilling deck ten feet above. It was on this steel floor the crew had erected the iron lattice of the derrick that rose up over a hundred and twenty feet. The rig and all the other support gear shipped in by an endless convoy of trucks, took time and skill to construct.

Yesterday had been tense. The drilling supervisor finally got word that the drilling programme had received final approval from the GeoPower company execs and the all-pervasive Department of Business, Energy and Industrial Strategy. The Department of the Environment had also been required to provide a nod of consent.

The DoE had been one of the original objectors to the drilling site location deep in the heart of a national park in Derbyshire. The inconvenient fly-in-the-ointment though was the cement factory. Very visible and very dirty - and smack bang in the middle of the same beautiful and aptly named, Hope Valley.

GeoPower was finally given a 'James Bond': a license to drill and then frack for gas in the Upper Bowland-Hodder shale layer, where they hoped trillions of cubic meters of gas were waiting to be extracted.

The uncertainty of the geology and capricious nature of politics and public opinion made it a high-risk gamble.

As the wind and rain eased a little and a large break in the clouds allowed a shaft of sunlight to pass over the rig site, the drilling supervisor and proud Scotsman, Simon Harding, grabbed the opportunity and called out to the crew to gather round him on the rig deck. They were expecting this. Simon always gave a speech just before they started a new well. A pre-spud they called it in the oil business. The crew called it, Simon's Sermon.

'OK guys. This is it. You know the routine. You're all professionals or you wouldn't be here.' For anyone else that might have been enough. Clocks ticking. Time is money! Not Simon Harding, 'This is going to be a straight forward well. Drill down three thousand feet and then a deviation south west for twenty-three thousand feet along the shale layer.'

Some of the crew joked about just how straight forward drilling 26,000-feet actually was.

'Yeah, well, were not in the middle of the North Sea are we, so you can get your mothers to come and tuck you up in bed every night.' Harding berated them like a sergeant major chewing out a batch of new recruits.

'Anyway, you know the routine. Be alert! Any downhole problems, environmental incidents, equipment failures, accidents, let your boss know. Or find me.' Then he got serious, 'This well is only happening by the skin of its teeth. There's been opposition from just about every pressure group and local politicians since the Blackpool debacle. They just don't want us fracking. We mustn't screw up. No bloody earth tremors!' He gave the geologist a glare. 'Steve is confident the geological survey assessments will hold up. Nothing grim lurking down there.' It was more of a question.

Steve Gardiner stepped forward.

'We can drill from this nexus to all points on the compass, except the north-west.' The geologist swept his arm around to indicate the points on a compass with the flat of his hand like a rudder, but used his forefinger to pick out Shivering Mountain, hidden in a shroud of heavy rain far beyond Rebellion Hill, on the western end of Hope Valley. 'We're not going to drill in that direction so we're good to go.' Steve Gardener had the confidence that years of experience on wells around the world brings.

The drilling supervisor nodded and looked around the gathered crew. Good people. He knew them well. Most of them anyway. He checked his watch to note the time and looked up through the steel frame of the derrick towering above with its rows of drillpipe held firmly in place to one side. Each one waiting it's turn to descend through sand and mud-rock towards the gas reserves waiting to be prized from the stony grip of the shale layer thousands of feet below.

Satisfied they were as ready as they'll ever be, he gave a simple nod to the driller waiting to operate the winch inside the dog shack - the cramped shed to the side of the drilling deck that housed all the drill operating equipment.

As Harding turned to leave, the relative quiet of the power generators muted hum was suddenly broken by the noisy clatter of the giant diesel engine that powered the drawworks winch starting up. Like the winding gear of a coal mine, the winch raises and lowers the sections of drillpipe up and down the derrick.

Getting up to the monkey board gantry near the top of the derrick where the derrickman works is a long hard climb up a steel ladder bolted to the side of the derrick, especially on a storm swept day. That's why the derrickman took the dangerous but fast way up. The winch also raises and lowers the top drive, the bright yellow hydraulic motor that turns the drillpipe. Getting on and off was all about timing - and nerve. It was a hell of a rush as it raced to the top of the derrick in just a few buttock-clenching seconds. The derrickman clung to the cable as his feet struggled to maintain a foothold on the rain soaked, grease slicked motor. He skilfully leapt off as the top-drive passed the monkey board 100-feet up.

Simon Harding saw this and glared at the driller, who simply looked back through the dog shack window and shrugged. What was the drilling supervisor going to do? He didn't have time to fire the derrickman and hire a replacement. Simon Harding made a mental note to talk to him later as he took the steel stairway down to the tarmac pad and headed over to the Portakabin offices.

High above, the derrickman, Sean O'Brien, fought against the heavy squall that had just roared in, throwing wind and drenching rain whistling through the latticework of the upper reaches of the derrick. Leaning out into the void he used his shoulder to guide the first 90-foot stand of steel pipe into the clamps under the top-drive motor. He snapped them shut with both hands just as the winch snatched it away, lifting it high into the air and out of reach. The pipe was now suspended underneath and swinging freely.

A hundred feet below, the driller in the dog shack released the brake and the pipe dropped swiftly down – screeching to a stop just four feet above the drilling floor, still whipping and jerking like a fish on a line.

The two roughnecks struggled to bring the wet steel under control as they guided it towards the drill bit, held temporarily by iron wedges in the flat doughnut of the rotary table. They lined the pipe up and stabbed it down with a loud clang into the drill bit's threaded connector and screwed it tight using the heavy torque wrench. The drawworks engine revved again as the winch took the weight and the roughnecks hammered the wedges out.

The first 90-foot length of drillpipe hung free for a moment, rainwater streaming off the drill's diamond-hard cutting blades like an open faucet, before being ripped away by the wind. Then came another clatter of gears and increase in noise level as the powerful winch changed direction and the drillpipe began its journey down through the rotary table and into the cellar below.

Just before it touched dirt, the top drive high above started up and the whole 90-foot length of pipe with its three-coned tungsten-carbide granite-grinder began to turn.

They were planning on dropping the bore hole straight down vertically for 3,000 feet. Nothing clever, just a dumb iron drill bit chewing through the rock. The clever stuff would come later when they changed the direction of the drill bit from vertical to horizontal, cutting through the narrow shale layer for a further 23,000-feet: That would be in about six to eight days' time.

The rotating drill bit was lowered the last few inches before it finally touched the muddy clay. In seconds it was lost from view as it chewed down through the soft top soil.

There were 25 drilling days ahead of them before fracking would begin.

This was day one.

Grand Cayman

Same day

James Stack had woken to another idyllic day of vivid blue skies and turquoise waters lapping gently on the shore of Grand Cayman's Seven Mile Beach on the western side of the island. Behind the hotel, to the east, the morning sun, already a fierce, golden orb, was hanging in a rose blushed sky just an inch or two above the curvature of the horizon. It sent long shadows of the hotel and island palms pointing across the coral sand towards the tranquil Caribbean Sea.

From the balcony of his luxury suite three floors up, Stack watched Summer jogging easily along the shallows of the water's edge. Her blond hair, brightly contrasted against the golden tan of her slender frame. The subtle brunette highlights already bleached out by the sun. Even from this distance it was clear she was strikingly beautiful.

Stack fell in love with her almost instantly when they first met in London. He thought he was hardened against any romantic foolishness. He'd had his heart broken badly once before. And anyway, he had other things on his mind when he'd arranged their *accidental* meeting in London's Canary Wharf. But there was no avoiding it. Out of the blue, there she was. An unbreakable spell had transfixed him the moment he looked into those bright, intelligent, cornflower blue eyes. Beautiful and smart, who could resist?

The morning beach run had become her daily routine as they settled into their new island-paradise life. London and the Bank of England job seemed a long way away now, both in distance and time.

He had finally got his hands on his share of the take from a precious metals scam that had run into trouble a few years earlier. It amounted to a serious pile of cash that had been secretly stashed in a Luxembourg account. Somehow, the Bank of England con had worked and the Luxembourg stash was now sitting in a bank right there in the Caribbean island of Grand Cayman.

Which is where they all ended up; James Stack and his accomplices Charlie 'Hollywood' Dawson and Summer Peterson. A new life in paradise. For the time being anyway. At least until they get bored.

He had moved back inside to shower and get ready for another lazy day. *Who wouldn't want this life!* Stack could think of one person who was beginning to notice the shine wearing off. He was staring at him in the mirror right now.

***

In his mid-thirties James Stack was a tough, intelligent man most women would consider attractive; six foot, short, dark hair, deep brown eyes, with an easy smile that brought laugh lines to his sun-tanned face. Though he had a compassionate nature that didn't anger quickly, he could bring swift and violent trouble when events called for it.

His career path had followed an unusual curve. Those who knew anything about it would agree that the height of it was in Afghanistan, when, as a respected and decorated Captain in Special Forces, he had, with the help of his sergeant, Charlie Dawson, saved eight soldiers and five civilians – family members of a tribe whose mud brick compound they had allowed the British squad to use as a temporary forward base.

They had come under siege one evening during a raid

by a large Taliban force. It was only by luck that Stack and Dawson found themselves behind the outer ring of fighters. Half an hour earlier the two of them had slipped out under cover of a dark, moonless night to recce a ridge to the east. Distant gun shots and a radio message gave them the bad news. Being too far from base camp to receive any meaningful and speedy back-up, they had no choice but to do whatever they could, and quickly. With so much gun fire being thrown into the besieged squad's position they wouldn't last long. Darkness and surprise was Stack and Charlie's only advantage.

Moving stealthily forward, they crept up behind the nearest insurgents who, in one and two man units, had taken positions behind rocks and outlying walls in a ragged perimeter around the small settlement. The Taliban fighters didn't notice them because their attention was focused on sending as much ordinance into the British position as they could. They were doing an effective job with their battered Kalashnikov semi-automatics and old bolt-action rifles from the Second World War, but one at a time, knives silently took them out of the fight as Captain Stack and Sergeant Dawson crept and belly-crawled across dry dirt ditches and rock-strewn terrain until they reached each new insurgent position. Sometimes, the robed fighters put up fierce resistance in hand to hand fighting. But Stack and Charlie knew their business well and slowly took out each militant with blade and bullet. Even so, Charlie received a wound to his lower leg and Stack took a round in his side.

Despite this, they kept pressing their silent attacks against whatever targets presented themselves. More than an hour passed before their activity was noticed by the rest of the Taliban force. But the degradation of their fighting ability was already critical. They were now receiving fire not just from within the British camp but from random positions out of the darkness beyond their own perimeter.

Stack had radioed his men, alerting them to their activity, reinforcing their resolve as they broke free from the protection of the walled compound and stormed out towards the rebels. Several received injuries but the insurgents had had enough and melted into the night.

It turned out that between them, Stack and Charlie had taken out eleven Taliban fighters.

Many lives of their fellow soldiers and the local villagers had been saved.

***

The low point came after leaving the army. Stack's next career choice found him in the City of London working for the precious metal trading company, Metro Metals. This led him into the scam that earned him and his partner, Victor Avery, plenty of money, but ended up with Stack serving two of a four-year prison term.

Short of money following his release because his old partner, Avery, screwed him out of his share of the take, he teamed up with his old army buddy Charlie Dawson. Together they'd entered into an unprofitable bank robbing enterprise. Their modest venture got a big shot of adrenaline when they came up with the con to take on the Bank of England and pull off the world's biggest gold bullion robbery. They had help from the London end of a New York crime syndicate, but that's when things got crazy and dangerous.

Long story short. The huge proceeds from the Metro Metals scam was eventually prised out of Avery hands and into Stack's Cayman Island account. Cash that Stack was about to share with his ex-army buddy and 'business' partner, Charlie Dawson.

***

The taxi took him south along West Bay Road. A strip that follows the luxury hotel lined beach for a few miles. Eventually, it pulled off into Eastern Avenue and what passes for the suburbs of George Town, Grand Cayman's capital city. For a relatively wealthy country it still had its share of third world poverty, like most of the islands in the Caribbean.

Though the taxi was clean and the driver friendly, the old Toyota's suspension was shot years ago. The driver didn't bother to slow down or drive around the pot holes. He laughed when he looked in the mirror and saw Stack clinging to the strap above the door, his other hand holding onto his sunglasses that threatened to fly off with every bone jerking bang. The seats didn't seem to have much spring in them either.

'Ya first visit to our beautiful island, sir?' The driver glanced in the mirror and lifted his chin in a questioning tilt. His cheery Caribbean accent had more than a hint of Jamaican. 'Don't expect it's goin' ta rain. Don't never rain at dis time o' year.' He gave a laugh, ''Cept in de afternoon.'

'Yeah, it's my first visit, but I've been here for a few weeks now.' He shouted above the noise of the radio, tuned into some local music station. Reggae for a change! They all play reggae.

The driver's window was wide open and as he turned into Main Street he gestured broadly to the world outside.

'Lots o' pretty girls in George Town. I like 'em on the big side, you know what I mean? Plenty to get a hold of.' He chuckled and waved in the direction of a couple of brightly coloured dresses wrapped tightly around two voluptuous bodies. He spent a good few seconds staring as he passed by. He eventually caught their eye and they waved and shouted.

'Hey Short List.' They laughed, 'We gonna see you tonight?' They turned and shook their arses at him, then burst out laughing louder than ever, raising their hands for a high five.

They passed out of view as the cab turned into Edward Street with the driver still laughing.

'Dems me cousins.' He looked at Stack in the mirror again and winked, 'Them a bit too frisky for an ol' man like me.' He banged the steering wheel at his joke, then grabbed some bottled water he had jammed in the pocket of the door and took a drink, his knees holding the steering wheel while he used the other hand to change gear.

'What did they call you? Shortly?' The cheerfulness of the driver had lightened Stack's mood.

'Me name's Short List Williams for me sins.' He gave another laugh at the absurdity of it.

The taxi jerked to a sudden standstill as a young guy ambled across the road nodding his head to music only he could hear on his oversized knock-off Beats headphones. Stack straightened his sunglasses again and was thrown back into his seat as the taxi leapt forward. The driver was banging his fist hard on the centre of the steering wheel to get the horn to work.

'Hey, you crazy boy! What's de matter wid you man, you got a death wish or sometin'?'

'He can't hear you, you're wasting your breath.'

'Yeah? Well it make me feel better y'know. Wakes up de blood.' He gave a quick laugh and began singing along to 'I

Shot the Sherriff'. That's all he managed before pulling up abruptly.

'Dis'll be you right here man. Da pink building over there by the T-Shirt Shack. Dat'll be twenty dollars US, from door to door.'

'I was told it was only fifteen.'

'Who tol' you that? Some people, they get confuse don't they man?'

'The hotel. Apparently there's some kind of government taxi tariff?' Stack didn't want a row. 'Look, stick around and you can take me back. I'll give you fifty including the tip.'

The driver lit up at this.

'You give me hundred an' you got yourself a chauffeur for the day, sir.' He started to go into his island tour pitch, but Stack cut him short.

'Look, just stick around here. I'll only be about twenty minutes. We'll see about the tour.'

'Sorry man, I can't hang around here. Some sore-arse policeman'll give me parking ticket an' I can't afford to give him no bribe, you know what I mean?' He reached into the shelf under the dash board, pulled out a card and handed it to Stack.

'See? Dat's me number right dere.' He gave a big wide, reassuring smile, all teeth and gold fillings, 'Just call and I'll be by, quick as lightnin', sir.'

'OK, I'll do that.'

As the taxi drove off the driver leaned out of the window and shouted, 'Don't lose me business card now. You make sure you call me. Ya still owes me twenty.'

Stack acknowledged him with a quick wave and turned to enter the building. Banque Privée du Grand Duchy: Grand Cayman, according to the small brass plaque beside the door.

***

The assistant manager showed him into an office just off the main reception area. It was a small, smartly furnished room which served as a discrete annex for private clients.

'What can I do for you this mornin' Mr Stack?' She had an attractive Caribbean lilt to her voice. Petite, well dressed and very striking, Stack knew instinctively she was all business. A real professional. They all were in the Cayman Island banking community. Other people's assets were the country's stock-in-trade. Discretion their unspoken guarantee.

'I need to transfer some money into this account.' He handed a note over with Charlie's newly opened bank account details. It also had written on it a figure that made the assistant manager's eyebrows raise and her lips purse.

'OK. So you want that amount transferred into this account, Mr Stack?' she indicated with her beautifully manicured finger.

'If you wouldn't mind, eh...' he paused to read the name tag pinned to the lapel of her suit jacket, '...Mrs Roberts.'

She skilfully tapped the keyboard while watching the screen. Seconds later, Stack's Cayman Island account flashed up.

'Hmm.'

It was the curious tone in that simple sound that worried Stack. That, and the puzzled look on her face.

'Do you have another account with us Mr Stack?'

'No, that's the only one.' He tried to swallow but his throat had dried suddenly. 'Is there a problem? Have I given you the correct account details for Charlie Dawson?'

'The problem isn't with Mr Dawson's account. I'm afraid there seems to be a problem with yours.'

Stack's heart missed a beat and his breathing got heavier. He didn't want to ask the next question.

'What kind of problem?'

There was a pause as the assistant manager tapped the keys again. Whatever she did, the result was obviously the same.

'I'm afraid you have no funds in your account at dis time, Mr Stack.'

Stack shifted in his chair his head spinning. He tried to bring his panic under control.

'Wait a minute, what do you mean no funds. It can't just go missing. Show me.'

Mrs Roberts browsed the account moving the debit and credit columns vertically up and down on the screen. Then she turned the monitor so that Stack could see.

'As you can see, not much activity since this account was created. Small stuff. A hotel bill it looks like and a little cash. Then three days ago a substantial transfer that emptied the account.'

The only thing that transfixed Stack's eye was the huge number in the credit column that had shifted into the debit column in the row below. And below that – a line of zeros.

'Wait a minute! This is crazy! Where did it go? Can you reverse it?' Has the account been hacked?' Stack was desperate. The shock was difficult to contain.

'To answer your first question, Mr Stack, all we have here is a number. If you didn't transfer the fund we'll have to trace it as far as we can. Might take time. Until then, in answer to your second question, we can't reverse it.'

'So, has the account been hacked?'

'If you didn't aut'orise the transfer, I'd say probably.' She shook her head slowly, almost reverentially. 'That takes some doin'.'

Stack sat there for a moment. He felt trapped. He couldn't see a way out. 'Look, I need to speak to the manager. Get him in here. I want him to explain how someone could get into my account and empty it.' He suddenly found his anger. 'Now!' It was the voice of authority from an army captain used to giving commands to his squad back in the day. It didn't need the A/C to drop the temperature to frosty.

Mrs Roberts left the room and came back a few minutes later with the manager. She was a little older and heavier than the assistant manager, a hint of grey in her immaculately permed hair and steel in her deep brown eyes.

'Mrs Roberts here has told me about your problem, Mr Stack. I've already instructed our security people to begin tracin' the source of the transaction. It might take a little time.'

'Yeah, I've heard that already.' Stack was now trying to contain his anger. He wanted to lash out.

'What hotel are you stay'n at, Mr Stack? We'll get in touch with you when we have some news.'

'Listen, I have hotel bills to pay. What are you going to do about that?'

'I'm sorry, Mr Stack. We can't take responsibility for those kind o' tings. We aren't that kind of bank.'

Stack could see this was going to go round in circles.

'So I'm going to be out on the street until you get my money back? All I have is some cash in my wallet. What happens when that's gone?'

'Just give Mrs Roberts here your hotel details an' we'll get back to you, Mr Stack.' It was a firm and final offer.

Stack could see no way around it for the time being, so he gave his hotel address and room number. The manager made some reassuring noises and left the room. The assistant manager stood up and went over and opened the door again. She was showing Stack the way out – the bum's rush for a penniless client!

Outside the temperature had soared. The sun pressed down and the humidity closed in, almost suffocating him. He fumbled for the business card and tapped in the number on his cell phone. His hand was still shaking from the shock of discovering he was broke again!

Short List answered with a rant complaining about the long wait. He had a long list of important things he had to cancel because he'd chosen to do 'sir' a favour and stick around. Stack wasn't in the mood for this.

'Just get over here, now. I'm outside the bank.' He red-buttoned the phone and slipped it into his pocket.

The reggae back beat was playing loud on the radio as they drove back to the hotel. Paying scant attention to the road ahead, the driver rambled cheerfully on about all the people he knew in Grand Cayman.

'Just ask anybody. Ain't nobody don't know, Short List. I tell ya man, dere ain't nobody I don't know in this town.' He boasted, 'You want girls, or maybe sometin' to smoke, y'know, some ganja? Or maybe sometin' stronger? I'm y'man. It help you relax.'

He looked in the rear view mirror. The tension in Stack's face was obvious. 'Ya' look like you could use somet'ing to relax you right now, man.' He said with a laugh.

'For Christ sake, just drive.' Stack responded sharply and instantly regretted it. He didn't want to take his problems out on the driver. 'Look, just get me back to the hotel... please.'

Short List, still looking in the mirror, frowned and shook his head slowly. He turned back to the road and shrugged philosophically.

'No worry, sir. Anytin' ya' want. I not say nuttin else', me mout' is zip shut.'

Without missing a beat he swerved across the road, just missing angry, horn-blasting on-coming traffic. He slammed on the brakes and skidded to a halt outside a scruffy, open-fronted bar that looked as though it had just been thrown together with old drift wood and oil barrels, but had probably been there for years. A long thin Rasta guy was slouched in a chair at one end.

'Hey Gladstone, you got somet'in' for me, man?'

The skinny guy ambled over and leaned into the car, giving Stack an indifferent nod.

'What you look'n for, man?'

'Don' mess me, Gladstone, you know I got to have me supplies.'

'You got der cheddar dis time, man?'

Short List indicated with a nod to Stack in the back.

'Me salt right now, Gladstone, but he got de money he owe me for the ride.'

Gladstone looked over to Stack.

'Dat'll be twenty dollars, man.' He put his hand out towards Stack.

'Don't mind Gladstone, man. It come out o' taxi fare.'

Stack thought about it for a moment and then with a sniff of resignation, reached into his back pocket for his wallet. He counted out two fives and a ten and handed it to Gladstone.

Gladstone snatched the money and passed a small plastic bag to Short List who threw it onto the shelf below the dash.

'More time, braa.' But Gladstone was already heading back to his beer.

The rest of the journey to the hotel was uneventful: Life threatening and noisy, but uneventful.

A Good Day for Bad News

'Summer, where's Charlie?'

Charlie Dawson was a pale skinned, clean-shaven, round-faced, wiry guy with black, collar-length hair. Older, and a little shorter than Stack, he was trained in all the same fighting and survival skills as his boss. Lethal abilities that were at odds with his amiable, easy going personality. He'd been Stack's wing-man for years. It went back to when he was Stack's sergeant in the elite Special Forces. Stack had arrived in Camp Bastion keen but green. The battle-hardened Sergeant instantly liked this new officer and provided the support the younger man needed to become the sure-footed commander Sergeant Dawson knew he could be. It didn't take long.

Summer was sitting in the hotel lobby reading. She looked up from her book. The stress in Stack's voice and his uncharacteristically anxious behaviour worried her.

'What's the matter James? Something's wrong, what's happened?'

The tension was contagious and the effects instantaneous, like catching a rampant variant of flu virus.

'I need all three of us together. The bar. I'll explain when we're all together.'

'I think Charlie's there already.'

As they headed through the hotel atrium and out towards the Tiki bar on the beach, Stack muttered something about Charlie spending too much time there. He needed something to distract him. *Well this news will bloody well distract him*, Stack thought.

Charlie was already celebrating his new life as a wealthy

man, so when Stack and Summer arrived he welcomed them with open-armed enthusiasm.

'Come on. What 'ya having? I'm buying.' He turned to the bartender. 'Two bottles of champagne. The best stuff, mate.' A South London accent that stuck out like an iceberg in a desert.

Summer put a hand on his shoulder and purred in her easy Canadian drawl. 'Let's do that later, Charlie. I think James has something on his mind. Perhaps we should hear that first.'

She looked at the bartender and gave a gentle shake of her head. The barman got the message and put the champagne back in the cooler and moved on to another customer.

Stack leant over to interrupt the bartender and asked for bottled water and three glasses.

'We'll be over there,' he said gesturing to a table far away from other guests.

Like most of the other tables, this one sat in the sand under the shade of a palm tree. In any other moment this would have been perfect: quiet music from the bar and the sound of shallow waves washing lazily onto the beach just thirty metres away.

Summer and Stack looked awkward, sitting up-right in their chairs, leaning forward, elbows on the table. Only Charlie was slouching back in his seat. Relaxed, legs outstretched, arms hanging down. Not a care in the world.

'Come on guys, why so serious? Look around you. Bloody perfect! And you're sitting there as though you've had all your toys taken away...'

He stopped there and began to straighten up as the penny started to drop.

'What's up?' You're starting to worry me now.'

The bartender arrived with a tray and set the frosted, ice

filled glasses and sparkling water on the table. Stack waited for him to finish and thanked him as he left.

He gave it a moment, gathering his thoughts. He'd been wondering how to tell the others. There didn't seem to be an easy way.

'Summer, Charlie. We're broke.'

Summer was ready for bad news. Only Charlie laughed.

'Nice one Jimbo. Come on, let's get a proper drink and we can tell each other jokes all afternoon.'

The silence that followed spoke more eloquently than any words Stack could think of.

Charlie slowly eased himself forward and rearranged himself into an up-right position, focussed and serious.

'Christ, you're not joking are you, Jim,' he said quietly as he reached for the bottled water, poured himself a glass full and took a long drink.

'What happened James?' Summer put her hand on his arm. 'What happened at the bank?'

Stack spent the next ten minutes recalling the visit to the bank in George Town and the shock of being told the account was empty. Charlie and Summer sat there listening in stunned silence. When Stack was done they batted questions and assumptions back and forth, no-one quite able to grasp the enormity of their predicament.

'Well, I could think of one person who is capable of screwing around with bank accounts.' Stack said. 'He did it for me when he moved the scam money out of Luxembourg and into the account here in Grand Cayman.'

'You mean Blackstone?' Summer speculated.

'What was that call you got a few of weeks or so ago?' Charlie asked. 'Wasn't that from him?'

'You mean the 'call this number' message? Yeah, that was Blackstone. This business has got his fingers all over it.'

'But you didn't call the number. You ignored it,' Summer reminded him. 'You didn't want any more to do with Blackstone. None of us did.'

Blackstone had provided a discrete and highly unconventional banking service for Stack. Each contact was initiated by a phone message, 'Call this number'. They never met and he didn't know his real name. What Stack did know was that Blackstone moved amongst the great and the not so good in the banking world. He made things happen. Opened doors. Funds magically disappeared from one account and turned up in another. The kind of things James Stack needed to happen in order to retrieve his money from the precious metals scam. Whoever Blackstone was, his handle was an extremely appropriate choice, taken from the brilliant nineteenth century American illusionist, Harry Blackstone.

'Perhaps we don't have quite as much independence as we thought we had,' Stack said as he pulled his cell phone out of his pocket and thumbed his way through to recently received calls. He clicked redial and listened as the '*call this number*' message was played back. He tapped the number into the keyboard, green-buttoned the phone and waited. Just three rings later a thin metallic voice answered. The condescending tone was discernible even over a tenuous, three-thousand-mile digital connection. The voice of someone who knew only one person would call him on this unique, one-off, private number. And why.

'Do I have your attention now, Mr Stack?'

'What have you done with my bloody money, Blackstone?'

'What have I done with your money?' Blackstone repeated as though it was some kind of philosophical conundrum. 'Yes, it must be worrying.' Blackstone was relishing this. 'How are you enjoying your newly acquired impoverishment?' He searched for another word, 'A little short are we, Mr Stack?'

What passed for levity was suddenly brushed away as Blackstone's tone became threatening.

'You ignored me, Mr Stack. I don't like being ignored. As a result, what was a trivial personal problem has now become your, much bigger problem.' Blackstone found this amusing, 'You know what they say, a problem shared is a problem doubled.'

'What was it you wanted me to do for you, Blackstone?' Stack's earlier formality with Blackstone had been terminated. He knew that would irritate him.

'Ah, yes. The problem.' Blackstone ignored the slight. 'The three of you have proved quite adept at fixing problems. I'm impressed. And I'm not easily impressed.' Blackstone paused for a beat, 'Here's where I find myself. I'm rather embarrassed to admit that a recent investment on behalf of some of my clients is proving less than profitable. A great deal of money is at stake. Money belonging to people who I really don't want to make unhappy.'

'I don't see why this should interest me, or what you expect me to do about it?'

'A little patience, Mr Stack and you'll see your part in it in a moment.'

Blackstone went on to explain that, as a result of recently discovered shale gas deposits found buried deep beneath large areas of the UK, he had advised close financial parties that this was an almost risk free opportunity. So much so that he had even added a chunk of his own fortune to the pot and invested the lot in shares in a relatively new oil and gas exploration company called GeoPower.

And then it all went belly up. It took only the most modest of tremors near Blackpool. A tiny quiver. Not much more than the movement of a passing train. That was all that was needed for the local pressure groups to cast doubt on the whole hydraulic fracturing business. Politicians quaked, licenses were suspended and share prices raced the drill bit to the bottom.

'And why should I care about that?' Stack cut straight to the chase.

'Because, my dear Mr Stack, I have taken all your money and invested it in the very same shares. You could cash them in of course, but by now they would be almost worthless.'

Stack took a moment to absorb this news.

'It doesn't make sense. Why you would do that? Why take my money?' Stack noticed Charlie and Summer watching him and gave them a bemused shrug of his shoulders.

'You have one chance to recover the value of your shares – and of course mine.'

'Oh? What kind of chance?'

'GeoPower began drilling earlier today, up in the North Midlands. Derbyshire to be precise. They have been given a conditional license. Any hint of seismic activity when they start to frack and they'll be shut down. Permanently. The only energy they create will be the burning of worthless shares by broke investors. On the other hand, if we can ensure a successful result and large quantities of gas are brought to the surface, the value of yours and my shares will rise - significantly! You can sell your shares, get your money back and perhaps even make a profit.'

'I don't need to make any more money. I just want my money back, Blackstone.' Stack's anger boiled over. 'I'm warning you, Blackstone. I'll find you, no matter how long it takes. You will return my money!'

'Locating me would be pointless. I don't have your money, nor do I have enough to replace it.' Blackstone remained irritatingly calm. 'You want your money back? You have just one chance. GeoPower has already begun drilling. I advise the three of you to return to the UK and ensure they are successful.'

'What the hell do I know about drilling for gas? What do any of us know? It's a stupid plan.'

'No more ridiculous than the one you devised to rob the Bank of England. You're a resourceful man Mr Stack. You'll come up with a plan. Don't waste any more time. The clock is ticking. The drill is drilling.'

***

It took a little while for Stack to explain what he had been told, and what Blackstone expected of them if they wanted to see their money again. The only one who had any experience in the oil business was Charlie. Ten months as a maintenance engineer on a rig in the North Sea.

'So, to summarise our position. As of now, I don't think we even have enough money between us to pay the hotel bill let alone buy airline tickets back to the UK. And I'm afraid, Charlie, that means you're still as broke as when we started. We all are.'

More silence, then Summer pushed her chair back from the table and stood up.

'In for a penny then. I agree with Charlie. We need something stronger than water.' She headed off, barefoot, back to the bar.

'Good girl, Summer,' Charlie said appreciatively. Then he too got out of his chair. 'I'll be back in a minute,' There was something about the look on his face as he made his way to the hotel. Amusement?

It turned out to be quite a bit more than a minute, by

which time the Tiki bar was beginning to buzz with late-afternoon drinkers just returning from island tours. Some, only three days into their holiday, attempted jokey banter with their new best friend, the bartender.

A whisky on the rocks and two chilled beers were dripping condensation onto coasters by the time Charlie returned. He sat down and the three of them raised their glasses to the perfidious nature of luck and life in general. Charlie was holding a scruffy backpack on his lap and a grin on his face.

He unzipped the larger of the pockets, reached in and pulled out an old T-shirt wrapped around something heavy. He placed it on the table, pushing the glasses away to make room.

Summer was bemused. Stack though, coughed a startled laugh of recognition. He knew what was coming.

Careful to keep it concealed from other eyes, Charlie lifted a small part of the cloth. Even under the shade of the palm tree that drooped lazily over the beach, the low afternoon sunlight found a small chink of space between the huge leaves and a tiny slither of sunlight reached down to spark a brilliant flash as it caught an edge of the bar of gold bullion.

Charlie was enjoying his moment of triumph as he looked at the others and declared with characteristic optimism, 'I reckon this should solve our money worries. All we've got to do is sell it.'

Roustabouts and Scoundrels

A thousand feet beneath Hope Valley the tungsten-carbide teeth of the triple-cone bit pressed hard against the tough sedimentary rock, scraping off thin cuttings with every turn.

Every now and then the GeoPower crew pulled the drillpipe out and lined the well with concrete sleeving to prevent contamination of any aquifer it passed through. At thirty-two inches across, this was the widest part. From now on the borehole got narrower as they drilled deeper into the Earths' mantle.

It was 19.00 hours in Grand Cayman. Midnight in the UK. The second day of drilling was about to begin.

***

They'd moved the conversation inside the hotel to a quiet corner of a bar, away from any inquisitive vacationers. The lighting was so low-key that the room was almost dark, apart from a dull glow spilling from ceiling recesses.

On the way, Charlie returned the backpack to the hotel safe. Summer carried a copy of a British newspaper she'd found, after noticing a small headline about protests at the site of a new drilling operation.

'Look at this James.'

She unfolded the paper and laid it out on the low table in front of her. They read it together, a short piece about GeoPower written the day before drilling was due to commence.

Angry protestors had set up camp outside the security fence of the GeoPower drilling site. They'd been there for weeks, hand-cuffing themselves to the entrance gates and throwing themselves in front of trucks that lumbered to and from the site. On one side of the argument they were heroes. On the other, they were a bloody nuisance.

'Charlie, you were out in the North Sea. Tell us what you know about drilling.'

'Well, Jim, I wasn't just doing maintenance. I was more of what they call a roustabout. A rig-hand. Haul that over there, clean this bit over here. It was tough work, mate.'

Charlie's eyes glazed as his mind wandered onto his specialist subject, movies, and the reason he'd earned the nick-name, Hollywood.

'Shame about Elvis wasn't it?'

Stack and Summer just looked at Charlie in dumb bewilderment and wondered how you could skip from oil drilling to the King of Rock & Roll in the same breath.

Roustabout? Charlie offered in response to the blank looks, his hands out in supplication, 'An Elvis Presley movie? You must have heard of it?'

Still nothing.

'Well anyway, it had nothing to do with oil rigs. Roustabouts are what they used to call casual workers in travelling circuses. Elvis played someone called Charlie something or other. Good choice for a lead character.' Charlie revelled in the reflected glory.

'So, can we move back to drilling, please?' interjected Stack. 'What can you tell us?'

What followed was Charlie's recollection of who did what on a rig. Mainly, what he knew about the crew on the drilling deck.

'Starting from the top you got the drilling supervisor. He

is God's representative on Earth and in overall charge of drilling operations. If anything goes wrong, he's the guy that knows how to fix it. He's also the guy in charge of safety and hiring and firing.

'The toolpusher is in charge of the actual business of drilling, making sure all the crew and equipment was good to go. Replacing stuff as needed which might include crew members.

'Under him you've got your driller, who's in charge of the actual drilling. He spends most of his time inside the dog shack where he operates the winch brake, looks after the mud pumps, measures the drillpipe. That sort of thing.

'You got a derrickman who spends a lot of his time up on his monkey board high up in the derrick throwing sections of pipe onto the elevator clamps under the top drive. That's the motor that turns the pipe when they're actually drilling. He also helps out mixing the mud slurry that they pump down through the drillpipe to lubricate the drill bit. When the mud comes back up the outside of the pipe, it carries the rock cuttings with it. I think they have to check that stuff to see what kind of rock they're drilling through.'

Stack interrupted. 'So they drill more or less by feel?'

'Not quite. If you hang on, I'll get to that in a mo.' Charlie was enjoying his moment in the spotlight – teaching the boss was a rare thing. Something to be drawn out and relished.

'Down on the drill floor you've got your roughnecks, there's two of 'em, who handle the drillpipe. They've got to screw all the drillpipe together to make what they call a drillstring. That's a tough job. You can't imagine how many ninety foot stands of pipe they have to screw together to reach right down the length of a really long borehole, fifteen thousand feet deep or so. And they have to take the drillstring out quite often to replace the drill bit. They call it tripping and it takes bloody ages to pull it out and stick it back down the hole again.'

Charlie didn't wait for a reaction – he just carried breathlessly on. 'Now, about how they know what's going on down the hole. There's all kinds of clever kit they stick on the end of the drillpipe to tell 'em where they are, you know, what direction they're drilling. Sometimes they want to steer the drill so it's going along horizontally. That's what the directional driller does and it's a highly skilled job.

It was Summer's turn to interrupt.

'But why do they want to make the drill go horizontally? I thought they just drilled down, you know, vertically, to reach the oil or gas.'

If Charlie had been wearing a gown, he'd have stuck his thumbs in the lapels and pontificated like a professor to an audience of students.

'You've got to understand that any shale layer that holds oil or gas generally runs horizontally. It's not necessarily a thick layer but it can be very wide and long. So instead of drilling loads of wells down to it, it's cheaper to run a single hole through it for as far as you can. They have to put an enormous pressure on the shale to fracture it to make it release the gas. That's the fracking business everyone talks about. And they frack the whole length of the borehole. The part of the hole that's in the shale anyway.'

'But isn't fracking dangerous? That's what everyone seems to be saying.'

'Look Summer, I think it's dangerous if you don't take care of where you're doing it, but these people know what they're doing. They're not going to frack where there's a fault in the ground for instance. That would be asking for trouble.'

'So how do they know if there are faults in the ground or not? Or where the faults are?' Stack asked.

'Jim, I'm not an expert. I think they survey the area somehow. Plot out where everything is. Then they make a plan of where they're going to drill and where they're not going to drill. That's all I know.'

Summer read from the newspaper.

'According to the woman in this report - she must be one of the protestors - anyway, she says that fracking contaminates the drinking water. The natural reservoirs.' She put the paper down. 'Why would they let them do that, Charlie?'

'Yeah, I'd heard that as well. Look, they wouldn't let 'em frack if they didn't think it was safe, would they?'

Stack butted in, 'I'm more bothered about rescuing the share price and recovering the money right now, so can we just stay with the technical stuff, please?'

'Oh yeah, I nearly forgot, the mud-slurry. They actually use that to transmit instructions to and from the bag of tricks at the end of the drillpipe, Christ knows how they do that. Stop me if I'm boring you,' he let out a sudden burst of laughter at his unexpected wit. 'Boring. Get it?'

Stack and Summer groaned, but they raised a glass to Charlie's knowledge before moving on to the more immediate problem of being broke and what to do about it.

***

One thing was certain. As long as they didn't check-out of the hotel, they could just keep signing tabs and put everything on the rooms - for the time being anyway.

Hunger drove them to the hotel's restaurant, a large low-ceilinged space with fifty or more linen-covered tables.

Each was placed in an artfully random fashion under discrete pools of gentle tungsten light. It was already busy with bustling waiters serving hungry guests. The best tables next to the large plate glass windows that looked out to the tropical waters had already been taken. Leather-bound menus forensically examined and choices discussed.

Once seated at one of the few remaining tables near the busy kitchen service door, they continued to press Charlie about drilling. It turned out he'd already given them everything he knew. It was sketchy, but compared to what they knew before, they were one hundred percent wiser.

Then, Summer's curiosity about Charlie's gold bar finally got the better of her.

'Come on, I've been really good about this. You dump a bar of gold in front of me like it's a piece of cheese and I've said nothing. I've been waiting for someone to explain. Fess up. It's got to be from the Bank of England. But I thought it all went back into the vaults after the heist?'

Both Charlie and Stack spoke at the same time, each trying to give their version of the story.

Summer broke in, 'OK Charlie, it's your gold. You explain.'

'And keep it short Charlie,' Stack said. 'Just the headlines.'

'Yeah, well, it was all pretty lively after the gold had been removed from the Bank. During the gun fight on the river there was an accident and a bunch of gold bars got lost in the river. One got lost to me. I hid it in my backpack. It's been in the hotel safe ever since we got here.'

'Why didn't you mention it before, Charlie?'

'To be honest, Summer, with a fortune sitting in the bank here, it simply wasn't on my mind.'

Stack shook his head in amazement, 'Until Charlie placed it on the table this afternoon, I'd completely forgotten about it.'

'Well, it looks like it's going to rescue us.' This was Summer at her most charmingly innocent, 'As Charlie said, all we have to do is turn it into cash.'

'Think about it Summer. Who do we know that would do that?' Stack didn't want to patronise her. He'd already had this conversation with Charlie but even he hadn't fully grasped the difficulty.

'We can't just walk into a bank and ask for its value in dollars. It's got Bank of England hallmarks all over it. They're gonna get a little suspicious,' James added sardonically, 'The kind of people who'd be interested in buying it from us are more likely to be crooks and villains.'

'Bit like us then.' Unintended irony from Charlie.

'These aren't going to be easy people to find.' Stack added grimly. 'Unless we marched through George Town waving it around. That'd get the local bad guys crawling out of every dive and gambling joint. But I don't think we'd survive their interest.'

They sat in thoughtful silence for a while. Charlie asked a passing waiter to refill their glasses.

'Same again mate.'

Stack stopped him. 'No, forget that. Let's take this conversation back outside. I could use a walk right now.'

'Me too.' Summer said, 'Come on Charlie. Bit of fresh Caribbean evening air. Do you good.'

After the air-conditioned cocoon of the hotel restaurant, the humidity out on the beach struck them like a hot flannel. They walked close to the placid water's edge through patches of pale yellow brightness cast by beachfront hotels. The light didn't reach more than a few yards into the water. Everything beyond that to the horizon was black. The horizon itself only visible when distant thunder-clouds gave off the occasional muted flash of sheet lightning.

Stars filled the sky above them. A perfect tropical evening.

'So, let me see if I've got this right. We're broke, but with potential liquidity of hundreds of thousands of dollars all tied up in a single bar of gold.' Summer laughed, 'If we were in the City of London I could probably find you a dozen scoundrel's that would do a deal for the gold. No questions asked.'

Summers' past experience in the commodities market gave her an insight, but not a unique one. James Stack had spent a few years skimming profits from precious metals transactions himself. Until his partner, Victor Avery, threw him to the mercy of the Serious Fraud Squad.

'We need someone who can put us in touch with the local villains. You know - the right kind of villains.' Charlie had a knack for cutting straight to the core of the problem. Summer picked up on the theme.

'That's right. We need someone who has contacts. Someone we can trust.'

'Yeah, but where do you find someone like that? Who do we know on the island? No one.' Charlie said.

Stack stopped suddenly and stared out to the horizon. The other two had taken a couple of steps further along the beach. They turned back to join him.

He pulled his wallet out of his pocket and began thumbing through the cards and paper that fattened it. Summer was the first to speak.

'What's the matter, James? You lost something?'

'Hang on a second.' He turned round to catch some of the dim ambient light coming from a hotel, 'Yeah, here it is.' He held a card in his hand triumphantly. 'Short List Williams.'

'Who?' Charlie and Summer chorused.

'Short List Williams! He drove me into George Town this morning. He reckons he knows everybody.'

'Do you believe him?' Summer asked.

'Can you trust him? Charlie added.

'And what kind of name is Short List Williams?' It was a reasonable question from Summer.

'In the first place, I think I believe him – up to a point. Can we trust him? Probably not. We'll have to be careful. Come on.'

Stack turned to walk back the way they had come. Charlie and Summer caught up and drilled him with questions

'Look guys, I'm going to call him. Get him to come over. You can meet him and make your own minds up. But it's the only contact we've got right now.'

***

Stack had left his cell phone on charge in his room. He returned with it to the Tiki bar where Charlie and Summer waited. He thumbed in the number and green-buttoned the phone. A few rings later, over the sound of loud music and party noises, a familiar voice answered.

'Dis is Short List Williams' taxi service. Cheapest and best on de island. What can I do for ya?'

Rebellion Hill

The nightshift was just like the dayshift: you go deeper, you add more drillpipe. Everything clicks. Routine is established. It's amazing how quickly it can all turn to crap.

They were down over two thousand feet when the driller first noticed a problem around two a.m. It started with a flicker of a mud slurry gauge, followed shortly after by a steady increase in pressure. Why do bad things always happen at night?

The drill bit made easy going of the first mudstone layer and had just passed through to the tougher sandstone. Grinding down on the rock face with the weight of the long drillpipe pressing hard on it. Progress was good. It quickly drove below the geological shear that separated the two layers.

It was the weakness in that geological flaw that water from nearby saturated porous rock exploited. First just moisture, but very quickly, thin jets under extremely high pressure, forcing its way through the wall of the well, mixing with the mud slurry that was returning to the surface. More liquid was coming back up than they were pumping down the hole. The noise of the heavy machinery outside suddenly doubled as the dog shack door was kicked open. It was a panic-stricken mud engineer. He came in yelling that something was wrong. Water was diluting the mud slurry. The volume was increasing. They've either drilled into an unknown reservoir or there had to be a break in the borehole wall deep underground. The driller kept a worried eye on the pressure gauge and told the assistant driller to 'get the drilling supervisor - and hurry!' Out on the deck the crew were standing-by to halt drilling.

Deep underground, a section of the borehole wall was being quickly eroded by the force of the water. If it wasn't brought under control quickly, they'd have a bigger problem on their hands. They call it a 'Kick'. Explosive pressure underground capable of firing the heavy drillpipes out of the well like rockets. It's as dangerous as hell, and expensive. Already, another digital gauge on a monitor screen showed the weight of the drillstring was measurably lighter. A sure sign the upward pressure of the incoming water was lifting it. Everyone on the rig deck could feel the vibration.

The drilling supervisor arrived. He quickly assessed the problem and yelled out an urgent command. 'Stop drilling! Close the blowout preventer. Kill the well!'

The drilling assistant had already turned the mud pumps off ready for the next dramatic step. The driller's finger hovered above the button that operated the rams in the blowout preventer down on the well head in the cellar below them. It was the only sure way to save the well. He punched the button hard. Nothing seemed to happen at first.

The crew had moved off the drilling deck, away from danger. Vibration was causing the deck to shudder and the steelwork of the derrick to rattle alarmingly. High above, drillpipes, loosely packed in the finger racks, clanged against each other. The derrickman had already taken the fast way down using the Geronimo escape line.

Still nothing! By now the ram should have closed tightly around the pipe, but the flow was still increasing.

A tide of mud coloured water had started spraying up through the rotary table and washing over the drilling deck.

He hit the off button to reset the valve and then punched the button again. The ram was either stuck or the hydraulic system was down. He rushed out of the dog shack, grabbed a fourteen-pound hammer and climbed down the steel stairs to the well-head below. Flickering strip lighting was bathing the big red blowout preventer in a cold pallid light. The driller placed his hand on the side of the giant valve stack. The increasing vibration from deep below ground could be felt through the heavy cast-iron casing. But he could feel something else. The hum of hydraulic fluid under high pressure pushing against an unyielding object. The hardened-steel piston of the ram was jammed in its cylinder. With the water pressure about to go critical. Only crude and brutal force remained an option. He took one great swing with the hammer and slammed it with a solid clang into the side of the cast iron ram housing. A definite change in tone from the hydraulic fluid as the ram moved - then stuck again.

A wave of fear swept over him. He knew the consequences if this didn't work. One final chance. He grabbed the hammer with both hands and swung it hard against the stack with all his strength. The impact sounded like a V8 engine-block being dropped onto the steel deck of a ship – but it was followed at last by a satisfying whirring as the ram closed tight against the drillpipe. The result was instantaneous. The vibration ceased and what passed for silence fell on the rig. Only the low rumble of diesel generators could be heard from somewhere on the site.

It took a couple of days, but eventually the flow slowed and then stopped. The only question that remained once they restarted drilling operations: why didn't the blowout preventer work and who was responsible? One person was fired, leaving an opportunity for advancement up the food chain for several of the drilling crew.

When the dust had settled, a new vacancy had been made for a roustabout.

The Facilitator

'What's this all about, man? You drag me out'o me way when I got business to attend to back in George Town.' Short List complained, 'Who gonna pay the fare for me comin' out here, man?'

At first, he played the beleaguered victim trying to spin a little extra money out of the journey. But his tone quickly changed as he realised this could be the lucrative tour of the island he had offered Stack the day before.

'Look Short List, we don't want a tour of the island. When we spoke on the phone last night, did I mention a tour of the island?' Stack was trying to get him to focus. 'I simply asked if you could help and there might be something in it for you.'

'I couldn't understand you, man, it was too noisy where I was hangin' out.' Short List quickly recovered, 'I mean, at me office.'

It was mid-morning and they were sitting at a table out on the beach again, near the Tiki bar. A cheery 'Hey, Short List!' from the bartender as they passed confirmed Short List's credentials as the guy who knew everybody.

'Listen Short List, when you said you know lots of people on the island, what did you mean by that?'

'Well, like I say, I know a lot'a people.' He looked at Summer and Charlie and shrugged in mock incredulity at Stack's apparent lack of understanding.

'What kind of *people* Short List? Just your old-school friends and family, or the kind of people that get things done. You know. Business people. Politicians... Other kinds of people who do business – shall we say – differently?' Stack hoped Short List would start to get where he was going with this. He didn't want to come right out and say, '*villains.*'

There was a pause as Short List looked at the three of them. His head swivelled from Charlie to Summer and then back to Stack. Weighing them up. Reassessing his assumptions. He gave a very slight nod of his head and a smile crossed his lips. He relaxed back into his chair, legs stretched out casually.

The relationship had suddenly changed from prospective taxi fares to something else. Something potentially much more rewarding.

His arm was resting on the table and without raising it, he pointed a finger at Stack.

'What is it dat you want?' Suspicion in his voice, 'What we talkin' about here, man?'

It was Stack's turn to reassess the man in front of him. Despite his easy-going, breezy Caribbean personality, he wasn't a fool. But could he be trusted? He looked at Charlie and Summer to gauge their opinion. He could tell they wanted him to go for it.

'OK. Cards on the table, Short List. We have something that we need to exchange for US dollars. It's not an exchange that can take place…' Stack searched for the right word, '... shall we say, legitimately.'

'What we talkin', man? Drugs or somet'ing?'

As dishonest as the deal he was seeking to arrange was, the dirty business of drugs made Stack's skin crawl.

'Christ! No! This is something completely different. We need you to introduce us to someone who might be interested in a precious metals transaction.'

'Go on,' he encouraged Stack. 'I still here ain't I?'

Without explicitly mentioning the gold bullion, Stack went on to explain what he had in mind.

'The item in our possession is worth quite a lot of money, and we want to get as much for it as we can.'

'What's in it for me? I need to make somet'ing.'

'Five percent of anything we make.'

'I do it for twenty an' no less.'

'Ten. Max. If the business is concluded quickly.'

'I gotta know what it is you got. Me contact will want to know.'

'Can you trust your contact?'

Short List gave that some thought.

'You gonna have to take a risk if you want the man to deal wit you. Whatever it is you got.'

'It's gold bullion.'

Short List's eyes widened and he sat forward in his chair and started to get up.

'Gold?' He seemed impressed. 'Den, me betta get goin'. I got ya number. I'll call ya later today.'

He was already leaving as he said it.

Charlie was delighted it went so well. Summer wasn't so sure.

'Be careful, James. We could walk into a trap. We don't know these people. We could lose everything - even our lives.'

'Yeah, it's risky. But I don't think we have an option.'

Stack had an idea that would take some of the risk out of it.

'Look, has anybody got any credit left on their cards? Mine's down to the last hundred at the most'

He eyed Charlie.

'Don't look at me. I'm stuffed.'

'How about you Summer?'

'The same. Two or three hundred at the most.'

'OK. Here's what we're going to do. We'll pool our

credit. I want you both on a one-way to London. Get up to Derbyshire. Summer, see if you can join the protest camp outside the GeoPower drilling site. Charlie. Check out any jobs that might be going on the rig. You can make a start on-line now. You've had experience, so you're in with a chance.'

Both Summer and Charlie were alarmed at the idea of leaving Stack behind to handle the bullion deal.

'No way, Jim. Who's going to get you out of trouble if it all goes pear-shaped? You're going to be dealing with local villains. Dangerous sods.'

'Thanks Charlie. That's really going to cheer Summer up.'

'I don't need Charlie to tell me how dangerous it is, James. I'll go, but I agree with Charlie that he should stay. It's the safest way.'

They argued back and forth, weighing the pros and cons. But Stack insisted his plan was the best way to go. Getting people into GeoPower and the protest camp was a critical starting point. The drilling was already underway and who knew when they'd start to frack. If they wanted to recover their money, nothing must interfere with the GeoPower operation.

Summer could see how getting into GeoPower might be useful, but what was the point of joining the protest camp outside?

Having been a captain in Special Forces a few years back, mission prep was instinctive and effective. But Stack had an ability to see a plan almost as though it was a three-dimensional object he could rotate and view from any angle. A rare skill. He turned the mental image a few degrees and explained his thinking to Summer.

'If I shared the objectives of the anti-fracking protesters and I knew that if the drilling operation that's going on right now could be derailed somehow by slowing them down, or even getting them to abandon the well, I would attempt to do just that.' He could see that Summer understood the point.

'You think they may have someone inside GeoPower. Perhaps an employee on the drilling crew? A sympathiser?'

'Exactly. If they do, they may well be in regular contact with him or her. Try and get yourself into the inner circle if you can. Charlie, see what you can find out on the inside. Talk to the drilling crew. Ask questions. Make friends. Eyes and ears. You know the routine.' As a sergeant in the same Special Forces unit as Stack, Charlie had been a reliable partner who could be trusted to get the job done. If there wasn't a job going at the GeoPower site, he'd find a way to engineer an unexpected vacancy. He was very resourceful.

***

Later that afternoon Stack got a call from Short List. A meeting had been arranged – more of a beauty parade. A credibility check before getting face-time with the money man.

'Tonight. Be ready.'

Gold Rush: Grand Cayman

This time Stack took the front seat, next to Short List. The ride hadn't improved and it looked like one of the headlights was out. The coast road heading south towards George Town was pretty good, but even the smallest jink in the surface felt like a bone jarring pot hole in the old Toyota. Like in the UK, they drive on the left-hand side. It's how they drive in most Caribbean countries. But with so many North American vacationers in right-hand-drive rentals, it could be life threatening. Especially at night, when the partying starts, and cars unexpectedly swing out of junctions and straight at you on the wrong side of the road.

***

The afternoon had been spent helping Summer and Charlie organise their air tickets back to the UK. They got lucky and found a BA flight to Manchester. The GeoPower drilling site was only twenty miles or so south east of the airport. It took two credit cards to cover the fare. They had counted out what little cash they had between them – $420 and change. They needed cash for hotels and car hire to tide them over until they achieved their separate goals. The plan assumed they'd get lucky and be embedded quickly. Stack hung on to a $100 and the gold bullion. He planned to join them back in the UK as soon as a deal had been done. What the gold was worth and how much he got for it were two entirely different numbers. If GeoPower screwed up and the shares became valueless, the gold bullion was their final asset. They couldn't take the risk of transporting it back to the UK, so he'd get what he could right here in the Caribbean.

All three were now set up and mission ready on the first part of James Stack's plan to recover his money. Again!

***

'Where's dis gold you want to sell, man?' Short List asked warily. He'd been eyeing Stack up and down from the moment he got in the car, seeing him differently. He'd moved him from the list marked 'tourist' to another labelled 'trouble'.

He drove casually, elbow out of the open driver's window. Sitting almost at right angles across the seat, smoking. There was a lot of knowing head nodding as they spoke, his attention shared unevenly between Stack and the road.

'Where are we going, Short List?' Stack tried to appear as relaxed as the driver, but his Special Forces skills were primed and ready if things got complicated.

'George Town. We're meeting me contact, like I told ya, man.'

Stack left it there. No point in pursuing it. He'd find out soon enough. They drove through the outskirts of the capital, coming in by a neglected back road, its rough, gravel foundation covered in patches of what remained of the old asphalt surface.

Old wooden bungalows with verandas clinging to the front squatted in neglected lots on either side. Some were populated with small groups of people from the neighbourhood, sitting, drinking, listening to music and staring suspiciously as they drove passed.

A few more turns and they were headed deeper into downtown and the busy harbour quarter. Eventually, the Toyota turned into Wahoo Close and then into a large derelict lot next to a car park. It was just fifty yards away from a water-side dive called, Randi's Rum Bar, according to the small red and blue neon sign hanging in the window. They parked up and waited.

'Dey'll be here momentarily,' Short List said looking at his watch. 'Ya got somet'ing to show them I hope, man.' He sounded a little anxious now.

Stack found the worry in his voice, contagious. His own radar was beginning to ping nervously.

They were facing Randi's Rum Bar and didn't notice a car pull into the lot, lights off, until it parked up alongside of them. It just sat there for what seemed minutes, but was probably only seconds. Finally, a guy got out, opened the rear passenger door of the Toyota and got in behind Short List. While he was mostly hidden in shadow in the back of the car, he had a good clear view of Stack, who was back-lit by the signage from the bar across the road. The new guy spent a few seconds eyeballing Stack, assessing whether he could be trusted and if things got tricky, whether he could be handled without resorting to the aging Rossi .38 special hidden in the belt of his pants under his short-sleeved silk shirt.

Short List made the first nervous introduction. 'Hey Montez, dis de man me tellin' ya about…'

Before he could finish, Stack twisted his body round as far as he could and leaned back against the door so he could confront the man in the back.

'I'm, Stack. That's all you need to know right now.'

'Dats right, Montez. Dis here is Mr Stack. Like I tell ya, he got a proposition for ya boss.'

'Show me.' That's all Montez said.

Stack stared at Montez for a beat and then slowly reached inside his pocket for his cell phone. His fingers swept across the screen and selected the images icon. Choosing one picture, he held the phone towards the guy in the back seat. The light from the screen revealed Montez to be not as black as Short List. Wiry, half beard and slick-backed hair, more Latin than African. Eyes hidden behind dark glasses.

'What's that?'

'It's what I have to sell.'

Always cautious, Stack figured it would be prudent not to carry such a valuable object into a potentially dangerous meeting. Better to just take a picture of the gold bar. As further evidence of its authenticity he'd taken the precaution of placing it on a copy of the day's local newspaper. The headline proved the image couldn't have been downloaded randomly from the internet.

'Where is it?' Montez didn't waste words.

'For the time being, just be satisfied that it exists and it's on this island.'

'How much do you want for it?'

'That's a conversation I'll have with your boss.'

Stack tapped the cell phone off, the screen dimmed, and Montez sat in deep shadow once again.

'Wait here.'

He got out and moved away from the parked cars in the direction of Randi's Rum Bar. He put his cell phone to his ear as he walked. From inside they could hear nothing, but it was clear he was conveying what had just happened to his boss and waiting for orders. Every now and then he'd turn a little and glance back at the car.

They watched him as he put the phone back in his pocket and returned to the car.

This time he came over to Stack's door and opened it.

'You, come with me.' And then to Short List. 'Wait here.' More Miami than George Town.

Stack followed him as he headed across the main road up the two steps to the wooden veranda where a few drinkers sat at tables playing dominoes, and into the darkness of the bar.

'Wait there.'

Stack watched as Montez made his way through the shabby interior filled mostly with locals and a few tourists. He ended up at a table tucked into the far corner overlooking the harbour. Barely supported by a spindly wooden chair a large man was filling his face with some kind of sea food. He didn't stop eating as Montez spoke to him. He merely leaned hard against the wheel back of the chair to peer around Montez and get a better view of Stack in the gloom over by the door. Satisfied, he turned his gluttonous attention back to the unfinished business of the dish of the day.

Montez turned and beckoned Stack to come over.

He took his place at the table opposite the big man who, apart from a grunt of acknowledgement as he sat down, continued to ignore him. He was shaved bald and had a tattoo creeping out of the open-necked gold-striped shirt. Dark blue against dark skin in a dark room, it was hard to make out what the tattoo was. Even in the tropical humidity of mid-summer, in a bar that seemed to have no discernible air conditioning, the man was still wearing a leather jacket. Stack felt hot and claustrophobic just watching him as the man paused only to dab the sweat off his face with a paper napkin.

The smell of the shellfish or whatever it was he was shovelling into his mouth was nauseating. Eventually, the big man pushed the plate away, gave his face another wipe and leaned back in his chair.

'You've got gold for sale.' The American accent surprised Stack. He nodded a confirmation.

'Show me'

Stack retrieved his cell phone and brought up the picture he'd shown Montez. The big man stared at it for a while. The background chatter and loud music in the bar gave the conversation a surprising amount of privacy.

'Tell me about it.'

'It's an old family heirloom...'

The big man interrupted. 'I don't want to know how you got it. Tell me about the gold. How many ounces?'

'400. Twenty-eight pounds of 24 carat gold.'

'That's a lot of gold.' The big man seemed impressed. 'What do you want for it? How much?'

'It's actual worth is in excess of $450k.'

'That's not what I asked.'

'At least ten – 15 percent.'

'That's quite a hit you're prepared to take. Where is it? I want to see it.'

'Do you have that kind of money?'

'I'll get you some money, once we've finished negotiating. But I want to see it right here, in front of me.'

Stack leaned back in his chair and took another look at the sweaty big man sitting in front of him – weighing him up. Then he took a quick look around the bar to see if anybody was taking an interest in their conversation.

'OK, it's in the car. Wait here.'

'I ain't going nowhere. Montez, go with him.'

They crossed the street into the darkness of the derelict lot, walking in silence until they reached the car. Stack had allowed Montez to walk a little ahead, just half a step. He'd noticed the bulge under Montez's shirt as they walked over to the bar earlier. Either Montez had a colostomy bag or the man was carrying a gun. Probably a small revolver. It was a clumsy way to hide the weapon. Perhaps it was intentional. An unspoken threat.

As they reached the car, Stack grabbed Montez's arm and swung him around, pushing him hard against the Toyota. His other hand pulled the gun free of Montez's carved leather belt. It happened so quickly Montez had no defence. He was a slim guy who depended on the gun to enforce his point of view.

Stack took a step back, holding the weapon at waist height. After the initial shock Montez quickly recovered. He relaxed back against the car and slowly folded his arms, his head cocked to one side. The arrogant demeanour of a man who didn't feel threatened.

'Now, what you do that for, man?' A whiny appeal to Stack's better nature.

'What's going on Montez? Who is that guy?'

'You're wasting your time. He doesn't have that kind of money.'

Stack had already guessed that bit of news, but hid his surprise at Montez's unexpected betrayal. 'Why am I here then?'

'I thought you were a tourist, not a player.' As Montez spoke he pulled a cigarette pack out of his pocket and lit up. 'You need a bigger organisation to handle that kind of gold.'

'What kind of gold do you think it is?'

'Not the kind you buy at Tiffany's.'

For the first time Stack noticed the Spanish flavouring the local accent.

'Go on...'

'There are people that would take an interest, but not on this island.'

'Where then?'

'Havana, Cuba. I can arrange it.' He nodded to the north as though Cuba could be seen from the car park.

'Montez.' Stack chewed the name over. 'It's not a Cayman Island name.'

'You find all kinds of history on this island. Real multicultural mix, man.'

Stack signalled Montez to move away from the car with a wave of the gun, then opened the door and climbed in. Short List's eyes widened and fixed like a laser on the old Saturday night special. Outside, Montez, cool and fearless, leaned through the open passenger window. He gave Short List a brief nod and turned to Stack.

'I guess the gold ain't in the car, no?'

'You think?'

'We need a bigger player for this kinda deal. I have people in Cuba that can handle it.'

Stack noted the 'we'. Looked like Short List just got himself a partner, because if Montez wanted a cut, it wasn't coming out of his end.

Short List turned the key. The motor struggled, then burst into life. One headlight came on. With his foot on the brake the old car gave a forward lurch as he put the shift into drive.

'What about the big guy back in the bar? How's he going to take it?'

They turned to look back at Randi's Rum Bar. The big guy had struggled onto the veranda. Two heavies were with him peering out into the darkness. The two guys stepped off and started towards them. They looked serious enough. Stack didn't want to wait around to find out.

Montez leaned in again. 'My people are serious business men. You're wasting your time on this island. Short List knows how to get in touch with me.'

'Yeah, braa, me got ya number alright.' Short List replied sceptically.

Montez stepped back and the Toyota very nearly put a black stripe on the tarmac as Short List jammed his foot down on the gas pedal. The tyres spun and they were gone in a shower of broken black top, gravel and smoking rubber.

Short List kept glancing at the gun. 'Don't look like it went too good, man.' He sounded disappointed. Looked like his percentage was starting to evaporate.

'A false start. The guy was just a small-time crook. He didn't have the kind of money I need.'

'What kinda gold ya talkin' about? How much ya got to sell?'

Stack took the cell phone out and showed the picture for the third time. The reaction was unexpected. Short Lists eyes nearly popped out of his head and the car swerved across the road, just missing an old truck careering past on the other side. He fish tailed a couple more times to the accompaniment of horn blasts from slower targets.

'We need to get to Jamaica, we're wasting our time here, man.'

'We?'

'I got to introduce you to me relatives. They know a t'ing or two about gold.'

'How are we going to get there? It's over 250 miles from here and apart from the gold bar and a few dollars, I'm broke.'

'As long as you cover it when you sell the gold, me brudda will get us there.'

'Your brother? Can you trust him?'

Short List burst out laughing and smacked the steering wheel.

'He's family. Course I can't trust 'im.'

While Short List continued with his commentary on the short comings of his relatives, Stack had a closer look at the weapon he'd just inherited. The Rossi .38 was old and rusty. It looked like it had been left out in the rain for years. He clicked open the barrel to see what, if anything was loaded in the six chambers. Just three bullets - probably as ancient as the weapon. Might be more lethal as a cosh. Still, Stack thought, with the amount of gold he was trying to get rid of, the sight of the old Saturday night special might be enough to get him out of trouble if it came looking for him.

As they arrived back at the hotel, the smile on Short Lists's face didn't improve Stacks's mood.

'Be ready tomorrow mornin'. Bring the gold wit you dis time.'

***

The rest of the evening passed easily. Stack spent a little while at the Tiki bar drinking beer from a frosted glass and chatting to the bartender. For some reason it wasn't busy, just the occasional hotel guest looking for company or couples taking their drinks over to tables on the beach, away from the lights. Looking for privacy.

Stack remembered the barman saying 'hi' to Short List that morning. He was curious. This was a chance to learn something about his new partner.

'So you know Short List?'

'Short List? Sure, who doesn't on de island.'

'Is he local? I mean, he talks about relatives in Jamaica.'

'Most of us got relatives in Jamaica. They used to run

the island, but it all change when Jamaica got their independence in '62. So the Cayman Islands are a British dependency now. Dat's cool. They leave us alone. Mostly.'

'It's an unusual name – Short List.'

The barman burst out laughing.

'You ain't heard?'

'Heard what?'

'The story 'bout how he got his name?'

The bartender topped up Stack's glass and continued rearranging bottles, cleaning glasses and occasionally serving as he spoke.

'Story goes he was born in Jamaica. His mother tried to come up with a name for the child but couldn't settle on anyt'ing. This went on 'til the day she gave birth. So she wrote down some names. The ones she liked the most. So, after she gave birth, she folded the paper and handed it to the midwife an' tol' her to take it to the registrar an' get 'im to pick a name.'

His flow was interrupted by more customers. Refills. Two white wines and a half-hearted attempt at chit chat with Stack. He wasn't in the mood so they moved off and the bartender continued.

'So, she gave the paper to the midwife, did I tell you that?'

'Yeah, you got that far.'

'OK, so the midwife handed the paper to the registrar. He unfold it and he look at the names. Then he asked the midwife which one he should choose. Well de midwife, she hadn't seen what's on the paper, so she just tell him, why don't you pick the one on the top? So that's what he did. An' that's why he's called Short List.' The bartender could barely get to the end of the story for laughing. Stack joined in.

'That's very funny. It can't possibly be true.'

'If it 'ain't true,' the barman said still laughing. 'How did he get his name? You tell me, man?'

'You mean it's not a nickname?'

'No, that's his name – Short List Williams.' The barman burst into renewed laughter. More customers arrived to interrupt the moment, giving Stack and the bartender suspicious looks. Stack gave a grin and a thumbs up at the story as he moved away from the bar and headed back up to his room.

***

As it turned out, Short List's brother was a busy man and two uneventful days passed before he was available. Eventually Short List called to say he'd be there in a couple of hours. Around ten o'clock that morning. Be ready.

Stack had breakfast and retrieved the backpack holding the gold bullion. At 28 pounds, it wasn't a light thing to tote around.

As he had no means to pay the hotel bill, what he didn't want to do was alert them to the fact he was leaving. If the deal went through he'd fly to London from Jamaica. He'd pay the bill later – maybe. He went back up to his room and stuffed what few things he had into the bag, including Montez's old hand gun. He'd arrived with nothing a couple of weeks ago, and that's how he was leaving.

The backpack looked completely innocent when he walked out to the front of the hotel with it to wait for Short List.

Ten o'clock arrived and went. Nothing.

He let another half hour pass before calling him. As he reached for his cell phone the taxi driver suddenly appeared on a path between a large planter filled with exotic palms and a tan coloured outbuilding that looked like some kind of storage room. He was in a hurry.

'Where's your taxi?' Stack hadn't expected Short List to be on foot.

'I parked it up. Come on, dis way, man.'

Stack was even more confused as he followed Short List through the foyer of the hotel and out to the beach. He stopped for a moment, looked at his watch and just seemed to be enjoying the view out across the beach. He started walking again along the sand beyond the Tiki bar, to the lot by the side of the hotel where, tucked away under some trees, the water sports and boat rental franchise hut was located. On the sand in front, various watercraft were beached – waiting to be enjoyed by fun-loving vacationers: twin-hulled Hobie Cat sail boats, wind surfing boards, kayaks, Waverunners and jet skis. The usual paraphernalia you can find at any beach-side hotel in that part of the world.

Stack joined Short List as he negotiated with one of the young sales guys. He was wearing standard beach bum issue, beaten up jeans shorts and, as a nod to the nature of his job, an orange life vest. They seemed to know each other which didn't come as a surprise. He turned to Stack.

'You got a card?'

This was tricky. He had a Visa card, but whether it would stand up to a credit check was another matter. He handed it over anyway.

He took Short List to one side while the guy put the card through the standard retail stress test – authorisation.

'What's going on? Are we rowing over to Jamaica?'

Short List took another look across the beach. And then at his watch.

'Don't worry. I got it all under control.'

'The guy handed a sheet of paper to Stack. A form that had to be signed. He wanted Stacks' room number. He still had the key in his pocket and showed it to the young man. In return he handed them both orange float jackets.

They followed the guy down to the water's edge and helped him push a Waverunner into the sea. He went through a cursory safety check with the small craft bobbing in the shallows. Both of them were wearing shorts, Short List wore a faded T-shirt, Stack, a short-sleeved cotton shirt over which was strapped the backpack. He took it off, pulled the life-jacket over his shirt, snapped the plastic buckles closed and slipped the bag back on again. Short List put his foot on the running board and pulled himself up and over onto the front seat as if he was mounting a horse. The guy took the key fob dangling from the nylon string strapped around Short List's wrist and plugged it into the ignition. It was a safety thing - you fall off, the key is yanked out, the engine slows to idle. He pressed a button and the Yamaha engine fired up with a low purr.

Stack got on behind Short List. He'd done this before. They had these as part of Special Forces mission tools. The backpack gave the rental guy a problem. He'd be happy to take it back to the hut, but Stack waved him away. As far as the rental guy was concerned it was Stack's problem. He waited, knee deep in the warm water as Short List gunned the engine and pulled away. The Waverunner bucked through the surf and out into the smooth waters beyond. The rental guy turned and headed back to the hut.

The spray was cool against Stack's sun-baked skin, sweltering under the brutal heat of the tropical, late morning sun. Behind him, the beach was already a hundred yards away.

'What's the story Short List?' He had to shout above

the whine of the engine and smack of the fibre-glass hull against the swell. 'What the hell are we doing out here in the middle of the ocean?'

The answer became immediately apparent and literally out of the blue. Short List was pointing at it as he leaned the Waverunner towards the object now dropping down out of the sky. A small single engine Cessna 185 floatplane already low at two hundred feet and making an approach that would place it not far from their position.

Short List kept the boat a safe distance back from the aircraft's landing path, the noise of its propeller already growing louder. The distinctive sound drew the attention of the rental guy back at the hut. He was used to light aircraft flying back and forth, following the water's edge at a thousand feet or so. This was different. He turned and stepped a few paces forward, shading his eyes against the glare of the sun. This was something he hadn't seen before, not round here anyway. Others on the beach were beginning to stand and point it out.

After a long downward swoop to bring the aircraft to a glide just above the water, the pilot dropped the plane the last couple of feet. The seaplane's floats pounded the sea causing a large bow wave that caught in the propeller, completely engulfing the aircraft in a salty spray. It bounced two more times and finally slowed enough to make a turn towards the Waverunner standing three or four hundred yards from the beach.

Back at the hut the rental guy ran towards the rows of beached watercraft, dragged a jet ski into the water, leapt aboard, fired the engine and headed, skimming and bouncing at full throttle towards Stack and Short List.

The Waverunner was closing the gap cautiously between it and the old Cessna, as it manoeuvred slowly towards them, engine idling. They came alongside as the pilot opened the door and stepped down onto the float under the shade of the wing, waiting to help them board. He held the Waverunner to steady it against the slow wallowing motion of the plane and introduced himself to Stack.

'You must be Mr Stack, the man with the gold.' He held out a hand by way of a hand shake and steadying arm to pull Stack onto the float.

'I'm Eric, Short List's better looking brother. Welcome aboard.' He roared with laughter at the joke at his brother's expense. Stack nodded an acknowledgement as he leapt across and made his way up the single step to the cabin. Before climbing in he removed the backpack, heaved it onto one of the rear seats, unbuckled the life vest and handed it to Short List.

Short List stepped over to the float without much difficulty then turned back to the Waverunner and yanked the key out of the ignition. He pushed the craft away from the Cessna with his foot and watched as it idled slowly towards the beach in a wide circle that would eventually bring it back. They had to be on their way before that happened. He threw the two life-vests into the water, climbed into the cabin and took the right hand, co-pilots seat.

Eric, still out on the float, looked up and spotted the fast-approaching jet ski.

'Looks like we got some company.'

'I reckon dat'll be one of the rental boys wonderin' what's goin' on. We better be makin' a move.'

Eric climbed into the cockpit, closed the door, slid into the pilot's seat and started the engine. Without any kind of brake, the plane started to move gently away. He did some cursory checks while strapping himself in. Set the flaps and pulled the throttle back a little. The seaplane was pointing away from the beach on a reasonably calm sea. Just a small chop. He watched for signs of wind rippling the surface and turned the plane into it. Ahead was miles of endless sea. He pulled the throttle fully back, the engine pitch rose to an angry scream and the propeller chopped noisily into the hot Caribbean air.

The effect was instantaneous. Acceleration pushed them back in their seats as the aircraft bounced forward, engine roaring at a deafening pitch. The floats cut through the water, sending spray into the prop which threw it back over the plane, drenching the cockpit windows and reducing visibility to zero. Not a problem – there was nothing ahead but open water. The pilot hung on to the yoke, kept an eye on the airspeed indicator, waited and waited as the speed reluctantly increased. It was as though someone had thrown an anchor into the sea. The plane kept leaping like a horse jumping fences, but the water just wouldn't let them go. Until at last, with a final aggressive roar, the plane pulled itself free of the ocean and headed slowly up and away. The last drops of spray were whipped away by the slip stream, and suddenly the view was clear. They were already well above the sea, leaving Seven Mile Beach far behind.

Down on the water, the rental guy was struggling to wrangle the Waverunner back to the beach. He looked up at the sound of the Cessna 185 making a 180 degree turn overhead. Watching until it was just a speck on the eastern horizon, heading for Jamaica 270 miles away.

Miss Direction

Drilling a well bore straight down doesn't take much more than a long pipe and a sharp drill bit. The really clever stuff happens when you want to turn the borehole from a vertical to a horizontal heading, and keep it going that way for thousands of feet. People who do that kind of work are specialists called directional drillers and are well known in the industry – mostly.

Sometimes one comes along with all the right qualifications. Their CV is packed with experience. But they turn up for day one and, among the drilling crew, the name doesn't ring a bell.

Debbie Blain didn't see this as a set-back. They'd just have to get to know her.

Her office was in the dog shack, the shed on the drilling floor which she shared with the driller. Her equipment, though, was much more hi-tech than the heavy industrial machinery he used. Once it was set up and running, the computer monitor she stared into would display the telemetry her systems received from the set of electronic sensors behind the drill bit way below ground at the business end of the drillpipe. The left, right, up or down direction of the well bore was achieved using a steerable drill bit responding to pulses it received. Actuators behind the drill bit would then send pulses back up to confirm the drill's precise position.

What made the system unusual was that the directional pulses weren't sent by wire or radio signals. Instead they travelled like ripples through the mud slurry that was pumped down to lubricate the drill. As the pulses travelled up to the surface from the drill bit deep underground, they were converted into a digital signal that could be displayed as numbers on the directional driller's monitor. Short of having X-ray vision to see through thousands of feet of rock, it was the only way they could be sure of the drill bit's exact location. Debbie Blain used the same system in reverse to send instructions back down to control the direction of the drill.

All very clever. But this peculiar technology was GeoPower's Achilles heel. A determined predator could use it against them.

***

During construction of the GeoPower site, many specialist services were contracted to install the long list of equipment all drilling rigs need to operate; heavy machinery, tanks to hold the mud slurry, generators, miles of drillpipe; portable cabins for offices, maintenance, canteen and accommodation; computer technology and the associated high bandwidth broadband.

At a glance, there was nothing unusual about the last two items to give away that something was different - that a specification had been changed.

Like all old technology, the crude analogue mud-pulses were almost tamperproof. But new is good. Data wranglers don't want valves and levers. They want binary code. Ones and zeros. So they put the old-world analogue pulses through a box-of-tricks called an analogue to digital converter, which screws around with it and spits it out as a new-world digital signal - a signal that can now be processed by a computer and displayed on a computer monitor. But that made the data vulnerable. Now, it could also be hacked into from a distance. Apart from the drilling crew in Hope Valley, there was no reason to suspect anyone else would be interested in such information.

But deep within a processor, fitted to a tiny circuit board hidden in the analogue to digital converter, lay an algorithm written by clever young minds. Code that was bought and paid for by a conspirator in a far-away country. It was a simple routine that had one very particular and devious purpose.

***

In a room nearly 1,300 miles away, a young man sat at a computer screen. Sitting next to him was a highly experienced directional driller. Displayed on a screen before him were the GeoPower geological surveys and drilling plans. These included the details of the proposed steerable drilling equipment. He knew exactly where GeoPower was drilling, when they intended to divert the drill from vertical to horizontal, and what heading they intended to drive the drill towards.

He had another set of surveys and geological data which he had laid over the GeoPower plan. The small cross in the centre of this new graphic lined up perfectly with the coordinates of the vertical bore hole in Hope Valley. From that point, two lines of dashes fanned out in quite different directions. One, shown on the GeoPower plan, headed through the shale in a south westerly direction for 24,000 feet. It ended at the place where they planned to start fracking. The other travelled the same distance but almost 90 degrees away to the northwest. This line of dashes ended in a cross-hatch shaded area that was sliced in two by a thick red line. The red line was marked with the legend: 'Mam Tor Fault', and recorded the location of a lethal geological crack in the rock strata over four miles down. This seismic anomaly lay just 20 miles southeast of the city of Manchester.

Mam Tor was the official name of the 1,700-foot-high prominence known to the locals of Hope Valley as Shivering Mountain.

***

After five days the well bore had reached down 3,000 feet. Drilling stopped as the crew spent the next couple of hours laboriously pulling the drillstring out of the ground. Unscrewing each 90 foot stand of pipe and leaning it against the finger racks at the top of the derrick.

Under instruction from Debbie Blain, the crew fitted the steerable drill bit, sensors and pulse mechanisms. When it was all screwed together the whole thing was almost 700-feet long and was already suspended down the hole. The crew then refitted the stands of drillpipe again until the drill bit touched the bottom of the hole, 3,000 feet below.

Back in the dog shack, Debbie Blain received the first mud pulse telemetry that confirmed the orientation of the drill and matched the coordinates on the GeoPower drilling plan.

The sabotage began when she typed in an instruction to turn the drill from vertical to horizontal in a south westerly direction.

That instruction passed through the hidden algorithm, which automatically rewrote the command before sending it pulsing down through the mud slurry to the drill bit. Slowly, as the drill chewed through the rock, the well bore began to bend away from vertical. It was a process that took quite a distance to complete. By the time the pipe was at last lying horizontally, the drill had travelled a further half mile.

To provide confirmation of its position, pulses were sent back to the surface and again, converted into digital data. As the data passed through the hacker's algorithm it was altered once more so that when it displayed on Debbie Blain's monitor, the numbers were exactly what she expected to see if the drill was heading southwest. Everything appeared normal.

***

In another time-zone, the young computer hacker and the directional driller could also see the data coming from deep below ground in Derbyshire. Zooming into the track, so that a hundred-foot section filled the screen, they noted with satisfaction their hack was working and the drill was under their control.

Debbie Blain's instructions had passed through their algorithm hidden in the processor, ensuring that way down at the far end of the drillpipe, the sensors received a completely different set of commands to follow a different course – their course.

Nobody at GeoPower, in their London headquarters or on the drilling rig, were aware that instead of drilling towards their target, safe from danger in the southwest, the tungsten-carbide drill bit was grinding its way remorselessly northwest, towards the massive geological fault line. The place where two large rock formations pressed hard against each other under colossal tension. One side pressed down by the enormous weight of Man Tor above - the other side pulled down with it and needing only a small intervention to cause a powerful upward jerk.

Dormant for centuries, in 20 days the fault will be given a highly destructive wake-up call by the explosive pressure of hydraulic fracturing. The resulting shockwave as the stresses are released would travel fast and violently towards the crowded metropolis of Manchester. An event that could cause death, injury and destruction on a massive scale and bring to an end all further attempts to frack for gas in the UK.

It was a plan of exquisite subtlety and ruthlessness, designed to benefit a single, foreign organisation run by a ruthless Russian businessman. It was Mikhail Ulyanin's intention that his company, Severgaz Postavka, would become the principle exporters of gas to the UK.

Home Coming

After an uncomfortable eight hour, overnight flight, Charlie Dawson and Summer Peterson landed at Manchester airport in northern England at 6:35 am. With a tail wind, the plane had landed 20 minutes early but was now docked and motionless at the jet-bridge, ready for disembarkation.

Passengers pressed against each other, tired and impatient along the aircraft gangways, hand baggage dragged out of overhead lockers and jammed into the slither of space between them and the person in front. Cell phones rescued from crumpled pockets were now switched from flight mode to full local reception. It seemed to be a race to see who would connect first: the noisy winners already chatting triumphantly with their friends and relatives. And still they waited, fretting and frustrated.

For Charlie, his main concern was Passport Control. He and Stack had left the UK unconventionally in a small business jet that had been arranged by Blackstone. There'd been a cursory passport check at Biggin Hill airport in Kent, just outside London, but that had happened right after the Bank of England caper when a barge full of gold had been stormed by a fully armed SWAT team.

The detective in charge, DSI Deakins, had allowed them to leave because Stack had provided information that led Deakins to scoring several major collars. As a result, the dog-end of DSI Deakins lacklustre career was given an uncharacteristically triumphant parting shot. This was despite his belief that Stack and Charlie had been directly responsible for a series of unsolved bank robberies during the previous year. Would the goodwill hold up? Or would they be waiting to grab him as he passed through UK Border Control?

He'd know soon enough. Shuffling off the plane through a seemingly endless rat-race of corridors and stairways to reach the passport check point. Summer to International, Charlie to UK control. Just a handful of bedraggled passengers stood in line ahead of them.

He waited on the white line in front of the passport desk, his weight shifting from one leg to the other in a restless, anxious motion. Finally, he was beckoned forward by an equally tired and irritated officer. Charlie tried a friendly 'Good morning' as he handed his passport over. No reaction. Wasted breath. It took a worryingly long time to flick through the pages of the document, pausing every now and then and turning back to re-examine a previous page. He thought the game was up when the officer turned to his computer screen and tapped some keys. But in the end, he simply handed the passport back to Charlie and gave a nod for the next customer back at the line to come forward.

Summer was already waiting in the customs hall. She'd had no trouble. Her VISA was for permanent residence in the UK. In her view, the only benefit that marriage and divorce to a philandering Londoner had brought.

They headed through a customs point manned by two uniforms; a woman and an older man. The woman officer watched them pass with disinterest. The older man, after seeing the beautiful blond in the company of a scruffy loser, with envy.

***

Shortage of cash was a problem. They planned to hire two separate cars to give each of them some independence, but Summer thought they'd get away with just one which they could share, at least until they were close to the rig site. From there Summer would get out and approach the protest camp on foot, telling them she'd thumbed a ride from Sheffield.

Charlie would take the car the rest of the way to the gates of GeoPower's drilling site. He'd already contacted them, telling them he would be in the area within a day. With Stack's help, he'd concocted a CV, some of which was based on fact. He was surprised how good it looked when he attached it to an email.

A quick reply offered a job as a roustabout if he could get there asap. It was the print-out of the reply that he showed to security at the gate. A pen tip ran down a list of names on a clip-board and stopped, presumably at his name. He was waved through and told to check in at the administration office a few hundred yards up the newly-laid asphalt road. There he would be given the full health and safety induction before going onto the rig.

It was two o'clock and Charlie was back in the drilling business.

There were no such formalities at the protest camp. They either liked what they saw or you were back on the road. In a tent city with no amenities, filled mainly with student drop-outs playing bongos and bedraggled women in baggy clothes wearing an odd mix of spirit-of-the-forest accessories or fancy dress, Summer, tanned and still dressed for the Caribbean, almost got sent away with a flea in her ear, until one of the guys took an interest.

It was 2.15pm and Summer was in the protest business for the first time.

The only person earning money now was Charlie Dawson. James Stack was still cash poor and gold rich.

Gold Rush

Jamaica

Nobody could take their eyes off the gold bar laying on the beaten up old wooden desk in the scruffy first floor office on the corner of King Street and Water Lane, just up from the harbour in Kingston.

The large woman behind the desk owned the jewellers shop on the ground floor. It wasn't much more than a long kiosk. A single florescent tube shone its pallid light down onto the top-brand knock-off watches, necklaces and bracelets displayed under a scratched glass counter. Watch-straps, earrings, hair pins and other assorted fashion accessories fixed to colourful cards, hung on hooks on an old wire wall fixture. More were hooked around a stubby carousel at one end of the counter.

There was nothing to suggest this grubby shrine to tat was a player in the gold bullion market. All the same he was assured the good stuff was locked in a safe in the back room.

Cluttered, claustrophobic and cheap are words that would never find their way into the quarter pagers that appeared occasionally in the Gleaner to advertise Jocelyn's Classy Jewellers.

***

It had taken an hour and a half to cover the distance from Grand Cayman to Kingston Jamaica. An easy but noisy flight. They wore headsets to communicate and at first, just after take-off, chat was brisk and comprised mostly of questions. Obvious stuff like; 'Where are we going?' 'Who are we going to see?' And, as far as James Stack was concerned, the essential: 'Can they be trusted?' Short List and his brother Eric made lots of soothing noises.

'Me brother tells me you got quite a bit of gold you want to trade, is that right Mr Stack?'

'Show 'im de photo, Mr Stack.'

Stack pulled the phone out of his pocket and leaned forward to show the picture to Eric. It wasn't quite the same reaction as Short List, but if he'd been driving a car, lives would have been at risk. When he eventually dragged his eyes away from the image on the phone, Eric pulled the plane out of a shallow dive and put it back on the correct heading.

'An' you got this with you now?'

'That's right.'

'What's something like that worth then?'

'Quite a lot.'

'Like I tell ya, Eric, me getting' ten percent o' whatever we can get for it.'

Inevitably, the question of payment for Eric's aviation services remained to be negotiated.

'What about me, what I'm getting out of it? I fly this for me boss, sightseeing and so on. He let me use it for this trip, but I've got to cover the fuel and other costs. Plus I need to make a tidy sum for me self. You know. To put away for a rainy day.'

Short List translated.

'Me brudda's got a bit of a gamblin' problem, Mr Stack.'

'Look, ten percent could be a lot of money. The more I get for the gold, the more money you make. Your brother can take his share from you. But I'll add something for the hire of the plane. How does that sound?'

'I can live with that,' the pilot said.

'This deal is gettin' worse 'n worse, man.'

'So that's a yes?'

They flew on in silence for a while. Until the next question.

'So, who is this Jocelyn? You said she was family.'

'She me brudder's aunty.' Short List said this as though, no further explanation was necessary.

A little more time passed.

'Wait a minute, Short List. Why isn't she your aunty?'

The answer explained a lot of obvious familial contradictions.

'Me brudda's the result of me mother marryin' twice, ya understand?'

'That's right, Mr Stack, Short List's my older stepbrother.'

'And this Aunt Jocelyn has a jewellery store in Kingston?'

'Yeah, it's a classy store.' Short List boasted proudly. 'She know all the right people in Kingston. The kind that want t'buy ya gold. Ya goin' to get ya money man. No worries.'

***

The seaplane came down, props feathered, to land in the sheltered waters of Palisadoes Seaplane Landing, to the east of Kingston harbour. It idled slowly round to an old timber landing stage that rocked back a little as the plane nudged against it. Standing back 15 feet or so from the edge, a weather-beaten shiplap structure served as a booking office and departure shelter. The only relief to the glaring whitewash paintwork was an advert promising spectacular views of the island, sun bleached into anaemic pastel colours.

Short List jumped across with a rope and tied the plane to an old rust encrusted bollard. Once the aircraft was secured, they walked down to the end of the harbour where Eric's Honda was parked.

They headed west along the Norman Manley Boulevard coast road that bordered the harbour and into Kingston. At the edge of town it splits into a one way system. The route into the centre via Port Royal Street leads through the endless cross roads of Kingston's busy commercial district. They turned into King Street, drove up a couple of blocks to Water Lane and parked up in the weedy lot behind the dilapidated, tin-roofed, two storey building that housed Jocelyn's jewellery store.

***

She had the scales out. Not the fine brass balances used to measure a few ounces of precious metal, these were bathroom scales. The gold bullion bar punched in at 28 pounds and a few ounces as advertised. She leant back, took a drag on the tiny cigarette stub jammed between her thumb and forefinger and breathed out a thin cloud of smoke as she spoke.

'So, Mr Stack. That's a whole lot a gold you got there. What do ya tink it's worth?' It was a rhetorical question to which Stack was about to give his usual reply of around $350K, based on not much in particular. He held his tongue as Aunt Jocelyn stubbed the cigarette butt into an overflowing ash tray, turned to a lap top and quickly found something that interested her. She pushed it to one side and leaned over to an oversize calculator that had finger worn numbers on big one-inch square tiles and an angled black screen. Fingers, with nails lacquered a brilliant green and pearl, danced a jig and the screen flashed glowing green numbers in response. She scribbled the number on a small pad. Her fat little fingers danced again and that number was added to the page. Her furious calculations at an end, she gave an appreciative nod to the final figure, underlined it and sat back in her chair again.

'In de real world the current value of gold is $1250 an ounce. That would make ya gold bar wort' about 560 t'ousand dollars.' she announced to the three men on the other side of the desk.

'Yeah, that's about right,' Stack said, coughing as he tried to hide his astonishment.

'Just like I tol' ya Jocelyn,' Short List said. 'We got some serious business here.'

Eric was initially speechless.

'And we're only getting ten percent?' He seemed disappointed. 'You should've held out for more Short List.'

The mood grew tense.

'Ten percent may be what you two boys goin' ta get, but I need to make somet'in' out of it too.' Jocelyn's earlier easy going friendliness quickly morphed into frank, cold business. 'Anyway, I said in the real world. Dis ain't the real world. Dis business here is the criminal world. Dat's who you going to be dealin' wit and that's a whole lot'a discount right there, Mr Stack. Ain't nobody gonna pay the full price.'

'Yeah, I know that, Jocelyn. Now, can you sell it, or am I wasting my time?...' He turned to accuse Short List, '... again!'

Jocelyn, Short List and Eric started in on each other. A family row. It sounded like each was accusing the other. The bickering went on in strong Jamaican patois that Stack was unable to follow. It ended with Eric storming out saying he had a phone call to make. Things to do. He'd be back. The other two didn't want him to go. He went anyway.

Jocelyn and Short List sat there in moody silence, the

only noise came from the busy traffic outside and the lazy whir of a dusty wooden four-bladed fan hanging from a rafter high in the apex of the roof. It chopped the air slowly, sending occasional downdrafts of sticky warm air drawn in from an open skylight.

The door was suddenly banged opened and a young girl of about fifteen years or so took a step into the room. She was wearing a simple lemon coloured dress that hung to her knees, her hair in braided buns. She looked around the room at Short List who she knew and James Stack whom she didn't and was about to say something when she spotted the gold bar on the desk.

The shiny golden brick held her attention in a wide-eyed, open-mouthed gape.

'What do you want, Serena? You can see I'm busy, child.'

Nothing. Just staring.

'Serena!'

Serena came to, but her eyes never left the gold bar as she explained she was just back from school and did her mother want a cold drink and by the way, can she go with Tiffany to meet some friends at Sharky's to listen to the music. She wouldn't be long she promised.

'OK, you can go with Tiffany but I don't want you goin' inside that place. No girl you age should be inside that bar. You can hear de music fine enough outside, girl. And one more ting. Don't mention what you seen here, Serena. Promise me girl.'

Serena was still staring at the gold bar.

'Promise me Serena. It's very important.'

'I promise, mom.' She turned to go – the spell broken.

'Serena!' Serena turned at the door.

'What do you promise?'

'To be back soon?'

'Just go and say not'in'.' Exasperated, Jocelyn turned back to Stack and Short List.

'Kids!' Jocelyn said.

'Don't worry about her,' Short List said, 'Serena's a good kid.'

Stack wasn't so sure. By the end of the day the whole of Kingston will know about the big golden brick. And that could be a problem.

Stack hadn't realised how difficult it was to find a villain when you need one. It seemed simple enough. A trade. My gold bar for your cash. Everybody makes some money.

He got up, leaned across the desk, picked up the heavy bar and returned it to the backpack.

'OK, Jocelyn. What's the plan?'

'I've been putting the word out to one or two people I know, since Short List call the other day. Discrete people. People I can trust. They're expecting me to call when the gold arrive here in Kingston. I'm going to make a couple o' calls and arrange somet'in' for later today. Where you going to be, Mr Stack?'

'He gonna be wit me, Jocelyn,' Short List butted in. 'We going t'be down on the corner havin' a nice cool drink. Ya got me number. Call me when you got somet'in' to tell me.' Short List didn't want to let Stack out of his sight. Too many people with their fingers in the golden pie.

Stack didn't have any other plans, and a drink would be perfect right now. Maybe, even something to eat. He hadn't eaten since breakfast.

Aunt Jocelyn was already reaching for the phone as they left the room.

The Oligarch

Mikhail Ulyanin was, by comparison to other Russian oligarch's, a modest man. Despite his multi-billion-dollar wealth, his tastes were simple, prosaic even. While others might prefer ostentatious gestures to confirm the world class scale of their breath-taking fortune, Mikhail Ulyanin, was practically a shrinking violet. He had no interest in the macho Olympian peeing contest that defined your average oligarch.

An example of his retiring nature was the Eba, his luxurious super-yacht, named after his mother and currently passing Castillo de los Tres Reyes Del Morro at the mouth of Havana Harbour. While other mega-yachts were in excess of 500 feet, Mikhail Ulyanin's Eba was considered small, measuring a mere 450 feet. A minnow.

Like most sea ports, the Port of Havana struggled in a perpetual fight against the briny assault from sea spray carried on Caribbean trade winds which left unprotected iron and steel, corroded and decaying. Under the port authority, Empresa Terminales Mambisas de La Habana, and being wholly owned by the people of Cuba, managed neglect was the best that could be afforded. A regime of painting and maintenance was merely something they'd get around to one day. It was a pitiful sight.

Private vessels were discouraged from entering the harbour which catered for cargo vessels and cruise ships. However, larger private yachts, the ones owned by Russian oligarchs, were accommodated and welcomed. A berth could always be found for Cuba's old friends along the western quays on the east side of the old town centre.

The motor vessel Eba was on a permanent world cruise.

Its seven expensively-designed and exquisitely-decorated floors contained all that was needed to run Mikhail Ulyanin's business interests in luxurious comfort 365 days a year.

Though he was a private man, he wasn't a recluse in the way Howard Hughes was. He did occasionally stay in one of the properties he owned here and there around the world. Cuba was one of the exceptions. He owned no property here and frankly, the hotels left something to be desired, but to wealthy Russians like Mikhail Ulyanin, Cuba offered something much more valuable. A deep friendship and a political kinship, especially within the house of Castro.

Cuba needed investment. Until recently America was off-limits. Over the years of stagnant state control, businessmen such as Mikhail Ulyanin were encouraged to find innovative ways to funnel some of their business activities through Cuban enterprises. And they were enthusiastic contributors.

In such an economy, it didn't take much for a modest investment to have a noticeable effect. Hospital equipment could be upgraded. Schools could be built. State salaries could be paid. As a result, a lasting and very useful friendship was welded. Cuba was Mikhail Ulyanin's base in the western hemisphere.

Ulyanin's main source of income was through his oil and gas corporation, Severgaz Postavka. It was that enterprise which brought him back to Cuba. An agreement had been reached to drill for oil in the Gulf of Mexico off the north-western coast of Cuba. This visit was just a formality. There was never any question - Severgaz Postavka would get the pick of the licenses.

And then of course, there was the entertainment. Intoxicating Latin jazz and exotic women. When he had

had his fill of these diversions it would be time to move on – but not yet.

***

The sea breeze did little to cool the humidity of the late afternoon temperature as the familiar Spanish skyline of Havana drew closer. The ancient city's decaying architecture always reminded Ulyanin of Seville or Cadiz. He felt somehow that attempting to rescue it from decrepitude would be like giving a beautiful older woman crude plastic surgery in a futile attempt to regain her youth. The city was what it was because of its age. Renewal would give it an air of artifice and imitation, like a casino in Las Vegas. Havana was the time-worn beneficiary of the inexorable passing of centuries.

A butler served ice cool refreshments as Ulyanin relaxed with his inner circle of close friends and business associates under the shade of the canopy that extended out from the fifth-floor salon, aft of the vessel.

Ordinarily, he was not a man with a naturally sunny disposition, but his mood had been lightened when daily reports began to reach him of the progress of drilling operations in Derbyshire. All seemed to be going well. It amused him that GeoPower was doing his work for him, and in their ignorance of his clever Machiavellian scheme, bring about the permanent termination of, not just their own drilling business, but all shale gas extraction in the UK. The irony gave Ulyanin an almost child-like thrill.

The hole was already at 12,000 feet. In about 18 days, when the well bore had reached its designated 24,000 feet, they would start to frack. That's when things would get interesting. He planned to sell his GeoPower shares just before fracking began – there was no point in going down with the ship.

Ulyanin was careful to ensure that knowledge of the sabotage scheme was on a need to know basis. Only a handful of people knew what was coming and that included the four men controlling the hack back in St Petersburg.

Derbyshire

Debbie Blain's computer screen showed the planned south westerly route of the borehole as a red line. Now though, more than fifty percent of its length had changed to yellow, confirming the trajectory of the drilling process so far. It matched the red line precisely. As far as Blain was concerned, everything was what she expected.

Deep below ground the rotating tungsten carbide drill bit was pushed hard against the shale, carving and scraping and grinding. Slowly, inch by inch, the distance from the wellhead under the derrick to the drill increased. Twelve-thousand feet ahead lay the great fault under Shivering Mountain. Waiting. Sleeping.

***

What surprised Summer most was the diversity of the protest camp population; Young and old. Students were inevitably over represented; A couple of young doctors; An old grey haired legal sage steeped in protest lore from the heady days of CND. Their numbers were swollen by assorted professional protestors who were on-call to join the ranks of any anti-capitalist, anti-war, environmental or animal rights campaign. They were the ones who arrived fully equipped for a lengthy battle. Some anarchists had simply taken a few days off work to join the anti-fracking protest, balaclavas ready to cover their faces when needed. They came across as earnest and motivated. But Summer guessed they were probably there for the craic, the adrenalin of battle and the chance to throw rocks at coppers.

In amongst them, though, were the true believers. Mostly women for some reason. Maybe they just cared a bit more for the world – for Mother Earth. Some had young children with them.

They had all the arguments carefully prepared and well-rehearsed, especially Clarissa Howden-Ffrench. Though the inner group professed no leader as such, Clarissa was their spokesperson, a representative who would provide passionate commentary and opinion to any journalist who cared to ask. They gathered each day at the 12 foot-high, barbed-wire-topped gates, shouting and screaming in frustration at the trucks entering and leaving the drilling site unhindered. Pushing and shoving against the police line protecting the corporate interests of greedy capitalists. At these times, Clarissa, full of middle-class guilt and sanctimonious zealotry, would seek out the TV cameras and reporters who consumed the mayhem with the feeding frenzy of sharks attacking a bait ball.

A reporter, live on Sky News, would merely have to ask why the issue vexed them, to have ten minutes of their story-hungry, 24-hour news channel, easily filled.

In the three days Summer had been there she'd noticed the numbers of permanent residents were swollen during the day by locals from nearby towns and villages. The daytime protest population almost doubled.

The camp itself was essentially a mini community that extended in an 80 foot arc out from the tall steel security fence into the neighbouring wooded area. After several weeks it now had a kitchen hut with food supplies sufficient to survive for months, catering mostly to predominantly vegetarian tastes. A shower arrangement had been constructed behind some bushes, and make-shift accommodation that ran from the modest bender

– a plastic sheet thrown over some branches, to tents, tepees, and a larger shelter that was under re-construction having been demolished by police and bailiffs in an earlier attempt to close the settlement down, or at least, make life as miserable as possible for the residents.

Another surprise for Summer was the diversity of nationalities within the camp, the most common accent, outside of British and Irish was Australian and then American, followed by French and German. Inevitably, to everyone else except the Americans, Summer was assumed to be American. As a Canadian, she was used to it and bore the careless slight with good nature.

The first day - the day she'd arrived, everything had appeared peaceful. As it turned out, they'd had a busy morning. A good day. This was the calm after the storming of the gates.

They'd distracted the police by throwing themselves in front of a heavy pipe-laden vehicle, while at the same time managing to strap two martyrs to the gates which had been shut fast after the last truck went through. The gates had, for a while, two humans lashed across them, making them impossible to open. Bolt cutters had to be found to free them under a bombardment of debris and insults from the protestors. Valuable time was lost and tempers tested.

A great skirmish won. A heroic struggle to be enjoyed in ever more embellished retelling around camp fires later that night.

The inner circle had developed a fiercely defensive scepticism of newcomers, especially any who looked like Summer. Not many did. She had a healthy tan, looked fit and was dressed in a bright summer blouse that was open over a T-shirt tucked into jeans. She didn't look like your typical agitator. She explained it away as merely the result of returning from holiday and wanting to do something meaningful. Fracking was the work of the devil, she told them and she'd come to join the cause. Man the trenches. Blow Gabriel's mighty horn and bring the walls crashing down on the evil empire. And bring an end to the dark side for ever. She hoped a confusion of Old Testament and Star War references would mark her as a hopelessly fanatical soul, passionate and romantic. Malleable cannon fonder. In other words – not a threat.

They welcomed her to their bosom, fussed over her and let their defences down, talking freely in her company. As far as Summer was concerned it was job done.

***

Charlie on the other hand found himself in the company of men and women who had already established a strong relationship. He was the new guy and it was up to him to fit in. It turned out his job had become available because someone cocked up and was fired. It was a long-standing principle that if a job becomes available, the next suitable candidate amongst the existing crew would be given the opportunity to take that spot, leaving a vacancy below for someone else to move up and fill. With the reshuffle complete, the remaining vacancy had to be filled from outside. For Charlie that meant the exhausting and largely menial roll of a roustabout on the nightshift. His 12 hour shift began at 6 pm, just four hours after arriving.

He'd had practically no sleep on the plane, so he grabbed some tea from the canteen and went looking for his berth in the accommodation block. It was better than he expected, A small white cubicle fitted out with moulded fibre-glass walls. The one opposite the bunk had a large window with rounded corners. At the other end was a tiny wardrobe with a couple of drawers. A ceiling light would provide stark illumination when it got dark, but at this time of year that wasn't until ten o'clock or so. A hinged board, more of a flap really, could be raised to form a small table under the window. He placed his cup on it and then fell back onto the thin mattress. Sleep didn't come easily. In fact, he was sure he hadn't slept at all.

A loud noise woke him. Sounded like a fist, hammering on the door.

'Oi! Come on. Wakey. Wakey.' Another couple of bangs.

Charlie dragged himself into a sitting position and looked at his watch: 5:30pm.

'Yea, OK. Give me a mo.'

He took a deep breath and leaned over to unlock the door. The door swung open into the room and banged against the wall opposite his bunk.

In the narrow hallway outside stood his immediate boss, Wayne, the assistant crane operator. A younger man than Charlie, but obviously glad to have someone of his own to chew out after all the aggravation his boss gave him.

There were two sets of crew: dayshift and nightshift. Nightshift worked just as hard as the dayshift and were just as important – after all, they're drilling the same hole. The same rules applied day or night. Nonetheless, the night crew couldn't help feeling a bit hard done by.

Charlie's heart sank a little. He knew what he was in for. A long, tough night. He'd promised himself he'd never go back and yet here he was. He consoled himself that this was different, he wasn't just a roustabout, he was a spy. Now that was cool. If things work out he'd be back in the money once Jimbo had sold his GeoPower shares.

He followed Wayne to the canteen to grab some breakfast.

Breakfast was served all day and all night. It was good and plenty of it. But breakfast at nearly six in the evening was hard to get used to. What he really wanted was a curry.

***

Fed and kitted out in overalls, hard hat and boots, Wayne led Charlie up the steel stairs to the drilling floor. He got a quick intro to the two roughnecks and the nightshift Driller. They were already busy with the hand-over from the day-shift guys, getting up to speed on progress and taking on-board any issues they may need to keep an eye on. They slipped easily into the rhythm. Pulling pipe out and stacking it. Working in close choreography with the derrickman high above. Seemed to Charlie they were about to do a drill bit change. You can get a couple of thousand feet out of it, but inevitably, even tungsten-carbide wears out.

Charlie was just a dogsbody and soon he was picking up, carrying, sweeping and cleaning oil and mud covered stairways and decking. Helping maintain the mud tanks, assisting the crane operator's assistant and endless other grimy tasks. Sometimes he had to visit the dog shack on the drilling floor to do something for the driller or just replace a couple of light bulbs.

It was on one such occasion that Charlie stole an extra couple of minutes just watching the directional driller work as he stared intensely at the screen; checking the well plans; keying in instructions; making notes. He was a younger man called John Stonebridge, a graduate engineer fresh out of university.

He seemed like a good kid, but for some reason, many of the older crew treated him with distain. Because of that, he welcomed Charlie's friendly interest. Directional drilling is a highly skilled job and while it was possible for someone to work their way up the ranks, get the education and do the homework, these days most directional drillers are college or university educated. Old rig hands understood this but it still irked them to see an inexperienced youth in charge of such a critical part of the drilling operation.

Noise from the drilling deck outside suddenly flooded into the room as Wayne stuck his head round the dog shack door and shouted across to Charlie.

'Oy, you!' Chewing Charlie out gave Wayne a misplaced sense of importance, 'You're needed over at the mud tanks – if you're not too bleeding busy.'

Charlie winked his irritation to Stonebridge and exited the dog shack.

***

The next three nightshifts ran pretty much the same. Charlie kept himself out of trouble and just got on with the job. On a couple of occasions, when he grabbed a break in the early hours, he found himself over in the canteen sitting across the table from the young directional driller. It was easy chit-chat and rig gossip. Charlie was keen to hear that everything was going well. Tonight was typical, all very routine. If he got a hint that anything was wrong, he wasn't sure what he could do about it anyway. But as James Stack had always maintained, information was king. The smallest amount of intel' might just put you ahead of the game. You have an edge.

On the third night, shortly after Charlie had consumed a heavy, stomach binding lasagne, Stonebridge approached. No food, just a cup of tea. Something seemed to be bothering him. He appeared less confident. Talking to Charlie seemed to cheer him up. Perhaps he suffered from depression. Who wouldn't, doing nightshifts week after week.

Charlie though, had other things on his mind. He hadn't heard from Stack since they left for the UK three or four days ago. Had he managed to sell the gold bar yet? That whole bloody scenario was very worrying. He should have stayed with Stack. He was his wingman after all. He'd got Stack out of trouble on more than one occasion. But in truth, back in Afghanistan, Stack had done the same for Charlie, in life threatening moments of battle, and too many times to count.

The Kingston Deal

Tivoli Gardens

The sun had dropped below the horizon a long time ago but the Caribbean night grew even more oppressively humid.

Earlier, as the sun travelled across the afternoon sky, what had been in shadow became bathed in the full blaze of its glare sending Stack and Short List inside the noisy bar to seek refuge. They found a table in the corner facing the door. Stack sat with his back to the wall, looking out into the room.

They'd already spent an hour or so sitting outside, drinking the local Red Stripe beer, but at these latitudes, with the sun defiantly overhead, the buildings offered just a thin strip of shade.

Short List had drunk two or three beers during the afternoon. Stack kept it to one. No news from Jocelyn yet.

Following a recommendation from the bar owner, Stack took a short walk along to nearby Orange Street where he found a cheap B&B. Economy was vital with just a hundred dollars in his wallet. He didn't know how long Jocelyn's deal would take, but he needed a place to sleep.

The walk took him past Sharky's, the place Jocelyn's daughter, Serena, spoke about. Worryingly, she was right there, standing in the doorway, not quite ignoring her mother's warning. She spotted him and pointed him out to her friends with a sly and clumsy gesture. He gave a friendly nod to let her know he'd seen her and kept going. The backpack must have looked temptingly heavy in his hand. Holding it by the straps, it was as though he was laying a trail of cheese for the local felonious rodents to follow.

He ducked into a doorway and reached inside the bag. Turning his back to the street, he pulled out the .38 special and tucked it into his belt. His shirt draped awkwardly over it, but he felt safer. He realised the last couple of weeks of lazy inaction had softened him. He needed to up his game. Refocus. The heat sucked the energy out of you. Made you lethargic. Careless.

He rebuked himself - *Wake Up!*

He took a couple of deep breaths, stepped back out into the street and was immediately engulfed once again in the colourful chaos of bustling, downtown Kingston as he continued his mission to find a bed for the night.

***

Later, back at the bar and with accommodation arranged, the smell of rich spicy Jamaican cuisine reminded Stack he hadn't eaten for a while, since breakfast in Grand Cayman. He checked out the menu but didn't recognise most of the dishes scrawled on the blackboard to one side of the busy bar. Short List came to his rescue. He was having the ackee fruit and salt fish and suggested Stack should try it. But it reminded him too much of the sickly smell of the fish platter the fat American was eating back at Randi's Rum Bar in Grand Cayman. Seemed like weeks ago now, but he didn't think he'd ever rid himself of the putrid aroma. He scanned the board for something he'd heard of. Jerk Chicken with rice and peas, which turned out to be more like a bean. Delicious none the less.

They ate hungrily and fast, washed down with beer. It was getting near nine o'clock and still no word from Jocelyn.

Inevitably Short List wanted to know how he came by the gold. Stack kept it quick and personal.

'None of your business.'

That wasn't going to do it for Short List.

'Well, me know it don't come to ya legitimately.'

Stack just shrugged.

Short List moved onto another issue that had bugged him.

'I saw your moves when you took the gun from my man Montez. You got some tricky skills. Ya know, like you been trained or somt'ing.'

Stack was proud of his earlier army career, but he kept that part of his life to himself and those close to him. The ones he cared about; Charlie Dawson, and more recently, Summer, who came out of nowhere almost a year ago, to add an unexpectedly wonderful confusion to his plans. Now though, he could see how telling Short List, the man who knew everyone, might be useful as a shield against low-life chancers.

'I was a captain in British Army Special Forces. Trained in a whole range of specialist abilities. The kind of skills that get me out of trouble and other people into it.'

'Yeah, I could see the kind of trouble ya talkin' about, Mr Stack.'

Stack changed direction.

'How about your aunt Jocelyn? 'Bout time you gave her another call, Short List. It's getting late.'

'Stay cool, Mr Stack. She know what she doin'.'

'Maybe, but I'm not sticking around with a bag full of gold waiting to be robbed.'

'Yea, well, I'm wit ya, can't ya see, Mr Stack. I got your back.'

Stack took a long appraising look at Short List. A wiry older guy. Easy going. Quicker with his wits than his fists he guessed. This place could be dangerous. Would he run to or from a fight? He hoped he wouldn't have to put that to the test. He took another sip of beer and leaned back in his chair.'

'That's very reassuring, Short List.'

Short List took a deep theatrical breath, arms stretching as his attention started to zone in on what was happening in the bar and out on the street.

'I tell ya what, Mr Stack. I goin' ta check out some of my local brudda's and sisters. Why don't ya get ya self another beer and chill? If I get any news from Jocelyn, I come and get ya. Know what I'm sayin'?'

Bored, Short List had obviously spotted an opportunity to catch up on some over-due horizontal relations with some of his 'cousins'. This bothered Stack and he leaned across the table to give Short List some close-up, face to face reality.

'Wait a minute. You're going to leave me here, the only white guy, in a bar in downtown Kingston, carrying a 28 pound bar of gold, on the edge of notorious, Tivoli Gardens where some of the worst criminals in Jamaica hang out?' Stack had grabbed Short List's shirt and pulled him in so he didn't have to shout this piece of news across to the gathered brethren.

Short List pulled his shirt away from Stack's grasp and stood up.

'Ya goin' t' be fine, don't ya worry 'bout these boys. Stay cool.' Brushing out the creases left by the Stack's grip, Short List gave him the ingratiating smile of a used car salesman. 'You got me number, Mr Stack. If you got a problem, just give me a call.'

He was in a hurry. He turned and pushed his way through the bar and out into the street.

Stack scanned the room to see what, if any, threat might exist.

On his own, without the risk of losing the bullion, he would be less concerned. But the whole point of being in Jamaica was to exchange it for the cash they so badly needed. He couldn't put that at risk.

One or two sets of eyes glanced over to him, but mostly they ignored him. Young men in baggy pants and shiny shirts adorned with loops of thick gold chain. A few wore dark glasses, but as cool as they looked, the dark shades meant it was unlikely they could see Stack, or anyone else. The young women dressed in skinny shorts and tight fitting brightly coloured blouses. Some with long jet black hair and others wearing it chopped short and blond. A few danced with moves that teased and promised. Others drank and smoked by the bar or chatted loudly at tables around the venue.

They all had other things on their mind – for the time being.

He decided that waiting around in the bar was pointless and potentially dangerous. Far safer to get outside and head for the B&B in Orange Street, where he could lock the door and keep an eye on the road outside from his scruffy first floor room. Basic rule of battle, find a position that's defendable.

The backpack hung from one shoulder as he stepped into the Kingston night. The bar must have had some kind of air conditioning because it was noticeably hotter now. The music followed him out to join the sounds pulsing from other bars and restaurants up and down the street.

Noise filled the traffic jammed road. Car horns played a few notes of popular tunes - 'la cucaracha' made an inevitable brassy appearance. It was busier than ever with stores still displaying their wares on the roadside. There was an awkward mix of locals just trying to get on with their life and tourists trying to look cool and fit in.

He turned to head towards Orange Street just as a black Mercedes pulled up along the sidewalk next to him. Out of the drivers window, a chubby arm threaded with a dozen assorted bracelets hung limply, a half-smoked cigarette dangled between a thumb and forefinger. But it was the brilliant green and pearl veneered finger nails that got Stack's attention.

'Where ya goin', Mr Stack. And where's that no good, Short List?'

'Jocelyn!' There was relief in Stack's voice, 'Short List suddenly had something urgent he needed to do.' Stack didn't think he needed to labour the point.

'That boy won't ever grow up. Get in. We got some business to attend to.'

Stack walked round to the passenger door and climbed in to the smoke tainted interior. As soon as his backside touched leather, Jocelyn floored the gas pedal and the car took off, slaloming between people and traffic as she navigated over to other side of the road. They were heading away from the carnival atmosphere of downtown and very quickly into the nearby darker, run-down streets of Tivoli Gardens.

If he was worried before, now it was getting dangerously hazardous.

'Where are we going, Jocelyn?'

'I got some friends who got friends. Politicians. They the ones with the money since the Dons and their soldier boys have been taken out.'

'You mean the local drugs lords?'

'They ain't what they used t' be, Mr Stack. Cost a lot of

lives to clear 'em out. But they still got influence, you can be sure. The ones that're still here, anyway.'

Back in May 2010, 73 people were killed and 35 others injured when the police and army came to the Tivoli Gardens district of Kingston, to arrest the drugs lord Christopher 'Dudas' Coke, the Don of the Shower Posse drug cartel. Four soldiers and policemen were also killed in a battle that lasted two days. Dudas had top politicians in his pocket including, it was alleged at the time, the prime minister of Jamaica.

'So, Jocelyn, what's the plan?' Stack didn't want to be driven into a trap. 'I need to know what's going on.'

'You want to sell ya gold don't you? We meeting the man gonna buy it. He's comin' here to meet us.'

'Why here of all places?'

'The man got friends down here. They take care of his business. Dey ain't the kind he can invite home to a posh place like Cherry Gardens, up there north o' Kingston, now can he?'

'I wouldn't know, Jocelyn.'

The Mercedes turned into another dark street, lit only by the grudging light of a single low-watt street lamp further down and what little light escaped through windows and doors of nearby shanty houses and dilapidated squat tower blocks, that splashed dim, angular, yellow rectangles across the road.

They'd almost passed through Tivoli Gardens and were just a few streets away from Trenchtown. Jocelyn pulled up behind another Mercedes. Hard to tell the colour. Might have been black. Looked newer. Shinier. Standing beside the car on either side were two guys the size of Smackdown wrestlers. Both were dressed in black and looked menacing, but wearing sunglasses - great for a threatening effect but pointless in low light. They were parked up outside a brick and concrete block bungalow with a short veranda clinging to the front. All the windows were boarded up, but the door was open a crack, allowing a slip of light to silhouette a man sitting on the veranda steps.

'OK, Mr Stack. Wait here.'

Jocelyn got out and headed over to the other car. She stood on the crumbling verge that passed for a footpath and spoke to the man in the back of the limo. It didn't take long before she waved Stack to come over.

Stack pulled the backpack onto his shoulder once more as he got out and walked over, carefully weighing up the two heavies as he approached. They were both six inches taller and didn't seem to think much of him.

The guy in the road on the driver's side beckoned him over and started to pat him down, looking for weapons. Stack held the heavy backpack in one hand, away from his body. Confident Stack had nothing hidden in his clothing, the heavy moved on to the bag, unzipping the pockets and checking the contents. Stack had been expecting this. He pulled the bag back against his body with both hands. The guy found the heavy gold bar and lifted it out to examine it. He pushed his dark glasses away from his eyes for a better look at the most valuable asset he was ever likely to hold. Placing it back in the bag, he nodded that he was satisfied Stack was unarmed. He opened the rear passenger door and indicated for him to get in. As he did, Stack looked over to Jocelyn standing on the other side. She gave a nod that was supposed to reassure Stack and indicated she'd be waiting in her car.

Stack slid in and found himself beside a middle-aged man in a business suite. The front interior light was on but it wasn't throwing much light into the back of the car, so it was hard to tell much. A thin, African Jamaican face and a neatly trimmed beard. Expensive eau de cologne. Something exclusive. It didn't smell like Old Spice.

The most annoying things about backpacks are the straps. Some people must find a use for them; hiking and camping probably, but in the general scheme of things, they just get in the way, constantly unbuckling and getting entangled with each other uselessly. But for once, Stack had found a practical and potentially life-saving use. Two straps at the back of the bag that might have been used for a rolled up sleeping mat turned out to be the perfect place to secure the gun. With the bag held against his chest during the search, the gun was invisible.

Inside the limousine and invisibly to the man sitting next to him, Stack used his right hand to stealthily unclip the weapon from its hiding place, slipping it onto the leather seat between him and the door. With a little sleight-of-hand, Stack had given himself an edge.

The businessman was also wearing dark glasses but he took them off as he turned to Stack.

'Is that the, ah, item?' He said, nodding towards the backpack. 'May I see it?'

An educated voice. He wasted no time with introductions, Stack noted. Well, as long as he had cash with him this was going to be a very short relationship. No broken hearts.

Stack's radar was turned up to full alert. His heart rate was under control but there was a definite zing of adrenaline coursing through him.

There was a briefcase on the seat between them. He placed the bag on it, opened the main zip and pulled the pocket open enough to show the gold block inside. The businessman reached over to take it.

'No. For the time being it doesn't leave the bag.'

'But surely, you understand I must be able to ascertain its value and authenticity?'

'What did Jocelyn tell you it was worth?'

'What she told me and what I'm prepared to pay are quite different things. You need to get rid of it and I have the means to dispose of it. Between those two conditions we need to find a number that represents a fair margin of profit for both of us, don't you agree?'

This bothered Stack. He didn't want to waste time with negotiations at this point. He knew what it was worth and how much he should reasonably expect in exchange. But he was in enemy territory and out-numbered. He may not have a choice.

'Your turn. Let me see some cash.'

'Of course. Your bag is sitting on it.'

Stack hoisted the backpack onto his lap. Turning to the briefcase the businessman snapped the locks and opened the lid.

'No touching.' A light-hearted rebuke that disguised a dangerous threat.

Even in the shadow of the dim light of the saloon, Stack could see the case was filled with wads of U.S. dollars. Problem was, in such low light, dollars all look the same if you can't see the number written on them. Could be fives. Could be fifties. Might only be one's. It was impossible to tell. And, if it was fifties, it might only be the top bill. It smelled real enough though. The leather lid was quickly closed and gold plated clasps shut.

Somewhere, out in the darkness, music could be heard echoing faintly from the surrounding neighbourhood as the two men silently assessed each other.

Stack's right hand rested on the hidden weapon. He had no idea if it would fire.

The limousine was an American import Mercedes. Left hand drive. He was aware of the heavy-set driver in front. He looked Relaxed. Indifferent. But Stack couldn't see the guy's hands. He didn't think he was praying.

'Let's get this over with. It's worth 560 thousand dollars.' Stack said. 'I'll settle for 15 percent. 84 thousand: Is that what you've got in the case?'

'Do you play the lottery? Are you a gambling man?' The businessman had a smirk on his face. There was something about him that reminded Stack of Blackstone's arrogant manner. Perhaps they went to the same expensive private school.

'I'm not in the mood for this.' Stack said. 'How much is in the briefcase?'

The businessman patted the case and slid it towards Stack. Turned out Serena had been very chatty.

'Things are worse that you think,' he tried to sound reasonable. 'My colleagues tell me that word on the street downtown talks excitedly of a white man walking around with a bag full of gold. You're a target.' His tone became more aggressive. 'Take the case. It's more than enough. Hand me the gold bar and you can go.'

The businessman's eyes flicked to the left. Stack followed his gaze. The driver had turned round, his arm was resting on the back of his seat, and the pistol he gripped firmly in his hand, was pointing at Stack.

'I think our negotiations are concluded don't you?'

As the businessman reached over for the backpack, Stack grabbed the old revolver with his left hand, lifting it up and jabbed it hard against the businessman's head. The man raised his hands away from the bag. Shocked. Surprised. But he recovered quickly, nodding his head towards the driver and his gun.

'Don't be crazy. You'll be dead. Take the case while you still can.'

The driver raised his gun provocatively, ready to fire. Stack had no doubts he would do it. He pushed his gun harder against the man's temple, his head jerking back with pain, cracking it against the window.

'What's more important? The gold or your life?' Stack's voice was low and threatening, playing a deadly bluff as he pulled the hammer back with his thumb. The sharp metallic double click underlined his threat. 'Your driver shoots me. He might kill me or wound me, but either way, the reflex will make this gun fire and you're a dead man. Tell him to put his gun down. Now!'

There was a pause as the businessman considered his options. He was clever, but he wasn't brave. Anyway, he had men outside. The man wouldn't getaway.

'Put your gun down.' He told the driver.

'This side. Drop it on the floor, over here.' Stack said, pushing the gun harder into the man's temple.

The driver did as he was told and the gun fell to the floor at Stack's feet. He reached down and picked it up with his right hand. Gave it a quick and appreciative once over. Not as old as the relic in his left hand. It was a Browning Hi Power semi, easy to spot even in low light. If the mag was full it had fourteen nine mil parabellums that kicked like a chorus girl.

He swapped it for the .38 pig-iron special and felt better for it.

As Stack pulled the backpack on to his shoulder once again, he gave the driver a simple instruction. 'Stay!'

He grabbed the businessman and dragged him roughly out into the street, holding him in front as a shield, the Browning drilling into his temple.

He'd got this far. The next bit was harder.

Both gangsters on either side of the car froze, their hands stalled over their weapons. The one sitting on the steps of the old wooden veranda back in the shadows began to grasp how things had switched. He went for his semi-automatic, but Stack turned the businessman around to show him the gun at his boss's head.

With the car door still wide open, Stack ordered the businessman to reach in for the briefcase. The guy hesitated for a second, but felt the muzzle pressing hard and painful and did as he was told. As he came back out with the case, Stack grabbed his collar and pulled him away from the limo, beyond the trunk and into the red glow of the tail lights.

That's when the driver suddenly popped up on the other side holding the old .38 relic. The businessman must have found it on the floor and tossed it over the seat while he was hidden from Stack. Clever move.

There were now four pissed-off Jamaicans waiting for the slightest opportunity to turn Stack into Swiss cheese.

'OK. Open the case.'

'What?'

'Pop the lid of the case open. Let's see what's inside.' Stack hit the back of the man's head with the barrel to emphasise, 'Now!'

Cowed, the businessman flipped the catches and opened the lid, holding the contents out like a cigarette concession in a clip joint. Stack leaned round a little to take a look. The case was packed with wads of cash.

What happened next came straight out of the James Stack book of surprises.

He gave the briefcase a hard kick, sending it tumbling upward and throwing a cloud of one, five and ten dollar bills into the air. They floated back down like giant confetti in a Mexican carnival. Stack noticed there weren't many fifties or hundreds. Just as he'd suspected.

An engine revved, headlights blazed and Jocelyn's Mercedes drove past at high speed sending the dollar bills flying into the air once again. She must have freaked out at the scene unfolding in front of her, guns and cash all over the place, and decided she had an urgent need to be someplace else very quickly. Everyone turned to watch as hundreds of low denomination bills chased her down the road.

Out of the darkness from nearby ramshackle homes and low-rise blocks, doors flew open spilling narrow strips of yellow light, rap music and people out into the street to grab a share of the windfall. Stuffing bills into pockets. Hoovering up what they could. Indifferent to the guns being pulled out of belts and shoulder holsters as the heavies turned their attention away from the money and back to Stack.

In the confusion Stack had legged it. He didn't look back, just turned off at the first junction into another of Tivoli Garden's dangerous, un-lit back-streets. His foot hurt from the kick.

He was only wearing running shoes, but that was what he needed right now - speed.

***

Having been driven to the location in an unfamiliar town, Stack was unsure of his bearings. The only clue was the brighter horizon to the east. No sign of the gangsters yet, apart from the occasional shout and the sound of running feet. What did they want? The gold was his and the money was theirs. All they had to do was pick it up. If a couple stayed back to recover the money lying on the road and in the pockets of the local population, Stack figured, there may only be two chasing him.

He turned another corner. A glow off to the east told him downtown wasn't much more than half a mile away. The boys chasing him had the advantage, they knew the area well, all the short cuts. He had one smaller advantage though and it wasn't far from the harbour area he was heading towards.

He turned yet another corner. No footpath to speak of, just overgrown yards leading to shabby, run-down properties. Some not much more than glorified sheds, others spruced up in bright colours. Stubby blocks of flats, four floors high their dark silhouettes randomly cut through with rectangles of light. More people around now as downtown grew closer. And always music and shouts and laughter heard from an indefinable somewhere else.

He kept running, breathing hard, the weight of the backpack heavy on his shoulder. Looked like he might make it. Then, from an alley, a dark shape the size of a barn door stepped out into the street right in front of him, arm held out towards him, holding a gun. His gun – the old .38 pig-iron special. The driver appeared like a large, shadowy wall blocking the path. A man of his weight had done well to get ahead of him. He was breathing heavily, the gun arm swaying with each breath.

'I got ya gun an I give it back to ya bullet by bullet if ya don' do like I tell ya,' A deep baritone voice. He paused to catch another gasp of air. 'Now put da bag down easy and hand ya gun to me, nice 'n slowy.'

Stack had almost run into him so he was only an arm's length away. He didn't think he'd survive an attempt to reach behind for the Browning semi tucked into his waistband, so he began to lower the bag. But then, holding it with both hands, he started to heave it around in a full 360-degree circle, swinging the bag as hard as he could against the driver's gun arm with the full 28-pound weight inside. Too slow. By the time the bag had swung round to meet the arm, the arm wasn't there anymore. The driver had stepped back a little, re aimed and fired.

Stack staggered back in anticipation of the fierce punch of the round. The slug would have struck him dead centre if it wasn't for two things: the momentum of the heavy bag spinning Stack like an Olympic discus thrower, pulling him away from the drivers aim. The second thing was - the gun didn't fire. Just a dull clunk as the hammer slammed down on a dud shell. The heavy Jamaican grunted in surprise but only a second later Stack heard another double click as the hammer was thumbed back followed by another dull clunk as the driver pulled the trigger again. Two dud cartridges. There was one left.

Stack didn't wait to see if his luck would survive a third time. He ran across to a narrow cut-through on the other side of the road and barged into a couple of girls coming the other way. As he muttered an apology a loud bang came from the dark street behind him, followed instantly by a ricochet as the round skimmed off the wall just above the girls' heads. They screamed. He kept running.

***

He'd been in the room about 40 minutes, no more than that. Resting on the old bed, still fully dressed, the gun on the covers next to him, ready. He'd tried calling Short List but had to leave a message.

He couldn't believe he'd got away. It was close and more than lucky. The luck of random choices as he made his way through the dangerous back streets of Tivoli Gardens, occasionally breaking into the larger highway of Spanish Town Road that led into downtown Kingston. It was well lit and busy, so he kept shy of it for most of the way, using it for navigation only.

He broke into Orange Street north of Saint William Grant Park. From there it was an easy, five-minute jog south to the B&B and his room on the first floor. He'd made it. The gold still stashed in the backpack and unsold.

The silence in the room was broken by a soft knock on the door and a whispered voice.

'Mr Stack.'

Stack grabbed the gun, but relaxed when he realized it was Short List. He eased himself off the bed to the noisy scratching of the rusty springs and cracked the door open enough for Short List to squeeze through. Despite everything, he was actually pleased to see him.

'I heard from Jocelyn 'bout ya troubles.'

'Yeah, she didn't hang around. And I can't stick around here either. Those guys will find me, and if they don't, apparently I'm big news on the street, thanks to Serena.'

'Don't worry. Grab ya tings. I got Jocelyn's car outside.'

'Where are we going?'

'I'll tell ya on the way.'

***

It was still early morning as they drove west along Norman Manley Boulevard. Short List explained how things had got even more complicated during the evening. His stepbrother, Eric, had been to see the casino guys he owed the gambling debt to, telling them he'd be able to pay what he owed within 24 hours. And then he told them how. It turns out they suddenly lost interest in the debt and wanted to know about the gold. They told Eric they'd write the debt off if he'd bring the man with the gold bar to them. Maybe they could persuade the man to do a deal with them. Eric didn't trust them but told them he'd see what he could do and left in a hurry.

He went looking for Short List but Short List wanted nothing to do with the deal, and anyway, didn't know where James Stack was. Later, Eric panicked after hearing from Jocelyn about what happened in Tivoli Gardens. He saw his share and the chance to pay off his debt vanishing into the night air. He clung to the hope that Short List would came up with something.

After hearing the message from Stack, Short List made a call to Montez. That's how they ended up back at Palisadoes Seaplane Landing, waiting for Eric to arrive.

Gold Rush: Cuba

Four thousand feet below the Peak District in Derbyshire, the shale layer spread wide but shallow, varying in thickness, as it followed the hills and valleys of the local topography.

The original GeoPower well plan kept the well bore within the shale layer, but the hacked instructions struggled to follow the different contours of the northwest route. Every now and then, as the shale curved away, the drill rose too high or too low, breeching the shale, and taking bites from the mudstone it was sandwiched between.

These rock cuttings were carried back to the surface by the mud slurry, now a distant 14,000 feet away. Routinely, samples of the cuttings were taken by the geologist. The unexpected rock type should have flagged up a warning.

***

It was just after 9:30 in the morning when they splashed down in the Gulf of Bataban, southwest Cuba, a sheltered bay where the old Puerto Batabano harbour was slowly slipping into irretrievable dereliction. Despite its rusting decrepitude, it still catered to a dwindling number of smaller container ships and freighters. Batabano was the location of the original settlement of Havana back in 1515. It turned out to be short lived. Not long after, a more suitable natural harbour on the northern coast was found and the old town was reduced to the ignominy of a forgotten, fly-blown, backwater.

It had taken nearly an hour to fuel and ready the aircraft for the journey. Four hundred and eighty miles. The very edge of its range. A nerve shattering hour in which all three of them expected bad news to turn up at any moment; for Stack it was the businessman and his crew of thugs, and any member of the population that had heard about the white man with the bag of gold; for Eric it was the fear that his gambling debt would catch up in the form of a car full of armed villains; Short List trembled with the nightmare that all of the above list of troubles was on its way right now, but more worryingly, Aunt Jocelyn would turn up in a cab and ask where her Merc was.

All the while, just beyond the curvature of the Earth, the sun was preparing to breach the horizon. Majestic rays of god-light were already painting blood-red brush strokes, long and fat across the eastern skyline in a glorious overture to another spectacular day.

The floatplane took off in a wash of sea-spray just as the first arc of golden light shimmered like a mirage above the horizon. The flight took nearly three hours.

***

Eric was unfamiliar with the harbour area and motored, prop feathered and noisy, slowly towards the oil-blackened spit of sand in the corner of the harbour jetty. As arranged, Montez was waiting with another man to help as the planes floats touched the polluted beach.

The sight of the seaplane coming in to land brought three or four kids, who'd been fishing off the jetty, scampering along the road and down though the jasmine and mangrove trees to the water's edge to greet them with noisy excitement.

After securing the aircraft, Stack and Short List heading up the short track through the trees to a car parked on the broken concrete edge of the deserted road, leaving Eric and Montez's man behind to guard the plane. They didn't plan to be long.

They took the only northern route available, through the hope crushing poverty of Surgidero de Batabano. The crumbling road beat a spine-cracking path through rural countryside for ten miles until it joined the auto route to Havana, and then, via the Prima Anillo de La Habana that edged the southern suburbs of Havana, into the centre of the old town.

Stack hadn't slept much in the last 24 hours. He'd managed to steal an hour or two waiting in the Mercedes for Eric to arrive and another couple in the plane. But it had been a bumpy flight that kept waking him. He drifted off a couple of times during the road trip to Havana but kept being woken by the bang of metal against metal as the suspension bottomed out on the chassis whenever the car jarred over a crack in the concrete road. A noise that coincided with the firing of another dud round from a big guy he couldn't seem to run away from.

Before they took off, he changed out of the shorts and shirt he'd been wearing for several days and into his old jeans and T-shirt which he'd stuffed, rolled up, into the backpack, back in Grand Cayman. That seemed days ago now, but it was only yesterday.

***

The view from Javier Fidel Henriquez's balcony on the first floor of his grand residence was heartbreakingly sad. A daily reminder of the irreplaceable loss of so much architectural heritage in Havana. It was simply a matter of money to restore the crumbling old Spanish colonial villa across the street. Money, and the will to take it on. There had been very little of either in Havana Vieja until recently.

Sadly, the villa across the road from Javier Fidel Henriquez was just one of many in a similar condition along Calle 21, the street just off Avenida Paseo, in the El Vedado district, just west of the old town. And Calle 21 was just one of hundreds of similar streets throughout the city lined with grand old casas in desperate need of TLC – many in a state of near collapse. Some already had. Each day another was lost.

It is true, that amongst these rows of elegant, time worn piles, some houses had been saved. They stood out like the occasional healthy tooth in a mouth full of neglect.

Javier's house was one such villa that had been restored to something close to its original colonial splendour, paid for by the Cuban administration on behalf of the People of Cuba and bestowed upon favoured sons and daughters of the revolution and those that had some measure of prominence within the government.

In the early years of the revolution, many similar villas had been partitioned into multiple apartments, to be shared by the local population. In one apartment might be the family of a bicycle taxi driver. In the apartment next door, a doctor. Both would be earning the same – just $20 a month. In all probability, the doctor envied the bicycle taxi driver and his simpler, less demanding life. Such are the rewards of communism, unless of course you are amongst the elite, like Javier Fidel Henriquez.

Most of the elite chose to live to the west of Havana in the leafy hills of Nuevo Vedado. Henriquez though, preferred to live nearer the old town, not like the peasants of course, but amongst them.

And then, when America began relaxing the decades old

trade embargo with Cuba following President Obama's state visit, things started to change. In Cuba the unthinkable had happened. A new term had entered the political lexicon: private ownership.

Javier's position high in the Ministerio de Relaciones Exteriores, gave him opportunities of travel that were impossible for other Cubans. Opportunities that were not wasted on mere affairs of state. Sure, Cuba benefited from the foreign relationships he nurtured and cultivated, but Henriquez's easy Latin charm was used to greatest effect when cultivating contacts and business acquaintances for his own private purpose. That's how he had found himself enjoying the luxurious hospitality on board the super-yacht, Eba. An all-expenses paid jolly, from which he had only just returned.

He'd been formally invited the week before by one of the islands' most generous friends, philanthropist to the people of Cuba and owner of Severgaz Postavka, one of the largest privately owned energy companies in Russia, Mikhail Ulyanin.

A flight to Barbados to board the Eba and a pleasant cruise back to Havana. It may only have been a few days but it was time that wasn't wasted. Already a trusted acquaintance, Henriquez was determined to turn the relationship into something more rewarding. He hadn't travelled alone. The minister for development of oil and gas resources was on board, but he didn't have the wit to see the obvious advantages a deeper personal relationship could bring. Nor did he have the inherited get-out-of-jail card that Henriquez' parents had bestowed upon him, recognised in his middle name in tribute to his great uncle, Fidel Castro.

As he was leaving the villa, Henriquez paused at the full-length mirror in the hallway to adjust his tie. He leaned in to inspect a fleck of lint on a lapel and fussily brushed it off before standing back to admire himself. The reflection was of a round olive face, smudged with dark, avaricious eyes behind thin-rimmed glasses.

His spectacles sat on a stubby nose underlined by a mean, charcoal stroke of a moustache. The toupee didn't look too artificial. Many men his age had a full head of rich black hair. Twenty years of plentiful lunches and excessive dinners made the face too full to be handsome. A taller man could have gotten away with it, but Henriquez was five foot six in Cuban heels and beyond the help of diets. He was too vain to admit he was short and fat, but, evidently, that's exactly what he was. In the tropical humidity, the toupee only added to his discomfort. He pulled a silk handkerchief from his pocket and carefully dabbed the beads of sweat from his forehead.

He was on his way to meet a business friend who had an 'opportunity' he refused to talk about on the phone. It sounded risky: Good. Risk meant profit.

***

The muffled energetic music of some kind of Cuban salsa fusion could be heard coming through the walls from the large cabaret restaurant next door.

The place was closed to customers at that time of day but the ten-piece band and a group of dancers were rehearsing their floor show as though they were entertaining a full house. Occasionally the music stopped as one of the dancers, probably the choreographer, complained excitedly about the other dancers' performance. The quiet periods lasted for several minutes punctuated by angry screams of frustration as the woman counted the other five through a particularly complicated dance step, again and again.

The Copahavana was located in the old town near the Hotel Miami. Both establishments were owned by a man called Gomez to whom Montez had just introduced James Stack. Following that meeting, Stack, Short List and Montez had been left to stew in an anti-room, listening to the repetitive Copahavana floor-show next door.

The meeting had begun without much promise. Montez had given an account of their proposal, during which Gomez appeared vaguely irritated and distracted by some annoying, trivial, restaurant business. The man sat there constantly relighting his cigar like some noble conquistador in his heavy, leather upholstered chair, behind the age blackened Spanish desk set amidst the dim shadows of his grand office. He seemed indifferent to the fact they had flown all the way from Jamaica to meet him. Stack wondered if this was going to be another wild goose chase.

Montez asked Stack to tell his story, which Gomez listened to with little interest, in between phone calls and interruptions and a frantic search for another cigar, after finding the humidor was empty. His secretary rescued him with a fresh box. That all changed with the spectacular, show-and-tell, gold bullion reveal. Even Gomez had to admit that was something you didn't see every day. His interest changed from cool to warm and then ingratiatingly friendly.

There were two doors that gave access to Gomez's office. One to his secretary's anteroom, the formal entrance to the inner sanctum. The other opened directly onto a passageway outside. It was to this door Gomez walked and told whoever waited outside that there were to be no interruptions for the next hour.

He went back to his desk and took the phone off the hook.

During the journey from Jamaica, Stack had worried that Cuba was a poor country. Who amongst its population could afford to pay what he wanted for the gold or had the means to dispose of it profitably? Montez explained that the people he knew in Cuba had long established, private business contacts in America and while there were no direct flights to the US, a restriction that was about to be lifted, there were many ways of doing business internationally.

This turned out to be the essence of Gomez's conversation with Stack in the hour that followed. But timing, as he pointed out, is everything. Now couldn't be a better time to do business in Cuba, he assured him. Things were about to change.

He broke off to make one call. Whoever he spoke to was clearly interested enough to come to Gomez's office on the basis of little or no information. It was just a promise of a business opportunity that might interest him. Stack was impressed. The contact would be there within the hour. In the meantime, would Stack, Short List and Montez wait in the room next door? His secretary would arrange drinks for them if they wish. He explained his business associate had a very privileged position within the government and therefore expected total discretion. Stack would be invited in to meet him to establish the authenticity of the deal by showing him the gold bar, but only if the visitor agreed.

***

To Stack, this deal seemed to have more going for it than the last two attempts. He was optimistic. Then Short List and Montez started to bicker about shares and who got what. This raised the issue of what Gomez expected to make from the deal. Suddenly Stack was pissed-off again. Maybe he was just tired and hungry. He looked at his watch, they hadn't eaten for hours. He needed cheering up. He took out his cell phone and speed-dialled Summer.

***

It had rained most of the night. Another summer thunderstorm. The deluge eventually ending around breakfast. The rivers of Derwent and Noe had over-spilled into both Bamford and Hope villages, flooding streets and homes along their banks. This depleted the usual sizable group of protesters as the villagers attempted to clean up the mess.

By early evening, the protest camp up at Donnybrook Hollow in the shadow of Rebellion Hill had dried out enough to become habitable. Belongings still hung from branches though, drying slowly under the grey sky, and the naturally boggy ground still resembled a muddy swamp.

Summer, miserable and missing James, wondered what the hell she was doing there. She was helping in the half-covered wooden framework that served as a kitchen. The plastic sheeting still sagged heavily from pools of rain-water that continued to gather during the day despite efforts to drain it. She was serving food to the wet and weary, when she heard a bright glissando. It sounded like fairies. She looked around to see if anyone else had noticed and piled another spoon of vegan delight onto a plate. Then, almost immediately, there it was again. The penny dropped. She hissed a profanity under her breath at her stupidity and pulled her cell phone from her pocket.

'James!' It was as though the sun had come out.

'Christ! It's good to hear your voice Summer.' Stack's mood

lightened instantly, 'How are things in Derbyshire?'For some privacy, Stack had walked over to a window that looked out onto a small park, not much more than a patch of dirt spotted with leafy trees and bushes, partially shaded from the sweltering afternoon sun by the Hotel Miami opposite.

'Well, what I'm looking at right now is about as far removed from the Caribbean as you can possibly get, James. Where are you? Heathrow? I hope?'

'No. Cuba.'

'Cuba? But I left you in Grand Cayman.'

Yeah, well that was five or six days ago. I've been to Jamaica since then.'

'Jamaica? What about the...' she moved away from the kitchen area for more privacy. 'What about the…the cheese…' She was trying to be discrete.

Stack laughed. 'I'm still trying to shift it. With any luck today might be the day. It's been tricky.'

'Jesus! James. Are you OK?'

'Yes, I'm fine. Tired, but fine.' Stack turned to see what Short List and Montez were doing. Montez had moved on to harass the secretary, 'I'll tell you about it when I get back to the UK. What's happening where you are?'

A bleep came down the line.

'What was that? Your battery?'

'Yes. I haven't charged the bloody thing recently. Too busy protesting.'

'Well, don't waste time. Give me the headlines.'

Summer gave Stack a precis of events. Not much to report, except she was being protected from the attention of sex starved youths and lecherous elder statesmen by the mother hens in the group. Though there were at least a couple of them she needed to fend off occasionally.

She had burrowed her way into the confidence of the inner leadership, mainly women, but one guy was a pretty fierce advocate for direct action. They mostly kept him under control, but with each passing day, his argument became more persuasive. She found out they did have someone, a sympathiser on the inside, working on the rig. But he got fired recently. She didn't know why.

'Any news from Charlie?'

Another bleep came down the line.

'I haven't seen Charlie since we split up four days ago, but he called me yesterday. He's working nightshifts so he sleeps during the day. From what I gather, he's got to know one of the drilling people on the same shift. He said…' Another bleep obscured what Summer had said.

'Say again, Summer?'

'He said he thought the guy was worried about…' Bleep! And that was it.

'Summer?' Stack realised with heart-crushing disappointment that she'd gone.

For just a moment the sound of her warm Canadian voice, seasoned with a hint of something that secretly amused her, had taken him far away from the mad chase across the Caribbean to offload the golden brick.

He tried Charlie's number. No reply. Must be on the rig. Nearly two o'clock in Cuba – eight pm in the UK. His shift started about two hours ago. Hopefully, the 'missed call' notice would alert Charlie that he'd tried to contact him. Just to be sure, he texted a short 'Get back to me' message.

***

The office was a health hazard of thick cigar smoke. Both men were chewing on fine Bolivar Libertadores, fat with hand rolled tobacco leaves and already half consumed. Gomez had buzzed his secretary to send Stack in and swept his arm in a grand gesture to the tooled leather chair, upright and severe, next to the visitor as he entered. Stack struggled to keep his eyes from watering in the choking atmosphere as he made his way over and sat down.

Gomez made introductions in English, but was careful to provide Javier Fidel Henriquez's first name only and no hint of his occupation. Discretion was essential. This was business that Henriquez was keen to keep from his fellow Communist Party members.

'Javier, please allow me to introduce, James Stack. He has travelled from Jamaica...'

Stack interrupted him.

'In fact, I've travel from Grand Cayman, via Jamaica, to be accurate.' Stack wanted the kudos of Grand Cayman's financial reputation to add credibility to his negotiating position.

The short and portly Henriquez was relaxing confidently in his chair, elbow on the thick leather armrest, his hand aloft, cigar between finger and thumb, waving it suavely to underline his words.

'Where you are from is of no interest to me, Mr Stack. What does interest me is la ingote de oro. Gomez tells me you have it with you. May I see it please?'

Stack shrugged. He'd shown the gold bullion to all kinds of dubious people. Why not show it to someone who looked respectable for a change?

Henriquez struggled with the unexpected weight at first, before resting it heavily in his lap. The office was darker now in the shade of the afternoon. Gomez turned his desk light around, throwing a pool of illumination over the gold bar. The bullion, brilliant against Henriquez's dark suit, sent sparkling, caustic ripples of golden light into the shadowy corners of the room.

Javier nodded respectfully. He was impressed. It just needed a simple test. Javier reached into his pocket and pulled out a pocket knife. He pulled the blade open and scraped the tip along one side of the bar. There was no doubt. It was solid. But was it gold? And if so, how pure?

'If it proves to be real gold of the purest quality as the hallmarks stamped on it suggest, what is your price?'

'It is the purest gold, I can assure you, Javier. Gold of such purity is currently worth $1250 an ounce on today's market. You are holding 448 ounces. In other words, $560 thousand dollars' worth. Henriquez didn't blink. He just paused as he took another languid pull on his cigar. Two centimetres of ash glowed fiercely for a moment before he blew the smoke lazily into the air above him.

'So, how much do you want?'

'Twenty percent.'

'Over a hundred thousand dollars? That's a lot of money for something that doesn't belong to you Mr Stack.'

Gomez leaned forward onto the desk with renewed interest as the numbers started to grab his attention. He hadn't realized quite how valuable the gold was and how much his end of any deal might be worth.

'For the sake of this conversation, let's say the gold does belong to me. No one else has a claim to it. Its existence is unknown.'

'So, why don't you just go to a bank and trade it for cash?'

Henriquez was toying with Stack. He cared little about the provenance of the gold or how it came to be in the Englishman's possession, but he knew perfectly well that legitimate is was not. Nobody in the room was pretending otherwise.

Stack could play that game too.

'So, do you have that kind of money, or am I just wasting my time?'

Gomez chipped in. 'Mr Stack, please don't insult my guest.' He implored, 'Of course he has the money. Be patient.'

Henriquez smiled arrogantly. Two desperate people. Each needing something from him. He enjoyed being in such a position.

'Yes, you must be patient as Señor Gomez has said. First, I must establish the gold is what it appears to be. Then we shall see what we shall see, Mr Stack.'

Stack realized Javier Henriquez had pulled the break hard on. Negotiations had come to a dead stop.

'The gold stays with me.'

'But of course. I will bring someone to this office tomorrow. Señor Gomez will inform you what time.'

He rose to leave.

'Does that suit you Señor Gomez?'

Gomez stepped from behind his desk to catch up with Henrique who was already heading towards the door.

'Of course. It shall be just as you say.' He took Henrique's hand, shook it firmly, and said something in Spanish, very quickly, in a deferential tone. The visitor was gone and Gomez turned to Stack, still holding the door open.

'You will need a room for the night. Please stay as my guest at my hotel. It's nearby. The Hotel Miami.'

Across the room, the office door opened and the secretary walked in ushering Short List and Montez through.

'Montez has his own arrangements in Havana.' Gomez continued, 'But I'm not sure about your other friend?'

'I'm sure you can find a room for him in your hotel, Mr Gomez.' Stack resisted the temptation of calling him cheap, 'It's small change compared to the sum of money you will earn tomorrow, and of course, we are guests in your country.'

'My country! It's the government's country – Castro's country.' Gomez heaved a bitter sigh of resignation, 'I'm afraid you know nothing of this impoverished island, Mr Stack. Of course your friend can stay at the Hotel Miami. It will be my pleasure. I will contact you tomorrow regarding the time of our next meeting. Today went very well I think.' He was corralling them firmly through the door and into the passageway as he spoke.

He stepped back into his office and closed the door, leaving them in near darkness, but not alone.

'Sígueme.'

'He wants us to follow him.' Montez translated.

The journey took them back across the floor of the cabaret restaurant where the musicians and dancers were still rehearsing. They looked on sullenly as the four of them passed.

Gomez's secretary must have phoned ahead because the rooms had already been reserved at the Hotel Miami. All Stack and Short List had to do was check in.

There was a small problem that both Montez and Short List had to deal with down in Puerto Batabano. Eric and Montez's guy were still waiting for them to return. Looked like they were in for an uncomfortable night in the cockpit of the seaplane.

Short List reported to Stack that with the plane's tanks nearly empty, a supply of aviation fuel had been located and a truck loaded with cans of the stuff would arrive tomorrow, and Eric wanted to know who was going to pay for it.

That conversation reminded Stack that he had yet to book a flight back to the UK. If tomorrow went badly they'd need yet another island hop to find yet another potential buyer. His heart sank at the thought. He might just take what he was offered anyway.

He'd taken his eye off the much more valuable prize up in Derbyshire. That's where his money was. He needed to get there to join Summer and Charlie PDQ – sooner if possible..

He had no idea how tricky it might be to get out of Cuba. And then there was the risk his credit card wouldn't hold up. But he went ahead and booked a seat anyway on the following night's Condor flight to London. More complicated that he expected, having to take an overnight via Frankfurt, but eventually ending up at London Heathrow courtesy of Lufthansa. Direct flights were almost impossible. Normalisation of relations between Cuba and the USA couldn't come soon enough for James Stack. Now, would be good.

***

Javier Fidel Henriquez was very confident he had a customer for la ingote de oro. He'd already spoken to him earlier, just after the meeting with Gomez. The man, an old friend was making a reputation for himself in the Cuban property market.

Ownership. The unobtainable was now attainable, if you had enough money. For a very small investment, a villa that had been restored could be sold for unimaginable sums. Many were valued up to half a million dollars or more and Havana was full of such dilapidated opportunities. The market was local only, and way beyond the reach of most Cubans. However, for those who knew the right people, Henriquez for instance, and who had contacts abroad, very good business was there to be had.

This was Henriquez's great business plan. Property. His cut from the sale of the gold bullion would form the basis of his investment fund.

He was in a mood to celebrate the inevitability of his impending wealth. This coming evening would provide the ideal opportunity.

***

A great friend of Cuba, and a personal acquaintance of Javier Fidel Henriquez, was being feted for his philanthropic contribution to the Cuban project. Speeches given and backs slapped. The dinner, though, was coming to an end. The guest of honour was becoming restless. Thoughts were turning to other diversions. Henriquez, sitting at the table with the honoured guest, suggested a venue that might please him.

The entourage arrived at the Copahavana in several limousines. A busy night, but the maître d' could always find tables for wealthy customers. This one in particular was a regular when he visited the island.

Henriquez, already feeling the effect of the rich Malbec wine imported from Argentina that had been served during the dinner, made sure he remained close to his new friend. Normally, he would have avoided the clichéd, pseudo-cultural, tourist shows that passed for entertainment in Havana. The dancers, he was amused to notice, seemed to struggle with the choreography. The room seemed to roll unsteadily as the night wore on, but his mood was light and he clapped and shouted approval along with everyone else, laughed at the bad jokes around the table and drank vodka. He hated the stuff, but tonight, for some reason, it slid down so easily.

They were sitting at a table in a large leather upholstered booth to the side of the floor show.

He looked around at the others.

Mostly an inferior rabble of bodyguards, leering at the dancing girls and touching the waitresses indecently. He though, came from the ruling political classes. It was inevitable he would have such wealthy friends. Soon he would be one of them.

He turned to the man sitting next to him and boasted drunkenly about his big business plan. He told him about the meeting he had had that day in Gomez's office, here, in this very building. About the deal that will be done here tomorrow. And he told him about the English man with the twelve kilo golden bar that he was trying to sell. And he boasted about its value. The man listened politely to the drunken rambling of the puffed-up, little apparatchik sitting next to him, so desperate for his friendship. A' useful idiot', to borrow from Lenin. His paltry ambitions were laughable.

Half a million dollars was merely the small change in the pocket of an oil-rich multi-billionaire such as Mikhail Ulyanin. Nonetheless, the story intrigued him.

***

The phone call came at 11:30 a.m. The meeting was in half an hour. Stack and Short List hadn't strayed from the hotel all morning. They'd breakfasted together in the restaurant. It had been a meal of questions and complaints from Short List. How much was Stack asking for the gold? When will he get the money? He had to get back to Grand Cayman soon. His brother was broke and probably in trouble with his boss for taking the plane for two days.

'What about Montez?' Short List bleated, 'I got to pay him out of me earnings. It don't seem fair when I got to do all the work. You know, what wit me step-brother flying the plane. I got a lotta over-heads all ready, without havin' to pay Montez somet'ing.'

'How much is Montez asking for?'

'He want fifty percent 'o what I get, man. But I tell him he should get it from Gomez. I tink he's gettin' it from both ends anyway. Me and Gomez. It ain't right, you know what I mean.'

Stack thought Short List had a point.

'Let me see what I can do. I'll talk to Gomez.'

That seemed to satisfy Short List for the time being. But the cast of percentage grabbing dependants had grown from one, Short List, to five or six, including; Montez, Eric, Gomez, Henriquez and whoever he sells it on to. He felt like a fat, juicy fish in a sea of hungry predators.

***

Getting to Gomez's office in half an hour wasn't difficult. It was practically next door. Just enough time to call Charlie. Stack tapped in the numbers and green-buttoned the cell-phone.

'Jimbo!' A surprised voice at the far end of a long line, 'Good to hear from you mate.'

'How you doing, Charlie? Working nightshifts Summer tells me.'

'Yeah. Just finished now. I can't get used to these stupid hours. I'm constantly knackered. You sold the gold yet?' Straight to the point. Typical Charlie.

'No. But it's been interesting. With any luck, today's the day. I've got a meeting in about twenty minutes.'

'So, you'll be back in England soon? Summer's missing you.'

'One way or another, I'll be there as soon as.' Stack moved the conversation on. 'Summer seemed to think you had some news or something. She got cut off before she could tell me.'

'Not really. Well, I don't know what to make of it to be honest. Drilling's going well, no biggies, just the usual niggles from time to time. Looks like they're on target to start fracking in about ten days.'

'So what is it that you don't know what to make of?' Stack asked, 'There are all kinds of people out there don't want them to frack.'

'Tell me about it, Jim. The protesters are pretty full-on every day. No let up. I'm pretty sure the guy who got sacked was a sympathiser. He pulled a really dangerous stunt that could have brought the game to an end a week or so ago.' Charlie sounded worried, 'I've made friends with the directional driller on the nightshift. He's a young guy. Educated. He knows what he's doing. He seemed a bit concerned about some rock samples that came up from the other end of the hole recently. I'm trying to understand what his concern is exactly. Something about the rock not being what the geologist should have expected at that point. I think it happened twice. Also, something about data from the drill that seemed unusual. Just one line of data that was completely off the scale. He made a report, but apparently the senior directional driller said not to worry. Just one of those things. I don't think they think much of him, you know, being so young and inexperienced.'

'Sounds odd doesn't it. What do you make of it, Charlie?'

'You're asking the wrong bloke, Jim . . . I must say, though, I like the kid.

'Despite what they say, I think he knows what he's doing.'

'But what does it mean, wrong kind of rock?' Stack pressed Charlie.

'At a guess, I'd say, because they have a pretty clear plan of what they're drilling through, if a bit of rock comes up that doesn't match that plan, it should ring alarm bells.'

'And it didn't.'

'No.'

Stack thought about that for a moment.

'I wonder why? You'd think with so much at stake they'd be curious at least.'

'Could be the schedule. They have to finish before a certain date, or the licence expires.'

Another pause.

'OK, Charlie. Good work. Keep an eye on it. Oh, and keep an eye on Summer?'

'You don't have to ask, Jim.'

***

As before, the office was thick with cigar smoke. There were three occupants. Two he'd met before. He was introduced to the third. Castellanos didn't smoke. An upright dark oak chair had been moved from its position over by the wall for Stack. Another was arranged for Short List who sat quietly to one side of the group, watching.

'I trust you slept well, Mr Stack?' A polite enquiry from Gomez who was eager to proceed. 'Do you have the gold?'

Stack removed the bar from his backpack and handed it to Henriquez, who put his hand up and indicated Castellanos.

Castellanos weighed the gold in his hands, giving Stack a nod of approval as he did. A few items were laid out on the low table to the side of his chair: a magnet, a ceramic tile, a small plastic bottle and a magnifying glass. He took the magnifying glass and examined the hallmarks carefully. He seemed satisfied and nodded again. He lay the bar on the table and did the simplest of all the tests. Was there any ferrous in the metal? The magnet would prove it one way or another. Stack watched as he played the magnet over the surface of the bar.

'So, no iron. What a surprise.' Stack thought.

They watched silently as Castellanos moved on to the next test. Lifting the heavy bar with both hands he attempted to scrape it against the unglazed surface of the ceramic tile, but the tile kept moving across the table as he did it. Stack leaned forward and held the square of pottery steady for him. Castellanos gave Stack a courteous dip of the head. This time he was able to scrape a corner of the bar along the surface, leaving a long, golden streak. On its own, this was a sure sign the metal was truly gold, but one final test would be the clincher.

He reached for the plastic bottle and opened it. A pungent acidic smell added to the heavy aroma of cigar smoke in the room. He explained that there were a number of levels of acid tests. Each one determined a particular carat value. As he was only interested in the very highest quality, he had brought with him only the test for 24 carat gold. The hallmarks stamped on this bar indicated that's what it should be. They all leaned in a little closer as the test was carried out. Stack was particularly interested in the result. What if this gold turned out to be something other than 24 carats? It would mean all the UK gold in the Bank of England would be worth significantly less than the Chancellor of the Exchequer expected and another great hole would open up in the beleaguered UK accounts.

One single drop is all it took. The liquid lay over the

golden streak, still and not reacting. Anything other than gold and the acid would have bubbled merrily away and that would have been game over.

Castellanos gave a final approving nod as he screwed the cap back on the bottle and returned his equipment to his briefcase.

'OK. How much do you want?'

Stack went through the same maths that he had for Henriquez the day before.

'Twenty percent?' Castellanos repeated. He chewed that number over in his head for a moment. It didn't seem to have alarmed him, 'OK. Twenty percent. But I don't agree with the value, Mr Stack. Current exchange rate is…' He paused while he browsed through a page on his laptop, 'Today's rate is…$1225 an ounce. Your bar of gold is worth...' A few taps on his calculator later, '$549,000 American on the international market. Give or take some dollars.' Having appraised the gold, he now sat back in his arm chair and appraised Stack.

'Let us not waste time with…what is that colourful Americanism? Ah yes, let's not waste time chasing each other around the table, Mr Stack. The gold in its present form is almost useless to you, that's why you are in a hurry to sell it. But I will give you a fair price. Remember, the gold has to be reduced to a practical, re-saleable product. I shall need the expertise of a…' He turned to Henriquez and Gomez, 'Cómo se dice, metalúrgico?'

Stack understood. 'Metallurgist?'

'Just so. A metallurgist - with assay equipment.' Castellanos nodded his thanks to Stack. 'This is not cheap. Other costs are inevitable. And of course, the value of gold can go down.' He paused again for a deliberately dramatic moment, 'I will give you 75,000 American dollars for your bar of gold.' Stack considered this figure. Ten percent is promised to Short List, whose eyes had nearly popped out of his head at the number. That leaves $67,500. And then there was Montez to consider.

'That seems almost fair. But let's make it $80,000, and Gomez here will pay his friend Montez out of his end and Javier pays Gomez out of the profit he makes.'

Gomez spluttered a protest, but Henriquez, confident of a much higher percentage from Castellanos, agreed without argument, which made it harder for Gomez to complain. Stack cast a quick look at Short List who nodded his thanks.

'OK. It is done,' Castellanos said, 'Bring the gold to my address later this afternoon and I shall have your money. Bring an account number with you and perhaps you'll also want some cash?'

They shook hands. Deal done. A relieved Henriquez left the office with Castellanos, the way they had come, through the private door to the passage way.

There had been a noisy exchange in the secretary's office next door which they had ignored a moment earlier. Gomez assumed it was a waiter or musician with a grievance. Suddenly, two men pushed their way through the door, followed by the flustered secretary who looked at Gomez, shaking her head apologetically, her hands spread out in a silent appeal that it was out of her control.

The remaining deal-makers in the room were busy congratulating themselves.

A jubilant Gomez was handing out cigars from the humidor.

They froze where they were, staring at the two intruders, surprised by the sudden and unwelcome interruption.

Gomez recovered first. He spoke in Spanish but they didn't seem to understand, then he tried English.

'You'll have to wait outside, please señores.' He appealed to them, 'We are busy here as you can see.'

Stack, his back to the men, had already returned the gold bar to the backpack. He turned around to face them, his hand still in the bag. He needed a plan to get out of the office as fast as possible, most likely, through the other door.

The two guys, dressed in dark trousers and baggy, black leather jackets, were of the large variety, grown for the purpose of intimidation. One struggled to speak in a guttural American English. It wasn't his first language.

'Mr Ulyanin sends you his invitation to join him on his ship, the Eba. The car waits outside. Please come now.'

'I'm afraid that won't be possible.' Stack said, 'I have other plans for this afternoon. Please send Mr…Olaf?'

The big guy corrected him.

'Mr Ulyanin.'

'Please send, Mr Ulyanin my apologies.'

'I too am busy.' Gomez added, 'Please thank him. Perhaps my secretary could make an appointment for later in the week?' Gomez had heard of Mikhail Ulyanin.

'Mr Ulyanin will be leaving Cuba this evening. There is no time. Please come with us.'

To Stack it was clear, this was not an invitation to a cheerful social event – to come take a look at my lovely boat. It was a blunt order.

The two heavies seemed to make themselves even larger as one went around behind them. 'Come. We go now.'

From the fit of the leather jackets, Stack was sure these guys were carrying. If they were Russian, or from that neck of the woods, then they're probably heavy Makarov PMM .38 hand guns. He wondered if they would actually shoot them if they refused to go. That wouldn't do very much for international relations.

Without any practicable alternative, they allowed themselves to be herded out of the building into the waiting car. On his way out, Gomez managed a quick whisper in the ear of his secretary as he went past. Stack couldn't pick out what he said, and anyway, it was in Spanish. The secretary was left standing alone in Gomez's office. She struggled to understand what had just happened. Was this a kidnapping? Still in shock, she wandered back into her own office. What was it her boss had said?

***

The man who welcomed them onto the wide, oak timbered aft deck was the far end of middle-aged and ten years past handsome. A lean, six-footer. Long thinning black hair streaked with grey, brushed back over his ears. Dressed for comfort in a light blue silk shirt, open at the neck, revealing a fine gold chain against tanned skin. White cotton pants and canvas deck shoes. A butler offered glasses of champagne to the men as they arrived. The host, Mikhail Ulyanin, was the very essence of urbane charm, which somehow made him more sinister.

***

They had arrived at the harbour via a temporary security cordon and parked on the quay alongside the gleaming white hull of the mega-yacht towering above them. A gangway led them up through a shell door built into the side of the vessel. It was the smell that struck Stack first: fine leather, new wood, expensive carpets and some other indefinable fragrances and luxurious aromas that screamed wealth. This was probably how a new Rolls

Royce smelled fresh out of the dealership. They were escorted through wood-panelled passageways all modern curves and precision carpentry, that led at last to a wide, gold inlayed glass and rosewood staircase that swept up to an exquisitely furnished, upper sun-deck in the aft of the yacht. A canopy provided shade, but the view was spectacular over the pantiled roof tops of old Havana.

They were invited through to the very rear of the broad, open salon where white leather fitted seating followed the curve of the brushed steel banister around the edge of the deck The sweep of the banister was broken in two at the stern by alloy and oak stairs that led down to an open private deck below. The heavies stayed by the formal staircase they had arrived by, almost ten yards away.

Stack could feel an occasional cool draught from air conditioning vents hidden somewhere. It provided a gentle, refreshing breeze that carried with it a cooling water vapour that must have taken five or six degrees out of the hot afternoon. Mikhail Ulyanin invited them to sit down, relax and enjoy the champagne.

Stack looked around, assessing his options. His field of play. If he had to make a stand, or a run for it, a ship was not a good place to be. Too many unknown passageways, state-rooms, galleys, decks, bulk-heads and narrow doors. And who knew how many tough guys like the heavies by the stairs. Hard standing on the quay-side, blue water on the other: If he jumped, he'd be taking twenty-eight pounds of ballast down with him. Great if you want to dive straight to the bottom of the harbour. All this happened in the two or three seconds it took Stack to reach for the champagne flute. For the time being he'd roll with it and see what happened.

He took a seat next to Gomez. Short List sat nearby, clearly impressed by the scale of the wealth the surroundings represented.

Ulyanin seemed very composed. The confidence only extreme wealth bestows.

'Where is that fat little Cuban, Javier Henriquez? I was expecting him to be with you?'

Gomez just shrugged. Stack stayed silent.

'Well, never mind. Thank you for coming at such short notice, gentlemen.' His English struggled with a thick accent redolent of borscht, kasha and too much vodka. 'We leave Cuba this evening, so there is very little time.'

Gomez sat there stiffly, his anger barely under control. Stack couldn't hold his tongue.

'Actually, Mr Ulyanin, with the greatest respect, I'm less pleased to see you right now.' Stack didn't feel like buttering his words, 'This is extremely inconvenient. What do you want?'

Ulyanin didn't miss a beat.

'I'm sorry Gentlemen for the...ah... inconvenience as you put it Mr...?'

'Stack.'

'So, Mr Stack. Is that the gold bullion Henriquez told me about last night?' Ulyanin was pointing to the backpack at Stack' feet.

'He seemed very impressed.' Ulyanin laughed as he said it.

'He told me his plans, you see Mr Stack. The gold represents opportunity and wealth. I believe he intended to go into the property business. I wonder if you would allow me to see it.'

Stack took a beat to consider the options. He sneaked a look at the heavies by the stairs. One way or another, Ulyanin was going to take a look. Why waste time.

He hefted the bar out the bag and placed it on the table in front of him. This required Ulyanin to get up and walk round to sit next to Stack. A small and probably pointless victory. The Russian took some spectacles from a case on the table and leaned in to scrutinise the gold. He seemed to be comparing the hallmark icons with something written in a small notebook he'd removed from his pants pocket. Eventually, he picked the bar up, weighing it in both hands and nodding speculatively, much as Castellanos had done earlier. He turned to Gomez.

'You had this gold tested this morning I believe. Is it what you think it is?'

'Yes.' Gomez said simply.

Ulyanin nodded thoughtfully before placing the golden bar back on the table. His next words would shock Stack.

'An Englishman with twelve kilos of gold bullion that is certainly not his own.' There was something about his voice. As though he was enjoying a private joke, 'It very much intrigued me when Henriquez gave me this news last night. So I have been making some research. You know, Mr Stack, a man of my wealth has almost limitless resources. It seems there was some criminal business in London recently. A robbery? The Bank of England? Does this mean anything to you Mr Stack?'

Stack didn't react.

'There was something of a small war that took place on the River Thames. A handful of gangsters, I'm told they were part of a New York mob and the police? There was a lot of shooting.' He stood up, walked around the table and over to the side of the yacht. Leaning back casually against the stainless-steel balustrade, arms folded, he addressed the two men like the denouement in an old detective thriller.

'The gold Mr Stack is trying to sell is from the vaults of

the Bank of England. The hallmarks, the weight, the carat - there is no mistake.' Ulyanin paused for a reaction.

The three men listening to the Russian remained silent. A gust of wind tainted with exhaust fumes from the old town drifted across the harbour to fill the moment. It carried with it the buzz of traffic, impatient car horns and occasional fragments of Latin music. Stack leaned back in his seat and waited. Gomez looked across to Stack before speaking.

'Well, Mr Ulyanin, this does not come as surprise to us. We are men of the world.' He cast his gaze back to Stack before returning his attention to the Russian, 'I think we would like to know what interest this is to you?'

'I think it is the British authorities who would be interested,' Ulyanin said. A note of amusement in his voice, 'Mr Stack would find it extremely difficult to return to his home country if they became aware of his involvement in one of the biggest heists in recent years.'

Stack spoke at last with a single inquisitive word.

'And?'

'And?' Ulyanin repeated mockingly. He could barely contain his laughter, 'You want to know what I want. Of course you do.'

There was an unexpected pause as the Russian seemed to be preoccupied for a moment. He walked over to the other side of the yacht, placed both hands on the gleaming hand-rail and stared out across the wide bay of Havana Harbour. He took a long, deep breath of ocean air, his face offered up to the warm sunshine, eyes closed, enjoying the caress of the gentle breeze. He appeared to be in no hurry. Reluctantly, his thoughts returned to the present and he turned to face his guests. It was as though he was seeing them for the first time. It was only a moment. Then he snapped out of it.

'What do I want? I will offer you $25,000 for the bar of gold. This is not a negotiation by the way.

Gomez was the first to respond.

'That is out of the question, and anyway, it has already found a buyer, isn't that right Mr Stack?'

'Yes. As far as I'm concerned the deal is done.' Stack turned to Gomez, 'Come on. We've wasted enough time here. We have an appointment to keep.'

As he was returning the golden bar to the backpack, in the distance, a new sound could be picked-out echoing forlornly through the streets of Havana. A police siren.

'I think not.' Ulyanin said, 'You will sell the bar to me, or the British authorities will be informed. Under the circumstance you have no choice.'

Short List had been watching in despair as his pay-cheque appeared to be slipping further away.

Stack asked the inevitable question.

'But you're a billionaire! How could you possibly be interested in something so paltry?' Stack kept his hand in the bag as he stood up.

'It is the unique history of the gold that interests me. It's provenance. I can buy hundreds of gold bars of equal value, but none will have become available under such circumstances. It will be kept in my private gallery, away from public gaze and political scrutiny.'

'I don't understand. It's just a bar of gold.' Curiosity got the better of Stack. 'All gold has the same value. What makes this one so special?'

'Rarity! The bar is one of a kind. As you know, as far as the Bank of England are concerned, it sank to the bottom of the River Thames with several others during the gun fight on the barge. They have recovered three. Only one is missing now, still presumed to be in the mud at the bottom of the river.' Ulyanin sounded almost reverential, 'Mr Stack, you may not realise it, but your grand caper created something worth far more than that single bar of gold in your possession.'

As he spoke, he motioned to his bodyguards. They started towards Stack, Short List and Gomez.

'Eventually, a legend will circulate about the missing bar of gold. In ten or twenty years that single ingot will become a priceless obsession to private collectors like me, but of course, I will already own it.'

Ulyanin said something in Russian to the heavies. They were going for the backpack. Stack anticipated it and stepped back, pulling the Browning semi out of the bag at the same time. He gave the heavies the full and unexpected attention of the 9mm threat, which stopped them dead.

'Throw your guns over the side'

Nothing. They just stood there. Shocked? Surprised? Or stupid?

'Now!' Stack shouted the command like he was back in a war zone, the boss of his elite Special Forces squad.

First one then the other reached inside their jackets, removed their guns and, to Stack's astonishment, threw them over the side.

He nodded to them as he turned his gun towards Ulyanin.

'You two! Stand over there with your boss.'

As they moved across the deck, Stack noticed the police siren was louder. It sounded close, maybe on the quayside.

'It's your last chance to make some money, Mr Stack. Accept my offer and leave my ship before it's too late.' The Russian was playing a big bluff. He had no idea what the police siren meant, why it seemed so close. Just a coincidence of course.

'Gomez, go to the stairs. I'll follow you.' Stack, his gun

pointing directly at the Russian, took a few steps backwards towards the stairway, as Gomez ran ahead and down the stairs, eager to get off the boat.

'I'll take my chances with the deal I've already made, Ulyanin.' Stack hoisted the backpack onto his shoulder, nodded for Short List to follow him and turned to go. But his escape was halted as unexpectedly, Gomez returned, walking slowly back up the stairs. Behind him came two police officers who stepped cautiously onto the deck of the salon, their hands resting on the flap of their leather gun holsters, ready for trouble as they moved forward.

Quickly adapting to the changing situation, Ulyanin raised his hands above his head, indicating to his bodyguards that they should do the same.

'I'm so relieved the Policía Nacional Revolucionaria have arrived at last.' Ulyanin gave the Cuban police officers – the PNR – their full title. He knew this would please them, 'As you can see, this man is attempting to kidnap me.'

Stack caught a look on Gomez's face. He knew something about this sudden turn of events. Responding to the unspoken cue, he turned and handed his pistol, grip first, to the nearest officer.

'I can assure you I am not trying to kidnap this man.'

'Then why did you sneak on to my ship with that gun? Why am I standing here with my hands above my head?' He turned to the officers, 'Please arrest this man and remove him from my ship.'

Stack could see no reasonable way to quickly explain how he came to be on Ulyanin's ship, and pointing a gun at the Oligarch, without giving away that he was carrying a 28 pound bar of gold stolen from The Bank of England. It looked like check-mate. He'd finally run out of options.

And then another head popped up the stairwell. A short,

fat man perspiring heavily. He finally made it up to the deck, took a cream coloured silk hanky from his pocket and wiped his brow.

'No, that is not quite what happened is it Mr Ulyanin?'

The Russian lowered his arms when he saw Henriquez. Game over. In a blink of an eye he flipped direction and deployed his two battle-hardened assets – cunning and cool.

'But, this is all a misunderstanding. I invited these gentlemen here as my guests. Who would decline such an invitation?' He was laughing and making light of the situation, 'There's no need for concern, is there Mr Stack?'

With little idea what would happen next, Stack kept his mouth shut and simply shrugged.

One of the PNR officers turned to Henriquez, awaiting orders. Henriquez just nodded.

'So, we are finished I think, there is no more to be said.' Gomez said, 'Thank you Mr Ulyanin for your kind hospitality. We shall be going now.'

Stack caught the fierce, cold glint in the Russian's eyes as they turned to go. He didn't look like the kind of guy who would leave it there. This was unfinished business. He should be careful.

***

As they drove through the boulevards of Havana, Henriquez explained he had received a call from Gomez's secretary. She had been trying to get hold of him for some time. She explained what had happened earlier and that they had been taken to Ulyanin's yacht. She didn't know why.

Henriquez had a pretty good idea though. A problem he had stupidly created that he had to fix. With the benefit of his position high in the administration it wasn't difficult to arrange a couple of PNR officers to visit the boat under his authority.

This would undermine his friendship with the Oligarch, but he had a more urgent need for cash from the gold deal right now. Needs must, as they say, and, as always, the politics of expediency have never spared friendships. The Russian and the Cuban will always find a use for each other.

They pulled up outside the address of Castellanos. All four got out.

***

For the first time in what seemed like days, the backpack felt as light as a feather, with only his shorts and a T-shirt rolled up inside. The deal had gone better than he had hoped, given his recent experiences around the Caribbean. Castellanos had been as good as his word. He'd given Stack the option of cash or credit transfer, or a bit of both. There was no way Stack could guarantee getting that much cash through all the airport checks from Cuba via Frankfurt and into London. So, despite the small difficulty of the apparent ease in which Blackstone had emptied his account in Grand Cayman, he really had nowhere else to put the money.

The credit transfer of $65,000 to Stack's Cayman Island account went through without a problem. Once the transfer had been completed, he phoned the bank directly to check all was good. The confirmation was the best news for days.

The remaining $15,000 cash was split $5,000 to Stack and $10,000 to the wiry Cayman Island taxi driver, a payment that included an extra two-thousand for the hire of the plane and fuel. Stack didn't think he had ever seen a human being so palpably happy. Gomez promised to take care of Montez from his cut. Henriquez's end would come out of the profit Castellanos made.

Stack asked one final favour. Get Short List back down to Puerto Batabano where his step brother Eric and Montez's friend were waiting. In a fit of untypical generosity, Henriquez said he'd be happy to oblige and arranged a car. It arrived ten minutes later.

Stack held the passenger door of the 1950s Studebaker open as the cheerful Cayman Islander climbed in.

'That's a lot of money.' Stack said. 'Don't blow it. And say thanks to Eric for me.'

'Don't you worry, Mr Stack, I got some investment plans in mind.'

Stack grinned as he slammed the door and watched the old car pull slowly away in a cloud of blue oily smoke. Short List wound the window down and called out to Stack.

'Any time ya want sometin', you just call me, right? You still got me business card.'

The last thing Stack heard was Short List's infectious laugh as the car disappeared into the noisy, traffic-filled street.

***

With a strong tail wind, the flight to Frankfurt took a little less than nine bumpy hours, most of which, Stack spent catching up on sleep, exhausted from the chase across the Caribbean.

Back in Cuba, trouble had kept coming at him to the very end. He'd noticed the car following a few vehicles back. Henriquez was taking him to the José Martí International Airport, southwest of Havana. He asked the Cuban to simply drop him off directly outside Terminal 3.

He had no baggage apart from the backpack, so he'd be quick.

They stopped outside the new passenger building with its stubby-winged rooftop architecture. Stack wasted no time. He'd already thanked Henriquez. A quick nod of the head as he slammed the car door. The briefest scan of other cars that were arriving and then he turned to walk the few steps into the shadowy darkness of the terminal. It was cooler inside, but not by much. He found some privacy in the space under the stairs up to the departures lounge. Unzipping the front pocket of the backpack, he removed his passport and the sheet of paper he'd written the reservation code and flight number on.

He stuffed both paper and passport into his pants pocket and turned, intending to make his way up to the departure lounge, but what he found was a wall that wasn't there a moment ago. He looked up into the smiling face of one of Ulyanin's goons. He made a quick hundred and eighty degree turn and ran straight into another leather-jacketed obstruction. They grabbed his arms and pushed him back under the stairs, away from any public attention and any PNR interest.

'You're wasting your time, fella's, I don't have it any more. Look.'

Stack held the bag out. It was obvious it carried nothing heavy, like a 28-pound bar of gold. Ulyanin's heavies had been instructed to find Stack and take the gold. With single-minded ruthlessness that is what they intended to do. One of them grabbed the bag and started to unzip the larger pocket. As he did, the other one, obviously capable of more independent thought, moaned at him in Russian. Stack guessed he was telling him not to waste his time. But the first guy kept pulling stuff out of the bag and throwing it on the floor. There wasn't much, just the shorts and T-shirt. Finally, in frustration, he threw the bag on the floor and grabbed Stack by the shirt, pulling him up so that their noses touched.

'You know what we look for. Where is?'

Stack pulled his head back and slammed his forehead hard against the goon's face. Shocked, the heavy stepped back and touched his nose, checking for blood. He was surprised to find none on his fingers when he took his hand away.

'I don't have it any more. It's gone.'

The heavy went to grab him again, but his partner stopped him. Independent thought marking him out for greater things in the Mikhail Ulyanin organisation. More words in Russian that brought the other guy under a measure of control. He turned to Stack.

'Mr Ulyanin will want to know who has it. You will tell please.'

'Somewhere in Havana. I don't know where.'

Stack bent down to pick up his bag and clothes. As he started walking away, the thinking guy grabbed his arm and pulled him in close – face to pockmarked, broken-nosed face. He had a grip like the jaws of a pit bull.

'You must be careful.' His voice was a low growl of threatening menace, 'Mr Ulyanin does not like to be made a fool of. This will not be forgotten.'

He relaxed his grip, nodded to his partner and they both walked off. Stuffing his clothes back into the bag, Stack had only one thought as he walked up the stairs to the departure lounge, *'You needn't worry pal, the sun will turn into an orange M&M before I cross paths with that slimy bastard again.'*

Stonebridge

In a basement room under the six-storey St. Petersburg headquarters of Russian energy giant, Severgaz Postavka, two men stared at a computer screen, concern etched across their faces. They had always known that undertaking such a technologically challenging task as managing a remote drilling hack for an extended period of time would carry risks. The main problem was the human component. Like the drilling site in Derbyshire, they needed two sets of crews running twelve hour, day and nightshifts: Two computer hot-shots controlling the hack and two directional drillers over-seeing the drill's hidden progress.

They had been confident in the robustness of the algorithm, but every fix added a new line of un-tested code. Some people are better at writing code than others, and the more lines of additional code, the harder it was to predict future outcomes. It was like having a docile horse that gradually becomes wild and harder to manage. Eventually, they'd need to reinstall the hack, which would make the real data showing the true direction of the drill bit visible for the few seconds it took to install. But not yet.

The computer monitor was displaying the third false data event. Like before, they had quickly corrected it. But they shouldn't have needed to. The algorithm in the drilling site computer should have taken care of it, invisibly washing the data before sending it through to the directional drillers screen.

The two questions for which they needed an answer, and quickly, were: why did it happen and had the directional driller on the nightshift noticed? If he had, it would be for the second time and he wouldn't ignore it. Which meant he would need to be 'managed'. Unlike the hack, they couldn't do that remotely.

Beneath the sunlit hills and grass-covered valleys of the Derbyshire Peak District, the drill chewed eagerly through the shale. Doing what the pulsed instructions told it to do. Indifferent to its deadly destination - the fault deep under Shivering Mountain. Just eight days away.

***

Mid-summer in the UK doesn't come close to the tropical heat of Cuba, or anywhere else in the Caribbean. Stack really noticed the difference.

In the two hours between flights, he'd taken the opportunity to pick up some new clothes at Frankfurt airport. Not an entire wardrobe, but jeans, regular smart pants, two shirts, t-shirts, underwear, toothpaste and brush etc. Nothing expensive, but the kind of stuff you'd pack if you started out from home rather than in the middle of a nomadic hike around the world.

He used the changing room of one of the shops to swap into the new shirt and pants. The old clothes were rolled up and stuffed into Charlie's backpack with the rest of the new purchases. He'd bought one other item, a black bomber jacket to replace the one he'd left behind at the hotel in Grand Cayman. He slipped it on and paused to check his appearance in a mirror as he left the shop. The outfit looked good, but he was shocked at the depth of the tan he'd developed. It didn't seem much back in the Caribbean, but here, in Europe, he looked like he'd just been rescued after six months in the Kalahari Desert.

The $5,000 had been reduced radically by the cost of the single fair to the UK, paid for in cash at the reservations desk back in Cuba and by the clothes he'd just bought. He had just over $3,500 left, plus some change in Euro's.

Like Summer and Charlie, the real test of nerves came during the passport check at Heathrow. Was he a returning fugitive, or just another sunburned holiday maker? The woman passport officer seemed to be making a lot of faces as she turned the pages, referring back to a screen and then to the passport again. She mentioned that he seemed very tanned and asked where had he been. Cuba was a name that had her flicking through the pages again. The fact that there was no evidence of a port of entry or visa stamp seemed to perplex her. Stack just shrugged and suggested it was not something he had paid any attention to. Eventually, noticing the long line behind him, or because the end of her shift was approaching, she waved him through.

***

It was mostly men from the rig that filled the crowded bar, so when Summer walked in to The Devils Pike, it was like Moses parting the Red Sea. All the guys stepped aside to get a better look at her and who the lucky guy was she was heading towards.

Summer wasn't entirely unaware of their attention, but knew that if they came any closer they'd be enjoying the strong odour of camp fires mixed with cooking smells and other assorted al fresco fragrances that the rudimentary camp washing facility couldn't remove.

Her heart missed a beat when she saw James. It hadn't been a week, but it seemed a lifetime. Not wanting to make an exhibition in front of the pub crowd, they kissed quickly. Stack bought a beer and a white wine spritzer and carried their drinks outside hoping to find somewhere to sit in the late afternoon sunshine. They were lucky, a table built from rough-hewn wood became available in the front of the pub looking out onto the road and the spectacular countryside beyond.

'The tan suits you.'

'You don't look so bad yourself.'

Small talk at first.

'Christ! I've missed you, Summer.'

They kissed again. Longer this time. When Stack pulled away at last, he wrinkled his nose.

'What is that smell?'

'Oh, you mean the new Eau de Summer? This year's must-have fragrance?' Summer laughed brightly, 'Every girl will be smelling like me before the year's out, James.'

'I certainly hope not. You smell like a bonfire!' Stack burst out laughing

'Get used to it, James. You sent me to the protest camp. It's how me and the sisters like to live. The honest and unvarnished smell of your everyday Earth Mother.'

'We'll soon see about that. I'm staying here at the pub, for the time being anyway. Stay here with me tonight. There's a thing called a bathroom. I'll introduce you to it personally. I'm sure you'll enjoy it.'

They both laughed again, happy in each other's company, oblivious to anyone else around them. Then the table rocked a little as someone joined them.

'Cheer up you two. You look like the world's come to an end.' Charlie 'Hollywood' Dawson gave a big hearty laugh and took a long swig from his dimpled glass of beer.

Stack leaned over and gave Charlie's shoulder a welcoming pat while Summer stood up and reached over to kiss his forehead.

'Now that's what I call a proper greeting guys.' He had a

broad grin on his face, 'Here we are, back together again. The Three Musketeers.'

'You're looking a bit knackered, Charlie.'

'Yeah, like I've said before, night time is for playing not working. I've only been up for an hour. I'm back on at six.'

Stack looked at his watch. It showed just after four.

'Well, we don't have much time. I'd better go through my story first. It'd make a hell of a movie, Charlie.'

It took the best part of half an hour to give them the highlights, with constant interruptions from Charlie and Summer, keen to know details Stack had skipped over.

Eventually, he got to the part where the deal was done and Summer and Charlie leaned in expectantly. He'd already texted them that he'd sold the gold bar, but not how much he got for it. When he told them, they both raised their glasses in celebration to him. Charlie's response was typical.

'So that bloke, Short List came through in the end. I must admit I had my doubts.' He held up his empty glass, 'Drinks anyone?'

'I thought drilling rigs were supposed to be alcohol free. You know, health and safety?'

'Yeah.' Charlie said despondently, 'Maybe just have half. Same again for you two?'

While Charlie was gone, Stack asked Summer if there was any news from the protest camp. It turned out that little had changed in the day to day protesting. They continued to make a nuisance of themselves - delaying things as much as they could. There was quite a crowd now at the camp, from around the country and from abroad. Many were professional agitators in her opinion, or independently wealthy. Some even had sponsors. Others had an axe to grind, or were just out for trouble.

One guy was pushing even harder for direct action. She'd mentioned him before, but now he had support from many of the new arrivals. The balance was shifting from rowdy but mostly peaceful, to brutality and carnage. A clear intention to stop the drilling at any cost. Then Charlie returned and he wasn't alone.

'Guys. This is David. David meet James and Summer – she's Canadian.'

Stack gave Charlie a questioning look, wondering why on earth he would bring a stranger back to their table. Nevertheless, both Summer and Stack offered their hands. Stack kept his mouth shut and waited for an explanation.

Charlie realised the ball was still in his court.

'Yeah, well, David Bennett here is a reporter. That's right ain't it pal?'

From the wide-eyed look of rebuke he flashed Charlie, Stack might just as well have yelled, *'A bloody reporter?'*

'Yes, I'm with the local press. I always pop in here to see if there's anything I can use. The place attracts people from the drilling site and the protest camp, so it's pretty convenient. And, you know…' He doffed his beer glass, 'It's a pub!'

Early thirties, average height, slim, dark hair brushed to one side. He wore thick-framed glasses on his narrow face. Dressed smart but comfortably in a loose fitting beige jacket over a white shirt, maroon tie that was dappled with a collection of darker smudges and dark trousers. Cigarette in one hand, drink in the other. Mid-career, but still fired-up with the undiminished enthusiasm of a cub reporter. He was easing his feet under the table and making himself at home as he spoke.

'Charlie here told me he works at the site. Nights. And apparently the lady's with the protest camp. I thought that was pretty intriguing. I wondered what you all might have in common.' He tapped his nose, 'Just curious.'

Charlie, ever the gregarious and sociable type, went quiet, suddenly realising that perhaps it hadn't been such a good idea bringing him over.

Summer and Stack just sat there, suddenly not feeling very chatty.

It was an awkward moment, but good reporters are born thick skinned. He looked at Stack.

'And then there were three. Are you a protester or a driller? I'd put you down as one of the drilling crowd.'

Stack thought about going along with the idea, but he changed his mind for some reason.

'Actually, I'm neither. Just a friend.'

Bennett gave a nod towards Summer.

'Her's I'd guess?'

Stack nodded the affirmative.

'So why are two people from opposing camps all cosy and chatty?'

'We're not. We're just friends.' Stack said.

'Come on guys. Give me something.' Bennett implored, 'I know something's going on. It's not just the protesters that want to shut the drilling down. I've heard from a couple of people about an attempted sabotage on the rig. Nearly cost lives.'

'That was before my time, mate. I've only been there a week.' Charlie said.

'So it's true then?'

Stack cut in.

'He didn't say that.'

'Why is everyone so defensive?'

'Well, there's a lot at stake.' Charlie said, 'We've got to make sure they complete the frack.'

Bennett looked at all three of them for a beat.

'What, even the protestors?'

'Charlie!' Another wide-eyed appeal from Stack.

Bennett turned to Summer.

'How long have you been up there, you know, with the protesters, Summer? About a week?' He turned to Stack, 'And at a guess I'd say you've only just arrived back in this country by the look of your tan.'

'What are you, some kind of Sherlock Holmes tribute act?' Stack wanted to close the conversation down, 'There's nothing of interest to you here. We're just friends, having a drink on a nice summer's afternoon.'

Bennett scratched his head for a moment, then reached for another cigarette from the packet on the table. He lit up, stuffed the packet back in his jacket pocket and reached inside his pants pocket for his wallet. He pulled a card out and snapped it onto the table.

'OK. Sorry guys. I'm just trying to piece something together. There's a story out there, I'm sure of it.' He tapped the card as he extracted himself from the bench, 'If you hear of anything…?'

He grabbed his beer, turned and pushed his way through the crowded entrance, back into the pub.

On their own again, all eyes turned to Charlie.

'OK. I get it. Not a good idea.'

'But a journalist, Charlie,' Summer said. 'He had our number from the moment he sat down. He'll keep sniffing around. He thinks he's on to something.'

'That's true, Summer. But it works both ways.' Stack saw an opportunity as he picked up Bennett's card. 'Who knows? Perhaps we can turn him to our advantage? He's a trained investigator. Might be useful.'

Over at the entrance, Bennett stuck his head out of the

door, threw his cigarette on the ground, stamped on it, muttered a profanity and went back inside.

***

It was the second false data event that raised John Stonebridge's curiosity enough to make him want to check out the first event over a week ago.

Ordinarily, the young directional driller would have discarded a one-off event like a row of stupid numbers. Especially as they were quickly followed by a new row that had the correct set of coordinates. But this second event, still just a momentary flash, took a little longer to be replaced and when the correct numbers finally appeared they had the unnerving appearance of being typed on, as though by a ghostly hand. He shuddered when he saw it. That was at around 2 am. For the rest of the night his eyes never left the screen, watching out for it to happen again. It didn't.

The extra effort of looking out for the strange telemetry had left him drained by the end of his shift. Tired and exhausted, he handed his chair over to dayshift directional driller, Debbie Blain. They had the usual de-briefing of the past night's drilling progress. Not much to say, everything was going as expected: on-time and on-distance. He turned to leave but hesitated. Last time, when he mentioned the false data event, she dismissed it out of hand as 'just one of those things'. She'd almost patted him on the head.

'Was there something else, John?' Blain could see something was on Stonebridge's mind.

Confronted with that question and the opportunity to say more, Stonebridge backed down.

'No... I... It's nothing really, Debbie.' His brain was like cotton wool. He knew he'd make a fool of himself if he brought the matter up.

'You look exhausted, John. You've done well. Go eat and get some sleep before you fall over.'

He nodded and left the dog shack. The route to the canteen took him across the drilling floor, down the metal staircase to the open passageways that led around the various areas of equipment that ran the rig. Past the mud pressure pumps, spares storage sheds. A right turn past drilling water tanks, electricity generators and compressors. Then a left past mud mixing pumps and the vast mud tanks containing the slurry that gets pumped down to lubricate the drill and through which the telemetry pulses travel. Finally, leaving the noise of the heavy machinery behind, the route crossed an asphalt apron to the accommodation, office and canteen blocks.

Stonebridge was about to enter the canteen but paused for a moment. Perhaps the crisp, early morning fresh-air had invigorated him a little.

He took a look at his watch. Still early, not many people in the office. The toolpusher was out on the rig right now, so his work station computer was free, for a little while anyway.

He brought up the access portal to the drilling data, entered his passcode and punched in the date and time of the first out-of-wack data event. It was displayed amongst a screen full of similar looking telemetry, except it just looked odd in some way. Then he realised what it was. All the other numbers changed sequentially over time. The false data simply dropped out of sequence. It had no logical relevance to the numbers that went before or after. He copied and pasted the line into a fresh page.

Then he looked for that morning's event. Easier to find.

Again, an odd set of numbers, which he copied and pasted under the previous set on the new page.

He sat back and looked at it for a moment. They were different. At first glance not sequential. But no! There was some commonality, some consistency in some of the figures. He began to wonder whether those two data sets were the only events. Have they happened before?

He took a breath, rubbed his hands together and entered the numbers into the search field at the top right of the data page. Pressed enter and very quickly that same data set came up. He should have expected it. A computer only responds to the question it's asked. He didn't think the search protocols were very intuitive. He'd have to do it the hard way, eyeballing each page of drilling data. How far should he go back? They'd been directional drilling for about two and a half weeks including tripping the entire drillstring out of the hole occasionally to replace worn out drill bits. He checked his watch, there wasn't much time. Decision made, he started from the first false data event just over a week ago. The data was recorded in 24 hour blocks. He scrolled it forward to the beginning of Debbie Blains shift, the one right after his had ended.

He knew what to look for, anything out of the ordinary from the usual sequence. It should spring out to him. The problem was fatigue. His eyes kept glazing over, or his mind wandered as he scanned through page after identical page. Sometimes he thought he'd just missed something, but when he scrolled back there was nothing. It was just as the drilling supervisor, Simon Harding entered the open-plan office that Stonebridge thought he saw something. He blinked and scrolled back half a page. There it was. He blinked his eyes to refocus. There was no mistake, right in the middle of Debbie Blain's shift, about 11.20 a.m. four days ago. He copied and pasted it into the new page of false data events. There were three of them now. Perhaps there were others, but he didn't have time to look as Simon Harding wandered over.

'Morning John. Bit late for you to be working? I'd have thought you'd have had enough by now.'

Harding was a good man, a company man perhaps, but always concerned for the well-being of his troops. It wasn't that Stonebridge shouldn't have been at the tool pushers desk, everybody hot-desks from time to time.

'Any problems that I should be concerned about?'

'No, Simon. All good. Just a bit of housekeeping. I'm done now.'

The last thing he wanted to do was alert Harding to something that may turn out to be nothing. Scaremongering. It doesn't look good and he'd already made a fool of himself last time.

He saved the page of three false data events to his laptop via the local intranet, logged out, left the office and walked on over to the canteen.

***

Charlie was just coming to the end of his meal, not breakfast or dinner really, a kind of hybrid. You can call breakfast and lunch – brunch. But what do you call dinner and breakfast? Dinfast? Brinner? He amused himself with these thoughts as John Stonebridge wondered in. He acknowledged Charlie with a quick wave and joined the line to get his food. Charlie hung around, wondering if he'd come back to his table. He often did, but not always. Stonebridge was a good guy, young and a little nervous perhaps, but steady, and as far as Charlie could tell, professional. Charlie reckoned

Stonebridge's main problem with the older members of the crew was that he still smelled of university: all eager and fresh out of the box. He didn't stand a chance until he'd got some real dirt and oil under his nails. But he liked the guy.

He reminded him of some of the college types who turned up as freshly hatched officers at Camp Bastion, bits of egg shell still sticking to them. When you've been out on three-day yomps across enemy infiltrated territory and back, fighting spiteful little skirmishes every other mile, when you've done that for a few years, a fresh face with none of the experience and all of the authority is hard to take. Some of them were better than others. Like James Stack. He was a born leader – eventually. He wondered whether that was a contradiction.

In the event Stonebridge made a bee-line for Charlie, placed the plate of sausages and mash and mug of coffee on the table and sat down. He unwrapped the paper napkin and the knife and fork tumbled noisily onto the table. His hands shook a little.

'Long shift?' Charlie said noticing the fatigue in his face and weary manner.

'Same length as always, Charlie.' He took a hit of the hot coffee. Black. No sugar. It seemed to invigorate him. 'How about you?'

'Oh, I'm just that little sod Wayne's lackey. When he screws up, and he does, often, he comes looking for me to spread the misery.'

'Why do you put up with it? I'd have pissed off long ago.'

There was a pause while Stonebridge cut a slice of sausage and chewed it listlessly. It was obvious, Stonebridge wasn't happy. That's why Charlie was there: to make observations; to spot unusual behaviour or activity; to keep an eye on things. To protect James's investment and ultimately his.

'Something wrong, mate? More Close Encounters of the Wrong Rocks?' Charlie 'Hollywood' Dawson always defaulted to his favourite subject when the opportunity presented itself. 'Close what?' That was often the problem. Many people just weren't on his cinematic wavelength.

'Rock. Have you had anymore unexpected rock types?'

'Well, yes. There was another odd sample that came up yesterday. It didn't match the expected profile at that point in the well-plan's geological projection.'

'I don't know what that means, but what are you going to do about it?'

'Not sure. It is possible that part of a sandstone layer squeezed through the lower mudstone and penetrated into the shale. That's what the geologist thinks anyway.'

'Or?'

'Or, we might not be exactly where we think we are.'

'Could that be a problem?

'The shale layer is all around us, so being off by a little bit shouldn't be a problem. It's just that drilling these days is quite a precision business. We always know where we are. Well, we should do anyway.'

'So you're not too bothered then?'

Another long pause during which Stonebridge played with his food, not quite getting round to eating it.

Charlie gently probed.

'What's on your mind, John?'

Stonebridge was obviously struggling with his thoughts.

'Oh, it's probably nothing.' This time he stuffed his mouth with food. He couldn't talk while he ate.

Charlie sat back and watched. He could see Stonebridge was troubled by something. He waited.

Eventually, Stonebridge put his knife and fork down, pushed the plate away and dragged the coffee mug towards him, cupping it between his hands as he stared into the rich, black liquid, struggling with his internal conflicts. Something was wrong he was sure, but he didn't want to make a fool of himself. He wanted to talk, perhaps he just needed to hear his concerns out loud. To see how it sounded before taking it further. Charlie was low in the food chain. A good guy but not a technician. A safe pare of ears. He was still staring into the coffee cup. He frowned as he spoke.

'There was another false data event this morning. I've checked and there have been at least three of them.'

'Three?'

Stonebridge looked up.

''Yes. The one this morning was different though.'

'In what way?'

'It's just how, when it corrected itself, the numbers seemed to type on, as though by hand. You know, on a keyboard. It was probably just some latency in the system, you know, buffering or something.' He tried to dismiss it, but he knew what he saw. It was creepy.

'So, it's happened three times on your shift?'

'That's the thing. It's only happened twice on my shift. I've checked this morning, just before coming here. It turns out it happened on Debbie's shift, mid-morning a few days ago.'

'What, just the once on Debbie's shift?'

'I didn't have time to look any further. I was interrupted by Simon Harding, so I copied and pasted the data into a fresh page and saved it.'

'Wait a minute. I don't understand. If these false data events self-corrected, how could you still see them? I mean, surely they weren't there to be found anymore?'

Stonebridge explained that they have lots of data on-screen which can get confusing, especially if you keep adding to it. To avoid clutter, they filter it. Only current data is displayed. The line of false data events wasn't corrected, it just dropped down into the line below and out of sight when the correct line was displayed. But when he was scanning through the continuous twenty-four-hour data pages looking for false data events, every event was displayed. It was a mountain of information and the false data events were easy to miss if you were in a hurry or tired. Stonebridge was both.

'Are you telling me that Debbie Blain, the senior Directional Driller, had one of these false data events but ignored it?'

'To be fair, she may not have seen it. It updates very quickly and if her eyes were on something else, you know, not on the screen, there's no way she would've spotted it.'

'And if she did spot it but ignored it?'

'That's the problem. Why would she do that? It wouldn't make sense?'

'Yeah. But if she ignored it…?'

'Then she would be either recklessly risking the whole drilling operation…'

'Yeah. Or…?'

The next words were the thoughts Stonebridge didn't want to speak out loud.

'Then…I suppose…she must be in on some kind of conspiracy.' His head dropped down to stare into his coffee for a moment. Then he looked up again sharply.

'But only if she saw the data and ignored it. She's a highly experienced driller, I can't believe she would.'

***

In a small basement room in St Petersburg, a sharp-eyed

computer hacker had noticed that pages of data had been called up on a computer in the Hope Valley drilling site. He watched as the pages scrolled up, moving forward in time, stopping every now and then, and then moving on. It looked as though someone was reviewing the history of the drilling data. Then, as the page stopped once more and the cursor highlighted a line of data, he leaned forward in shocked comprehension. He watched the data being copied and pasted into another page. Information that if you joined the dots would leave an unmistakable trail to the fault under Mam Tor. Making a note of the account and username, he waited until the user had signed out. After a few moments, he signed back in. He knew how many false data events had occurred. It wouldn't take long to find them all.

Hope Valley

She wasn't on wages. She didn't have to clock in and she didn't need a sick note if she didn't turn up. The bloody protest camp would just have to manage without her for the day. Summer stretched lazily under the white linen sheets of the four-poster bed, her arm reaching over for James, still curled up asleep next to her. She lifted her head and blinked her eyes into focus a couple of times. The red digital figures on the bedside clock seemed to say 9.35. She squeezed her eyes and then rubbed them with the back of her hand. No, it was definite. 9.35. Apart from the, how much time had they'd spent making love - two - three hours? They'd slept a good nine hours. They both needed the rest. She was worn out with the relentless misery of life under canvas. Hard ground, hard work and hardcore prejudices. And James had barely slept after nearly five days chasing across the Caribbean.

The sun found a narrow gap in the drapes allowing a thin bright strip of warm golden light to fall across the bed. Outside, there seemed to be plenty of traffic, so the day was already up and running.

She pushed James to rouse him, leaning over to kiss his neck, tickling his ear with a lock of blond hair.

'Come on. Breakfast.' She whispered in his ear, 'We've got twenty minutes.'

He turned over and kissed her lips. Falling back again for a moment, he yawned, stretched and swung his legs over the side of the bed.

'Yeah, OK.' He rubbed his face with both hands. 'I'll just have a quick shower. Coming?'

'Well, if we want breakfast, quick it had better be.'

***

'Tell me about this guy back at the camp. The one who wants all-out war on GeoPower.'

They'd made the breakfast sitting with a minute to spare and a resentful glare from a waitress who had hoped her shift had ended. They were both famished and went for the full English: sausage, eggs – poached – beans, tomatoes, mushrooms and toast. Coffee was served in elegant cups. They'd drunk two refills before the delicious hot food arrived.

'Danny Finnegan. Charmless bastard.' She said. 'He must be a professional agitator. His arguments seem very well thought out. People find it hard to counter his reasoning.'

Stack sniffed his contempt.

'It's the classic politician's trick where you produce a fact that nobody can contest, at least not immediately. You know, something like; *yesterday's rain was the worst in living memory.* You claim it's a statement of undeniable fact. Then you follow up with; *that being the case, the following must be true.* And you go on to make your incontestable point.'

'Maybe.' Summer conceded. 'Anyway, there are plenty of people in the camp who support him, unconditionally. They sit with him in the evenings and he preaches to them like some kind of religious messiah. It's almost a cult. Very scary.'

They ate silently for a while, just enjoying each other's company without the pressure of needing to be somewhere urgently. A day off. A guilty pleasure. Stack struggled to ignore the ticking clock over at Rebellion Hill.

'Charlie reckons they're about eight days away from fracking.' He spoke in between sips of coffee, 'If we can get it past the finishing line without any hiccups, eventually the share price will go back up and we can get on with our lives.'

'It does sound a bit mercenary doesn't it? You know, get the money back no matter the cost.'

'We can't afford to be philosophical about it, Summer. I didn't invest the money, Blackstone did. I'm just trying to rescue it again.'

'I know. But helping GeoPower bring more gas to the surface, just when the world is trying to use less fossil fuel. And our motivation is money. It doesn't feel right. You know - morally.'

'Careful, Summer. You sound like you've gone native!' Stack tried to make a joke of it, 'You've spent too much time at the camp, or Finnegan's cast his spell on you.'

Summer sat back thoughtfully.

'I might not agree with them, James. Well, not everything anyway. But they hold their principles dearly. I have to respect that.'

Stack's moral compass didn't always steer a true course. His recent past was evidence of the elastic nature of his relationship with it. Summer on the other hand was a better navigator of ethical issues and Stack new it. He didn't want to spoil their first day together in a while, so he dropped the subject. He checked his watch, dabbed his mouth with the linen napkin and started to get up.

'Come on! It's a fantastic day. Let's go for a drive. Take a look at the countryside. People come from all over the world to visit the Peak District.' He put his arm around her waist as she rose from the table. To the annoyance of the few remaining diners in the small breakfast room he used the voice of a fairground barker 'Last chance for a magical mystery tour of the Peak District – the Switzerland of the north. Hurry up! Only one seat left on the coach, missus.'

Summer tried to hide her embarrassment, but laughed happily anyway.

***

The camp had been buzzing since the night before, when a steady stream of supporters had started to arrive. Danny Finnegan had got his way. The game had changed. Direct action was the new religion. He'd sent out a message calling the faithful to prayers and they turned up in their hundreds.

It started with the odd one or two in the late afternoon, but soon they were arriving in tens and twenties. Coming in on trains and buses. Walking the last few miles. Those that drove had to abandon their vehicles along the verges of the narrow country roads without concern for the comings and goings of the local population, but providing an early bonus for the cause by strangling access for trucks going to and from the drilling site. News which cheered the activists at the camp when they heard about it.

Most brought tents and sleeping kit with them. Many just wrapped themselves in old plastic sheets and whatever they could scrounge to get them through the mild summer night.

They were old hands, familiar with the routine. Veterans of many political campaigns and violent demos.

The new arrivals swelling the numbers of camp residents didn't go unnoticed. Rumours of the steady influx of strangers began to spread throughout the valley. The few police in the immediate vicinity were slow to respond. Their first reaction? It was high summer, lots of holiday makers and tourists passing through. Nothing unusual. But the local kids saw an opportunity to liven up a dull weekend. The word was eagerly spread around the local pubs where teenagers gathered on a Saturday night that something cool was happening up at Rebellion Hill the next day. Bored with valley life, they arrived early in the morning all high spirits and eager.

The camp population was now so large that it swelled out through the trees and on to the adjacent hillside.

By the fading light of the midsummer evening, one police car managed to thread its way up to the security gates. After exchanging pleasantries and then concerns with the guards, they took a tentative walk around the nearby camp environs. Local police, unused to the cruel indifference of inner city dwellers, tried to be friendly but were met with hostility and retreated back to the safety of their patrol car. They radioed in a report but were given little sympathy from dispatch who accused them of being soft, making light of their concerns by joking that a safer option was the report of two escaped sheep on the road up to Hathersage they may like to attend.

The day began early with zombie-like creatures wrapped in blankets and ground sheets, wandering aimlessly around the camp, some stopping to pee against a tree, the women preferring somewhere more private. Others foraged for food wherever it could be found. Gradually, they coalesced into large groups around one of Danny Finnegan's half dozen trusted lieutenants.

Each group were given specific tasks and timings. But it boiled down to two main forces: one large group assembling around the main gate; the other, smaller task force of about 50 hardened activists, melted into the woods to take a position hidden from view, further along the gully on the other side of the rig site.

This group included specialists with petrol-driven

grinders and other heavy industrial cutting equipment. They had radios for communications which they used sparingly and in code only. The hidden assault force was waiting for a single word: 'Pelican'.

Danny Finnegan knew the press would be looking out for him. He'd put the word out at the last moment to the national and local news media to ensure secrecy for as long as possible. He'd given them just two hours to get their act together. There was no point in kicking off the main event without having TV cameras around to show the world.

Finnegan's reputation as a hard-boiled anarchist was well earned. When his name got associated with a demo, picket, protest, street march or civil disturbance, you could be sure nothing good would come of it. That's why he made himself very visible leading the great army of protestors at the main gates. Lots of noise and angry shouting, air-horns and bull-horns. Professional banners and scrawled signs filled the area 20 yards thick. The camera crews sought Finnegan out as he knew they would, and he made sure they found him. As long as all the attention was on him, no one was taking an interest in anything else.

After some quick interviews with several news teams, he melted into the crowd to join the other activist leaders at the edge of the wooded area. He checked his watch. It was ten o'clock and things had gone exactly as planned. He raised the palm-sized radio to his mouth and pressed the transmit button.

***

Far away, behind the fence at the back end of the drilling site, a small two-way radio hissed into life and a tiny metallic voice crackled through.

'Pelican. Repeat. Pelican.'

'Copy that. Pelican.'

The lieutenant pocketed the radio and nodded to the stocky guy next to him. The man reached for the pull-cord of the cutting equipment. Until that moment they'd been hidden out of sight in nearby bushes and trees. The sound of the steel grinder's petrol engine buzzing into life, was the cue to rush the fence. It took under a minute to cut a hole large enough for several people at a time to push through. Inside the site no one was watching. Those who weren't directly involved in the drilling operation were all paying attention to the chaos in the opposite direction down at the main gate.

The mob of protestors quickly rushed across the empty space between the breached fence and the drilling rig. Thirty or so sacrificed themselves by running directly around the rig and towards the main gate. A deliberate tactic to get everyone to watch them and not what was happening back at the fence. As they'd planned, security guards and nearby rig workers began chasing after the interlopers around trucks loaded with pipe, spares containers, compressors and equipment bays. They ran through offices and into the canteen, shouting and cursing, anywhere but back towards the rig. Keeping the GeoPower crew distracted while the remaining ten or fifteen activists headed for the rig itself. There weren't enough men remaining to stop them as they quickly stormed the drilling deck and began to scale the framework of the towering steel derrick.

The driller immediately saw the danger and shouted to those nearby and others on his two-way that he was shutting down the drill. The roustabouts and roughnecks clambered up after the activists, prising them off of the iron work when they could reach them and just clinging on to others with all their considerable strength, preventing them from climbing higher.

By the time the winch engine and top drive motor had fallen silent, five had already made it half way up the tower. Three secured themselves to the steel framework as a sacrificial defence against any assault from below. The remaining two, laden with backpacks and climbing gear, clambered the final 30 feet up towards the monkey board. The derrickman decided to get the hell out of the way. He finished securing the ninety foot stand of pipe he'd been making ready, strapped his harness to the Geronimo escape line and abseiled down, away from trouble.

With no one left to stop them, the remaining two experienced climbers, made their way the last few feet up to the monkey board and unpacked their rucksacks. They attached the strings of two tightly rolled bundles to nearby girders and threw the packs out and away, allowing them to unroll as they fell.

A light breeze toyed with the material, occasionally lifting it high into the air like enormous ribbons, before dying down and becoming still, allowing the cloth to fall again. The group halfway down grabbed the strings that still flutterred like the tails of a kite, and secured them to the ironwork.

The main gates, only a few minutes before a place of anarchy and chaos, on Finnegan's cue, became silent. An air of expectancy buzzed through the crowd like static electricity. The TV cameras had already spotted the activity on the derrick. Finnegan didn't want anything to distract from this moment. Heads turned and cameras panned and then a great cheer went up as the hundreds of activists clapped and screamed their delight at the sight of their spectacular propaganda coup. Two long banners hanging down from the top of the derrick were displaying an unequivocal message for the whole world to read. Two very clear and simple words with the unambiguous instruction: *Frack Off!*

***

They'd explored all the minor roads that linked the villages and hamlets nestling in the folds of the Derbyshire hills. Driving through narrow, tall-hedged corridors that wound around and up and down. Alongside rivers and edging fields. Stopping every now and then to enjoy a view, or take a walk. In the early afternoon they'd stopped at a pub, built of wooden beams and local stone like most of the old buildings in the area.

Eventually, they passed beyond Castleton and on through the twisting gorge at Winnats Pass to the foot of Mam Tor. They left the Ford Focus rental in the car park and took the hikers path that rose 1500 feet to the domed summit. It was like standing on top of the world with the valley spread out below them under a cloudless, pastel blue sky. An endless horizon in every direction. The view was breath-taking.

They'd been drawn towards the massive feature dominating the landscape from the moment they stepped out of the hotel to begin their tour of the valley. In the pub, they'd asked about it. A local legend held the population transfixed. Mam Tor had large buttresses of loose shale rock that slithered in whispering streams down its slopes, changing the mountain's shape over time. Perhaps these collapses were caused by small tremors deep beneath the ground, or simply the natural instability in the layers of broken stone. The locals preferred an old legend that blamed a mysterious life force. To them, the monumental rock that loomed over the valley was Shivering Mountain. As far as Stack and Summer were concerned, the walk to the top was worth the effort. From high up, the view east along Hope Valley was spectacular, overlooking one of the most beautiful and peaceful scenes in England. The undulating countryside spread out before them, from the nearby town of Castleton and across to Bradwell far beyond. The meagre waters of the River Noe twinkled fleetingly in the distance through thickets of trees before disappearing behind low hills and then reappearing as it headed towards Bamford where it became the River Derwent. In the hills to the left, another stream fed the River Noe at Hope, a village whose name was recorded in the Doomsday Book in 1086.

It was a green-shaded vista of rural perfection under the powder-blue skies of a sublime midsummer afternoon, with one notorious exception. It was as though someone had taken a knife and hacked a jagged slice across a much love Turner landscape. Half way across the valley an enormous quarry had been gouged out of the ground creating a very visible grey scar. It sat next to a concrete factory with its tall white chimney rising over 400 feet above the valley floor. How such an industry could have been allowed to blight the outstanding natural beauty of the valley was beyond understanding. Yet there it was and not a protester in sight.

They sat on a small rocky outcrop drinking in the view, trying to ignore what was after all, only a small patch of scenic discord.

The views in every other direction were rewarded with the unspoiled landscape found only in romantic poetry and forgotten love songs. He found himself beginning to relax for the first time in a long time. Summer leaned against him, a strand of her blond hair caught in the gentle breeze brushed lightly against his cheek. Purpose and urgency forgotten. He closed his eyes and breathed a deep contented sigh.

The serenity of the moment was broken suddenly by a jarring noise. The acoustic equivalent of the jagged hole torn out of the valley floor below. A loud, brash, nerve-jangling interruption assaulted the calm silence of Mam Tor. Stack's cell phone had sprung into life. Shaken from her reverie, Summer jerked back to the present.

'Bloody things should be banned up here.'

'It's been a while,' Stack sighed as he reached into his pants pocket. 'I was wondering when I was going to hear from him again.'

A questioning look crossed Summer's face.

The ringing blared louder until Stack answered it and held the phone to his ear. It didn't take long. By the time he'd stabbed the red button to end the call

four or five seconds later, he hadn't said a word.

Summer understood.

'Blackstone? A *call this number message?*'

Stack nodded as he replaced the phone in his pocket.

'Yeah. He can wait.'

He was determined not be at the beck and call of the man who was the architect of his present financial problems.

As he settled back, trying to recapture the sublime tranquillity of the mood of only a moment earlier, Stack's attention became snagged on a distant shape. He stood up to see it more clearly, his gaze seeking something further out across the valley. He held his hand over his eyes to shield them from the sun and asked Summer to stand next to him so he could share it with her. With his other hand he pointed to a feature just below the horizon, where trees filled the space between two low hills.

'Can you see it yet?'

'What, by the village over there?

'No. To the right. There's a small barn or house of some kind. The hill to the right of that. Keep going right a little and you'll see the trees.'

It took a moment. It was quite a distance and a light haze reduced the clarity.

Eventually, Summer thought she had it.

'OK, I see the trees between the hills. So what?' She squinted, trying to resolve the shimmering image.

'Once you spot it, you'll wonder how you missed it. It's the top of the drilling derrick. It's mostly hidden behind Rebellion Hill, but it's a distinct shape.'

'Yes, I can see it now. Wow. That must be almost three miles away. It's barely visible.'

She spent a little while looking at it, surprised that the drilling site didn't impact on the countryside as much as she thought it would.

'It's not what you'd call 'prominent' is it. I mean, compared to the concrete factory. That industrial site and the hole in the ground is an unbelievable eyesore.'

Stack agreed.

'You know, I don't remember seeing the drilling derrick much as we drove around today. I guess that's a good thing.'

'Yes, but they're doing all the digging under the ground. It's still heavy industry.'

'It's not creating the mess that they've made down there at the concrete factory. You can't compare it.'

'Well, to some people it's worse. They think fossil fuels are just bad news for the climate.'

Though Stack didn't disagree his response was pragmatic.

'We've got to put those issues to one side, Summer. We've got a different objective. Come on, let's get back to the pub. Charlie will be there soon.'

They took off at a run, down the steep, winding path back to the car.

***

Charlie was already there, sitting at the same table as before, talking to the journalist, David Bennett. Summer slid on to the bench next to Charlie. Stack said 'hi', gave a polite nod to Bennett and went inside to order drinks.

When he returned, the others were deep in conversation.

'Hey Jimbo. Where were you guys? It all went off up at the rig today. The shit really hit the fan. Bloody riot.'

'It looks like we missed out on all the fun. What happened?' Stack asked.

'The bastards cut through the fencing.' Charlie said excitedly, 'It's tough, reinforced steel. They must have used some kind of heavy cutting equipment. Came in through the back end of the site. Loads of them swarmed through. I was fast asleep in the dorm. The racket woke me up. I threw some clothes on and went outside to have a look. I was nearly bowled over by the crowd screaming and shouting running past the door. It was like a rugby game in a mad-house. Security tackling people down to the ground. I tripped a few up. One bloke was really out of order. You know, looking for trouble. I gave him a slap. I got the feeling he wasn't used to people fighting back. The drilling guys seemed to be enjoying themselves so I left 'em to it. Looked like a bar-room fight in Dodge City.'

He laughed as he said it. 'A couple of 'em made it up to the top of the derrick. They've got bloody great banners. It's all on TV.'

Stack turned to Bennett.

'Were you there by any chance?'

'Yeah. I got wind of it because they put the word out to all the local and national media. They were making a big fuss at the main gate. There was a hell of a lot of them. One of them is a rabble rouser called Danny Finnegan. He's behind it I'm certain. He's a well-known, gun-for-hire, agitator.'

Summer interrupted.

'Finnegan spends a lot of time up at the camp. He's not interested in peaceful demos. He's been agitating to do something spectacular. Sounds like this was it.'

'Well, he wasn't alone. The usual suspects were there on the front line too. The local MP who's been campaigning against fracking, along with his sidekick, Don Hutting, leader of the local council. He's a notorious slime-ball. All three of 'em were doing stand ups for any news crew that had a couple of live minutes to fill. Finnegan used social media to get more troops to turn up, and boy, did they turn up!' Bennett reported with breathless enthusiasm. Ever the cynic, he found it all very amusing, 'Well, while all that circus was going on at the gate, a crowd of hard cases were busy round the back, hacking away at the fence.'

Charlie interrupted again.

'Security was caught completely off guard. They managed to get a few of 'em attempting to climb up the rig, but as I said, two of 'em made it to the top. They've strapped themselves to the monkey board.'

'TV are having a field day now.' Bennett said, 'But I've already filed my initial report. I was the first reporter there. Scooped Sky and the BBC. Their early news coverage used the wobblycam footage I took with my cell phone.' He laughed hysterically and banged the table with his hand. 'Normally they're not interested in my stories of rivalry and mayhem at the local parish elections.' He took a gulp of beer while he was laughing and snorted Theakston Old

Peculiar out of his nose, which made Summer and Charlie laugh.

'So, are they still drilling, Charlie?' Stack asked, concern about the progress of GeoPower's operation at the top of his mind.

'Christ! No! There's no way they can run the rig with those bozo's up there. It's bloody dangerous. But I don't think they can remain stopped for long with twenty-two and a half thousand feet of drillpipe laying in the hole. They can't circulate the mud so the whole bloody shooting match will probably get stuck. That could take a long time to sort out.'

'Where are they up to in terms of timing? How many days do they have left once they start drilling again?'

'About two or three days. Everything's been going pretty smoothly, except for some worries John Stonebridge has.'

Bennett's ears pricked up at this.

'Worries? What worries are these? And who is John Stonebridge?'

'He's the nightshift directional driller,'

'Is this the same person you told me about before, Charlie? The wrong kind of rocks guy?' Stack asked.

'Rocks? What do you mean wrong kind of rocks?' Bennett zeroed in.

He wanted answers. He scribbled the name *John Stonebridge* on a scrap of paper. He wasn't going to let this slide.

'Look, you'd be better off talking to Stonebridge. But from what I understand they know what kind of rocks they should be drilling through. But recently there's been a couple of times when the rock chips that came to the surface aren't what the geologist had expected. And then there's the business of the data.'

'Wait a minute!' Bennett said, 'These rock chips you're

talking about. Why would they be different to what they expect?'

'Look, it could be nothing. Drilling isn't a perfect science. No matter how clever the geologists are, they only have a good guess at what's deep below ground and where it is.'

Bennett deflated a bit, sensing this might be nothing after all. He tried another tack.

'But, it alarmed this John Stonebridge guy, yes? Is he a whistle-blower?' Bennett was still trying to make something out of it. Looking for an angle, 'What about the data?'

'Now this is much more technical. He did try to explain it to me this morning.'

'Give it a go.' Bennett encouraged Charlie.

Stack and Summer leaned in. This was the first they'd heard of it.

'First of all, I don't think you could call him a whistle-blower. He just seems concerned enough to want to talk it through, but he doesn't want to throw his job away.'

'Fair enough. Now, about the data?' Bennett pressed.

'OK. The directional driller steers the drill bit. He receives numbers, you know, the data, from the drill which tells him where the drill is. And he steers the drill by sending directional instructions back down to it. It's the only way they have any idea of where they're drilling. Without the data they'd be completely lost.'

'So you're saying the numbers have gone missing and they don't know where they are?' Bennett asked hopefully, thinking this would be a real scoop.

Charlie struggled to explain.

'Look. The numbers aren't exactly missing, they're the wrong numbers. It's happened a few times. I don't know why this might be a problem, mate, but it seemed to bother Stonebridge. From what he tells me, his boss on the dayshift doesn't seem to think it means anything, so perhaps it's nothing. You know. Just one of those things. A computer glitch.'

'I need to speak to him. Does he ever come to the pub?'

'Bloody hell, mate. I don't baby sit him. You're the blood hound. Go and sniff him out.'

Stack cut in.

'So if they're not drilling, what happens to your shift, Charlie?'

'For the time being I guess nothing has changed. Six o'clock start as usual.' Charlie checked his watch, 'Which isn't far off now, I'd better get a move on soon.'

Bennett didn't stick around for long. He wanted to get back to his office to file his story and follow up on the Stonebridge angle. He gulped the last of his beer and hurried off through the pub to the parking lot at the back.

Which left Stack, Summer and Hollywood alone at last to review what had happened and what they should or could do about it.

'These protestors can be pretty persistent. They've got nothing to lose, so they'll try and stay up on the derrick for as long as possible.' Stack said. 'That's bad news. We've got to make sure they come down and pretty bloody quickly.'

'Yes, but you can't touch them. It'll be all over the news.' Summer said. 'There are plenty of sympathetic journalists with an agenda.'

'Yeah. Touch 'em and it'll be all about their human rights.' Charlie said.

'So, who said anything about touching them?' Stack said.

'What you got in mind, Jim?'

'Yes. Come on James. Do tell.' Summer said.

'I have the kernel of an idea but I'll need help on site. Who's the best guy to talk to? Who do you trust Charlie?'

'Best bet is the drilling supervisor, Simon Harding. He's the bigshot running things. He's dayshift, but with this going down, and the drilling stopped dead, he'll be working through the night. I'll get back to you.'

'Good man Charlie. You better get going. And keep your phone close by.'

Charlie got up to leave still holding his beer glass, but Stack had another thought.

'Look, if we get the protester problem fixed and they start drilling again, this Stonebridge guy, the one with the wrong rocks and screwy data, do you think you could get him to come here? I think we should all meet him and see if this business of his could present a risk to the drilling. It's better for us to know what problems might be creeping up.'

'If he'll talk to you. As I said before, he won't put his job at risk.' Charlie downed the last of his beer put the empty glass back on the table, nodded a goodbye and headed back to the drill site, a brisk yomp a mile or so away.

On their own now, and with a heavy heart, Stack asked Summer to return to the camp this evening, but added that he was coming with her this time.

'Well let's have dinner here first? It's your last supper before camp food destroys your will to live.' She laughed as she spoke,

'I'll share your polyester palace with you, if two people can squeeze in.'

'Ah, yes, my luxurious sleeping accommodation in the People's Democratic Republic of Rebellion Hill. I'd forgotten about that. You'll love it.'

***

Instead of using his smart phone, Stack played it safe and

used the pub's PC to check his UK bank account. He wanted to see if the money transfer from his Cayman Island account had arrived. It wasn't much. He didn't want to raise the suspicions of the authorities. A sudden tranche of money, especially from an offshore banking facility like the Cayman Islands, raises suspicion of money laundering and tax evasion, and gets all kinds of nosey government people snooping around. All good as it turned out. The money had arrived.

Then a final bit of financial housekeeping. He transferred some money to his almost exhausted credit card. With no bank or ATM nearby, he checked to see if he could raise a bit of cash from the pub. They wouldn't give him much, just a couple of twenty's out of the till which they added to the bill for his room. He'd already changed a few hundred dollars into pounds at the airport and given most of it to Charlie and Summer. The few pounds from the pub wouldn't last long. He'd have to sort out something more substantial later.

As early as it was, the restaurant was busy with the tired and hungry. Bold adventurers returned from a hard day exploring the bucolic landscape and fearsome ruminants of the local countryside. They finally got a table in the pub rather than the restaurant. The bar food was OK, but Summer assured Stack it was a big improvement on the fayre served up at the camp.

They ate hungrily with fragments of intermittent chat strewn like stepping stones across a broad river. Eventually, the conversation got around to the coming attempt to eject the rig-top protestors and get the drilling going again. Stack reached for his cell phone and started tapping in numbers.

'I need a legitimate reason to get onto the rig-site,' he punched the green button. 'Maybe Blackstone can help.'

As before, it didn't take more than three rings for an irritated Blackstone to answer.

'Stack!' A pause as he brought his anger under control. 'You continue to test me. If I contact you it will always be for good reason. I have no time to waste on games.' He attempted the reasoned tone of a long-suffering mentor.

'It's a one-way game though, isn't it, Blackstone. And somehow it's always bad news.'

Blackstone interrupted him, uninterested in Stack's protests.

'You may by now have heard about events up at the drilling site. How will this affect your mission?'

Stack took a breath and raised a sceptical eyebrow to Summer, who shrugged a '*what's happened?*' back.

'Yeah. We've had a meeting about it. We've got two big problems.'

Stack went on to explain about the protesters chained to the top of the derrick which Blackstone was aware of. And moved on to the more grievous technical issue of the seized drillpipe, which Blackstone wasn't. For good reason, the second problem bothered him more.

'How soon before the problem is irretrievable?'

'The clock is ticking. They've got to get the drill turning again PDQ. The more time passes, the more stuck the drill gets. There's almost three horizontal miles of it. The top drive is powerful but eventually it won't be able to overcome the grip of rock against steel. They won't be able to turn it or pull it out. It could result in weeks of delays.'

Stack wasn't sure he had it technically right but it was probably close enough for this conversation.

'You say you've had a meeting. What plans have you made?'

Stack thought he could detect a metaphorical *gulp* in

Blackstone's voice. Good. He needed him at his most resourceful.

'They can't restart the drilling until the protesters are brought down. I have a plan to do that but I need to get on-site to carry it out...'

Blackstone butted in. All business now.

'You need access. What background shall I give?'

'Security. Keep it simple. Let's call it Special Projects. They should expect some specialist expertise to be sent up from head office. No questions asked.'

'Give me twenty minutes. I'll call when your pass is ready at the security gate.'

Conversation over. No goodbyes. Stack red-buttoned the phone.

'Change of plan. I'm going onto the rig site tonight. Blackstone's getting me in through the front door. In about twenty minutes or so.'

Stack rose from the table moving round to Summer's chair.

She got the message. They were on the move.

As they drove towards Rebellion Hill, Stack explained Summer's part of the plan.

'Do you think Finnegan will be up at the camp tonight?'

'Wouldn't surprise me. He'll want to keep an eye on things. But he's a real little Napoleon. He'll want to bathe in the glory of today's big victory. Make sure he gets his money's worth. Why do you ask?'

'OK, that might be a problem. Do you know him well enough to distract him for a while?'

'What? I think so, why?'

'What I have in mind will really piss him off and if he's the smart operator I think he is he'll get on the phone to every sympathetic lawyer he knows to stop us.'

'Wow! Sounds like I've got my work cut out. I'll do what I can.'

'Yeah. Try to get him away from the camp. You know, away from his pals. They'll be looking for him when this thing goes off. But be careful. Don't give him ideas.' Stack began to worry Summer might be putting herself physically at risk.

'When are you planning to do whatever it is you plan to do?'

'Later this evening. As soon as possible. Assuming they're up for it of course.'

'So come on. Do tell.' Summer had become used to Stack's abstract thought processes when crafting a scheme, only revealing details when he was confident the plan would work.

'Don't worry. You'll know when it happens.' Stack said enigmatically.

Dead Stop

Day 20 and the tungsten drill bit lay at rest for the first time since drilling started. It had stopped just 2,300 feet short of its target distance of 25,000 feet, directly under the eastern escarpment of Mam Tor. The fault that sheared deep down into the bowels of the Earth lay just 50 feet ahead.

Soon, the intense pressure of mud slurry being pumped down the borehole would force the drillstring hard against the rock. At three and a half miles long, the friction of the steel pipe pressing against the wall of the borehole would make turning the drill bit or even pulling the drillstring out, all but impossible.

Nearly 13,000 feet above, Mam Tor loomed close and threatening. Another scattering of loose shale slid down its western flank, shaken into motion by an almost immeasurable micro-tremor as the hyper-stressed fault shivered even as it slept.

***

'So, what are you telling me? They can see what we're doing? What the hell am I paying you for? I was told you were the best in the business.'

Still bruised after allowing the gold bullion to slip through his fingers, Mikhail Ulyanin, a man who tolerated no dissent or failure, had lowered his voice to a whisper. The two men at the focus of his displeasure knew he was at his most lethal when he ran his thumb slowly along the blade of his cold, calm, rage.

He had flown them via London to L.F. Wade International

Airport in Bermuda, 700 miles north east of North Carolina, and from there by helicopter out to the Eba. The super-yacht made no concession to speed as it passed the island, forcing the chopper to make a precarious landing on the helideck at the stern of the vessel. A feat only the very best pilots, or the craziest, would attempt at night and in the long heave of an Atlantic swell.

The news that the hack was leaking arrived while the Eba was still in Cuba. This was a worrying development he expected his technicians to quickly fix. He wanted to hear no more about glitches. They'd assured him everything was under control.

Mikhail Ulyanin was Aviophobic. He didn't fly. He would do anything to avoid doing so. Apart from the childish logic that man simply wasn't designed to fly, there were too many crazy people out there trying to blow planes out of the sky. For Ulyanin, flying was transportation of the last resort. It was the one place, on or off the surface of the planet, where he had no control.

It was as the Eba was making its way out of Cuban waters en route for London when the bad news arrived from St. Petersburg.

Ulyanin was on his way to join his UK counter-part, a civil servant of the British government. The visit was to celebrate the signing of a new gas supply agreement. An urgent need after the imminent GeoPower disaster in Derbyshire. Fracking for shale gas would have been dealt a fatal blow in the UK and gas shortages were sure to follow. But news of a third data breach sent the Russian's explosive wrath off the scale and a call went out to bring the principal hacking team out to the Eba to explain themselves.

The second team remained in St. Petersburg to handle the covert drilling, while the first team travelled half way across the globe to deliver their explanation, a meeting that terrified them. Which meant by the time the team arrived and set up shop in one of the Eba's exquisitely decorated state rooms, the second team had been on shift for over 30 hours straight.

'There could be any number of reasons for the interruption in the data conversion, Mr Ulyanin. Power supply failure might be one.' The young hacker had been rehearsing what he might say during the journey over, 'They are generating their own power. If it drops low enough for some reason, the system trips over to battery back-up. That could allow a single string of real data to get through to the directional drillers' screen.'

For a while, the only sound in the Russian's office suite, a sanctuary of olive burl panels and Zuber hand-printed wallpaper, was the low hum of the twin, MTU 10,000 bhp engines thrusting the vast yacht through the dark, cold, waters of the North Atlantic Ocean. Despite the effort of the vessels' stabilising system the room still pitched and rolled gently as Ulyanin pushed his leather chair back from the desk and prowled over to where the two men stood. His face an inch from the young computer expert.

'So, you're telling me you didn't plan for this contingency. You knew this might happen, yet your software didn't anticipate or ameliorate such an event?'

'We weren't able to supply a computer of our own design, we had to adapt one of theirs.'

'There is some good news, Mr Ulyanin.' The older directional driller cut in. As a long-standing employee of Ulyanin, working on the oligarch's many drilling platforms in the bleak Siberian tundra, he mistakenly assumed he was on safer ground. 'The record of the data leaks has been erased.'

'That's right.' The young hacker agreed eagerly, 'I went through all of the data history and deleted those navigation strings. There are no others. And now there is no record they ever existed.'

'No record, you say.'

Ulyanin smiled as he said it. And then he directed a laugh towards the barrel-chested suit standing arms folded by the door.

'No record he says. Then everything is fine. There is no problem.'

Ulyanin didn't expect a response, but the guard attempted a toothy, sycophantic laugh anyway. He shook his shoulders to give it some authenticity, but he couldn't help the small shake of the head, and a slight raising of his hands, palms up. He had no idea what they were talking about. Ulyanin told him no secrets. The boss laughs. The hired-help laughs. It is, and always has been, the way of the world.

Ulyanin turned abruptly and leaned into his two victims, scanning each exhausted face with a brief, disdainful glare.

'So you think there is no record?' His whisper turned into a roar, 'Someone saw it. He reported it. The record is in his head. Did you erase that one as well?'

The two men stood open-mouthed. There could be no answer to that impossible question.

Satisfied the men quaking before him had been crushed, Ulyanin returned to his desk.

'Is your equipment set up and running?'

It took a moment for the two of them to switch to the new topic.

'Ah, yes, Mr Ulyanin. Everything is running perfectly.' The young hacker was back on familiar territory, 'We have a good strong link to the satellite. It's holding steady. We can take over from the other team when you're ready.'

'And you?' He said pointing to the directional driller.

'The same. My control systems are up and running.' He tried to sound confident.

'And you will be able to control the drill from the mid-Atlantic?'

'It should make no difference, Mr Ulyanin.'

The small matter of a 50,000 mile round trip to the satellite and back, introducing a delay of more than two seconds, wasn't mentioned.

'Then you had better get back to it. There will be no more errors.'

The young hacker turned to leave but the directional driller bravely stood his ground.

'Well? You have something else to say?'

'But. The rig.'

'What about the rig?'

'They've stopped drilling. They may not be able to restart after such a long time.'

'You think I'm not aware of this problem? Go to your station and be ready.'

The directional driller wasted no time. He turned and joined the young hacker waiting by the door, closing it behind them, grateful to get away from Ulyanin's volcanic temper. The Russian paid well but demanded excellence and obedience. Penalties for those who incur his displeasure were harsh, and occasionally fatal.

The powerful forward motion of the yacht, ploughing through increasingly heavy seas caused the hull to shudder along its length as the Russian, alone in the opulence of his private office, picked up the desk phone and dialled. He had two calls to make. The first to the eager early adopter of the Russian Oligarch's conspiracy. A highly placed civil servant who saw it as easy, risk-free and lucrative. It merely required whispers in ears, pressure placed on malleable committees and the occasional oiling of wheels.

Ulyanin told him it was time to get the oil can out. A message to be passed on. An immediate result expected.

'Get those stupid protesters down. Now! I want that rig drilling again by tonight.' His final angry words before slamming the phone down.

The second call was of a different nature entirely.

Somewhere on the rig-site, in the valley behind Rebellion Hill, the midsummer evening light had been reduced to colourless gloom when a cell phone rang. The person who answered it straightened, becoming alert and attentive. Heart rate increased. Apprehension moistening the palms of hands. With the phone shielded, the conversation was taken outside, away from prying ears. A command was given. Only one answer was expected.

'Yes, I understand.'

***

'I've got enough problems without having to nursemaid some bureaucrat from London HQ. No offence intended.'

Standing outside the Portakabin office, drilling supervisor, Simon Harding, was direct as always. It saved time.

'None taken. Do I look like a suit from London?'

Harding stepped back and appraised the man in front of him for the first time.

'OK. Not an exec from HQ. So what are you?'

'You've got the email in your hand. I'm here to help with your problem.'

'Harding surveyed Stack again, sniffed and lifted the print-out to catch the light from the open office doorway. Holding his glasses to his eyes, he read the message again.

'What the hell is Special Projects?'

'Let's just say, for example, two guys are chained to the top of an oil rig. You can't restart the drill until they're removed. Time is critical. That scenario might come under Special Projects.'

'What do you know about drilling...' he glanced down at the email again. ' ...Mr. Stack?'

'Not much. What do I need to know? I do know we're wasting time.'

'There are TV journalists and cameras with long lenses out on the perimeter just waiting for us to screw up. We don't have many friends. It's a political minefield. We've asked them politely to come down. We even tried bribery, but these people aren't interested in money. I'm afraid those bastards up there are in for the long stay and we're looking at weeks of delays and huge cost to the company.'

Stack allowed Harding his pessimistic review of the situation. He looked around and observed the activity on and around the rig - or lack of it. Nobody was running. No sense of urgency. They'd been brought to a standstill both physically and mentally. They were in a state of siege. The protestors had already won.

'So, nothing to lose as far as I can see. I'm here to help. What do you say?'

'I'll listen to anything right now. What do you have in mind?'

***

Most of the adoring crowd lounging on the sun-baked dirt around their leader were already drunk by the time Danny Finnegan addressed them. To say Finnegan was pleased with himself was to understate the man's nauseating smugness and overwhelming arrogance. Now that the beautiful Canadian woman, Summer, had taken an interest in him, his authority over the protesters was both endorsed and complete.

He'd seen her return to the camp earlier in the evening after being away for a couple of days. Shame. She'd missed all the fun. An opportunity to see him at his dazzling best. The great plan - his plan – a coup by any definition, executed with ruthless precision. At least she could see now, with his ragged band of star-struck soldiers fawning over him, hanging on his every word, what a natural, perhaps even charismatic leader of men he was. Women liked strong men. She'd taken no interest in him before, but now, well, perhaps it was his turn to play hard-to-get. Not too hard though.

Slime-ball. There was no other adjective. Summer had nailed Finnegan's personality upon first meeting two weeks ago. The slick agitator. An answer to everything, except the question you asked. Rehearsed responses. Clever, street wise and the possessor of a 2:1 in political science. He spoke in convoluted paragraphs of radical text. Throwing in long, unfamiliar words awkwardly and often inappropriately that unfailingly impressed the gathered crowd of eager young anarchists. A classic manipulator of opinion. Just the kind of troublemaker you need on your side if you want to bring down the corrupt citadels of capitalist greed.

The thing was, for all his sanctimonious posturing, he was as easy to manipulate as his acolytes. Summer knew which buttons to press. She played him like an accordion. Easing her way through the crowd to sit next to him. Smiling, applauding and encouraging him. By mid-evening it was job done.

At one point she excused herself to go for a pee. Once

safely away from the crowd she texted an up-date to Stack. It was a short message: *'All good. Alcohol. Putty!'*

By the time she returned the crowd was already thinning, wandering off to form smaller groups of friends around the campsite. High on the heady mix of success, booze and drugs. Invincible, righteous youth. Look out world here we come! Pass the joint.

She got up and started to walk away. He caught her arm.

'Where are you going? Why don't you stick around? Have another drink?'

'No, I need some space. Get my head together.'

Finnegan got up still holding the bottle of red wine. He was a little surprised that he missed his step. Staggering slightly. He waved the bottle towards the glass she was still holding, pouring, but mostly missing, then filled his own glass to the brim until it washed over his hand.

'I'll come with you. I could use some space too.'

Summer pretended to object but then, already turning to walk away, nodded her head. Finnegan didn't need a gold embossed invitation. He walked next to her, submissive, happy and drunk, leaving his cell phone behind in the pocket of his jacket neatly folded on the dusty ground. She led him away from the camp at a slow and easy, almost aimless ramble, up past the southern boundary of the rig-site.

They followed the curve of the shallow valley until the hind quarters of Rebellion Hill hid the drilling site from view.

Summer knew she had to be careful. She was talking a big risk with Finnegan, drunk though he was. But Finnegan was now away from the protest camp and, for the time being, out of the game.

'OK, James. You're on'

***

Ten giant Caterpillar diesel rigs mounted on trailers had already been lined up on the remaining half acre of space on the drilling lot. It was an impressive sight. They were the engines that drove the pumps that powered the hydraulic fracturing process. If the pressure from the combined output of all ten wasn't enough to frack the shale rock, there was room for a few more heavy power units to be parked alongside. For Stack's plan, ten should be more than enough. At his request, the engineers had fired up all ten and they were now turning over at high speed. Standing next to them the noise was deafening. Charlie, wearing ear defenders, had sent roughnecks over to the maintenance depot to get as much used oil as they could lay their hands on. Barrels and jerry cans of old sump oil had already started to arrive. Flexible hoses from hand pumps snaked into the barrels and up to jerry-rigged nozzles fitted to the diesel engine's massive exhaust manifolds. They were nearly ready. Soon the engine exhausts would be hot enough.

Stack had made a big noise about bumping into Charlie. Lots of happy surprise and what the hell are you doing here? Simon Harding got the message: they were old army buddies. Stack appealed to Harding that Charlie and he had worked well together in the past and can he borrow him if he had nothing more important to do right now? All innocent and spontaneous.

To Simon Harding, Stack's plan seemed simple enough to execute. Too simple? It was certainly audacious. They had the equipment on-site to carry it out, but could it possibly work? Harding was under orders to give Stack as much help as he needed. Make all facilities available, within reason. But he was by nature, a steady, by-the-numbers manager not given to seat-of-the-pants, madcap schemes. Madcap though the plan might be, it was the only cow in the cattle auction. They had nothing to lose but time, and the well bore itself. That thought sent a shiver of worry down his spine.

He'd already taken a major gamble making the decision to reduce the pressure of the mud slurry. Not by much, but enough to slow the inexorable push of the drillpipe hard against the wall of the well. There was a downside. Now the well pressure was unbalanced, the earlier ingress of water deep in the well was pushing back up the borehole to the surface and washing over the drilling floor again. Though under control it was a dangerous compromise.

***

It wasn't business as usual in the dog shack. The small room to the side of the rig floor packed with data-filled computer screens and control panels loaded with dials, switches and buttons, was the control centre and heart of any major drilling operation. It took only a few people to make it feel crowded. The young nightshift directional driller, John Stonebridge had turned up for his shift like everyone else, perhaps a little earlier, but much of the dayshift was still on station including senior directional driller, Debbie Blain, all unwilling to walk away from the drama of the day's costly events.

Around mid-evening, the roar of the Caterpillar diesels being fired up sent the curious out to see what was going on. A few stayed behind. Strange to see Steve Gardener, the lead geologist, there in the dog shack, sitting at a computer terminal. Not his normal patch. He seemed to be taking the issue of the unexpected rock samples seriously because he was reviewing the drilling history, page by page. It gave Stonebridge a chance to peer over his shoulder and check for himself once again. He was shocked when he noticed a page that before had contained the rogue data, now had continuous numerical sequences. No sign of out-of-place data strings. Then he remembered, someone named Bennett had tried to get in touch. An office junior had made a note of the number and handed it to him earlier. Maybe he should call him while he still had time.

He stepped out into the warm twilight of the midsummer evening. The sun had gone down an hour or so ago but the sky above Rebellion Hill still had a pale blue iridescence that turned pink to the west, and arriving from the east, the darker blue of the brief night of the solstice. With no drilling crew around, there was an eerie stillness on the drilling floor, wet now from the upwelling water. The night air though throbbed with the rumbling chorus of the Caterpillar engines 50 yards away.

He took the stairway down from the elevated platform and followed the walkway past the shale shakers, mud tanks, pumps, agitators, degassers and the mud lab until he stepped into the gloomy shadow of a long corridor of steel containers now used as storerooms and maintenance sheds. The steel walls formed a bulwark against the noise from the giant diesels.

He glanced at the post-it note and dialled Bennett's number. It took a few rings before a bored voice eventually answered.

'I'm returning your call? From earlier today? I'm John Stonebridge.'

You could almost hear the cogs in the journalist's brain whirring - bringing his attention into full, needle-sharp focus.

'Yes, I did indeed try to get in touch. You're the guy that knows Charlie Dawson up at the rig?' Bennett replied brightly.

Stonebridge was cautious.

'Yes. What of it?' It was a hesitant confirmation.

'Well, how shall I put this?' He paused a beat while he gathered his thoughts. 'He tells me you've been getting some crazy numbers and something about wrong kind of rocks. What would he mean by that?'

It was Stonebridge's turn to pause.

Eventually, Bennett prompted him.

'Are you still there?'

'Yes.'

Another pause. Bennett tried another tack.

'What kind of rocks are the right rocks?'

The sound of the Caterpillar diesels roaring in the background filled another hesitation.

'I'm not a rock man.'

'Sorry? You're not the right man? What do you mean?'

'No. Rocks. I'm not a geologist. I'm a directional driller. I deal with telemetry. Coordinates.'

'OK. Why would there be wrong numbers? What do they indicate?'

'The coordinates, ah, the location of the drill bit, sometimes they show a different coordinate.'

Another pause while Bennett waited for him to say more.

'So?'

'They're gone.'

'What's gone?'

'The numb...ah...the coordinates. They've been erased.'

Bennett stopped to consider his reply.

'Why would they be erased? Who would do that?'

'Someone who didn't want them to be seen?'

It was as Stonebridge said it that he realised this was precisely what was bothering him.

Stonebridge's answer raised the hairs on the back of Bennett's neck. A conspiracy?

'It's a pity they've been erased.' Bennett mused out loud. He thought about that for a moment, then made a decision. 'How do you feel about meeting, you know, to chat. Maybe tomorrow?'

'You're a journalist.'

'Yeah? So?'

'I don't want...I can't have my name mentioned. I'm not a whistle-blower.'

'OK. No names. So how about tomorrow?'

'Where?'

'The Devil's Pike? It's nearby.'

'No. Too local. Chance of being seen.'

'OK. Do you know the Scotsman Pack Inn at Hathersage? It's just a few miles further east.'

'Yeah. I've been there. It'll do.'

'So. Tomorrow then. Say, midday?'

Another pause.

'I made a copy.'

'A copy?'

'The data. The false readings.'

Bennett tried to control his excitement at this news. 'Good, bring it with you.'

Yet another silence – then...

'OK.' Almost a whisper.

Click.

On his own again in the monochrome twilight of the corridor of containers, Stonebridge thought he heard a noise. A metallic scrape. The sound a container door makes as it opens.

***

There were a handful of hand-picked rig crew gathered on a bald patch of asphalt a safe distance from the thundering diesels.

Standing on the wooden pallet next to Simon Harding facing the men was the stranger who'd arrived just an hour or so ago, but who now seemed to be the in-charge guy. Harding spoke to the crew, outlining the hard facts of the problem facing them and then, with a detectable note of cynicism, turned to Stack to explain the plan. Some had already guessed what he had in mind.

'Ordinarily, I understand there are around 150 people crewing this rig day and night. Right now, you're the only people I need, so everybody else has been told to stay inside and close the windows,' Stack nodded to Charlie. 'Most of you know Charlie Dawson. He's coming round with material for you to tie around your faces. It's to protect your breathing. Make sure you use it.'

Stack indicated the row of trailers with their load of powerful engines. 'When that lot goes off, the air's going to get pretty toxic.' He stepped down from the pallet and picked out two of the crew, the derrickman and a roughneck. 'Shaun here, and Tom have volunteered to join Charlie and me to do the dirty deed. The rest of you, I need you to take positions around the rig to keep everything corralled in. We don't want any strangers running loose again.'

It was the performance of a man used to giving orders to his squad before setting out on a mission into the remote hills of Helmand Provence in Afghanistan. As in the past, the rig crew responded to Stack's natural authority without question. He shot a glance at Harding and nodded. Harding raised his radio and gave an instruction.

Though there was still daylight enough to see by, the big lighting towers were suddenly turned on, throwing bright light and hard shadows across the site. They weren't on for illumination.

Then he gave another instruction to the engineers waiting over by the Caterpillars. With so much noise, Harding also waved an emphatic 'Go!' signal to be sure the message was received and understood.

The engineer waved an acknowledgment and turned to the men standing by at each trailer, ears protected and faces masked. They each grabbed the lever of the nearest hand pump and started working it back and forth. Nothing seemed to happen at first.

***

The camp dwellers were initially curious when the roar of the diesels drifted across from the rig. Some tried to find a position that gave them a better view, but the Portakabins, containers and other equipment had been circled around the high value, central drilling platform like a wagon train fending off an Indian attack. A deliberate obstruction to direct sightlines. And anyway, the security fence formed a perimeter that was set back, well away from the drilling operation itself. A good 50 yards of scrub and boggy marsh stood between the protesters and their quarry. The only thing clearly visible was the tall derrick with the banners hanging down. A comforting vision. Their fervour reinvigorated, the anti-frackers eventually drifted off, heading back to the benders and shelters they called home for another nightcap and a smoke.

The noise had also raised the curiosity of the remaining news crew. Though the main event was long over, they'd hung around in case the duty news editor wanted a final live report from the location. Nothing for a couple of hours, so they'd started packing up, leaving the camera mounted on its tripod – just in case.

Alerted by the unexpected noise, the cameraman went over and took a look through the view-finder.

The tripod was essential to give a steady, telephoto close-up view of the two protesters on the monkey board near the top of the derrick. They appeared at almost touching distance through the optics of their Canon 1,500mm ultra-zoom.

Even in the reduced light, the picture was clear and unambiguous. Two young men tied to the steelwork with bicycle anti-theft cables. They could be seen talking together and occasionally looking over to the campsite and waving. Now they were pointing down at something out of shot and hidden at ground level. Suddenly, the lighting towers became ablaze with light, over-exposing the picture, forcing the cameraman to roll down the aperture by a few stops. He zoomed back to a wider focal length that showed the full height of the derrick framed in the shot. The picture had been pin sharp but now it seemed a little fuzzy. Perhaps it was the change in temperature this late in the evening causing the lens to mist up. He took a Kleenex and wiped the big glass at the front of the lens. He looked again. If anything it was getting worse. And now a darker shape seemed to be noticeable at the bottom of the frame. He looked away from the viewfinder to see for himself. There was no doubt. A great black cloud was lifting up from the centre of the rig site. Billowing dark smoke rising up, thick and opaque. Drifting slowly into the air. Climbing higher until the bottom half of the derrick was completely hidden from view. The bright light from the towers bounced back off of the swirling pall like headlights in fog. An impenetrable cloak.

***

As the crew operating the hand pumps worked, a fine jet of black oil squirted out of the nozzles fixed inside the burning hot exhaust manifolds. On touching the scorching metal the aerosol instantly vaporised, sending thick black and grey smoke into the hot, turbo-charged jet of exhaust fumes blowing through pipes the size of drains that had been rotated to point skyward. The ten 9,000 bhp behemoths soon became hidden in clouds of super-heated oil-fog that rushed to fill the open space in the centre of the compound. As more smoke was generated the volume of cloud in the column became displaced, quickly pushing up higher like the mushroom head of an atomic explosion. At its centre, the iron latticework of the derrick peered like a skyscraper above a city swathed in mist. Hidden from sight inside the cloud, four resolute men, mouths covered by cloth already blackened with soot, climbed steadily higher - keeping pace with the enveloping cloak. Each carried a small canister of air and a breathing mask to be used only if necessary. It wouldn't last long. Half an hour at the most. On the way down, if all goes well, two more will have need of it.

***

News quickly reached the protesters of the strange phenomena at the rig site. Their first hope was that the Gods of Justice were at last on their side and the dammed place was on fire. Then they remembered their heroic compatriots helplessly chained to the derrick and about to get charbroiled. Maybe they were too high up for the flames to reach. But as they rushed to see for themselves, it was obvious there were no flames, just thick oily smoke. Even as they watched, the last few feet of the derrick vanished into the swirling cloud. Alarmed, several went looking for Danny Finnegan. Nobody had seen him for the past twenty minutes or so.

The TV crew sent pictures of the strange smoke event back to the studio via the satellite link. Between them, the three members of the crew had a pretty shrewd idea about what was going on and kept the lens pointing at the top of the derrick. They had actually managed to get a shot of the two protesters disappearing into the smoke. They locked the camera off and waited.

Still doing her job, the reporter tried to get a reaction from GeoPower but received the inevitable 'No comment'.

***

The sudden arrival of the sour, eye-watering cloud panicked the two activists up on the monkey board. Earlier, when they were full of self-righteous swagger, they'd taken pictures from their lofty point-of-view and sent them to the world via Instagram, Snapchat and WhatsApp. Now though, the last snap taken as the fog was billowing up remained unposted. Self-preservation forced them to turned their attention to unlocking the padlocks to the bike cables, but the density of the eye-watering caustic smoke caused a coughing reflex that made it all most impossible. In a nervous fit of haste, one of them managed to drop the key through the boards of the platform. They could hear it tinging its way down as it bounced off the metal-work. The other, now free from his self-imposed imprisonment, struggled with the dilemma to remain and help his 'associate', a word that offered less of a moral encumbrance than 'friend', or simply attempt to climb down and save himself.

The decision was made for him. Materialising out of the thick smoke someone was climbing through the hand-rails onto the monkey board, followed by another. Finally, two more ghostly figures just visible back at the ladder.

The first and second wasted no time. They leapt forward and grabbed the two protestors. Pinning them by their arms and forcing them face down onto the platform. The protestor still tied to the railing had trouble getting fully down. The second man pulled a set of bolt-cutters from his belt that easily sheared through that problem.

Hands moved into pockets searching for cell phones.

'You'll get these back once you're off the site, OK?'

The authority in Stack's voice smothered any thought of defiance.

'Now, turn over.'

The two young men, docile now and coughing in the cloying smoke, allowed themselves to be turned face up.

Stack offered the facemask to one and opened the valve on the bottle. The activist struggled at first, thinking it was some kind of lethal gas, but Charlie reassured him by putting the mask to his face and took a deep breath, which he had to admit, made him feel a whole lot better.

'It's for the smoke. You'll need it.'

Both protestors took the mask and were grateful for the fresh air. It was a brief interlude broken quickly by being hoisted to their feet and marched to the steel ladder. The two men waiting there, had already started down and were waiting to support the youths as they descended, making sure they didn't miss their footing. Giving them no reason to complain. It was slow progress, with stops on the way for each of the six climbers to take a lungful of clean air from the canisters.

Halfway down, Stack radioed Harding to stop the diesels. It took a minute, but one by one the great engines came to a stop and the rig site was silent once again. By the time they'd reached the drill floor, the smoke had thinned noticeably.

Stack and Charlie guided the protestors to the stairs that led down to the walkway. Crew members held them while Stack thumbed his way through the files on each cell phone, deleting any photographs relating to rig operations and the invasion by the protestors before handing them back.

The protestors were put in a car and driven quickly past the main gate and down to the highway a mile away from the rig site before being released.

At the same time the rig started coming back to life. The drawworks winch engine turned over noisily and the crew returned to the drilling deck.

The next few hours were going to be tricky as they began teasing the drillstring away from the wall of the wellbore. Maybe, there was still a chance.

***

One hundred and twenty miles off the Scilly Isles on the Western approaches to the UK mainland and the English Channel, the Eba slowed as its helicopter was made ready. The closest helipad was near the village of Rock on the northern coast of Cornwall. By the time the chopper was ready to lift off, the distance would have shortened to nearer one hundred miles, an easy hop for a twin-engine machine. On board was a man who would arrive in the UK expecting imminent employment as a directional driller. GeoPower didn't know they needed him. No vacancies had been posted. Yet.

***

Finnegan's face was a picture of red-blooded rage as he looked across to the derrick now denuded of banners.

'Where the bloody hell are they?' He screamed. For Jesus Christ's sake. Somebody tell me what the hell happened!'

'We didn't see anything.' The voice of someone who thought he was one of Finnegan's favoured lieutenants. Big mistake.

'How could you not see what happened you stupid bastard?' Finnegan shouted.

'The smoke. One minute they were there and when the smoke cleared, there they weren't any more.'

Unimpressed, Finnegan walked fast and purposely over to the news crew.

'Did you get any footage?' he demanded. 'Did you film what happened?'

The cameraman wasn't about to be bullied by Finnegan. He let him stew for a bit, pretending to be busy fiddling with the camera lens.

'I'm talking to you. Did you film it?' Then he added the magic word absent from most of his conversations. 'Please.'

'I might have done. Wait a minute.'

Finnegan was almost apoplectic with fury that his demand hadn't been instantly met. But he had no power over this man.

After a deliberately long time going through movie files, the cameraman stepped back.

'Is that what you're after? Take a look in the view finder.'

Finnegan peered through the rubber eyepiece at the tiny screen. It was true. As the video played his two men were there. Then came the smoke. Then the protestors were gone. Smoke and mirrors. No evidence. No possible claim of violence or breach of human rights. What kind of clever sod could manage that?

Walking back to the campsite he was greeted by one of his followers holding his jacket. The cell phone's muted ring could be heard coming from within the folds of the cloth. Finnegan rummaged through the pockets until he found it.

'Yeah? Finnegan.'

A pause as he listened. He raised his eyes in mock disdain to Summer, who had just arrived.

'Well, if you've seen the news, that business is over. They're down. I wouldn't have told them to come down for you or anybody else. Why would you ask me to do that?'

Another pause.

'Well, that's your problem not mine. This event has been massively successful. We got their attention and now they know we're serious. If I get a chance, I'll do it again.'

A beep as he ended the call.

'What was that all about, Danny?'

Finnegan was sanguine but cryptic.

'I turns out I've got my very own mandarin in Westminster.' Somehow, he managed to be both irritated and flattered.

'But who was it?'

Nothing from Finnegan.

As they continued back to the encampment, Summer wondered how she could inveigle a name from him. Then she remembered – booze and putty.

Missing

At first the drill bit remained stubbornly jammed against the shale. A vibration from the top drive nearly four miles upstream was all that reached it. Eventually, there was a small shift in the drillstring as the powerful engine of the drawworks winch pulled the drill bit a few millimetres away from the rock face. The driller, highly skilled but praying silently, delivered just enough power to gently ease the 22,000 foot length of steel tubing without risking the calamity of pulling the pipe apart deep underground. If that happened retrieval would be all but impossible.

A small shift - a few millimetres, but just enough for the powerful torque of the top drive's hydraulic motor and the 250 tonne pull of the giant drawworks winch to gain a foothold against the irresistible forces of gravity and friction.

It took another hour before the well bore's stony grip was finally loosened.

***

Bennett was downing the last of his beer when he realised John Stonebridge wasn't going to turn up. He'd tried the cell-phone number logged in the received calls list several times, but got no answer. When it finally went to the *leave a message* option after one particularly long and dispiriting wait, he did just that. Eventually, he rationalised that as Stonebridge worked the nightshift he might easily still be asleep. Giving up, he headed back to The Devil's Pike. If his new friend, garrulous Charlie Dawson was there, perhaps he knew something.

***

The morning after the day before brought with it bright sunshine and blue skies that contrasted sharply with the glum mood in the protest camp. The collective double-dip hangover didn't help. Booze to celebrate their great victory, and later, more booze to console Danny Finnegan's disheartened group of true believers. Everyone else, the 100 or so who'd arrived just for the craic, and others who were there to make their voices heard, had left the camp and moved on.

But Finnegan's hardcore loyalists had gone into a tailspin of impotent indignation. Where was the evidence that showed how badly their boys had been treated? How dare the lackeys of the capitalist oppressors remove their heroic martyrs? And worse, do it in a way that left no opportunity for the grievance-fest that normally followed any confrontation with authority. No pictures. No video footage: Just angry, arm waving frustration. It was mighty depressing.

During Summer's attempt to get the name of whoever called Finnegan last night, she had to fight off his pathetic drunken groping's until she was rescued by her self-appointed chaperone, Clarissa Howden-Ffrench. No names were finessed, though it did seem to be a name he knew well, but not personally. Not someone he particularly respected either as far as she could tell.

***

The mess was busy with an endless stream of hungry people coming off shift and those about to go on. A mix of hard-hat and hi-viz and ironed shirts and smart pants.

Men mainly, but women accounted for a good percentage. Breakfast and dinner all at the same time. The room was filled with the percussive sound of cutlery and plates and the rowdy buzz of conversation. A sign that business was quickly returning to normal on the rig.

Stack carried his tray across the room in a winding route around tables, trying to avoid other customers looking for a chair that was free. As soon as one was sighted, at least three people made a dash for it. He could have waited. It would thin out in half an hour, but he wasn't familiar with the morning routine.

Then he spotted a hand waving from a corner table. A head popped up above the sea of hungry employees: Drilling supervisor, Simon Harding. Tough and respected, but not a man your typical tray-carrier would seek out to sit next to. Stack headed over and sat down with a nod of thanks.

Nothing was said at first as they tucked into their meal - Harding dinner, Stack breakfast. Eventually, Stack put his fork down.

'Long night?' Not very original. Just an opening gambit.

'Yeah.' A mouth still full but then gulped down. 'It was a bastard getting the drill moving again. They nearly had us.' He saw Stacks questioning look. 'The protesters. You know. It was a close call.'

He stuck his fork into his steak and Guinness pie and took another mouthful. Just as he did, his two-way handset squawked an electronic hiss and a thin electronic voice spoke.

'Boss?' *Hash click.*

Harding clicked the send button and spoke through a mouthful of pie.

'Go ahead.' *Hash click.*

'Still no sign, but we've located a replacement.' *Hash click.*

Harding swallowed before replying.

'Today?' *Hash click.*

'Should be on station by this evening – subject to your approval.' *Hash click.*

'This evening! Is he any good?' *Hash click.*

'He's available.' *Hash click.*

'Fair enough. How about Debbie?' *Hash click.*

'Not yet. Still sleeping' *Hash click.*

'Give her a couple more hours. She had a long shift' *Hash click.*

'OK Boss.' *Hash click.*

Harding put the two-way down and shovelled another mouthful of steak and Guinness pie into his mouth. The business of eating continued for a few moments before he spoke again.

'We've had someone go missing – our night-shift directional driller.' Harding explained, referring to the com's call. 'I assume they found you accommodation? You got some sleep?'

'Yeah. Fine.'

Another mouthful.

Then a grudging acknowledgement. Not resented, but not given easily.

'You did well,' a pause as he swallowed. 'How did you come up with that stupid idea?' His Scottish accent, broader suddenly.

Stack laughed. It was a good question.

'I have a talent for smoke and mirrors. You know, distract the enemy. Look over there while we're up to something nefarious over here.' He was thinking of the small-town bank jobs he'd done with Charlie as he said it.

'I wasn't sure how it would work here, but we've used

smokescreens on the battlefield quite successfully in the past. Navy too.'

'You got lucky with the weather.'

'Yes, but this drilling operation sits in a valley. That hill west of us protects us from wind coming from the southwest, the most predominant direction in this part of the world. But as you say, we had a bit of luck.'

Harding nodded as he chewed, then finally gulped a mouthful of coffee.

'Well...thanks anyway.' He looked at Stack, sizing him up, revising his first impression. 'Are you going to stick around? We're getting close to completing the drilling operation. Pretty soon, in a couple of days, we start fracking. You can be sure the bloody eco-warriors and their political masters won't make it easy for us.'

Harding's offer solved Stacks central problem. *How to keep a eye on my unwanted investment?*

'I'd want a roaming brief. All aspects of security.'

Harding had pushed his plate to one side and turned his chair a little towards Stack, now more interested in the direction of the conversation.

'That could be a problem. The man who oversees that job might object.'

'I don't want his job. Tell him to think of me as a ghost. Eyes and ears only.

'Yes, that might work. Reporting to me in the first instance. If I think anything is worth taking further, I'll bring him in.'

'Not on the payroll though.' Stack suddenly remembered his somewhat unconventional recent past. 'That might be a problem. Some kind of freelance arrangement would suit me.'

That didn't seem to bother Harding who simply shrugged an agreement. He looked just beyond Stack's shoulder and gave an upward nod, indicating the direction Stack should look.

Stack turned and noticed at a few tables over, a shaven-headed man with a ginger goatee who was in a deep and animated cell phone conversation. By the self-satisfied look on his face, someone was slapping gobbets of honey all over his ego.

'That's Andy Saunders. He's Operations Manager responsible for security and to be fair, he's reasonably competent.

'Coming from you, that's probably a big complement.' Stack joked.

'Well, it wasn't meant to be.' Harding didn't hide his disdain for the man. 'Right now he's probably taking the credit for clearing those boys off of the mast. Like I said he's competent, but watch your back.'

'Duly warned. Thanks.'

Harding sighed a deep breath of resignation.

'OK. Let's get it over with. I'd better take you over and introduce you to him. Come on.'

'Andy, this is James Stack. The man who came up with the smokescreen plan. Thought you two should meet.'

Andy Saunders tried to hide his discomfort, placing his hand over the mic of the cell phone.

'Oh, right.' He coughed nervously and told whoever was on the other end of the phone he'd call them back. 'Sorry, I didn't catch the name?'

Stack offered his hand.

'James Stack? I'm surprised we didn't meet yesterday.' Stack replied mischievously.

'Yes. Well, I was busy, Mr Stack. I was in conference calls with head office. You know. They wanted a first-hand appraisal from the expert on-site, which is me by the way.'

A beligerent, excuse-laden response, more for Harding's benefit.

Harding leaned in, one hand on the table.

'I've got some good news, Andy. Stack here will be joining us to provide additional security oversight. He'll be reporting directly to me.'

'As long as he doesn't get under my feet - I've got a busy operation here. Runs like clockwork. I'm not sure we need another cog.'

'Nice piece of clockwork precision yesterday, Andy, when the Sons of Anarchy ran free and loose throughout the rig. I suppose those two at the top of the mast were going to pop out like a cuckoo clock and ring little silver bells once an hour?'

'Very funny, Harding. We can talk about that in my office later. Right now, I'm advising you I'll be raising an objection with head office to this unnecessary additional staff member.'

Classic Andy Saunders. Running to Head Office whenever he thought his position was at risk. Unfortunately, he did have friends in London and wasn't afraid to use them. The unpleasant underbelly of office politics.

'Calm down, Saunders. Stack will be here on a freelance basis. The lightest of touches. Eyes and ears only,' he said, borrowing Stack's words. 'And as I said before, reporting to me. OK? So don't get your knickers in a twist.' When he needed to establish his authority, Harding's roots were laid bare, delivering his admonishment in the rich Scottish brogue of a Dundee accent.

***

It was well past midday, by the time Summer arrived at

The Devil's Pike. She'd had to share duties at the camp along with everyone else, apparently with the exception of Finnegan and a handful of grubby youths who thought that was what mothers were for. But she was also keen to maintain the illusion of enthusiasm for the cause by not rushing off at the first opportunity. Even as she made her way down the gully road she had to brush off the clumsy attentions of Finnegan who had caught up with her, in the hope of spending the day with her. It was getting awkward. She tried to strike a balance between interest and distance, keeping him on a leash. Finnegan had information and she was determined to extract it from him. I'll see you later, was the unspoken promise in her gestures and tone. At least, that's how Finnegan read it.

'Well, that was some show last night, James.'

'Yeah, it was, wasn't it. You should have been in the middle of it. I can still taste the smoke in the back of my throat.' Stack paused as he picked up his beer glass and took a long draft, 'It got the job done. They're drilling again. What was the reaction back at the camp?'

'They seemed a little disappointed.' Summer joked.

She went on to give Stack a full account of events from the protestors perspective. He was curious to know how she handled Finnegan. Her reassurances that while Finnegan hadn't been much of a gentleman, she had been quite safe, didn't convince Stack. He was intrigued, though, to hear about the phone call from Finnegan's Westminster mandarin. Such civil servants were the elite of the elite. Probably a 'Sir Somebody or other' having been ennobled for some modest service or act of cronyism.

'Sounds like he has all kinds of interesting contacts.'

'I don't think he was a personal friend. I got the impression he was surprised to hear from him. Impressed even.' She paused to recall the moment last night, 'You know, I think he'd called to instruct Finnegan to do something.'

'Why do you think that?'

'Well, Finnegan said something like *'I wouldn't do it anyway'*.'

Stack took another swig and emptied the glass.

'I think we need this bureaucrat's name. What's his interest in drilling here in Hope Valley? And what did he ask Finnegan to do?'

'I've already tried to get it out of him. Maybe I'm being too subtle.'

'Stay with it. Even if you have to break the bastard's heart.'

They were sitting at a table near the open fireplace. Some kind of ornate brass shield stood in place of the roaring flames that would normally entice travellers in during the cold winter months. Stack turned to go to the bar but was prevented from getting up by a hand on his shoulder and then a familiar voice from behind.

'No, Mr Stack. Let me get these. What'll it be?'

The offer came from, David Bennett, who struggle with the meagre expense account of a journalist. This though was a genuine expense in Bennett's view. Two people in possession of information he needed. A possible lead in a developing story.

He returned shortly with drinks for Summer and Stack, as well as his second of the day.

Stack and Summer waited for him to settle next to them. See what he had to say.

'I just came from a meeting with John Stonebridge. Except he didn't turn up. Should have been there at twelve.'

Stack and Summer looked at each other.

'So?' Summer frowned quizzically.

Bennett struggled to provide a follow up.

'Well, did he turn up here?'

The question was met with a mute shaking of heads.

'I left a message on his phone. Perhaps he'll get back to me.'

'When did you last speak to him?'

'Last night. It was the only time we'd spoken. He called me.'

Stack was about to say something about giving it some time. He could be sleeping. Or changed his mind. But before he got the words out, Charlie arrived. Same question.

'Drinks anyone?'

No sale.

By the time he'd returned to the table and borrowed a chair from the table next to them, the conversation had moved on.

'Strange night last night.' A curveball from Charlie.

'Well I was just telling David about the smokescreen plan James came up with last night.' Summer, proud to boast of Stack's ingenuity, aware he was unlikely to mention his part in it.

'Yes, it worked a treat. But I'm talking about later,' Charlie said. 'You know, once they'd got the drill running again.'

They all sat there waiting to hear the rest of it. Bennett almost twitching in anticipation.

'S'posed to be the nightshift, but things being how they were, they had Debbie Blain take charge of the directional drilling - just to get it started again.' He took a long draught of his beer.

The others leaned in, impatient for him to go on.

Charlie looked over the top of his beer jug at the three pairs of eyes staring at him.

'Yeah, well. Debbie needed to go off shift. She'd been up

all day. But I'd noticed he wasn't around a couple of hours before.'

'Who wasn't around?' Bennett said, unused to Charlie's rambling, story-embellishing ways.

'Stonebridge. Didn't I say that? He didn't turn up all night. They looked for him in his room. Everywhere. No sign. Very strange.' Another gulp of beer.

Stack was intrigued. 'So who did the shift?'

'Well, they couldn't stop drilling or they'd have the same problem as before. You know. With the pipe getting stuck? So they're just keeping the drillstring turning slowly where it is. Until Debbie Blain has had some sleep or they find a replacement directional driller: Whichever comes first.'

'And John Stonebridge hasn't turned up yet?' Summer this time. They all had questions.

'No. If he does turn up, unless he's got a bloody good excuse, he's toast. They're really pissed off.'

'Well that explains the radio chat I overheard at breakfast with Simon Harding.' Stack took a sip of beer before continuing, 'My guess is Debbie Blain is back at the helm now and drilling has restarted. There's a replacement coming this evening, if I interpreted it correctly.'

'This evening? Christ! That's bloody quick, and very lucky.' Despite his incomplete understanding of drilling operations, Charlie was impressed, 'These guys are hard to locate at short notice. Very often they'll be on the other side of the world.'

David Bennett had been listening to all this, looking for a connection to something bigger he was certain lurked amongst it.

'So, let me draw up a list.' Bennett counted on his fingers as he spoke. 'We've got several incorrect drilling numbers that John Stonebridge had made a copy of and was going to show me. Stonebridge's boss, Debbie something or other, didn't seem fussed about it when Stonebridge told her. There are inconsistencies with the rock samples coming up from the bottom of the borehole. Again, no bells seem to be ringing. And now the man who flagged up these issues has gone missing. I could add to this the arrival of a replacement directional driller who just happens to be available at the drop of a hat, which is an almost magical coincidence, according to Charlie here anyway. Call me an old newspaper hack, but something smells.'

'You've missed something, but I don't know if it's connected.' Summer said, 'Danny Finnegan had a call last night from a top civil servant. I don't think it was someone he knew. A call out of the blue. I think he was under pressure to do something he didn't want to do. I'm working on Finnegan to give me the name.'

Stack gave Summer a look of total respect. She had drawn the short straw with the protest camp. It was a miserable job but she hadn't complained and she'd remained focused.

'Just be careful, Summer.'

Stack turned his attention to the group. 'So, if we're agreed that something shifty is going on, what are we going to do about it? If there is an 'it' to do something about.'

Summer threw her thoughts in first.

'What about the copy Stonebridge claimed he'd made. Shouldn't we try to locate that?'

'Does he use a laptop, Charlie?'

'I saw him with one occasionally when he came on shift.'

'OK. If he's gone missing – you know – left his job and gone walk-about, did he take anything with him? Charlie, see if you can get into his room to check it out.' Stack paused for a moment to gather his thoughts. 'Listen everyone. If we take what we have as evidence that something's going on at the rig site, then, assuming it's not being perpetrated by the company itself, I think we should play it very softly. Tell nobody outside of this group, which now includes Bennett here.'

It was Summer who asked the $64,000 question.

'But why?'

'What do you mean?' Bennett asked.

'We all know who wants this operation stopped. Environmentalists, political groups and of course the protestors holed up in the valley alongside the drilling rig. But this reeks of a subtler conspiracy. If it exists, what is it trying to achieve?'

They all fell silent as they considered what Summer had said.

Charlie and Bennett reached for their drinks.

The bar had begun to fill with lunch time customers, mostly tourists now, but still quite a few from the GeoPower rig site, as well as a handful from the protest camp, noisy and sullen as they stole resentful glances at the representatives of their avowed enemy in oil stained hi-viz jackets. The rig crew just turned their backs and ignored them.

The thoughtful silence ended when Bennett gulped the last of his beer and placed the glass on the table. He glanced around at the other three, James Stack, Summer and Charlie, giving each of them a few seconds of appraisal.

'I'm wondering whether there's another question I should add to my list.'

The others just looked at him. They knew what was coming.

'I'm looking at an ex-army captain, his sidekick who works on the rig and a beautiful Canadian who's posing as a protestor. Yet here you all are, working together. On the same side. It's as though you're expecting trouble. Are you undercover? What are you doing here? I'm beginning to wonder whether in fact you're the story I'm looking for?'

***

At the bar, one of the protesters was ordering drinks. Taking advantage of the sunny weather, most of her friends had moved to tables outside and the pub was less crowded. It was while she was waiting for the drinks to be poured that she casually gazed around, taking in the low ceilinged rustic architecture and the walls and shelves cluttered with brass nick-knacks and equestrian paintings, and then, over near the fire at the far end of the room, someone she recognised – sharing a table with strangers.

The Dump

The London Stock Market was experiencing the usual summer doldrums. Share prices just seemed reluctant to do much more than enjoy the short siesta after some earlier buying and then profit taking towards the end of the day. The FTSE 100 hung on doggedly to what modest gains had been made after a recent and very popular privatisation share issue. Most of the shares bought by the general public had now already been sold to institutions, putting an end to that particular bubble as the share price sank back to what most investors thought was their true value.

The only significant blip was a new low for GeoPower shares.

A few days ago, when protestors had brought drilling to a standstill and the situation looked like becoming permanent, the price dipped below a pessimistic 146 pence for the first time. It rallied a little to an optimistic 193 pence once the drilling restarted, but overnight, a large tranche of shares was offloaded unexpectedly. A few nervous shareholders followed suit in the morning, dropping the share price dramatically.

Anyone brave enough to hang in there had just had a 50p-a-share haircut. GeoPower shares could be picked up for below £1. Even at this price there were no takers, just sellers.

The drill was making easy progress as it chewed into the shale layer.

At some point during the previous night the tungsten carbide bit screwed its way through the crack in the earth that dropped 20,000 vertical feet under Mam Tor. It was an event too small to impact on the hyper-stressed fracture, but one that was noted with some satisfaction in the English Channel, on board the Eba. The two events: the breaching of the fracture and the sale of shares were not unrelated.

The Russian had sold at a few pence more than he'd paid for them a month or so ago, when the share price had taken a hit from the Blackpool fracking debacle. Such was his confidence in his scheme, he saw no reason he shouldn't profit from a little side bet on the stock market. With the kind of foresight only omnipotent Gods possess and the wealth of billionaires create, Ulyanin knew GeoPower was about to go belly up.

***

The '*call this number*' message from Blackstone came early the same day, over breakfast. Stack had taken to having breakfast later to avoid the crush. Some called it, 'the nosebag', such was the functional nature of the bland anaemic box they ate in. Stack wasn't surprised how quickly the mess emptied. It wasn't a place you wanted to spend any time in. Looking around after receiving the message, he saw only five other people scattered randomly, drinking coffee and reading newspapers. Quiet enough to make the call.

As before, it rang three times before Blackstone answered in his usual haughty voice. But no, not so arrogant this time. There was a worried edge to it. Not quite the chippy Blackstone he was familiar with.

'So, what is it this time, Blackstone?'

'Do you ever take an interest in the value of your shares, Mr Stack?'

Stack had to admit he'd not checked GeoPower's share value since Blackstone gave him the bad news way back in, how many weeks was it? Three? Four? He'd lost track of time.

The thought hadn't crossed his mind since.

'Why should I be interested in that now, Blackstone? The only time I need that figure is when I cash the shares in in a couple of weeks.'

'Well you should be. Last night GeoPower's shares took a big hit. Somebody dumped a whole load and the price has slumped even further.'

'Thanks, Blackstone. You should work in advertising.'

Blackstone ignored him.

'Give me an update on drilling. I get the usual PR bullshit from the company. I want to hear it from you. What do the technicians think?'

'They are drilling again. It's going as well as it should from what I understand. They had just over 2,000 feet to go before the idiots climbed the derrick. That was four days ago. One of the directional drillers went missing. His replacement arrived two days ago, so they're back in the saddle and fully crewed and doing what they do best. You know. Grinding rock.'

'Listen to me Stack. Something's not right about the share dump last night. They frack in a few days. If it goes well the share price should go up. Selling now makes no sense. Unless they know something that everyone else doesn't.'

'Such as?'

'Well, think it through. It's not rocket science. If you knew the well would definitely not bring in the bacon, armed with such knowledge you'd sell.'

'You think the owner of those shares has got wind that this is a dry well?'

'Look Stack, the Upper Bowlan-Hodder layer has proven reserves of trillions of cubic metres of gas. Why on earth would someone who had invested a great deal of money, suddenly decide to sell now?'

Stack paused as he considered the implications.

'But someone has sold. What do they know that we don't?'

'Do you trust everybody on the rig, Stack?'

Another pause from Stack as the hairs on the back of his neck rose up in the frosty chill of unexpected coincidence.

'How are your government contacts in Westminster, Blackstone?'

'Extremely good. Why would you want to know that?'

Stack went on to tell Blackstone about the call Finnegan received from some high and mighty civil servant. He didn't have a name but when he did Blackstone should follow it up. Then he told him about John Stonebridge, the weird data and the rock sample anomalies. And finally, how Stonebridge himself had now gone missing.

'I wonder. Is there a connection?' Blackstone mused, 'There is vehement opposition to GeoPower, but that's not a secret. They make no attempt to hide it. This is something else. Something hidden. It feels bigger. More dangerous.'

'I think the answer could lie in the three lines of data. We think Stonebridge has a copy on his laptop. I'll need to be able to contact you.'

'Use this number. Call as soon as you have any news. Time is running out.' Click.

Once again, Stack found himself listening to the jarring silence of a disconnected line.

***

'Nearly there, just another 1,200 feet and we start fracking.'

It was around midday and they were out by the metal stairway that led up to the drilling floor. Simon Harding, not a man to waste words, had taken to telling Stack about the progress of the drilling operation. He had the usual meetings with company execs and his team of experts at the site in Hope Valley. But somehow, talking to Stack had become something of a confessional. He could say things to Stack that he'd keep to himself in the company of the GeoPower crew. Stack had a different way of seeing things. A fresh mind.

Stack on the other hand gave little away about himself and nothing away about the possible conspiracy. Not yet anyway. Everyone was a possible candidate for corruption, though he had to admit, Harding seemed the least likely.

The conversation paused as they headed up the stairs to the drilling deck and entered the dog shack. Harding spent time in turn with both Dean Turner the driller, and Debbie Blain. Turner was busy tripping pipe, pulling the 90 foot stands of steel tubes that make up the drillstring out of the borehole. He didn't have much time to spare for conversation. Debbie on the other hand had nothing to do right now because the drill bit was on its way back to the surface.

As before, pulling out the drillstring was done to replace the drill bit, but on this occasion an additional possible problem had also been identified with the mud motor. This was the critical bit of equipment that directional driller's use to steer the drill bit.

Outside, the noise from the drawworks winch as it strained to raise the 200 tonne weight of the drillpipe, was multiplied by the clanging of steel against steel as the powerful jaws of the huge yellow hydraulic torque-wrench clamped hard against the pipe joint. With immense force, it spun the upper section until it was unscrewed from the pipe below. The jaws were released and the pipe swung free, hanging from the top-drive clamps high above. The two roughnecks wrangled it across the drill floor and racked it against the side of the derrick. Then the process was begun again as the next 90 foot stand of pipe was winched up out of the ground.

Each cycle took 2 minutes to complete, a hard 30 hours of work to pull all 23,000 feet of pipe, out and then reverse the process to run it back down the hole ready to start drilling again.

With so much noise it was hard to hear what was said between the two engineers and their boss. After a while, Harding stood back and watched the operation. He seemed content that everything was going well. A good crew. Tough and hardworking. Roustabouts and roughnecks. The derrickman a hundred feet above them. The expertise of the driller working the winch. It was slick and professional. Everybody knew their job and did it well. But for the roughnecks especially, the prospect was relentless, repetitive and brutal They earned their pay the hard way over the next two and a half days.

Stack went over and stood next to Harding.

'So, what is this mud motor and what makes you think there's a problem with it?' Stack, was just making conversation. He had no idea one of the questions on their riddle-list had officially raised its head.

'The mud motor is a clever piece of kit that receives the mud pulses from the directional driller. Each set of pulses deflects the motor in a different direction. Not much, just a couple of degrees, up down and left and right. As far as we know it's working fine but one of our geologist has been making a nuisance of himself worrying about a few samples of rock that have come to the surface.'

Once again, the hairs on the back of Stack's neck rose

in the frigid chill of another coincidence. He turned and stared at Harding.

'Rocks?' He tried not to give away his foreknowledge, 'Why should that be a problem?'

'The drilling plan is a thoroughly well prepared three-dimensional map of the geology we're cutting through. We know what's up down and sideways, more or less. You know. The kind of rocks that form layers above and below the shale. On a couple of occasions, we've had chippings come to the surface that aren't what the geologist was expecting.'

'The wrong kind of rocks?' Stack offered cautiously.

'Exactly.' Harding nodded respectfully at Stack, 'Sometimes the drill has unexpectedly broken through the shale layer and cut into rock types that shouldn't be there, at least not according to the drilling plan. We need to know two things. Is the mud motor cutting exactly where we think it is, or is it off course by a degree or two?'

'And the second thing?'

'It's not something we can do much about, but why are we cutting through rock types that are different to the plan? How did we get that wrong?'

Stack thought about that for a moment before asking the one question that was relevant to his objective.

'If that's a problem, does it make a difference to the outcome?'

'Possibly.' Harding looked concerned. 'We may not be able to frack the whole length of the borehole if it passes above or below the shale layer, which means the anticipated gas yield could be lower than we hoped.'

Stack pictured a number. The one in his bank account in the Cayman Islands before it went missing.

The share price hangs on what the experts think the well

was capable of delivering. A low yield could mean a low share price. But the plain fact was, if the well didn't come in as profitably as expected he couldn't see what the hell he could do about it.

***

'We may have a problem.'

The call to the Eba came via the ship's satellite systems and had a distinct choppiness to it as though not all the digital content had got through.

'I'm listening.'

Just passing Falmouth on the Southern coast of Cornwall, it was 4 am and the first light of morning was already breaking when Mikhail Ulyanin took the call in his Stateroom. There was a 50,000 mile, two-second delay before the reply got through.

The long distance voice shook with handwringing anxiety.

'The guy they brought in to fix the protest problem is still here. They want to keep him here permanently, snooping around.'

'He did us a favour. Why should I be worried? What does he know?'

'Nothing, as far as I can tell. Not yet anyway.' A series of frantic concerns spilled out, 'He's no fool. I get the impression he's looking for something. And now they've started asking questions about the kind of rock that's coming out of the ground. They're going to check the mud motor. What if they find out what's going on? This business with the data. Has it all been deleted? What if Stonebridge made a copy? What if they discover the hack? I can't afford to be discovered, Mr Ulyanin.'

The Russian remained calm. 'What do you know about him?'

'He's professional, perhaps ex-military. Like I said. He's not stupid.'

'Are you using yourself as a comparison? Am I not paying you enough? Would you like to renegotiate our arrangement?'

The voice became more agitated. 'No, no. I, I, This is not…'

Ulyanin interrupted him. 'Should I be worried about you? The man you brought onto the rig site to take care of the Stonebridge problem, he is still in the valley. It would take one call…'

He paused for a moment to allow the threat to sink in. Digital hash grew in volume to fill the silence.

'But you make an interesting point. You must ensure no copies remain.'

'How should I do that?'

'His office computer. A laptop. Look among his personnel effects. Do I have to explain this to you?'

'No, I understand.'

'Let me know when it is done. Waste no more time.'

The Russian replaced the receiver and laid back on his bed and stared at the wood-panelled ceiling above. He reviewed the conversation that had just taken place. The hack into the drilling telemetry must never be discovered – now, or in the future. If any copies of the three lines of rogue data existed, they must be found and erased, as should anyone who had knowledge of the plan. Therefore, he would wait before putting an end to the problem he had just spoken to.

Lock-Out

It took three days and three bolshie computer propeller-heads before they managed to get Stonebridge's laptop open.

Charlie had managed to get into Stonebridge's room during one of his nightshifts. It looked like it was still occupied. If Stonebridge had left permanently, he'd taken nothing with him; clothes, travel-bags, shaving gear, everything was there including his laptop.

The first contender to play 'crack the password' was in his late teens and super confident He didn't care whose property it was. He treated it as though it was some kind of cool, crime reality show. Problem was, you get six goes before the software locks up. He screwed up three times leaving three chances remaining. They hustled him out of the hotel room before he pressed any more random keys.

So much for, Colin – Bennett's best friend's son. Next up Alice's Computer Oasis – out of the local want ads. Her ad promised the alluring, 'When your precious PC bluescreens or your mighty Mac crashes and they're not worth their weight in sand until they're fixed, call Alice's Computer Oasis, the only hardware and software solutions expert for PC and Mac in the valley.'

It was a local number and she seemed worryingly available and a bit too eager. Perhaps the ad wasn't working for her.

She was quite a bit older and had probably retrained after becoming superfluous to the needs of whatever company she had worked at before.

It was explained to her that the password had been forgotten and the contents were urgently needed. Again, the ownership of the laptop didn't seem to bother her. She put up a bit of resistance at first just to salve her conscience. It was two in the afternoon and the laptop was booted up and the security screen offered the password field once again. The curser was blinking away waiting for the first digit to be entered. But Alice just sat there, frozen, hands just above the keyboard. And there they stayed hovering in mid-air, her eyes fixed on the screen.

Alice didn't move or breathe for a long moment. And then her hands moved away from the keyboard and up to her face to adjust her glasses. Another breath as though a decision had been made. She brushed a strand of blond hair away and sent her hands back down to hover over the keyboard again. She did this a couple more times. Then she tapped in some random digits. '*Ding*'. Two more goes left.

Stack asked if there was a problem. She took her hands away from the keyboard and revealed she hadn't actually cracked open a locked computer before. She had misunderstood and thought this one was just frozen, but unlocked.

She adjusted her glasses again and said she was prepared to have another go. This alarmed Stack. Or maybe she could download some specialist software. Stack declined the offer, gave her some cash and sent her on her way – back to the oasis.

The following day, Bennett came back with another name after talking to some of his contacts. This sounded more promising. Someone based in Manchester. Didn't travel. Cautious guy. Might be able to fit the job in over the weekend. They agreed a price – not cheap. Cash only. And security was a big issue. They were to meet at a venue of his choosing for a preview of the job and to scope out these strangers that were prepared to pay good money for what he considered, a simple crack for any self-respecting hacker. They gave him a cell phone number. The plan was to travel into the city centre tomorrow, Saturday, around noon. At some point he would call and give a location. They would have 15 minutes to get there. Stack thought this was all over-dramatic bullshit, but didn't have a choice.

They'd made the call up in Stack's room, out of earshot of strangers. After, they'd headed back down to the bar, where Charlie was waiting. The weather had returned to the norm for a British summer in this part of the country: Cold and wet. So they gathered around a small corner table inside.

Stack gave Charlie the rundown on what was planned and the game they had to play to get to meet the hacker. This news threw Charlie into full 'Hollywood' mode as he recalled the plot of the Clint Eastwood movie *Dirty Harry*, where Eastwood had to run from payphone to payphone to deliver money to a psychopathic kidnapper.

'This boy, what did he call himself?"

Stack rolled his eyes.

'Mani-hack' you know, like maniac but with an 'h'. Apparently, the 'h' was silent when spoken.'

'You're kidding me. So, you're going to be part of this Mani-Hack's wet dream,' Charlie emphasised the 'H'. 'Running around Manchester all Saturday and then you have to pass some kind of 'Spy' test to meet his approval?'

'I'm told this kid is the real McCoy. Still at university, almost a savant.' Bennett explained, keen to establish credibility with his new best friends. 'I'm told he can sing code like sheet music. These people, these computer hackers are like a community. It's all about credibility. They boast about the stuff they get up to. They become legends. The trick is to be just a turn of a corner away from getting caught. It must be something to do with the risk because most don't seem to make any money out of it. Just enough to pay for their exotic specialist kit. Some do it as a protest. You know, like that WikiLeaks guy, Julian Assange.'

'I think he just publishes the stuff hackers give him, David.' Stack said.

'Well, you know what I mean. They think they're on some kind of moral crusade.'

'Bit like you journos then.' Like most reporters, Charlie's dig skipped off Bennett's career-hardened skin. He was used to it.

It was early Friday afternoon and they still hadn't made much progress. If something was brewing - a conspiracy of some kind - Stack felt sure the answer, if there was one, lay in the rogue data they believed was buried somewhere inside Stonebridge's laptop. The 'what?' 'why?' and the 'who?' remained a stubborn, impenetrable barrier. On the other hand, if you can't find a rational reason why unexpected data pop's up from time to time then perhaps it's just a matter of computer glitches and nothing else and they were all just wasting their time.

Stack brought them up to date on the mud motor problem. It turned out there wasn't one.

'They put the motor through all kinds of tests and couldn't find anything wrong. It still does exactly what it did when they took it out of the box all new and shiny a few weeks ago. So they've put it all back together and are in the process of sending the drill bit back down the hole.'

Charlie added to that.

'Yeah, I think they're just about finished tripping the drillstring back down. They'll drill the last of the well later today. Tomorrow they'll pull it all out again for the last time and start prepping for the frack. Going to be a busy night so you're on your own tomorrow.'

'Don't worry, Charlie. I need you here anyway.'

'So, no explanation for the wrong kind of rocks then?' Bennett asked.

'I'm on pretty good terms with Harding. He keeps me in the loop. He's worried that if there are no mechanical or technical issues, then the drilling plan isn't as accurate as they believed. All heads are turning to the geologist and seismologists. Those boys are defending their work but the GeoPower crowd in London are pissed off. Apparently the drilling plan took months of careful preparation. Anyway, they've gone through all the numbers again and again and as far as the geologists are concerned, it's all solid.'

To a tenacious old hack like Bennett who sees conspiracies everywhere, the more the facts seem to support one thing, but the evidence stubbornly says something else, the more his nose twitched and his teeth bit harder like a dog pulling on a rag.

He leaned back in his chair and shook his head sagely.

'You've got two conflicting pieces of evidence here. Both defended by highly professional people who, let's give them the benefit of the doubt, know what they're doing. The machinery functions as it should. The geology is accurate. But the result is unexpected. Does anyone else think something smells? Something is definitely wrong.' He paused before asking Stack, 'Do you know what they're going to do about it?'

Stack leaned forward, elbows on the table.

'I think they're just going to carry on. They've only got a thousand feet to drill and then as Charlie said, they start fracking. Harding says the yield might be lower because the drill came out of the shale layer occasionally. He couldn't say by how much though. Looks like they have a real problem. They can't trust the well plan now.'

Then, needing to clear up something that had been bothering him, Stack turned to Bennett.

'Listen, Bennett, I know you're looking for a story. Be very careful. We are not your story.' There was danger in Stack's voice, 'You may think we share the same objectives. We don't. You can help but don't get in our way – no freelancing. Whatever this turns out to be - if anything - it stays out of the media until we get to the end of it. Are we clear?'

Bennett, surprised by the sudden change in tone, took this news badly.

'I'm a journalist. It's what I do…'

Stack broke in before he could finish.

'Are we clear? Nothing goes to press.'

'But…'

'Nothing. Not yet. I'll make one concession. However this ends up, when it ends, we'll answer any question you like. But not now. I repeat, are we clear, Bennett?'

Bennett shrugged his compliance. He didn't have a choice. He needed these guys more than they needed him. No brainer!

***

When Clarissa Howden-Ffrench asked Summer to step into her office, Summer was surprised to find Danny Finnegan sitting there under the tarpaulin covered shelter. Sitting next to him was one of the furious few: A true believer. Not one of the inner circle, but a young woman that Summer had noticed around the camp, and tried to avoid. No more than 20 years old, she advertised her commitment to the cause in highly illustrated ink-work over her arms, torso and legs, not all of it by a professional. Some looked like scratchy self-inflicted scribbles. Her long unkempt hair had been shaven close to the skull on one side revealing a Goth-like tattoo from an earlier obsession. Her face, untouched by cosmetics, bore metalwork in nose and tongue that completed the deliberate vandalism of her femininity. A rejection that sent out a strong, not-for-boys, signal. Like a schoolgirl's crush for her teacher, Bryony had the hots for Summer.

Summer stood in the doorway out of the weather, bent slightly under the low roof and scanned all three with a suspicious eye.

'What's up?'

Danny Finnegan spoke first.

'Would you sit down please, Summer. A serious accusation has been made against you.'

'What's this, some kind of kangaroo court?'

'You've been accused of consorting with the enemy.'

Summer's first reaction was to laugh.

'Is this some kind of joke?' She was irritated, but reluctantly sat down.

Howden-Ffrench spoke up before Finnegan had a chance to reply.

'Now calm down, Summer. Bryony here thought she saw you with some strangers down at The Devil's Pike the other day. She didn't recognise any of them. Can you tell us who they were?'

Summer's indignation started to boil over into anger.

'What the hell has what I do outside this camp got to do with any of you?'

'Quite a bit.' Finnegan said, 'There are people who'd be very interested to hear what goes on amongst the righteous people of this protest movement. We have to protect ourselves from infiltrators. Are you a spy, Summer?'

The accusation stunned her for a moment. So what, if

she'd been in the pub with Stack, Charlie and Bennett? They didn't have any interest in the activities of the protesters, unless those activities conflicted with their goal. But she wasn't about to admit to that or anything else. On the other hand it was pretty obvious that Bryony had a crush on her.

It had been an awkward few weeks of keeping some distance without offending her. Bryony had many friends in the camp. She could make things difficult if she felt rejected. The business with Finnegan didn't help. Bryony had gone into a sulk. Feeling rejected, her attitude tipped into resentment. Summer knew there'd be trouble.

'What was I supposed to have been doing?'

Bryony leapt in, her anger clear in her vindictive accusation.

'You were there with some men.' She said '*men*' as though Summer had been sitting with the devil himself.

'Yes, I was. I'd bumped into them at the bar as I'd brought myself a drink. Two of them had been here for the big protest. You must have seen them, Bryony. Actually, I think they're gay. Not that that matters does it, Bryony.'

'What about the other one?'

'A friend of theirs. They seemed like nice guys. I left after a while and found a table by myself.'

This last bit was a risky embellishment. She didn't know how much Bryony had seen, but she had to ease the pin back into Finnegan's grenade. With the name of the big cheese civil servant still unknown, she needed him onside.

Bryony scowled as Summer turned to Finnegan and smiled.

'You saw me leave the other day didn't you Danny. I told you I was looking for some solitude away from the camp.'

'Yes, well, that's true. But we have to be clear about security, Summer. No fraternising with the enemy, OK?'

Finnegan's mood was lighter. He still saw possibilities.

Always playing the calming den mother, Clarissa Howden-Ffrench brought the meeting to a close.

'So, I think were done here everyone. Everything's good. Nothing to worry about. Sorry about this, Summer.'

Bryony didn't agree.

'Are you all blind?' she raged at Clarissa and Finnegan, 'She's a bloody spy. Who were those people? And for that matter, who is she, coming into our protest and taking over?' She got up in a jealous fit, threw the canvas cover of the doorway open and turned to Summer, 'It's not over. I'll be watching you...you bitch!' She rushed out into the drizzle.

'She'll get over it,' were the final words from Howden-Ffrench.

Finnegan winked at Summer as she stooped up to leave.

'See you later?'

'Sure. I look forward to it.' Her fingers firmly crossed as she said it.

The Civil Servant

As far as the hacking teams in St. Petersburg and on-board the Eba were concerned, with the drill bit now safely beyond the massive geological fracture, their work was done. No real suspicions had been raised according to Ulyanin's contact back in Hope Valley. Confusion over some unexpected rock chips had them chasing their tails for a while, but the rogue data which, if discovered, would have put the whole sabotage plan in jeopardy, had stayed off their radar. All that remained was to nurse the drill bit the last thousand feet. Keep it out of trouble until drilling was completed, probably by later today

The final part of the plan had nothing to do with them. It was to be a self-inflicted calamity caused by the explosive pressures of hydraulic fracturing. A technology fraught with well-known dangers the world's many anti-fracking activists had warned about for years. Chickens coming home to roost.

The remote hack would have been closed down well before then, the perpetrators melted into obscurity – if they were ever there at all.

***

It was early evening and the sun, now a large ochre ball resting just above the distant London skyline, speared fiery god-rays through giant cumulus clouds in a biblical tableau that promised another majestic sunset.

The Russian, Ulyanin, was standing on the bridge of the Eba with the captain. An experienced River Thames pilot who had boarded further downstream was navigating the massive yacht the final leg of their 4,500-mile journey. Right now they were passing under the spectacular sweep of the Queen Elizabeth II bridge that provided the north-south link in the M25 motorway that encircled London.

Finding space to moor a 450-foot super-yacht in one of the world's largest cities is harder than you might imagine, even with a river the size of the Thames running through it. Mostly they get roped against the quays at Canary Wharf in East London. Nearby Royal Albert Dock and the King George V Dock also have facilities for bigger boats, or, if you plan ahead, there's a prime central London berth beside HMS Belfast on the west side of Tower Bridge.

Some people like to flaunt their wealth, and though Ulyanin wasn't a shy man, he preferred a lower profile, if that was possible for the lucky few in the superyacht league. Canary Wharf suited him just fine, and anyway, if you had people to impress, the vast glass and steel office towers provided the perfect backdrop to show off the Eba's expensive curves.

This visit to London was the final stage of a brilliant plan put in place with great stealth by a man whose unsubtle business maxim: 'Whatever it takes – whatever the cost', made him a feared adversary.

In a few days an important guest will arrive in great secrecy. A fine meal would be shared, a little business discussed - nothing too formal, just a restatement of an agreement already established. No overt threats would be made but a tacit understanding that 'failure to deliver was unacceptable' would be conveyed in the most delicate and regretful of terms. Later, the guest would enjoy some friendly divertissements in one of the Eba's luxurious staterooms. Every detail of the evening's performance captured with the pin sharp clarity of high definition video.

Later still, the girls would leave in one direction, the guest more discretely in another.

Until then, the arrival of the Eba sent a powerful message the civil servant couldn't ignore.

***

Small camp fires were burning here and there lighting the darkness in the protest encampment on Rebellion Hill. With most of the dry wood scavenged from the woodland floor consumed long ago, the fires were fed with branches ripped from trees and bushes still damp from the day's rain. Choking smoke rose up as the green wood spluttered and dried in the flames.

In a central clearing a larger group fuelled with cheap booze and some light recreational drugs were chanting to the beat of South American bongos and African djembe drums. Others grabbed anything that made a noise: pans, pots, sticks or simply clapped. Someone had a whistle which she blew enthusiastically and annoyingly, though no one seemed to care.

It had been one of the better days. By late afternoon it was still cold but the rain had eased to intermittent. Another noisy protest had taken place down at the gates. More had arrived crowding the narrow gully road, slowing the comings and goings of site vehicles. A crowd had taken to pulling on the fence. They got into a rhythm that actually managed to sway the tall steel structure. Seeing a chance to inflict even more damage, others joined in, pushing and pulling, loosening the footings until a large section was listing dangerously outwards. Some climbed up and grabbed hand holds near the top, the sheer weight of numbers finally pulling the fence over into a V shape supported on either side by sturdier fence structures. By this time security guards and police had arrived, but it was too late to prevent the protestors climbing over and pouring on to the access road that led up to the drilling rig itself.

They hadn't expected to make as much progress and didn't have a plan, but the assault was shown live on TV. The demonic forces of capitalism overwhelmed by the valiant few defending the rights of the weak and the oppressed.

Inevitably, they were corralled and led back out through the main gates, noisy and jubilant. Damage had been done.

While this was going on, a half mile further up Rebellion Hill and much closer to the rig itself, Finnegan was overseeing the release of a tiny drone, piloted by Bryony. It turns out she was a highly-regarded drone racer in a new techno-sport dominated by men. She'd brought her drone to the camp in the belief it could be useful. Finnegan immediately saw the possibilities.

It flew up and over the fence, its four propellers buzzing like a swarm of angry bees. The camera on the tiny palm-sized Hubsan Quadcopter allowed Bryony a real-time, first person point of view through the monitor on the handheld control unit. The drone was so small it could fly through the length of a drillpipe without touching the sides if a pilot was skilled enough.

In ordinary circumstances, the buzzing of the drone would draw instant attention, but the heavy industrial noises and powerful rig machinery drowned out everything below the 90 decibels of a shout.

She kept the drone low, dropping to hide behind containers and machinery every now and then. Even with a more powerful battery on board to power the four tiny rotors, camera and transmitter, the maximum flight time was measured only in minutes. Crossing the 50 yards of open land and weaving in and around obstacles consumed time and power.

They had only a few minutes to observe the lay of the land. Finnegan watched over Bryony's shoulder. After it had dodged the cab of a truck he asked her to fly it higher to get a wider view. In the view-finder the cab zoomed back to reveal the full length of the truck and the pump equipment on the trailer. More than that, it revealed nine other identical vehicles parked alongside. Men were attaching large flexible hoses to each pump. Other pipes criss-crossed and connected into heavy steel tubing that led off in the direction of the rig. Finnegan instantly understood that the pumps were being rigged in preparation for the high pressure frack that would soon take place. The battery indicator showed less than half a charge left. Just enough time to take a quick flight over to the rig.

Again, keeping low and flitting around whatever cover was available, the drone closed in on the rig structure. The tiny craft rose up the ten feet to the rig floor. Its wide angle lens gave a deceptive field of view. The drone was much closer than it appeared on the monitor. As it rose a couple of feet above the railings, something blurry obscured the image. Then she realized with a shock what it was. The hard hat of someone leaning with his back against the rail, the drone was practically touching it. She flew the miniature aircraft away and off to one side just as the man turned round to look out across the site. Bryony had a clear view of a three quarter profile. The man was practically looking at the drone, but his two-way radio must have squawked. His attention was diverted and he turned back around as he raised his radio to speak.

'I know that man.' Bryony said, surprise in her voice, 'He looks familiar. But I can't place him.'

A bleep alerted her that the battery life was almost exhausted. Without waiting for Finnegan she set the drone on a return course. Dodging and skipping like a nervous insect, it flew back across the open ground and over the fence. As the tiny craft hovered restlessly in the light wind just an arm's length away, she clicked a switch, the buzzing stopped and the drone dropped lifelessly to the bracken covered ground at Finnegan's feet.

The recce had given him an idea. It was risky, but it could deal a blow to the very heart of the problem.

***

Stack had been watching the endlessly repetitive process of raising and unscrewing lengths of pipe as the drillstring was being pulled out for the last time. He was hoping a clue to the puzzle would suddenly reveal itself. In the end his mind wandered back to Summer and the risks she was prepared to take to get the name he needed from Finnegan. He turned away from the activity on the drill floor and looked across to the tree line that hid the protest camp, where Summer was right now. Frankly, he'd rather just get hold of Finnegan and beat the information out of him. It might just come to that.

Two things happened just then. A glimpse of something caught his eye off to the left. Something that seemed to dance in the air and then was gone. At the same time the radio squawked. He raised the two-way, turned back to face the roustabouts struggling with another length of pipe and pressed the switch.

'Stack – go ahead.' *Hash-click.*

He pressed the radio hard to his ear to listen to the thin metallic voice of Simon Harding.

'Seems like they've got things back under control at the gate, Stack. Today's entertainment appears to be over.'

'Copy that. Thanks. Stack out.'

He turned round again and tried to locate what had fleetingly caught his eye. Nothing. He tried to picture what he thought he'd seen. Not an insect. Bigger. Not a bird. No wings. More like a hummingbird. That was it. But *not* a hummingbird. Artificial? Could be.

***

Later that evening in the protest camp, fuelled by their previous success, emotion was at a jubilant high. But Finnegan threw more flammable rhetoric onto the impassioned fires of the devout, true believers. He told them how the weeks of protest were nearly over and they had inflicted costly damage, slowing the drilling down. Stopping it on one heroic occasion. A loud cheer went up at this.

But now they were moving towards the endgame and a great opportunity that had presented itself to inflict substantial wounds on the evil, anti-climate change morons at GeoPower. Even now as they gathered bravely under the stars, the fools on the hill were preparing equipment to begin fracking. He warned them to be ready. Our destiny is to end this obscenity for ever!' He roared. More loud cheering as Finnegan walked away, Summer at his side.

Glamping is the word they use for luxurious camping and it described Finnegan's accommodation perfectly. Not for him the crude bender or cramped one-man hiking tent. You could stand up, even walk around in the space the polycotton enclosure provided. Though Summer was unwilling to see for herself, she was sure Finnegan didn't lack for the basic necessities inside. The door was unzipped and pinned open. They sat outside on comfortable picnic chairs.

She'd been considering how to broach the subject of the civil servant after so many days had passed. What little she knew of Finnegan, it was clear he was a man who held grudges. The issue wouldn't be buried too far. Booze and putty. Alcohol and manipulation. It had worked before, up to a point. This time though, she would add an additional ingredient - shared irritations. First though, she persuaded Finnegan to draw on his private stock of Rioja. He would share it with no one else. Added to the many drags on joints that had been passed around during the evening, the heavy red wine ran like Valium through his veins. Not too much, he needed to be awake to play Summer's game.

Fortunately, Finnegan offered Summer the perfect opening.

'I don't know you at all really, do I. Tell me something about yourself, Summer.' His eyelids half closed as he gazed adoringly at her.

Summer paused and looked thoughtfully off through the trees to the distant fire, now not more than an unattended glow that occasionally sparked a yellow sprite of flame. She wanted to give the impression of a reluctance to reveal anything about herself. Still staring into the distance she wove her story.

'Oh, there's not much to tell really. Before I was married – and then divorce...' Summer knew that the trick to telling a convincing lie was to include some measure of truth, '...I used to work in London at the Canadian Embassy. Boring job really, but it brought me into contact with the Foreign Office. Arranging meetings for my boss. The bloody civil servants treated *him* with all kinds of respect, but to them, I was just a dog's body. The senior civil servants were worse. What is it about those supercilious bastards that make them like that? Private education I guess. The right kind of tie or club or something.'

Finnegan stirred, rising to the bait. The chip weighing heavily on his shoulder.

'Tell me about it. I'm a politician but I've got working class roots. The clowns look at me as though I'm dirt.'

He took another gulp of wine as Summer continued.

'It's the way they talk to you. Where do they get that accent? Nobody talks like that in real life.' And then in a softer voice, 'I don't know how you put up with it, Danny.' She turned and looked into his eyes as she said it.

Finnegan was already topping up his wine again. He passed the bottle over her glass and she let him fill it. Revved up and pissed off. He was ready for a confession.

'Have you heard of Sir Sebastian Winstanley? One of those bastards that run the Department of Business, Energy and Industrial Strategy.' Summer held her breath. *'Could this be it?'*

'Called a few days ago. You know, just after we put those banners on the derrick. I was busy as hell. You won't believe it. He told me to shut the protest on the rig down. I mean, how dare he? Threatened me with repercussions. Things could become difficult he said.'

Summer sat there listening and nodding sympathetically. Encouraging him.

'And then, seeing that his threats weren't working, he said 'you may not believe me but we're on the same side. I want what you want'. I got the impression he was even prepared to bribe me. He sounded desperate. I mean, what was that all about? Slimy sod. The joke was, he didn't know they'd already brought our guys down.'

Summer burst out laughing at the unexpected image of the mandarin waving bank notes at Danny Finnegan. Finnegan joined in. They raised a glass to 'the shits in the Civil Service!'

'*That worked better than it had a right to*', Summer thought. She had a name – Sir Sebastian Winstanley. Now all she had to do was extricate herself from what Finnegan thought might be on offer next. Tricky.

Manchester

At least it wasn't raining. Miserable weather is a cliché for Manchester, England's, most prominent northern city. They put up a good fight to defend what the locals regard as unfair meteorological prejudice, but records show a dismal share of the nation's sunshine, averaging just four hours a day, plus an overabundance of rain.

The weather made no difference to Stack's mission.

He'd taken the 10.36 train from nearby Bamford to Manchester Piccadilly station in the centre of the city, a place he was unfamiliar with. All he needed was somewhere to park his arse until Mani-hack contacted him. A nearby café would do.

While he waited a text came through from Summer – just a name: '*Sir Sebastian Winstanley*'. Progress at last. He tried hard not to imagine how Summer had prised that info out of Finnegan. He texted back for her to meet him later at the pub. Her reply bothered him: '*That might be tricky. Problems!*' He texted back: '*I'll call you.*' Her worrying reply: '*Not a good idea! I'll call you.*'

He tried to put his concerns to one side and get through to Blackstone right away with the name, but he didn't want to miss the call from Mani-hack.

The café was no more than a simple corridor of a space squeezed between a newsagent and a curry house. A row of tall stools, rocking on the uneven floor, were pushed against a chipped and cracked Formica-laminated strip of wood that served as a shelf to put cups and plates on. Facing it was the grubby shoulder high glass counter from which, if they had a customer, tea and coffee-to-go was served in polystyrene cups by a skinny man whose tattoos seemed to have wormed their way around his arms and up the back of his neck. Although he had his back turned, Stack noticed through the reflection in the window that without something to keep his hands busy, one of his fingers seemed to be lodged permanently up his nose.

Bearing in mind the personal hygiene issues, Stack wondered which side of the cup he should drink from, if at all. A dilemma resolved by the sudden buzz of his cell phone. He green-buttoned it and held it to his ear. He listened, agreed that, yes, he was James Stack. Listened some more.

'Sorry, where is that? I don't know Manchester.'

A pause.

'OK, don't worry, I'll take a cab.'

With the rail station nearby, a cab wasn't hard to find, but it took a couple of attempts to explain the address he'd been given. The cab driver eventually translated it from Home Counties English into Mancunian and sped off into the traffic.

Stack looked up at the weather-beaten spire that topped the derelict church he was standing in front of and wondered if the driver really had understood him. The Church of Evangelical Martyrs sat on the corner of a busy junction. A large sign welcomed all to come in and enjoy refreshments and shelter. He took the few steps through the stone porch into a large echoey room of unwelcoming dreariness. Half a dozen wooden pews had been pushed down towards what once was the nave and a trestle table dressed with tea making paraphernalia was set up to one side. Old S-shaped tubular chairs, probably donated by local businesses were laid out randomly. One or two small groups of tea drinkers were sitting apart from each other in muted conversation. The low buzz halted for a moment as the stranger walked in. They watched Stack choose a chair as far from them as he could find. He sat and waited. The laptop in the backpack on his lap.

He didn't know what should happen next. He didn't have to wait long to find out.

'Follow me.'

A voice from behind him. He turned and saw whoever it was already walking away towards an open door that led to a flight of wooden stairs that corkscrewed up in a sequence of steep right angles.

The ancient woodwork creaked as Stack climbed in near darkness. The musty smell of old books and dusty neglect increased with each step until a final narrow turn led onto a gallery furnished with a few pews that were raked to give worshipers a view of the pulpit below. Mani-hack had already taken a seat. Stack slid in next to him. The gallery was in permanent gloom. What light there was came from the open space below and the grudging daylight that leaked through the narrow grime-covered windows behind them.

'The cash first.'

Straight to the point. Good. As far as Stack was concerned he didn't want a long conversation with this guy.

'Just to confirm. You're Mani-hack?'

'Maniac! You don't pronounce the 'H'.' He sounded pissed-off. Stack thought it was his own fault for choosing such a stupid handle.

He passed him a wad of twenties and fifties. Mani-hack used the light from his mobile to count it. He stuffed it in his pocket and nodded to the backpack.

'Is that it? Pass it over.'

Mani-hack took it and before opening the screen, checked it from all angles, noting what ports it had, model number and other stuff that had him sniffing and sniggering as though its obvious inadequacy and age were beneath the talent of a man such as him.

Next, he opened the lid and switched it on. The boot up was fast, and pretty quickly he was presented with the same logon screen that had defeated the last two timewasters. More huffing and sniffing.

'The battery level is low.'

Stack didn't know what he could do about that so he said nothing. He watched by the dim light of the boot up screen as the hacker delved into his own backpack. Stack guessed he was five foot five, over-weight, probably through lack of exercise and a lifestyle of sitting for hours on end, staring at computer screens. Small darting brown eyes in a youthful, chubby face that was hidden in the cowl of a hoody pulled over a baseball cap.

He pulled a USB stick out of his bag and plugged it into the side port. His fingers moved quickly over the screen and keyboard: Too fast for Stack to follow. A second screen overlaid the logon screen. This one was text based and had a constantly changing sequence of digits flowing up from the bottom edge. It took no more than 30 seconds before all the asterisks in the logon field had been filled. Mani-hack punched the enter button, the screen cleared and was replaced by the desk top. Stonebridge's laptop had been opened!

Mani-hack sat back in the pew and folded his arms.

'OK. What else do you want?'

'Can you keep it open? Disable the password?'

More key strokes.

'Are we done here?'

'Just wait a moment. I need to find something I think has been stored in this computer. I'm not sure what he would have called it. You may have an idea of how to retrieve it.'

'Give me a clue. Tell me what you're looking for.'

Stack gave Mani-hack the short version of Stonebridge's rogue data story without mentioning GeoPower, which took more than a little dodging around the facts. Some kind of conspiracy: Just up Mani-hack's alley.

'How long ago was the file saved on this laptop?'

'I think it would have been more than a week or so. But the owner disappeared a few days ago.'

'So if I look up the most recently saved files going back a week or so, what do think?'

He was doing it as he said it. Again, a few key-strokes and a window opened with a list of files.

'See anything? Nothing familiar?'

'I don't think so. Try going back a little further.'

More tapping. Another, longer list appeared. This took Stack time to go through.

'You'd better hurry. Battery is about to go.'

He went through the yellow icons, bringing more up from the bottom with each stroke of his finger. Then he paused and went back over the last few before stopping at a likely candidate.

"Errors'. Could it be as simple as that?' Stack wondered.

Mani-hack double clicked on it and the file opened in a simple text app. And there they were: three lines of data. Looked like navigational coordinates to Stack, along with time and date info.

'This is it I'm sure.'

'Do you want me to copy it onto a stick?'

'Yes. Do that.'

The hacker reached in to his bag and brought out another USB memory stick, plugged it in and swiftly copied the file. He handed the stick over just as the laptop blinked off, its battery exhausted.

'OK? Now, are we done?'

'I guess so, thanks. Look, I might need your help again. Give me a direct number. I don't want to go through all this spy crap again.'

'Give me your phone.'

Stack handed it over and Mani-hack inputted a number.

'Your eyes only. Check?'

'Copy that.'

The First Frack

They finally got all the drilling done and the drillpipe, pulled out, unscrewed and stashed back in the racks. Down on the drilling floor the roustabouts worked with the crane operator crew to line the hole with concrete and steel sleeving - another tough job that had to be completed before fracking could start.

The fracking process happened in two stages. The first involved exploding perforation charges to break through the steel and concrete lining. The force would create small cracks that travelled a few inches into the shale rock. Then comes the serious stuff. High pressure hydraulic fracturing. A shock so powerful, it creates great webs of cracks that rip deep into the shale to release the gas.

Just another day in the office for your average fossil fuel extraction company. Everything's under control. What could go wrong?

***

Back in his room at The Devil's Pike, Stack dialled Blackstone's number. There had been no opportunity on the way back. The train was both too noisy and too busy with passengers travelling from Manchester to Sheffield, the city east of Hope Valley.

'Yes?' Blackstone's curt answer. 'Do you have the name?'

'And hello to you to.' Stack didn't really want to exchange pleasantries with Blackstone, the sniffy superiority of the man just made him contrary. 'Summer managed to get the name out of Finnegan. Sir Sebastian Winstanley. Ring a bell?'

'Sir Sebastian Winstanley.' It was said in a wistful tone, 'Why am I not surprised?' There was a short pause, 'You know something, Stack? I do like your girlfriend, Ms Peterson. She's clever and resourceful. It's why you and she make such a good team.'

'Thanks. Sebastian Winstanley?' Stack prompted.

'King of the sideways shuffle. No golden goodbye has ever been sufficient to prevent him from turning up like a bad penny in some other lucrative or lofty perch. I've had dealings with him on occasions. No matter what you think of me, Stack, this man is of a different order of Machiavellian deviousness.'

'How does he end up in such privileged positions if his dubious nature is so well known?'

'It's the Civil Service. At a certain level they all look after each other. He was knighted against the advice of respected opinion. He spent a lifetime nurturing friendships and contacts, many of whom I suspect are indebted to him in some way. I must admit, he's a smooth operator. On the surface, if you met him, you'd think he was a decent enough chap: charming, erudite, a straight bat, but... well...' There was a regretful tone in Blackstone's voice as though Sebastian Winstanley had gone over to the dark side. 'Anyway, the point is, if his name was mentioned then we must assume he's playing a crooked game.'

'What kind of game is the question?' Stack pondered. 'Could it affect our business?'

'Exactly. What was it he asked Finnegan to do? Stop the protest on the derrick? The government might have had a hand in it, after all, Energy and Climate Change is within his remit, but there's a risk Finnegan would whistle-blow it into some kind of political interference. The government is walking a fine line with fracking licences. It's making them extremely unpopular. Local elections are coming. No, this is something different.'

'But it can't be bad if he was asking them to stop protesting so that drilling could continue.' Stack ventured, 'Did he do it for GeoPower?'

'Unlikely. There's much more to it. I need to turn over some rocks, see what's crawling underneath. You'll hear from me.' *Click.*

Again. Dead air.

Stack pocketed the phone and was about to call Summer when he remembered, she was going to call him. She was very clear about that. Still, a text wouldn't hurt: '*Call me.*'

There was a nagging question. Should he go straight up to the drilling site and let Simon Harding in on their little rogue data secret?

He left Stonebridge's laptop in the room and stuffed the memory stick in his pocket.

Before he took off for Rebellion Hill he checked out the saloon downstairs to see if Bennett was in his office. Unsurprisingly, he was. Sitting on a stool by the bar, his eyes glued to a tabloid newspaper and his fingers wrapped tightly around the handle of a pint glass in permanent readiness to down the remaining dregs of draught beer. He looked up and threw the folded paper onto the bar, narrowly avoiding a pool of spilt ale.

'What you having?' Bennett's usual cheerful greeting.

'Let's get away from the bar. I have news.'

Stack was already walking over to a table in a bay window. Bennett grabbed his paper and beer and followed.

'So? What news?' He said, placing the paper and beer glass on the table as he sat down.

'That kid, Mani-hack got the laptop open. He was very good. Knew his stuff.'

'The dodgy data?'

'All there.'

'OK. What are we going to do with it?'

'A good question. I was wondering whether I should go up to the rig site now and show Simon Harding. I suppose he really needs to know so he can make up his own mind if it's relevant or not.'

He reached in to his jeans pocket and brought out a folded paper.

'This is a print out. Used the pub's printer as soon as I got back from Manchester.' He unfolded it and laid it over the newspaper for Bennett to see.

'These aren't really coordinates as I understand them – north, south, east and west - but I'm guessing one of these is an azimuth reading, left and right, and another is inclination – you know – up and down. There are other numbers that, if you compare one line of telemetry to the other two, you'll notice the figures jump to higher numbers, as though they were nipped out of a sequence or a timeline. These numbers should relate to a known value, such as where north is and probably the starting point of the well itself.'

'So it's to do with the direction of the well?'

'That's the tricky bit. These numbers need to be compared to the regular coordinates. The ones we must assume Stonebridge was happy were correct. If these numbers are wrong, what is it that's wrong about them? Stonebridge would have been able to tell us if he hadn't disappeared.'

'Talking of Stonebridge, looks like GeoPower have reported him missing, the police have been up there. I'm going to be filing a story tonight. I spoke to the local coppers and they're treating it as 'not suspicious' for the moment. Though they can't explain why he disappeared and left all his belongings behind. They've put a description out and been in contact with his family.'

Bennett saw the look on Stack's face.

'Look. I've got to report this. It's local news. A missing person. My editor's on my back. I'll keep the other stuff out of it – OK?'

Stack shrugged a tacit agreement.

'Ok, but how can the police not find it suspicious?' Stack said, 'Just how 'missing' do you have to be to get in the 'suspicious' category? He was due to meet you the following day.'

Surprisingly, Bennett was more sanguine.

'Coincidental maybe?'

'Come on, Bennett, you're a journalist.'

'Yeah, well I haven't told the cops he was supposed to meet me. I just took notes. If I had told them, they would have wanted to know why he was meeting me. I'd have had to tell them. That would get complicated. You see the problem?'

Stack nodded.

'Well, I'm glad we got his laptop out of his room before this all blew up. Could that be seen as tampering with evidence?'

'Only if they know about it.' Bennett had spent his career weaving a dubious path around the blurred edges of legality.

Just then, Stack's cell phone played a muted glissando. Bennett saw the chance to refill his glass and indicated with an extravagant mime that he was going to get a round of drinks.

It was Summer.

'Thank God, I've been worried about you.' Stack's voice was buoyed with relief, 'Where are you? How are you?'

'I'm fine. How did it go with the lap-top? Did that Mani-hack guy pan out ok?'

Stack quickly gave her the good news about the data, but he was more concerned about her and what had happened up at the camp.

'It's been…interesting.'

'What the hell does that mean?'

Summer told Stack about the evening's activities in the protest camp. Finnegan's speech to rally the troops and how he told them GeoPower were getting ready to frack and he had some kind of plan to stop it. Then she explained how she had tricked Finnegan into revealing the name.

'He was quite drunk by then. I'd been leading him on quite a bit and he was starting to get very…well let's just say he was assuming a very happy ending to the evening. I could handle him, but it was becoming awkward. We may still need him. I must admit I wasn't sure what to do beyond getting up and walking away. I was hoping he might have fallen unconscious. He'd drunk so much. But the problem was solved for me.'

Stack was intrigued. 'Do tell.'

Summer explained about the earlier meeting with Finnegan, Clarissa Howden-Ffrench and the young woman, Bryony.

'Well it seems she recognised you.'

Stack was shocked. 'Me? What in the pub?'

'No, later. Finnegan was secretly surveying the GeoPower site with a tiny drone that was being flown by Bryony. Turns out she's a top cat in the new techno-sport, drone racing. Very skilled, and it turns out, extremely useful to Finnegan.'

The mention of a tiny drone immediately clicked with Stack.

'I know what you're going to tell me. She saw me on the drilling deck the other day.'

Summer was surprised. 'Yes, how did you know?'

It was Stack's turn to tell Summer what had happened. How he'd glimpsed a tiny hummingbird that wasn't a hummingbird.

'Yes, well she came crashing into Finnegan's party last night, full of alcohol and indignation. Pointing fingers at me and screaming how the man in the pub she'd told Finnegan about worked for GeoPower. She thought she had recognised your face during the recce, put two and two together and hey presto, I'm consorting with evil capitalist devil worshipers. She ranted on quite a bit about this. Oddly, she was pissed off but quite tearful as well.'

'How did Finnegan take it?' Stack asked.

'Mixed emotions. He was all revved up to take his chances with me. Then this little firecracker comes along and spoils the moment, for him anyway. She had no idea she'd saved me from Finnegan.'

'Yes, but what did Finnegan say?' Stack urged.

'I just reminded Finnegan that I'd only bumped into you both in the pub. I had no idea what you did for a living. Coincidence. Finnegan was prepared to give it the benefit of the doubt. Probably trying to rescue the moment in an attempt to put his pathetic imaginary love life back on the rails. I made out I was angry with Bryony and walked off.'

Stack reached over for the data printout and started folding it.

'So what's the situation now?' As he was putting the folded paper in his pocket he noticed a story in the newspaper about the arrival of a superyacht in London. There was even a picture. It looked very familiar! He turned the paper a little towards him and read as he listened to Summer.

'I'm keeping a low profile. Trying not to bump into Finnegan or Bryony.'

'It might be best if you come back to the pub. Stay away from the camp for a while. You've done all you can.'

'Yes, but I still need to find out what Finnegan's got in mind to prevent the fracking...and when. But he's definitely going to be suspicious of me now.'

'Look, fracking starts very soon. Maybe today. I'll get them to step up security on the Hill. Get down to the pub as soon as. OK?'

Summer agreed but then remembered something.

'This might be nothing, but Finnegan mentioned something Winstanley had said, 'we're on the same side. I want what you want'. What do you think he meant by that?'

'Could just be manipulative bull shit. But it is a curious thing to say isn't it.'

They ended the call just as Bennett returned with the drinks.

'Something interesting?' Bennett asked as Stack opened the paper and gave the story his full attention.

'This story here. It's another coincidence.'

Even as he said it Stack shivered as though a ghost had brushed passed him. He realised there had been too many coincidences recently. He reached for his beer and sipped a mouthful, then turned the paper to show Bennett the page. He tapped the picture with his finger.

'I know this boat and I've met the owner. I'm not going to tell you what circumstances brought us together, but I can tell you Mikhail Ulyanin owns one of Russia's largest oil companies.'

Bennett zeroed in on this information.

'I read somewhere that coincidences are the whispers of gods. We should pay attention to them.'

'You should lay-off the Chinese fortune cookies, David.'

Bennett ignored then sarcasm.

'I guess that was Summer on the phone. Did she come up with a name yet?'

'Yes she did, Sir Sebastian Winstanley. Heard of him?'

Turned out Bennett had heard of him, but that was all.

'I'll see what my contacts have got on him.'

With Blackstone already on the case, Stack tried to slow Bennett down.

'Can you take a rain-check on that for the moment. I have someone much closer to the centre of things looking into Winstanley's connection with Finnegan, or with GeoPower, if any. I don't want him tipped off that people are asking questions.'

Bennett said he would, but his journalists instinct was like an itch that needed scratching. This was his story. If it turned out to be a live one, he wanted the glory.

Stack gave Bennett a sideways glance. He didn't trust him but couldn't see what he could do about it. He let it pass for the time being. Rebellion Hill was where he needed to be right now. He asked Bennett if he'd keep an eye out for Summer.

'Tell her I've left the room key on the hook behind the bar.'

As he rose to leave, Bennett said, 'So that's another one added to the riddle list.'

Stack turned.

'Sorry?'

'The arrival of this Russian. You know. The big-time oil guy. It's an odd bit of timing.'

'You journo's see conspiracies everywhere.'

Stack turned and left the pub. He had intended to go straight up to Rebellion Hill, but decided to call Blackstone first to tell him about the curious timing of the arrival of the Russian, and the cryptic info that Summer had extracted from Finnegan about Winstanley.

***

The business end of the drilling site was a hive of activity. To a layman like Stack it looked as though they'd started drilling again. Something was being stuffed back down the borehole. Stack approached Simon Harding. He was at his desk in the pre-fab office unit.

Harding looked up from his computer screen and nodded a greeting as Stack rolled a chair over from another unmanned desk.

'What's going on?' He nodded in the direction of the rig, 'I thought drilling was finished?'

Harding didn't look up from the monitor as he spoke. 'It is. That's just the perforating gun loaded with explosive charges being lowered into place.' Harding stopped what he was doing and turned his attention to Stack. He saw the look of concern on his face, 'Well, they're big bangs. Not the kind of bangs you ex-army guys are used to though. Anyway, it's small stuff compared to what's coming next.'

He explained that these preliminary explosions are needed to perforate the wall of the borehole which had now been lined with steel and cement casing. The sleeving was in place to prevent contamination of the water table and stop the hydrocarbons seeping out of the well.

'The explosive charge penetrates a few inches into the shale layer. It's a starting point for when we begin fracking.'

'It sounds alarming. Big explosions underground.'

'Not as big as the high pressure fracks. Anyway, it's over three miles down.'

'You said 'fracks' I thought it was just one?'

Harding told him how fracking was done in 1,000 foot sections.

'The first frack would happen right after the first lot of charges had been set-off.' He looked at his watch, 'Soon now.' He turned back to his computer.

Stack hesitated as he considered how he was going to broach the issue of Stonebridge's data. Now he was here, at the drilling site, sitting next to the drilling supervisor, somehow it all seemed a bit far-fetched. These are professionals. They know what's going on. He was way out of his depth.

He pulled the printout from his pocket, unfolded it and looked once again at the three lines of telemetry sent up from deep below ground that had bothered Stonebridge so much. Doubt clouded his mind. Who was Stonebridge? A young inexperienced college graduate working the nightshift. One of his first solo directional drilling jobs. Everyone else around him was vastly more experienced. Was Stonebridge right and everyone else wrong? It seemed unlikely.

Though Harding was focused intently on his computer screen, he became aware that Stack was still sitting next to him.

'Something else I can do for you, Stack?' He glanced at the paper Stack was holding.

Stack shook his head, folded the printout and slipped it back into his pocket.

'No. It's nothing.'

He rose to leave and then remembered.

'Yes, there is something. I think you should get security stepped up right away.'

Harding swivelled his chair to face Stack.

'We already have pretty comprehensive security. It should be enough...well according to Saunders, anyway.' He didn't sound confident, 'What makes you say that?'

'I've heard on the grapevine that Danny Finnegan over in the protest camp has some kind of plan to stop you fracking. I don't know what it is yet. I'm trying to imagine what kind of fun and games I'd come up with if I were him.'

'You'd better talk to Saunders. Let's not take any chances.'

Stack nodded and walked away. He stepped outside and was just closing the door when Harding yelled a final piece of advice.

'And Stack, don't take any crap from him.'

***

Saunders took the news with his customary bad grace. Thanking Stack, but explaining in a supercilious sneer that he had everything under control and needed no help. Especially from someone as inexperienced in the highly specialised field of oil rig security as Stack.

Standing his ground, Stack reminded him that he wasn't without skills and neither was he trying to undermine Saunders' authority. He was simply advising him that the information came from a reliable source and constituted a real and present threat to GeoPower's operations.

Stack couldn't see how he could force Saunders into action so he left and went looking for his partner in crime, Charlie. He tried the mess first.

***

Saunders sat staring at the door long after Stack had gone. Resentment over Stack's interference on his patch made him seeth. Not just Stack but Harding. He had overstepped his authority by bringing in a rank amateur. A lucky up-start with a stupid and dangerous scheme to bring the protesters down from the mast.

Then Saunders remembered with a shiver the commitment that was required of him. The scheme he'd been invited to join. Invited? Perhaps not invited. How about 'manipulated'. That was kinder. It implied a reluctance to take part. He shrank in his chair and covered his face, hoping like a child that when he removed his hands a different reality would present itself. If he was honest, money, on an uncountable, life-changing scale, had been the motivator.

***

It turned out Charlie wasn't in the mess. Stack found him hovering around the drilling deck. Not actually working but taking an interest in the final preparations to fire the explosive charges. He always loved things that go bang.

'Hey Jimbo.' Charlie's typically breezy greeting, 'Any trolls and orcs lurking below ground are about to get a wake-up call.'

'Let me guess – *Lord of the Rings*?' Stack had learned to roll with 'Hollywood's' movie obsession. Sometimes it had provided an unexpected but incisive clue to a problem. It was Charlie's indefatigable fan worship of the film Goldfinger that had led to the successful recovery of Stack's fortune, the stash of cash from the precious metals scam that ended with two years of four behind bars. The same money he was trying to recover again!

'How did Manchester go? Mani-hack come up with the goods?' There was a mocking tone to his voice.

Stack removed the print out and showed Charlie.

'Yes. He was impressive. The problem is I don't know what to do about it?'

'Well, what do you know? The new Captain Cautious. Captains should never tell the guys in the squad 'I don't know what to do'. It's not a democracy. You're God. You're... what's the word? Omnipotent?'

'Omnipotent!' Stack sniffed.

'Come on, boss, if you've got the proof, you've got to tell them.'

'Yeah, but proof of what?'

Stack turned and looked across to the Portakabin where Harding was still working.

'I was with Harding earlier. I was going to show him the print out, but I bottled it. It all just seemed too crazy. These guys must know what's going on. They're professionals. What the hell do I know about this game?'

'James, John Stonebridge was unhappy. These numbers really freaked him out, but no one would listen...'

'That's what I mean.' Stack said, cutting Hollywood off, 'Nobody would listen to him. Why would they listen to me?'

'But they haven't seen the numbers have they. I think he only told Debbie Blain the first time it happened. Anyway, she's gone.'

'Gone? Why's that?'

'They only need directional drillers when they're drilling. They're expensive inventory to keep around. I reckon she'll be back when they start drilling the next well.'

Across the asphalt pad, the door to the office unit opened and Harding stepped out and headed towards the rig.

'Harding's on his way. They could be about to fire the first charges.' Charlie said.

On the rig deck the crew moved away from the well. The shaped charges in the perforating gun concentrated the blast into a narrow, focused beam that cut through the casing into the shale. But the shockwave could travel the length of the well bore.

Harding took his place in the dog shack, Stack and Charlie followed. With service company engineers contracted to handle the explosives already there, the shed was getting full. The prep for the first frack always drew a crowd.

'We good to go?' The drilling supervisor was the go, no-go guy.

'All set and ready.'

'Clear the drilling floor.' Harding again.

'All clear.'

Whoever was out on the drilling floor a moment ago, was now squeezed into the dog shack.

The chief service company engineer shouted 'Stand-by.' His fingers gripped the key that operated the electronic ignition.

He got a nod from Harding.

'Firing!'

He turned the key and pressed the button.

Nearly 5 miles down and 2,500 feet beyond the fault, deep under Shivering Mountain, it sounded as though war had broken out. A series of machine-gun-like bursts of explosions cut through the steel casing and cement lining. A thousand-foot length of hard shale rock was perforated by a series of small cracks. The explosive assault ended just 1,500 feet from the fissure. The next one would be closer.

Above, a silent moment passed during which Stack looked at Charlie and then at Harding. He wasn't sure what he should be have been expecting.

According to the engineer whose equipment showed a row of green lights, all was good.

'OK, pull the gun out.'

The dog shack emptied and the drilling deck was a hive of activity again.

'Not bad! They'll be getting this well operational and delivering gas by tomorrow or the day after.' Charlie said, 'Your shares should be worth a few quid by then and we can all pack up and go...' He paused as he considered exactly where they could go. '...Home...where ever the hell that is.'

'It can't come soon enough for me, Hollywood.'

'You've got to show that print-out to Harding, Boss. He trusts you. Those dodgy numbers must mean something, otherwise Stonebridge wouldn't have worried so much.'

Stack looked over to Harding and nodded. 'OK, but I want you to do something for me.'

Charlie shrugged.

'You merely have to command me, master.'

Stack gave a short laugh.

'Fair enough. Look, Summer's had enough of the protest camp and frankly, it's getting too risky for her.' Stack put his hand on Charlies shoulder. 'OK, Charlie, I'll talk to Harding. But I want you to go back to The Devil's Pike, I think Summer should be there about now. Buy her a drink. Keep her company.'

'You think she's in danger?'

'Danny Finnegan's a crazy self-obsessed agitator. He's on to Summer, and there's another crazy woman who could be out for revenge. I have no idea what either of them might do, but I don't want to take a chance.'

Charlie didn't need to say anything, but as he turned to go, he gave Stack a nod towards Harding who, with little to do now except wait while the engineers set up for the frack, was walking over towards Stack.

'I saw the look on your face after the perforating charges went off. It's always like that. There was no chance those explosions could be felt or heard on the surface.' Harding gave a quick nod to the activity outside and said ironically, 'Hydraulic fracturing. Now that's a different ballgame.' His Scottish accent made it sound all the more terrifying.

'When does that start?' Stack was keen to see an end to the whole business. A successful end. A cashing-in and getting his money back kind of an end. It couldn't come soon enough.

'As soon as they've cleared the perforating gun from the wellbore.' Harding said. 'Everything's set up. They just have to connect the high-pressure lines to the Christmas Tree valves on the well head.'

Out on the pad behind the rig, all ten massive Caterpillar diesel pumps were turning over noisily, ready to draw slickwater fracking fluid from the nearby mixing tanks. The Slickwater was 99.5 percent water, but contained some chemicals and minute quantities of sand to keep the cracks open.

Flexible hoses snaked out from each heavy pump unit and fed into large diameter hardened-steel pipes. They'd been plumbed up, around and down until they emerged in the cellar below the drilling deck. Engineers were already tightening the bolts that connected the two pipes to the Christmas Tree.

The first hydraulic fracturing of GeoPower's Hope Valley well was good to go.

***

There is big science involved in fracking. It sounds like dumb brute force and in a way it is, like the brutal power used to launch Saturn rockets to the Moon. But in exactly the same way that they don't just load a giant silver tube with kerosene and liquid oxygen, press a button and hope for the best, hydraulic fracturing requires many measurements to ensure a precise amount of pressure is brought to bear on the shale rock. Not enough and you don't get enough flow to make the well viable. Too much pressure and you create unwanted seismic events. Small, but occasionally measurable surface tremors that GeoPower were keen to avoid.

In the dog shack, Stack watched as the engineer scanned the readings on his monitor. Bore hydrostatic pressure was nominal. The mud slurry used for drilling had already been replaced by the slickwater.

This wasn't strictly Harding's responsibility, but he was there anyhow, and they all looked to him before the frack job began. He simply nodded for them to proceed.

One at a time, engineers out on the pad began to open valves. Powerful pumps forced pressurised fluid along the bore hole to the freshly perforated section at the far end. Initially, at a rate of 5,000 pounds per square inch, but gradually increasing until all ten, 900 horse power, Caterpillar power units had come online and were forcing fluid down the well at a rate of 200 litres a second – some 70 barrels a minute. The rig floor shook and the drillpipes stowed in the derrick above them rattled in the finger racks. Flickering needles on dials and graphics on digital displays showed the scale of the pressure being driven against the rock.

Twenty five thousand feet from the drilling site, and almost five miles down, the tiny webs of hairline cracks punched into the shale formation by the explosive charges shrugged off the assault. A few had weakened, permeating a little more into the formation, but refused to go further.

Harding had been present at many fracks and the signs

for this one were not good. Sometimes the stubborn rock just won't give. The engineer and his crew were also old hands with hundreds of frack jobs under their belt, but they were already working at big pressures. No question, they had the power out on the pad. Ten Cats driving behemoth pumps. But winding them fully up can do a whole lot of damage.

He gave the call to increase the flow rate. The technicians manning the pumps opened the valves a little more. The big engines worked harder to compensate. The noise was like thunder.

The tension in the shack matched the pressure in the well bore. Everyone looked worried. Even Stack, a man who could remain calm under the most terrifying combat conditions, was alarmed. The look on the faces of the experienced professionals didn't help. It seemed like the force of a powerful hurricane was bearing down on them.

Harding watched the pressure increase, passing 11,000 psi, then twelve. 90 barrels a minute was being pushed against the rock. The fluid pressed harder into the small initiating cracks, but there was still no sign of fracturing.

At 14,000 pounds per square inch and rising, with the flow rate nearing record levels at just short of 100 barrels a minute, the rig and the ground around it shook and vibrated with the violence of the pressurised flow. The noise was unbelievable.

This was heading into unfamiliar territory. It had been a long time since they had used this kind of force and that didn't have a happy end. The engineer's attention was fixed on the gauges, but his vision blurred. He used the back of his hand to wipe a bead of sweat from his eye.

And then suddenly, the needle kicked and the pressure dropped slightly.

There was a palpable sense of relief from the fracking team. Harding, not a man to show excitement, breathed for the first time in ten minutes. The rattling and vibration eased as the first hydraulic fracturing came to a successful end.

They'd set up seismometers above ground in the general area south west of the well-head. The area where the well bore should be. They were there to record any seismic activity as a result of the frack. In the dog shack, the set of white lines that traced across the live monitor screen stayed motionless. The only evidence of the event was a small shifting of loose shale on the flanks of Shivering Mountain. But that was far off to the north west.

The Pugin Room

Luxurious and relaxing, the room was everything you might expect to find in a gentleman's club. Somewhat under lit and very old school: rich flock Gothic tapestry wallpaper dating from 1850, specially woven carpets, a large gilt and brass crystal chandelier hanging from a ceiling that was hand-stencilled with patterns of roses surrounded by leaves. And on the wall, portraits of Augustus Welby Pugin, the benefactor and interior designer of the Palace of Westminster, the home of the Houses of Parliament.

A niche had been created in a bay window where a raised dais gave an enviable view of the River Thames and a perch from which to spy on other members and their guests. Though it wasn't in fact a gentleman's club, the Pugin Room was Sir Sebastian Winstanley's favourite bar. Governing the United Kingdom must be thirsty work because there are many such bars to choose from in the Houses of Parliament.

The raised dais in the bay window, and in particular, the winged leather chair that dominated it, was regarded by Winstanley as his exclusive realm. Fledgling careers had been known to falter on the misjudged resting of backsides on the leather of 'his' chair by the young and naive when Winstanley entered the room.

Today was different.

As well as the wingback, the dais had two old leather tub-like club chairs arranged around a low table. Sitting in the wingback, known as Winstanley's throne to the regulars, sat a man of evident substance. Easily recognised by the Savile Row business suit, silk tie and luxuriant silver-grey hair brushed back over his ears. There was something formidable about him and the easy way he sat: legs crossed, left elbow resting casually on the arm of the chair and a glass of Scotch in his hand. His head was turned to the bay window and the view of tour boats, tugs and other vessels traveling up and down the busy river. Irritatingly, even from a distance, it was clear the man carried the authority of one who could not be easily intimidated or embarrassed. He had metaphorically planted his standard on the dais and for the time being he was King. He reminded Winstanley of another equally dominant personality he had recently come into contact with. The thought made him shudder involuntarily.

As Winstanley walked through the room he asked a waiter if he knew the man. He was told the stranger had been escorted to that very seat by a member of the government no less, a cabinet minister, which explained his confident presence. Most bars and restaurants within the Houses of Parliament are off-limits to ordinary members of the public. This bar was even more exclusive, which was why Winstanley liked it. Ministers of State, their Permanent Secretaries and the higher echelons of the civil service only, unless, like the stranger, you had a prestigious contacts list.

Winstanley continued over to the bay window where the man was still enjoying the view. Looking up from the floor, a demeaning foot lower than the dais, he coughed politely to attract attention. Slowly, the man turned and from his elevated position, looked down, weighing the intruder, assessing him as though he was a boy sent on an errand. It was an unnerving experience that placed Winstanley at a disadvantage, which was precisely where the man wanted him. He indicated with an elegant motion of his hand one of the other chairs.

'Please, take a seat.'

The wind removed from his sails, Winstanley stepped obediently up and did as he was told. As he did so, the man spoke again.

'Can I get you a drink?' The voice was very public school.

He didn't wait for an answer but simply looked across the room to attract a waiter.

Winstanley settled into the chair, not one he was used to sitting in and inordinately more uncomfortable than the one the stranger was sitting in. His chair.

The sides of the tub chair were a little narrow for Winstanley and his elbows couldn't decide whether they were more comfortable inside the chair or resting awkwardly at almost shoulder height on the curve that formed the arms.

Through all this the stranger watched silently, relaxed and urbane - almost amused. The glass of whisky held elegantly in his hand, his attention wavering, preferring to study an annoying blemish on a highly polished shoe at the end of his crossed leg, as though it might have sustained a scuff.

He indicated to Winstanley with a nod of the head as the waiter came over. The waiter, familiar with the civil servant's preferences didn't wait to be told.

The stranger, took a sip from his glass, placed it on the table and sat back again.

'You are familiar with Danny Finnegan.' It wasn't a question, more a statement of fact.

Shocked by the totally unexpected opener, Winstanley wondered where such an enquiry might lead. And what drove the man to ask it. It was obvious that this was no accidental meeting. This was an interview. He wondered if he might be MI5, or MI6 even?

'Danny Finnegan? Why would you ask me that I wonder?'

The stranger, cool and indifferent, simply turned his head lazily to the bay window again. His fingers drummed on the arm of the chair, a deliberate device to show irritation and impatience. A warning. A moment passed before he spoke again, calmly, still staring out to the river.

'Finnegan confirmed that you spoke to him recently.' He turned to Winstanley, 'What is your interest in drilling operations in Derbyshire?' The man delivered the words with a pleasant smile.

'Who the hell are you to question me this way?' Winstanley replied indignantly.

The waiter returned with a tray holding Winstanley's drink. He placed it on a coaster on the table and withdrew. Winstanley waited until the man was out of earshot, leaned forward and spoke in a low threatening voice.

'Do you know who I am…?'

'It is precisely because I know who you are, or more accurately, what you do, that we are having this conversation.'

Winstanley bristled.

'My role in the Department for Business, Energy and Industrial Strategy has a direct bearing on acquisition of fossil fuels within the UK…'

'But you are not a decision maker are you? You are a facilitator – a factotum.' The inquisitor knew which buttons to press.

The civil servant brazened it out.

'Look, you're a man of world, I can see that. Yes, I ensure the BEIS runs smoothly. Call me a factotum if you like. But our interest is in securing the continuity of supply to run our industries and heat our homes.' Winstanley was playing the 'reasonable man' card, 'We've licensed a very sensitive drilling operation that's going on right now in Hope Valley.

Protestors had brought it to a standstill. I thought I could appeal to Danny Finnegan to bring it to an end. Just doing my little bit, you know.'

As Winstanley reached for his drink, confident he had deflected the direction of the inquiry, the stranger threw in another name.

'Ever heard of a Russian called Mikhail Ulyanin?'

The drink didn't quite reach Winstanley's lips, it hovered in mid-air as he hesitated.

'Sorry? Who?'

'Ulyanin,' he repeated, 'You're in the fossil fuels business as Permanent Secretary to the Secretary of State for Business, Energy and Industrial Strategy, Winstanley, you must have heard of one the world's richest oil billionaires. He owns Severgaz Postavka.'

Winstanley regretted his earlier guilty response. The line of enquiry had Winstanley worried.

If the man in the chair opposite was MI5, what did they know?

'Yes, of course. I didn't get the connection with Finnegan for a moment.'

The stranger was following a vague lead. Nothing that proved anything. A string of coincidences really. That, and the character of Sir Sebastian Winstanley with his rather elastic notion of service in the interest of the nation. He was fishing, but trying not to make it look like it.

'I believe the drilling operation in Hope Valley is at an end and hydraulic fracturing is due to start, if it hasn't already.'

'That is how I understand it.' The civil servant replied formally.

The questioner considered Winstanley's response before pushing his luck with the next statement.

'Do you not find it curious that the Russian should arrive

at precisely the same time? Do you imagine he may have an interest?'

Even as he said it, he knew how Winstanley would reply.

'I can't imagine why Ulyanin chose this time to visit London.'

'Severgaz Postavka has vast oil and gas reserves.' The stranger said. 'Ulyanin is man who is always looking for new customers. Has he not been in touch with your department? Wouldn't it make sense to use this visit to do some business with the UK?' Has the phone not rung?'

'The BEIS is not seeking further contracts with Russia or anyone else at this time.' Winstanley was on more certain ground as he spouted the government line, 'It is the government's intention that the UK should become self-sufficient in energy and rely less on foreign suppliers.'

The stranger reached for his drink. With Winstanley's confidence returning, the sip of 13-year-old single malt gave him a moment to consider his next question. To lever apart a seam in Winstanley's armour.'

'Of course, the government doesn't actually sign the contracts, it just approves them. Gives them the green light, doesn't it.'

'That's a simplification, but I suppose that is how it could be characterised.'

Again, like a lawyer cross examining a witness, the stranger considered his next question.

'Are you that man?'

'Pardon? What man?'

The questions came faster.

'Is it you who gives the green light?'

'Me personally? No. A committee is involved.'

'Have you ever recommended a course of action to this committee?'

'Yes. Of course.'

'How often do they take your advice?'

'Occasionally.'

'So you are the man. That's quite a powerful position you hold.'

The businessman sat back in his seat and studied Winstanley for a moment. He took another sip of whisky and turned to look out of the window as he considered his next move. He knew that Sir Sebastian Winstanley terrorised the committee. His opinions often held sway. He imagined drawing a triangle with GeoPower, Winstanley and Ulyanin at each point. Take the triangle away and you're left with just three coincidental actors, but put the triangle back...

He turned back to Winstanley and asked a final question, straight out of left field.

'Why would you advise Danny Finnegan that - *He shouldn't worry. We're on the same side.*' The interrogator had read the words from a notebook. He closed it and slipped it back inside his jacket pocket as he ask. 'Whose side are you on, Winstanley? Finnegan wants to stop GeoPower. You call to tell him to stop the protest on the derrick, yet you expect him to believe you are on his side. What is it about allowing the drilling to continue that Finnegan would approve of?'

Nothing from Winstanley. He just slowly shook his head at Finnegan's betrayal.

The stranger thanked Winstanley, drank the last of his whisky and left.

Sir Sebastian Winstanley sat there, staring at the space where the businessman had been. He wasn't sure what had just happened.

The Second Frack

The print-out had existed for less than a day, but after being folded and unfolded and stuffed into his pocket a few times, it was already looking scruffy. The filthy environment on the rig deck quickly turned any pristine sheet of white paper into a dog-eared, oil-stained mess.

Simon Harding held it up and moved into a patch of daylight coming through the dog shack windows to examine it. His folded glasses held to his eyes. It took only a moment.

He handed the paper back and, as Stack had anticipated, asked how he'd got hold of it. This presented a problem. It's known as breaking and entering.

Stack had already explained the background and how concerned John Stonebridge had been. He also mentioned the associated problem with the rock samples and how Stonebridge had freaked out when the last set of erroneous numbers magically re-typed on the screen as he watched. And of course, how Stonebridge had gone missing after he'd made plans to talk to a journalist. This last part didn't impress Harding. You just don't go to the press.

'So you, or was it Dawson, just decided to break into his room and steal Stonebridge's laptop,' he said matter of factly.

Put like that, it was hard to defend. Stack didn't try.

'Look, can we get past that for the moment. What do you make of the numbers?'

'Until they're compared to the other data it's impossible to know, and I'm not sure I could tell you anyway.' He scratched his head as he considered his options, 'Debbie's not around, but the new nightshift directional driller,

Kramar, is still on site. Let's talk to him. If anyone should know he's your guy.'

He pressed the TX button on his radio.

'Is Pete Kramar on site?'

A female voice responded. 'Not in the office.' *Hash-click*

'Yeah, Kramar here. I'm in the mess.' *Hash-click*. The American accent surprised Stack for some reason.

'Meet me in the office. I need to check something with you.'

'Roger that.' *Hash-click*.

It took just a minute to cross the pad to the prefab units. Kramar was already entering the office as they arrived.

Harding did a quick introduction.

'Kramar, this is James Stack.'

Kramar, a tall broad-chested man with a day's growth of blond fuzz on his narrow, almost skinny face, gave a broad grin.

'Hey, glad to meet you.'

Stack amended his first impression of Kramar's accent. American, yes, but it sounded as though it had been superimposed onto something else. What was it, German? No, further east. Maybe Poland.

Kramar turned to Harding, 'So, what's up?'

Stack handed him the print-out.

Stack couldn't help noticing the initial shock on Kramar's face. It was fleeting, and quickly recomposed to bland and expressionless.

'Well, these are obviously error messages, they happen all the time. Or they're from another rig.'

'Error messages?' Stack asked.

'The mud telemetry can get confused. It has to travel a hell of a distance, and as good as the analogue to digital converters are, the background noise, you know, vibrations or sudden lurches as the drill bit hits a void, these can screw around with the data. Last job I was on, we had lots of these.' He turned to Harding, 'Why do you ask?'

It doesn't matter, Pete. Sorry to bother you.'

Kramar nodded in the direction of the mess.

'Coffee's getting cold.'

The directional driller screwed the printout into a ball, threw it into the waste basket and walked out.

As Harding turned to leave, Stack removed the printout and ironed it flat with his hand on the desk. He folded it as he walked back to the drill floor with Harding who nodded at the creased paper Stack was stuffing into his pocket.

'Not convinced, Stack?'

'I have to accept what he said because I have no way to counter his explanation.'

'But?'

'Did it sound plausible to you? This is your neck of the woods. What did you think?'

Harding walked on silently before replying.

'I know about error messages, but they are very different to those on your printout. They have rows of question marks and other obvious differences from regular data. But he is the expert. Why should I not believe him?'

Stack stopped for a moment as Harding walked on a few paces and turned to look back.

'He didn't compare it to the data history.' He pulled the paper out again, unfolded it and held it up for Harding to see, 'Look at these lines of numbers. I can't explain what each part of it means, but to anyone who knows anything about navigation coordinates there is one very obvious commonality with all three lines.'

'OK, Sherlock. Impress me.' Harding's Aberdeenshire cynicism coming through strongly.

'There might be a long time lag in between each line of code, probably many days, but there are sections that are broadly consistent.'

Harding waited for Stack to make his point.

'Look, if these relate to directional coordinates, this group here, are all heading in the same direction.'

Harding walked back to Stack, held his glasses to his eyes again and peered at where Stack was pointing. He said nothing. Sniffed, and put his glasses back in his shirt pocket. He turned and continued back to the rig floor.

'Come on Harding. You've got to compare these numbers with the drilling history.' Stack shouted as the ten Caterpillars roared back into life again.

***

Kramar's coffee remained untouched on the mess room table. He cut across to another office. He didn't knock, he just barged in, went over to the desk and leaned across practically nose to nose with the Operations Manager.

'I know where the laptop is.'

'I'm waiting.' Andy Saunders wasn't in the mood for long stories.

'Your friend James Stack has it.'

'And you know this, how?'

'Because I've just seen him and he had a printout of the data. He was with Harding.'

Saunders was shocked but said nothing.

'They asked me what I thought the figures meant, I just blew smoke at them, you know, unimportant error messages, that kind of thing. But if they get their act together, it's like a finger pointing to the northwest. The game, as you say, would be screwed.'

Saunders breathed a deep, despondent sigh. He knew what he must do.

After the last call to the Russian almost a week ago, he had broken into Stonebridge's room. It wasn't difficult. He was Operations Manager after all, security was part of his brief. Like most of the accommodation in the block, it was a small unit with few places to hide anything. The laptop hadn't been there. But now the question 'had it ever been there or had someone else beaten him to it?' had been answered.

He grimaced in disgust at himself, flicked a glance at Kramar and reached for the phone. He dialled the number he'd used before, but looked away as he raised the phone to his ear. Trying to imagine it was someone else making this call. He knew bad things happened as a result of the things he said.

***

Summer finished showering off the stench of the camp and reached for one of the large fluffy towels piled invitingly on an old chair squeezed between the sink and the shower. She found a bathrobe hanging behind the bathroom door and put it on. Like bathrooms in many taverns that provide accommodation, the room wasn't big, or particularly luxurious. The floor creaked and the showerhead delivered a grudging flow through the remaining unblocked holes, but to Summer, right now, this was incomparable luxury central. The Dorchester would have struggled to compete.

***

A little earlier as she entered the pub she'd spotted Bennett over by the bar with his back to her. Tired and not in the mood for conversation she had intended to sneak past. But inevitably, when an attractive woman arrives in a bar populated mostly by men, her arrival was unlikely to go unnoticed. The sudden interruption in the noisy bar room buzz caused Bennett to look up. He caught her reflection in the mirror behind the bar, turned and greeted her brightly. That of all the men in the room, this attractive woman was a friend of his, had him basking in the unfamiliar envy.

Keeping his promise to look out for her if she turned up, he offered her a drink. Summer chose a sparkling water for now. Perhaps something stronger later when she'd showered. She apologised for any camp odours she'd brought in with her.

Alone, in the company of a beautiful woman, Bennett attempted small talk, sending an awkward, one-way stream of commentary to her about the successful cracking of the laptop security code and the discovery of the data file and that Stack was up at Rebellion Hill right now showing the numbers to the rig guys.

She listened for a few polite minutes before thanking him for the drink, turning to the bar to asked the landlord for the key to room seven and heading wearily upstairs.

***

Somewhere, out in the Valley, a cell phone rang and an urgent instruction was given, 'Get John Stonebridge's laptop.' The Siberian was glad to have something to do again. The message included a location: A pub, not far away.

It seemed a while since he'd been called upon to take care of the problem up at the drilling site. The operations guy, Saunders, had snuck him in and out hidden in his car. That was probably only a week ago. It seemed longer. He'd been stuck in a shabby hotel in the Derbyshire wilderness since then, bored out of his mind. It was pretty enough, but the gentle pastoral countryside and benign weather softened a man. Gave him too much time to think. You could only stare at a TV screen for so long.

For a man with his skills, who worked for an uncompromising boss who expected results without excuses, doing nothing was dangerous. His talents needed continuously honing: Something to grind against, to keep the blade of his violence sharp.

***

Summer pushed the laptop to one side of the bed and spread out blissfully on top of the cool linen bed sheets, her head resting in the depths of the down-filled pillow. She had no intention of moving even if the hotel caught fire. She lay on the bed, eyes closed and in a state of blissful exhaustion. It wasn't long before she dozed off.

***

Stack was on the drilling floor when he received the '*Call this number*' message from Blackstone. Now wasn't a good time.

He walked into the dog shack to find Harding in deep conversation with the geologist, Steve Gardener. They were interrupted by the engineer telling them they were ready.

As before, the explosive charges of the perforating gun had created the initial cracks and now they were ready to start the hydraulic fracturing of section two.

They knew to expect tough, ungiving shale rock after

their experience with the first frack. They went right in at 10,000 pounds per square inch. It took all ten caterpillars to ramp the pressure up quickly. They hoped the initial shock would force the shale apart. It didn't. The pressurised fluid hit the rock layer like a steam-hammer. The tiny cracks barely moved. The engineer gave the technicians out on the pad the word to continue opening the valves slowly to take it up through 11,000 and 12,000 psi. Fluid was already being delivered 24,000 feet away at the rate of 90 barrels a minute. And still the shale wouldn't give.

Worried faces told a story of pressure levels reaching the outer envelope of their professional experience. When the shale cracks, as it eventually would, the kind of force they were deploying could create the unwanted tremors above ground they were so desperately trying to avoid. But, like all prospectors, the lure of hidden treasure became an irresistible urge, driving them to take terrible chances.

The needle hovered over the red as the pressure rose over 13,000 psi and 100 barrels a minute. The engineer exchanged worried glances with the rest of the fracking crew. He was about to call it a 'no-frack' and maybe try a second perforation, perhaps with bigger charges. But first, maybe just a little more would do it. This would be one for the record books.

He radioed the engineers operating the pumps back at the trailers. Reluctantly, they pushed the valves towards their limits. One or two joints in the network of pipes started hissing thin jets of high pressure slickwater that could cut like a knife.

It was beyond dangerous now.

The indictor needle bounced against the end stop in the red zone. At over 14,000 pounds per square inch, the reading was off the scale. Over on the pad the rate of flow was draining the water bowsers dry. The engineer let it run for a few seconds with his hand hovering over the Emergency Shutdown button – the ESD. Ten, 15, 20 seconds. His hand shook and not just from the vibrations coming up from the rig floor. He kept touching the button but not quite pressing it. Twenty-five seconds...

What started as a small pulse produced by the power of the ultra-high pressure fluid was forming into a dangerous, low frequency sine-wave that oscillated back and forth across the crack in the earth. The two faces of sheared rock had been under pressure for centuries, but now a simple harmonic resonance could cause them to suddenly slip in a stress releasing jog.

It was at the exact moment an involuntary muscle movement caused his finger to press just a little harder on the ESD button that the needle of the pressure dial ducked back momentarily. Dropping to 7,000 psi. Then it returned slowly to 10,000. As before, a noticeable lowering of the deafening cacophony announced the sudden fracturing of the shale. Stack had no idea whether what had just happened was typical or unusual. It was way beyond his experience. He wandered over to Harding who was once again talking to Steve Gardener, the geologist.

Stack tried to be cool. 'That was quite something!'

'It was more than bloody something.' Harding said fiercely, 'If that was felt at surface level and someone complains, we're screwed.'

This was not news Stack wanted to hear.

'There's no evidence from the monitors of any shocks, but Steve's going out to double check the seismometers and see what, if anything came to the surface in the area directly above the frack. The first frack didn't cause a flicker so perhaps we'll be OK.'

Despite his bravado there was something else in his voice: An unanswered question.

'I heard what you said before and I agree, there's more to those fragments of data history than Kramar suggested. I'm going to call Debbie Blain and get her opinion.'

'I think you could do better than that.' Stack reached into his pocket and brought out the USB memory stick, 'It's all here. Email it to her. Let her see for herself.'

Harding took the stick with a nod of thanks.

'There's more, Stack.'

Stack waited.

'Steve Gardiner tells me not only did the seismometers not record any noticeable shock waves from the first frack, the sensors didn't pick up anything at all.'

Stack waited.

'These are incredibly sensitive instruments. When they don't pick up any seismic activity it's because there was none.'

'That's good isn't it? The well is what, four - five miles down? That's a long way from the surface.' Stack said tentatively.

Harding shook his head. 'In geological terms five miles is nothing. It's as though we didn't frack. But we did. Heavily.'

***

Shivering Mountain sat under a blanket of heavy rain clouds coming in from the west causing most walkers to abandon their trek and escape back to their cars. One lone walker, still 700 feet up was surprised to find herself sitting on her backside as the ground beneath her boots turned to liquid, pulling her feet from under her in a river of shale. She put it down to the heavy rain shower.

The Siberian

It was one of those summer afternoons when the heat hung oppressively over the countryside. The air had been still and sticky with humidity all day. Now though, convection was drawing up great cumulonimbus clouds from the west that billowed several miles into the stratosphere. The jet stream savagely ripped away the highest reaches into anvil heads. Thunder, lighting and heavy rain had been predicted. It looked like the show was about to start.

Charlie arrived at The Devil's Pike as the first large drop, pregnant with water, splashed heavily on the flagstones. He looked over to Mam Tor in the distance and noticed it was already hidden behind the dark cataract of a stormy squall. He ducked inside.

The room had started to fill with other customers taking shelter from the coming storm. He spotted Bennett sitting at a table over by the window. A near empty beer glass in one hand, the newspaper in the other. He looked up and raised a hand to Charlie in acknowledgment. On his way to the bar, Charlie silently asked with a motion of his hand whether Bennett wanted another pint. He wondered why he bothered to ask. This guy was always thirsty. What was it about journalists and beer - or whisky for that matter?

Charlie waited in line while the man ahead of him ordered liquor of some kind. He had an accent that reminded Charlie of the kind of clichéd casting in gangster films where all the bad guys came from Russia or some dodgy ex-communist country like Albania or Romania. Perhaps he worked up at the rig, not that he'd seen him around. Maybe the protest camp? Na, not likely, he thought.

He seemed to take an interest in accommodation. Asking

if there were any spare rooms. The barman, a youth barely out of his teens, said they were full. The foreign guy pointed to the room keys hanging on hooks in a wooden box screwed to the wall next to the optics. The barman told him those rooms were taken. But guests left their keys behind the bar while they were out.

'So only two people in rooms right now, yes?' foreign guy said, pointing to the two empty hooks.

The young barman turned to look.

'I suppose so. Unless they're down here in the bar.'

The foreign guy nodded his thanks and took his shot glass of clear liquor to a table by the door.

Charlie ordered his drinks and took them over to join Bennett.

'Have you seen Summer?' Charlie's first urgent question as he sat down.

His chair gave him line of sight of the foreigner. He couldn't put his finger on it. The man seemed oddly out of place. Strangely, he wouldn't have appeared out of place if he was on a station platform waiting for a train. Charlie looked around at other single customers. They may have been on their own but they were here because they wanted to be. They looked settled. That was it. The pub was irrelevant to him. He was waiting. Observing.

Charlie tried to ignore him and tune into what Bennett was saying.

'...she arrived about 40 minutes ago. Said she was going to have a shower and come back down.'

'Just so long as she's okay.'

Charlie made some small talk about how the fracking had just started up on the hill. He didn't mention Stack's hesitation about telling Harding.

Bennett lifted the dimpled glass and took a swallow.

'I've got to get back to the office, the editor will be expecting a story from me and right now, because your friend James Stack has told me to keep my mouth shut, all I've got is a missing person. Well, they're not going to lead with that on the *News at Ten* are they?' He could see Charlie wasn't paying attention.

Charlie was looking over to the door and noticed the empty chair.

'No mate, that won't float their boat,' he said absently.

Bennett touched his newspaper.

'Talking of which, this business about the Russian arriving in his fancy boat. Maybe that deserves a follow up.'

As he said it, Charlie pushed his chair back, stood up and scanned the room.

'What's up?' Bennett asked.

'That bloke sitting over there by the door. Did you see him leave?'

Bennett's view was of the bar.

'I think he headed over there. Maybe going to the gents? Why?'

Something was wrong. He couldn't say for sure what it was. Just something. An instinct. There was a soldier like quality to the foreigner's manner. Something that screamed 'trained'.

'Do you know what room Summer is in?'

'I think I heard her ask for the key to room seven.' Bennett was starting to become alarmed.

At first Charlie just walked over towards the bar. He asked the barman if he'd seen the foreigner go to the WC. Negative to that.

Then the worry turned into concern as he headed towards the gent's washroom. He pushed the door open, expecting, no, hoping to find the foreigner peeing into a urinal.

Nothing. He pushed the cubicle door. It swung freely. Panic. Summer! His heart-rate instantly doubled.

He turned and rushed back out, looking for the '*Guest's Only*' entrance - he'd not been upstairs before. The door to the stairway was in a small alcove behind the bar. He tried to control the sudden adrenaline hit. To stop himself rushing up the stairs. If the guy was up there, best to have a plan. Bollocks to a plan! He took the stairs two at a time.

Summer had fallen into a deep untroubled slumber. Even the occasional rumble of the approaching thunder storm was unable to rouse her. It was the tiny squeaking sound of the brass door handle being gently turned that drew her out of her siesta. A tentative rising into consciousness at first. She had turned in her sleep so that she faced the window. The door was at her back. Then she smiled. James had returned. The thought warmed her. The door opened and closed quietly. Too quietly. She began to turn over. Still groggy.

'James?' She whispered.

It was quite a big room for a pub, 12 feet by 10, but it took just three strides for the Siberian to reach the bed and place his hands around Summer's throat. Her airway was quickly restricted. The Siberian had made no attempt to conceal himself. There would be no witnesses.

At first Summer put up a violent fight, thrashing her legs and scratching her assailants face. Hitting and kicking. But the man's grip grew stronger. A horrifying comprehension took hold as she realised her life was about to end. The man's face was just inches from hers, the smell of coal tar soap filling her nostrils. He pushed his whole weight into the effort of squeezing the life out of her.

A big lightning flash brightened the room. Her assailant's cruel, dead eyes and pale, expressionless face was illuminated for a second. It was a look that sent waves of panic-born adrenalin to fuel her final battle for life.

Then a crash as the door was flung back against the wall. The sound of two heavy strides crossing the room and a powerful thud as the attacker was kicked away from Summer. The force pushed him off the bed, dragging her with him. He tried to maintain a one-handed grip on her throat as he pushed himself back up from the floor. A deafening thunder clap rattled the window drowning an angry shout from the rescuer. It sounded like the war-cry of an ancient warrior rushing into deadly hand to hand battle. Shouting profanities and raining blows against the Siberian, Charlie was a man possessed.

Freed from the man's grip at last, Summer dragged herself off the bed and down onto the floor. Pushing with her legs until her back was hard against the bathroom door. As far away from her assailant as she could get. Her hand went up to hold her bruised throat.

Charlie cursed. Punching and kneeing. He'd caused some damage to the Siberian, but being a wiry guy, he didn't have much bulk. The Siberian pushed Charlie back and threw a hard, disorienting punch to his head, followed quickly by a powerful left to his body that sent him flying back over to the door.

Charlie tried to recover, holding onto a table. Knocking the light over as he shakily pulled himself up. The Siberian slid over the bed, grabbed the laptop and rushed towards Charlie, head down. Charlie side-stepped just in time and let the man rush past, tripping him as he went by. Sending him tumbling through the open door and out in the hallway. The Siberian landed in a half crouch against the wall. The laptop fell to the floor. He scooped it up and, still off balance, headed down the short hallway, through the fire door and down the stairs into the pub. Charlie got as far as the fire door but couldn't make it any further.

Several brilliant lightning flashes that seemed to come from all directions at once, lit the hallway.

Something didn't seem right. His chest hurt. He'd been holding himself where he was punched. He took his hand away and found a patch of blood on his shirt just below his rib cage. Knife wound? Then he noticed the blood on his hand. He put the hand back to staunch the flow and headed back into the room to check on Summer.

The noise of the fight had been heard downstairs. Bennett was among the first to arrive. He was shocked when he saw Charlie and his blood-stained shirt. Summer was nursing him despite the injury to her neck.

'We need to get him to hospital, quickly!'

Bennett wasted no time

'There's a hospital nearby. My car's outside.'

They set off as another growling roll of thunder rumbled threateningly across the dark sky.

Blackstone

It took three rings before he heard the familiar pompous voice of a man he had yet to meet, and the reason why he was stuck on a grimy drilling rig in Derbyshire, instead of a pristine beach in the Caribbean. His mood matched the weather.

Blackstone didn't waste time on pleasantries.

'I have intriguing news. Our friend, Sir Sebastian Winstanley is probably in the pocket of Mikhail Ulyanin. There's some kind of deal, I'm sure of it.'

Blackstone waited for a response.

Stack knew he was required to unpick the riddle. Weigh what little he did know against this new information.

'So. Let's see. Winstanley is the Permanent Private Secretary who runs the Department of Business, Energy and Industrial Strategy. I imagine his boss, the Minister would probably dispute that. Anyway, Winstanley is the go-to guy for fracking licences because he heads the committee that hands out contracts for that sort of thing. Is that right?'

'In a way, except you'll probably find that he tells the committee what to think.' Blackstone said. 'Go on, Mr Stack.'

'Ulyanin, has large reserves of gas that he'd like to find customers for.' There was a pause as a cog dropped into place.

'The UK want to become self-sufficient in gas. Ulyanin would prefer that we didn't?'

'Exactly.' Blackstone said. 'The Russian would like to stop GeoPower. If he achieves that, it's highly probable Winstanley will offer him the contract to supply gas. You can be certain a great deal of money will exchange hands.'

'But Winstanley told Finnegan to call off the protest. To keep GeoPower drilling. How does that square?'

'Yes, that is curious isn't it? What is it about keeping the rig drilling that could put GeoPower's drilling plans in jeopardy? Now, that is a riddle. Do those false readings provide a clue to the answer?' Blackstone asked.

'I've already raised that issue with the drilling supervisor and he's not convinced. He's waiting to hear from one the senior directional drillers, Debbie Blain.' Stack was becoming frustrated, 'I'm going around in circles here. There's something I'm staring at, but I don't have enough technical knowledge to see it.'

'Has fracking begun yet?'

'Earlier today. They've just fracked the second section. You wouldn't believe the amount of pressure they're pumping down the hole. It's practically off the scale. The strange thing is, with all that energy blasting into the shale, nothing is registering on the seismometers. That seems to bother them.'

Blackstone was thoughtful.

'You'd think they'd be pleased there were no noticeable tremors…'

There was silence for a long moment.

'Blackstone? You still there?'

'Tremors, Mr Stack. If there were tremors the contract would be cancelled.'

'But, there were no tremors. In fact there was no noticeable evidence that they had fracked.'

'It's about tremors, I'm certain. Get those false readings analysed. Don't wait.'

'Click'

The Third Frack

It was one of the fracking engineers who brought the bad news. Everybody had ducked out of the deluge, taking refuge where they could. Harding was in the dog shack when the guy busted in, his rain slicks dripping.

As good as Finnegan's word, under the cover of the storm, a couple of his boy soldiers had cut their way through the fence, made their way to the mud ponds, taken the big water hose and stuffed it into one of the tanks containing the slickwater additives. It had been flooding the tank for a good while, which meant the slickwater recipe cooked up for this particular shale layer was now unusable. Fracking couldn't continue until the tank had been emptied and replaced with fresh slickwater mix.

Harding looked out of the window at the monsoon-like rain. Thick black thunderclouds had reduced the early evening light to near darkness.

'Looks like we're taking a rain check on the next frack,' he said to the fracking crew behind him. He looked over to Stack to explain, '...until they replace the fracking mixture.'

'When's that?' Stack asked.

'Later this evening, if they pull their finger out.'

The chief fracking technician agreed. I'm on to it now. Let's call it nine o'clock.'

Harding looked at his watch and said. 'That's nearly four hours.'

He turned back to the window and the storm outside. The wind could be heard howling through the steel latticework of the derrick above them.

Stack went over to join him.

'Have you heard from Debbie Blain yet?'

Stack had an urgent need for answers after the call to Blackstone.

'Nothing. She's on leave until the next drilling contract. Could be anywhere. Have patience.'

Stack's cell rang. He green-buttoned it. Harding could tell by the expression on his face that Stack was at the wrong end of bad news.

'I'm on my way.' He thumbed the red button as he pocketed the phone and ran to the door.

'Summer and Charlie. They're both in hospital. Some kind of assault.' Stack shouted back to Harding.

'Go! Don't wait to explain it to me, man.'

Stack was already gone.

***

The journey over to Buxton Hospital 13 miles away filled Stack with a sense of dread. His wild imagination conjured terrible injuries. Bennett had told him Summer had been badly assaulted. He hadn't waited to hear more. He threw himself into the Ford rental parked on the pad outside the prefab offices and took off at high speed through the main gates, down the gully road. Speeding recklessly along the winding roads of the valley floor, cutting corners and skidding into hidden junctions. The wipers beat furiously against the heavy rain hosing onto the windscreen. The car's headlights tried vainly to punch a path through the storm as the summer evening turned as dark as his fears.

Bennett had driven Summer and Charlie to the hospital. After the phone call to Stack he'd taken off again back to the office in nearby Macclesfield to file his report. He had a story at last. One that didn't conflict with his promise to Stack - or so he believed.

They were already waiting in the reception area of A&E where a nurse was fussing over Charlie's bandages. He was buttoning up his blood-stained shirt telling her he'd had worse. Both she and the doctor had commented on the faint jagged tracks of scarring on his torso. The embossed white tattoo left by an IED that had blown him off his feet in another life, several years ago.

No, he'd take care to not to pull the stiches out. And yes – he promised no strenuous movements. And yes, again, he would definitely take the anti-infection tablets.

He livened up when Stack walked through the door.

'Hey Jimbo!' Charlie said with a hand wave, unable to move from the nurse's ministrations.

Summer rushed over and wrapped her arms around him in a desperate embrace. Stack leaned back to see her wounds. He was expecting...well he didn't know what he was expecting, but his imagination filled in the blanks with terrible injuries. He lifted her chin to examine her neck, moving her head slightly one way then the other.

'Blue: Matches your eyes.' Then he kissed her.

'Thank God you're okay. The way Bennett told it, it sounded as though you'd been beaten half to death.'

'No, that was Charlie. He's a 22-carat hero. He saved my life, James. The guy was trying to kill me.'

Stack could tell she was putting a brave face to it, playing the attack down. But clearly, she was still in shock. Who wouldn't be?

'He got away with the laptop.' Summer said.

'Don't worry, I have a copy of the data.'

He looked over at Charlie and gave an enquiring upward nod.

'I'm cool, Boss.' Charlie said, 'Got in the way of a blade. Small scratch.'

It looked much worse. The blood stains on his shirt were witness to a deep flesh wound.

'He was eastern European. Maybe Georgian or Russian.' Charlie was walking over to Stack, dragging the nurse with him as she took his pulse one more time, 'Definitely trained. Army or some kind of special forces. He was trying to kill Summer, no doubt about it. Just for the laptop. It doesn't make sense.'

Stack saw the sense of it if you were a greedy man undertaking a world-class sabotage. For that, Stack realised, was what was going on. The pieces were beginning to fit together. The 'why' of it was becoming clearer. Stop GeoPower. But what was the angle? The Russian, Mikhail Ulyanin and Sir Sebastian Winstanley were involved in some way.

Blackstone thought earth tremors would put an end to any future fracking in the UK. But how could Ulyanin ensure there would be tremors. What was it he knew that no one else did? Did he know that the Shale was tough to crack and needed powerful fracking? Enough to be felt on the surface? But that information was available to GeoPower's geologists. And anyway, nothing had been felt on the surface.

'Those three lines of false data are the key.' Stack said as they drove back to The Devil's Pike. 'They don't want us to see that data. They'll do anything...' Stack looked over at Summer sitting next to him as he said it, '...*anything*, to prevent anyone from seeing it.'

'So, what's next, James?' Summer asked.

'I'm dropping you off at the pub.'

'You're not leaving me out of it after all I've been through.'

'You're still in shock, Summer. I've seen it before. You think you're fine and then later, it'll hit you. I want you to have a least one night's sleep to get over it. It won't be enough. See how you feel tomorrow morning.' Stack was just as determined.

Blue flashing lights of a police car outside the pub reminded them that the local law enforcement officers still had an interest in what happened earlier.

'Shit! We don't have time for this. I need to get Simon Harding's attention. Now.'

Summer saw the look on Stack's face.

'Okay. Don't worry, let me talk to them. You and Charlie get over to the rig.'

She climbed out into the rain. Then leaned in to give Stack a kiss before closing the door.

'Make sure you lock the door to the room, okay?' Stack shouted as she ran over to the pub entrance.

They drove off, wheels spinning on the gravel. During the drive up to Rebellion Hill, Stack dialled a number on his cell phone.

'Who're you calling?'

He glanced at Charlie's reflection in the rear-view mirror.

'Mani-hack.'

***

Only one car had passed as the Siberian waited along the gully road. Earlier, he'd fled the pub, jumped into his car and headed back to his digs. He had another appointment that evening and he needed to be tooled up, ready and on time.

The navy-blue and white-striped nylon sports bag lay on the wet ground beside him. He wasn't getting much cover from the heavy rain cascading through the branches of whatever kind of tree he was standing under. Nature wasn't his thing. He'd had to park his car in a field further down towards the village of Brough and walk the rest of the way up through the deluge to get to the meeting point.

Eventually, another set of headlights came into view from the other direction, their brightness dispersed into a halo of shimmering light by the incessant rain. Then a flash of lightning that seemed directly overhead, but was probably a few miles away illuminated Andy Saunders' car. The operations manager pulled up beside the Siberian as he stepped into the road. The trunk popped open an inch or two. The Siberian lifted it higher and threw the bag in. He stepped around to the rear door, climbed in and squeezed down as far as he could into the well of the floor. The sudden crack of thunder hit as Saunders took his yellow rain slicks from the passenger seat and placed them loosely over the back seat to provide cover. No words passed between them as he threw the car into gear and did a clumsy three point on the narrow black top. Another crunch of gears and the car took off - heading back up to the drilling site with the Siberian for the second time.

***

The rain had eased a little by the time Stack and Charlie made it back to the dog shack. Harding wasn't there but the fracking crew were and they looked busy. Out on the drilling deck technicians were just finishing putting the perforating charges in place. Stack guessed the fuses were about to be fired anytime now.

Charlie went over to see if he could learn anything about the state of play with the slickwater mixture. He passed Harding on the way and told him Stack was on the rig and needed to talk to him. Harding made a cursory enquiry into

Charlie's health and grumbled that he was in charge here so how come when Stack snaps his fingers, he is the one who's expected to do the running?

The drilling supervisor was in a foul mood. The protestor's stupid games had pissed him off. Andy Saunders had pissed him off. Stack had warned the operations manager this might happen just hours ago.

These thoughts coincided with the arrival of Saunders as he parked his car outside his Portakabin office. Harding didn't see why now wouldn't be the perfect time to get something off his chest. He strode over to the driver's side window. He stood there in the drizzle, arms folded. Waiting for Saunders to open the door and get out. He noticed Saunders seemed agitated for some reason. Eager to move away from the car towards his office.

'A little rain bother you, Saunders?' Harding's jeering Scottish brogue cut deep.

'What's your problem, Harding?'

Saunders attempted to be confrontational but it came across as anxious.

'Stack warned you about the possible attempt to sabotage the frack. What did you do about it? Nothing. We're behind schedule and you are directly responsible you useless, superannuated idiot. This is the last time. God knows how you got the job in the first place. I don't think your pals in London can save you this time.'

Ordinarily, Saunders would have come back with a sneering reply. A threat supported by a boast about his close friends at GeoPower. Not this time. He merely grunted something, turned and entered his office. He seemed in a hurry to get away.

Not what Harding was expecting. Nor was it as satisfying, but he felt better for having vented his anger.

He turned and headed over to the dog shack.

Hidden in Saunders' car, the Siberian stayed low and waited.

***

'Debbie?' A one-word question to Harding as he walked through the dog shack door.

'Nothing yet, Stack.'

'Have you called her again?'

'She's not picking up. Or maybe there's no signal. Anyway, I've sent her a text.'

Harding walked over to the technician waiting to fire the perforating charges.

'Where are we up to?'

'We're about to blow the third section. Just waiting for the drilling deck to be cleared.'

After his conversation with Blackstone, Stack had a heightened sense of urgency. The answers were all around him. Everyone had a bit of it, but he couldn't find a way to draw it all together.

'Listen, Harding, I can't explain why, but I just don't think we should frack again until we know for sure what's going on. At least wait until you've heard from Debbie.'

'Look, we're going ahead because on the balance of probability, there's nothing to worry about.'

Stack pulled the folded printout from his pocket again but Harding held his hand up before he could say anything

'For Christ's sake, Stack. let me show you something.'

Harding went over to the directional drillers computer. Pete Kramar was sitting in the chair. He pushed it back to make room. Harding waggled the mouse. The screen came up and he hunted for the drop-down list of options. He found the history tab and clicked. A second window, filled with rows of numbers, overlaid the main screen.

'See this data here? While I don't understand everything, these numbers are exactly what we expected to see, isn't that right, Kramar?'

Kramar nodded. 'Just like I told you before.'

Harding pulled up page after page going back over weeks of drilling, 'There is nothing about these numbers that are remotely wrong. They all agree with each other. Look.' His fingers ran along the lines to a random group of numbers and then followed them as they changed incrementally in the rows above, 'This is what we would expect. It's all perfectly normal. The drilling plan may be slightly out, but that's all.'

Then Harding grabbed the grubby dog-eared sheet from Stack and waved it.

'I can't abandon the frack because of the figures on this scrap of paper.'

Kramar tried to hide his surprise. This was the paper he'd screwed up and thrown away.

Behind him the engineer called out that they were ready to blast the charges. Frustrated, Stack stood back and watched. Everything went as it had before. A button was pressed and nothing happened – on the surface.

***

The crack five miles below Mam Tor had been skewered by the well bore. Both rock faces seemingly pinned together by the concrete and steel tube. Five hundred feet in either direction a series of cylinders lay in place, armed with hundreds of small charges.

The silence of the rocky underworld was torn apart when

at the far end, the first charges exploded in a sequence that rushed towards the massive tear in the rock. In seconds, it came up and passed through the fault line with an ear-splitting concussion. It sped on until all the perforation charges had been detonated along the entire length of the section. The fault took the assault with just the faintest shiver. But its grip had been weakened.

***

Stack's cell phone buzzed and vibrated in his pocket. He pulled it out. It was a text from Mani-hack and right on time.

The next bit was going to be tricky.

He waited until Harding had finished talking to the senior fracking technician before approaching him.

'Have you got a minute?'

'What now, Stack?'

'Walk with me...please?'

Stack wanted to get Harding's full attention. He needed him away from all the activity on the deck as they prepped the well for the next frack.

Harding sighed, but followed Stack down the stairs to the metal walkway between the services containers. The drizzle had stopped but bigger spots were occasionally falling. Harbingers of another thundery squall.

'OK Stack. Let me have it.'

Harding was stubborn and by the numbers. But he wasn't stupid.

'Now, hear me out, Harding. Some of this is going to get... interesting to put it mildly. I have very good contacts in all kinds of useful places. One in particular has been extremely helpful to me in solving a very unique business problem that frankly, couldn't have been fixed without him. He has the ears of the great and the good. No door is closed to him.'

'I'm impressed,' Harding said ironically, 'And the point is?'

'I wouldn't be here without him. I didn't just turn up out of the blue. I was placed here. So was Dawson.'

Harding stop walking, turned to face Stack, and waited.

'I'm here to protect some investments. To ensure the drilling is successful. To watch out for anything that might interrupt that success.'

'Who's paying you for this service?'

'I am. Part of the investment comes from me.'

Harding raised an eyebrow but again said nothing as he started walking.

'I'm here because I can help. But I need you to listen to me.'

Without naming him, Stack told Harding about his recent conversation with Blackstone and their conclusion that the owner of a large Russian oil company currently visiting the UK, has a good reason to want the fracking to continue. He explained how they believed that by some means or other, the Russian wanted to deliberately create a tremor that would end the fracking license. Not just for this well, but a permanent termination of all hydraulic fracturing. The UK would start to run out of gas and the Russian's oil and gas company would step in to fill gap.

'It's this detail - the how he intends to do it, that I'm struggling to figure out. I'm absolutely sure those three lines of data have something to do with it. They wouldn't have stolen the laptop from my hotel room if it wasn't important.'

'Come on Stack. That may have been just an opportunist robbery. It happens all the time. And anyway, are you saying, this Russian of yours hacked into our systems somehow? You've been reading too many spy stories.'

Stack saw his chance.

'Well, it's funny you should bring that up. I have someone waiting down at the main gate who is an expert in just that kind of thing. I want your permission to bring him onto the rig to check out the computers.'

'We have IT for that kind of thing.' Harding responded, testily.

'No, you have IT to install cables, reboot software and replace circuit boards. They don't have the skills this guy has.'

Harding thought it through for a moment.

'OK. No damage. And definitely no sniffing around GeoPower security. Everything outside the specific task is out of bounds. OK?'

He lifted his radio and clicked the transmit button.

'Andy Saunders, over?' *Hash-click.*

A pause...then.

'Saunders, over.' *Hash-click.*

'I'm bringing someone onto the site. He'll need a security pass. Can you tell the gate?' *Hash-click.*

'Why is he here?' *Hash-click.*

'Because I want him here.' *Hash-click.*

'Come on, Harding, I need some kind of contractor name or purpose. Is he rig-safety approved?' *Hash-click.*

'I'll take responsibility. He's here to check the directional drilling computer systems.' *Hash-click.*

A long time passed before Saunders replied.

'Saunders? You still there?' *Hash-click.*

Eventually a feeble voice came back. Sounded as though his throat had suddenly gone dry.

'Okay. Copy that. Out.' *Hash-click.*

Stack and Harding both looked at each other and shrugged. Harding was about to turn back to the rig, but paused to ask Stack a final question.

'Who is this Russian oil guy?'

'Mikhail Ulyanin. Heard of him?'

'Yes, I've heard of him.' Harding replied grimly as he turned and walked away. Stack watched him go. Pulling his collar up against the wind driven splashes of rain, he headed down to the gate.

***

The door to the small flat in the suburbs of Manchester opened and Debbie Blain stepped across the threshold and reached for the light dimmer.

It was a modern two-bedroom apartment furnished with an almost Japanese sense of clutter-free living. The rotary switch turned on six discrete ceiling lights to whatever level of illumination suited the moment. Right now, low key was what Debbie needed. She'd been on a date with one of the rig guys. Always a mistake. At first, he seemed charming and interested in her. But as clean as he had scrubbed up, there was still the indelible hint of crude oil below the skin. The macho characteristic she hoped had gone out of fashion with John Wayne.

The restaurant had been painfully right-on. All the hippest of hipsters wanted to be seen there. Couldn't last though. Current trendy idea – put in Faraday screens to prevent mobile signals getting in or out. Debbie liked it, but pretty much everyone else ended up standing outside with the smokers, catching up on the last pointless Snapchat or Twitter message. Or worse, to broadcast another stop-the-presses Instagram announcement about their own fascinating lives along with a picture of their meal of course. No, they'll be ripping the screens out before long.

She'd had a bit too much to drink. Didn't improve the company though. Worse still, she very nearly allowed him back to her place – *for coffee*! It was a close thing. Maybe that's why the evening had ended early. He'd lost interest.

Her mobile had texted into life as she left the restaurant. She couldn't be bothered to read the message. It could wait until she got home.

Well, here she was, at home – alone – again. She kicked off her shoes and threw herself down on the couch. Somehow the phone was still in her hand. She didn't remember how that had happened. Her thumb swiped the screen and she clicked her text messages. She had to squint, but it looked like it was from Simon Harding. What did he want?

***

The container was in a neglected part of the rig's operational area, behind the services corridor Stack and Harding had walked down only minutes before. It had taken Saunders a little while and some skilful dodging to get the Siberian safely inside with his holdall. Kramar had joined them there.

They were working off the grid. They hadn't been able to contact Ulyanin since the laptop had been recovered, so this was strictly freelancing. With Stack making so much noise about the rogue data, and more alarmingly, bringing a specialist onto the site to examine the computer systems, the sabotage was at risk of being discovered. Pete Kramar couldn't understand how they hadn't pieced it all together by now. Once you knew how the scheme worked, it all seems so obvious.

With the Siberian and the reluctant help of Saunders, he had put together a contingency plan. One way or another, the massive geological fault under Mam Tor was going to get fracked.

***

When Harding first laid eyes on Mani-hack he tried unsuccessfully to hide is shock. He signalled Stack and walked over to a corner of the dog shack for a private conversation.

'You got a minute, Stack?'

Stack knew what was coming.

'What is that?' He said pointing to the scruffy chubby black kid with his hoody up over his baseball cap. The kid was unscrewing the side panels of Harding's expensive computers. 'Is he even out of school yet?'

In for a penny, Stack thought.

'That, my friend, is Mani-hack.'

'Mani-hack?' Harding said it too loud.

Mani-hack looked up and gave him a gang sign with his index and pinkie.

'It's Maniac. You don't say the 'H'.'

Harding nodded a wary acknowledgment and turned back to Stack.

'Tell me he's older than he looks.'

'In fact he's at university, Harding. I don't know his real name, but he's a genius. Practically lives in cyber-space.'

'What's he doing now?'

'It turns out that because you've finished directional drilling, any hacker will have long gone. Ask him yourself.'

As they walked over, Harding gave Stack a startled look.

'Hacker? What hacker?'

Stack introduced Harding. Mani-hack looked up and offered his hand which surprised Harding. Before Harding had a chance to pull his own hand out of his pocket, Mani-hack was back inside the tower, probing with a tiny torch into the darker recesses.

'Can you tell me what you're looking for...' Harding struggled to say, 'Maniac?' without the H.

'It's easier to trace hackers when they're active.' The youth's voice came back muffled as he worked, 'If the system had been hacked it would need to be very sophisticated. Especially if it was played out over a few weeks. A simple hack would have been detected at some point. If I was going to do it, I would have got at the computers while they were being installed and retrofitted a card. That would have been my gateway. Any hackers would have been talking to that and nothing else. Your IT guys would have no idea it was happening.'

'If it was hacked. All we've got are three bits of data that prove nothing. Harding said'

'Mr Stack here, tells me someone saw one of those lines of data being typed on the screen in real time. That's a big hello from a remote keyboard right there. I'd say you've been hacked.'

'I ran that passed our IT guys and they thought it was just latency, you know, the computer catching up with itself.' Harding played devil's advocate, still unconvinced.

'I know what latency is. That could be the reason. Anyway, I can't find anything here.' Mani-hack pulled himself out of the tower and started screwing the side panel back on. 'Tell me how directional drilling works again, where does the data come out of the ground. Is there another box of tricks somewhere?'

Harding took him the few steps over to a tall rack

of equipment. They went behind into the service area between the rack and the dog shack wall. As smart as the front looked, the back was a mess of cables, circuit boards, fans and dust. Nearly seven feet tall, most of the space was filled with slide-in 19 inch rack units.

Harding followed a cable from a conduit that came up from the floor. The cable led to the first unit, one blank panel above ground level.

'The analogue signal comes in here and comes out as a digital signal that is sent to the directional drillers computer over there.'

'So this is the analogue to digital converter. If I was going to hack into your drilling system, this could be the best place to do it.'

Mani-hack went around to the front of the rack and checked the unit from that side. Only one tiny light was on, glowing green. It flickered occasionally. He pulled a screwdriver out of his canvas shoulder bag and started to unscrew the four chrome screws that held the unit in place.

***

Down below the drilling floor, the engineers had finished checking the pipes from the Caterpillar pumps to the Christmas Tree.

After the last frack, joints had been breached by the intense pressure. Now they knew just how much power was needed to crack the shale rock beneath them. They weren't taking any chances.

The senior technician running the fracking crew sat at his station checking the on-screen numbers. To one side was a control board covered in buttons, switches and gauges. Needles flickered with readings from equipment out on the pad, waiting to deliver the newly prepared slickwater mix.

He looked at his watch. It was long past nine pm – closer to ten. He turned to Harding.

'We're ready to go.'

The dog shack door burst open. A wet gust swept into the room on a blaze from the flood lights. Pete Kramar was momentarily silhouetted against the dazzling glow, his rain slicks dripping wet. He used his shoulder to pushed the door closed against the gale. He removed his hard-hat and placed a navy-blue sports bag on the steel floor.

'Pissing down again.' He said.

A brilliant lighting flash emphasised his point.

'OK, let's get on with it. We've wasted enough time.' Harding gave Stack an accusing glance as he said it.

The technician picked up his two-way and told the crew out on the rain-drenched pad to start the Cats. It took only a second and ten powerful diesels coughed into noisy life, jetting clouds of thick black smoke that was quickly whipped away by another whistling gust of wind. Power increased and valves opened allowing the slickwater fracking fluid to flow to the well bore: low pressure at first but building quickly. As before, deep below Mam Tor, the first few inches of pre-cracked shale shrugged off the assault.

But the ancient fissure that had ripped a jagged split for miles in either direction began at last to show signs of weakening. The first small reactions to the energy being levied against it.

In the dog shack the technician was becoming irritated with the delays and the stubborn resistance of the shale rock.

'Get that pressure up. I need 10,000 psi now. Let's get this bloody frack-job done.'

No problems had come to the surface from the last two super-high-pressure fracks: no seismic activity of any significance. In fact, nothing recorded at all! Unusual, but reassuring that the rock layers in this area were very stable and able to absorb the shock. That's how they read it, anyway.

***

The scene at the mud ponds was like a nightmare story-line from the crime series, NCIS. While the fracking process was underway, the maintenance crew were getting on with general housekeeping - tidying up and repairs. Roustabouts had been given the task of emptying the mud ponds where the mud slurry was stored once it had passed down through the borehole and back up again. There was a lot of it and it took a while to drain. They were only part way through the job when one of them spotted something a few yards out. Nothing solid goes into the ponds so it was unexpected.

One roustabout had found a long-handle rake. After wading out boot deep into the slurry, he began trying to catch whatever it was on the tines.

This was one fish he wished he hadn't caught as he started heaving it towards the edge of the pond.

Charlie had gone to get his yellow rain slicks and arrived back just as they pulled the object clear of the slurry. The mud ponds were some way away from the main area and received only a spill of light from the floodlight towers. With a rain squall beating hard against their faces it took a moment for them to recognise what it was.

***

Flickering nervously as it climbed higher on the scale of the digital gauge, the needle hovered over 11,500 psi and continued to edge towards the red zone. Another screen showed 88 barrels a minute and climbing. Vibrations shook the floor and rattled steelwork. Above them the gale screamed through the lattice-work of the derrick adding to the ground-shaking roar of the ten Cats. Only shouted commands could be heard above the cacophony in the dog shack.

'Keep going. We're nowhere near the pressure we need.' The technician shouted into the radio handset.

Others didn't share his confidence. They got lucky twice. This was the third time. The superstitious in the room had their fingers firmly crossed.

Stack felt his cell phone vibrate in his pocket. He checked it. The screen showed Charlie's number. He green buttoned it and held it hard against his ear. His other hand pressed firmly to the other ear to mute the noise. He had to shout several times before he understood what Charlie was telling him. Harding had looked over as Stack took the call. He couldn't hear what he was saying above the roar of the noise but it looked serious. Stack looked over to Harding and held the phone up for him and indicated with an upward lift of his chin he should take the call. As he handed Harding the cell phone he shouted into his ear.

'They found John Stonebridge's body.'

Shocked, Harding listened to what Charlie had to say and handed the phone back. Stack thanked Charlie, and pocketed the phone.

'Keep that pressure coming, boys. It's going to take 13,000 psi at least.'

The technician put the radio down and watched the needle climb to over 12,000. Harding stood there, arms folded, and brow furrowed as he peered over the technician's shoulder at the screen.

'Aren't you going to tell them to stop, Harding? You've got to stop the frack now!' Stack shouted.

'What's the point?' Harding shouted back, 'Stonebridge will still be dead whether we frack or not. It proves nothing.'

A strong surge of guilt swept through Harding. He knew the discovery of Stonebridge's body added to the weight of evidence. But was it conclusive?

He couldn't admit the lure of a completion bonus played heavily in his decision.

Crouched on his haunches and poring over the insides of the analogue to digital converter with his torch, Manihack took an interest in a small circuit board riding on the back of a larger board. He eased it gently out of its socket and gave it a closer inspection. Confident it was what he thought it was, he took it over to show Stack.

Over by the door, Kramar watched and waited.

***

Twenty-two thousand feet away from the dog shack, the 1,000-foot section of well bore that crossed the fault-line was receiving the full force of 14,500 pounds of naked brute force. An ultra-low frequency resonance was already sending pressure waves radiating out along the length of the fissure. When a sympathetic resonance had built up sufficiently, one face of the fault would lose traction and catastrophically slip, jerking up no more than a metre or so, but letting loose a gigantic seismic wave that would be felt far beyond Mam Tor. Towns and villages in all directions for miles around would take the brunt of its force. Manchester was directly in its path.

***

As soon as Debbie Blain looked at the three rows of data downloaded as an attachment to Harding's email, it was obvious what was wrong. The correct numbers were practically burned into her memory after weeks of drilling. Almost nothing about these three rows of numbers seemed right.

She remembered John Stonebridge mentioning something about something a few weeks back. She'd told him to ignore it. Just a glitch.

This wasn't a glitch. It was deliberate. The shock of that statement frightened her.

Right now the question of why, didn't concern her. What did bother her though was, where?

Using the original drilling plan as a reference, she drew a mathematical line through one group of numbers and converted them into a heading. If she'd been drunk when she arrived home a little while ago, she was stone cold sober now. She couldn't believe what she was seeing and she didn't need a map to prove it. She did the calculation two more times. The course didn't change by the slightest degree. Her heart rate increased, her breath shortened and her fingers trembled as she dialled Simon Harding's cell phone.

***

Another plea from the technician to push the valves hard open came through the radio coms. Noise from the diesels made it hard to understand, but they guessed he wanted more. Levers were pushed. More pressure was delivered.

The needle was jogging hard against the end stop as the

fluid pressure nudged towards 15,000 pounds per square inch.

At first, Harding didn't feel the cell phone vibrate in his jacket pocket. The second buzz got his attention. He had it to his ear on the third.

Stack watched as he took the call. It was extraordinary to see his face change from mildly irritated, to concerned, to disbelief and finally to panic.

Harding leapt forward shouting as he grabbed the technician's shoulders to get his full attention. Despite the overpowering noise in the room everyone heard the terror in his voice.

'For Christ's sake. Stop the frack! Now!'

It took a moment for the fracking technician to grasp the meaning of the drilling supervisor's command. Harding tried to reach over and hit the Emergency Shutdown button himself. The tech's hand got there first. The effect was instantaneous. Vibrations around the rig ceased and the noise from the ten mammoth diesels dropped to a low murmur.

Behind Stack, Kramar had dropped to his knees and begun unzipping the bag. Unseen by anyone else, the contingency plan was triggered when Kramar turned his back to the room and spoke one word softly into his cell phone.

'Go!'

Stack moved across the room to Harding who still carried the wide-eyed stare of someone who had just missed being hit by a train.

'Christ Stack. I hope we're not too late. I just heard from Debbie. You were right, but it's worse than you can imagine.'

Stack waited. The 'what?' was finally about to be revealed.

'All the drilling data confirmed we were drilling in the

correct direction towards the south west. But those three random lines of telemetry data show that we have in fact been drilling in a completely different direction. Towards the north west.' He pointed in the direction of Mam Tor as he said it, the full enormity of what might have happened clear in his voice, 'My God! Below that mountain is a large geological fault. We know about it because it's recorded in the geological surveys. A powerful frack could disturb it and cause at the very least, a large tremor, or worse, an earthquake that would be felt for miles.'

Stack jumped in.

'And that my friend would mean the end of fracking and the production of shale gas in the UK. To say nothing of the lives that might have been lost'

'It's unbelievable.' Harding was shaking his head slowly at the impossible trick that had been played on them, 'Day after day. Week after week. Everything was just an illusion.'

'I think I know how they did it….' Mani-hack was cut off by an angry voice from behind Stack.

'Keep fracking!'

Stack and Harding spun around and found themselves on the wrong side of two semi-automatic hand guns. Stack recognised them both. Kramar held a SIG P226 pistol at waist height and the other guy had a Glock G19 at arm's length. The Glock had 13 nasty 9mm parabellums plus one in the chamber. The SIG packed a little less: just nine of the mean little hollow-pointed suckers. At close range, the 7.45 grams of lead wrapped in copper alloy could hammer a hole in a body, exit through the far wall, and get storm-washed clean of blood before it hit the ground. Together, they could end life in the dog shack several times over. Kramar and his pal looked capable of doing just that.

Standing next to the two gunslingers was Andy Saunders

looking extremely anxious. The picture of a man who wished he was somewhere else.

'Whose side are you on, Saunders?' Stack asked.

Kramar replied for him. 'He's with us.'

This information didn't make Saunders look any more comfortable.

Kramar's pal, the Siberian, walked over to the fracking technician still seated at his equipment and planted the Glock hard against his head. The cruel look on his face was more terrifying than the weapon.

Kramar, clearly in charge, told the technician to restart the frack.

'You're not finished. Let's try it again with more pressure this time.'

The technician looked over to Harding for help.

'Listen Kramar. Have you any idea how dangerous that fault is?' Harding appealed. 'You're putting thousands of lives at risk. It's crazy. The shock wave would cause destruction across central England.'

Kramar ignored him and gave the technician a hard stare that said 'do it now'. He waved his gun to underline the threat.

The technician picked up his radio, but before he pressed the transmit button, he gave Kramar a final, pleading look. An act of hopeless futility. The Siberian pressed the gun harder against his skull, forcing the technician's head down towards the two-way radio in his hand. He clicked the button.

'Bring the diesels back up to full power.'

Unaware of drama in the dog shack or the danger underground, the fracking crew increased the revs of the power units. The fracking fluid immediately starting flowing again at high pressure.

Noise and vibration returned to the dog shack. Harding turned to watch the gauges on the control board. The needle was already hitting 13,000 pounds per square inch.

'Get them to open the valves fully. Now!' Kramar shouted above the noise.

Another push of the barrel and the technician clicked the send button again.

'Turn them up. Open the valves fully.' His voice was weak with fear.

A tiny metallic voice was just audible coming back from the Cats.

'Repeat. You want the pumps fully open? Over.'

'Just do it.'

If it was possible, the rumble of noise and vibration increased in the dog shack. Outside on the drilling deck the noise was insane. Steel juddered against steel. Loose pipes rattled a jig against each other high up in the storm swept derrick.

Already travelling through the red zone, the needle was swinging across 15,000 psi.

Stack saw the look of horror on Harding's face at the catastrophe about to be unleashed.

Deep below Mam Tor the tiny perforations in the shale finally gave way to the pressure. Jagged cracks spread like frozen lightning throughout the shale layer and filled with slickwater fluid.

The ultra-low vibration started once again, transforming slowly into a cohesive resonance that matched the long wavelength of the borehole. The two halves of the geological weak spot vibrated in unison as a single layer. But eventually, the grip of one rock face against the other would fail. It was only a matter of time.

Kramar had the room covered from his position. One gun

against four: the technician, Harding, Mani-hack and Stack.

Saunders was part of it. He wasn't carrying a weapon though. His wide-eyed terror marking him out as an untrustworthy partner brought along to keep an eye on him.

Stack tried to catch his eye. To see if he could be manipulated into helping.

'Saunders, you know this place is in the direct line of any earthquake. We'll get hit first. The whole bloody derrick will come down and kill us all!'

He saw the fear in Saunders' eyes. But he just stepped back and shook his head without saying anything.

Suddenly, the room was filled with a strobing blue-white brilliance as lightning arced across the sky, one jagged branch struck the ground nearby. The explosion of thunder was instantaneous, rattling the window and startling the already jumpy, Saunders. At the same time the flood lights outside and the strip lights in the dog shack flickered and died.

In the split second it took the super-hot plasma discharge to hit the ground Stack spotted someone coming up the steel stairs to the drilling floor. Their rain slick jacket a stark yellow brightness against the stormy black night beyond.

The door opened and Charlie burst in.

'Christ! Did you see that? I nearly got fried!'

Another double flash of lightning threw harsh, cold arc-light flickering across the dark room. That's all it took for Charlie to spot the guns and the men holding them. He got the picture immediately.

He dropped to the ground as his old Special Forces training took over. This was familiar territory. He'd spent many hours in this room. He knew the layout.

In the darkness that followed, Stack took his chance and

leapt at Kramar who managed to get off two shots. One skimmed Stack's side as it punched through his jacket and a cry went up from the direction of the fracking technician.

The Siberian still had the technician by the collar of his hi viz jacket, but the weight of the wounded man was dragging him down as he collapsed onto the floor.

Another gun shot went off by the door, the muzzle blast blinding everyone for a second. The round went high. It clanged noisily as it ricocheted across the steel roof. Then another flash from over by the fracking control desk. Harding cried out in pain as he was spun around by the force of the impact. He'd been fumbling for the ESD button when the Siberian fired at close range. Charlie was still close to the door when another lighting strike lit the room. Saunders had pulled a semi-automatic out of the canvas bag. He'd decided to take part in the shoot-out. He let off another three shot burst that went high. Or perhaps it was deliberate. One of the light fittings dangled dangerously. A gale blew in cold and wet as the door opened and he slipped out into the thunderstorm. Charlie let him go. Save it for later.

Stack had his hand around the boxy barrel of the SIG, twisting it this way and that as Kramar use his other hand to punch him in the ribs. Stack pushed back and they both fell over the directional driller's chair, punching and kneeing each other. Kramar squeezed the trigger again. The bang was loud in Stack's ear as the bullet flew across the room, zinging off the tall equipment rack in the corner.

In the darkness, Harding had managed to crawl behind the steel fracking control desk. The part with the dials and gauges was raised at a 45-degree angle making the back of the unit higher than the front. Weakened by loss of blood and shock, he struggled to pull himself up until he was standing. His left arm dangled uselessly by his side. The top of the unit came to just above his waist. He couldn't see it, but he knew the ESD button was down on the flat part of the desk more than an arm's length away. He tried to fold his body over the high back of the unit to reach further across, sweeping his arm this way and that. Hoping his fingers would find it.

With the lights out and the noise of the generators and high pressure fluid pumping down the well, the Siberian couldn't see or hear Harding, but he sensed him somehow. He let off two more shots. One came close. It gouged a groove in the sheet steel of the desk, causing Harding to duck back down again.

The only light came from tiny yellow tell-tails on dials, or red numerical readouts on equipment dotted around the room. It was by the faint glow of the pressure gauge light that Harding knew they had run out of time. The needle had reached 15,500 psi and still rising.

***

The ultra-low resonances had formed a perfect sine wave, vibrating like the string of a double bass, but at a frequency far below the range of the human ear. Lower still than the call of a whale. These were primitive oscillations on a massive scale that shook the walls of the rocky fissure for many hundreds of meters along its length. Where the borehole passed through the fissure, a jagged crack was splitting its concrete and steel sleeving in two.

***

The battle for Kramar's gun was fierce and deadly. They'd

rolled into the narrow space between the desks and equipment benches. Punches, elbows, kicks and head-butts began to take their toll. Stack went for broke and grabbed the gun with both hands, bending Kramar's wrist back abruptly. He let out a grunt of pain as his finger, trapped in the trigger guard, was dislocated. The shock seemed to make him fight more furiously. Reaching deep into the last of his reserves, Stack forced the gun away from the man's weakening grasp and rolled free just as Charlie jumped on the assailant from behind. His arm wrapped around Kramar's neck in a choking grip.

'I'll hold him. You get the other one,' he gasped as the attacker struggled. Charlie's stitches had started to rip painfully apart. But still he tightened his hold on the struggling man's throat, squeezing until the fight went out of him.

Armed with Kramar's gun, Stack crawled around the desk to the back of the room. The sound of his journey hidden under the volume of noise. Another multiple lightning strike gave him the Siberian's position. He was down on the floor, taking cover behind the injured fracking technician. He must have been aware that Kramar was out of the fight and someone else has his gun. He was pointing the Glock in the direction of Harding behind the control desk. Waiting to pick him off if he tried to go for the Emergency Shutdown button again. He hadn't seen Stack.

Once in position Stack didn't wait. He aimed a double tap into the Siberian's legs. A safe shot. They were the part of the Siberian furthest from the technician. The bullet wounds had an instant effect. Shocked by the sudden bone smashing assault, he let out a shout of pain and turned to face his attacker somewhere in the darkness behind him. He fired randomly in Stack's direction.

The round was close, too close, as Stack leapt forward, throwing himself onto the gunman, knocking him back against the wounded technician. Stack hadn't finished. He raised his gun and brought the butt down hard against the Siberian's skull, cracking him into oblivion.

On the floor, the injured technician raised his head towards Stack and spoke in a weak, breathy voice.

'Stop the frack! Quickly.' It was, barely audible above the noise.

From his kneeling position, Stack couldn't reach the Emergency Shut Down button on the control unit above. He grabbed the edge of the desk to pull himself up, but blood from the wounded technician had spilled across the panel and Stack fell back as his fingers slipped in the viscous fluid.

Fracking pressure continued to tear into the weakening fault as Stack grabbed the desk once more and reached out to grab the back of the control board with his other hand. He began pulling himself up but lost his balance again as his boots slid on the blood-drenched floor. His feet searched for something he could push against and found the Siberian's body. Hauling himself up again, he began searching for the switch with his free hand. More precious seconds were wasted as his hand groped blindly back and forth across the control board. Then his hand caught on something. The kill button. Lightning flashes strobed across the desk as he punched down hard.

For the second time in five minutes the room fell silent as the ten diesels dropped back to idle.

Everyone held their breath. Had they stopped the frack in time? They'd soon know. It would only take seconds for the seismic wave to hit them. They waited. Five seconds. Ten seconds...

Suddenly the room shook with an explosive crash sending everyone diving for cover under desks and against the walls: anything that could provide shelter. Stack threw himself over the engineer lying wounded on the floor and covered the back of his own head with his hands. He tried to curl into a ball, grimacing as he anticipated the rig crashing down through the roof of the dog shack upon of him.

They waited, but the derrick didn't crash down. The world didn't end.

It took a heart-stopping moment before their fear turned to relief and then nervous laughter as the summer storm flashed another jagged blue-white lightning strike across the storm ripped sky, sending blinding light flickering through the windows again. Seconds later, the dog shack shook violently with another double-crack of thunder.

The End Game

The morning was running late at The Devil's Pike. It had taken the three of them a long time to get through their full English breakfasts. Long pauses interrupted the meal as Stack and Charlie told Summer what had happened. Before they'd finished, Bennett had joined them. He wanted the full press award-winning story.

***

The drama up at Rebellion Hill during the night got Bennett's full attention when the call went out to police and ambulance services. By the time he'd talked his way onto the rig site, the pad was swarming with vehicles. Still without power, flashing blue and red lights of the emergency services and hand torches were all that lit the rig area. Some vehicles arriving, others rushing off. Sirens blaring despite the empty roads and time of night.

An armed SWAT unit had arrived in the early stages of the aftermath. It didn't take them long to find Saunders. He'd gone back to the container where the three had gathered before the attack.

Stack had watched as they pushed him, handcuffed, into a squad car. He looked pathetic. By contrast, Ulyanin's two men still had fight in them, despite the Siberian's leg wounds.

It was well past midnight before the engineers got the power back on and the flood-light towers threw their harsh glare down onto the scene once more. Bennett tried vainly to catch Stack and Charlie's attention. The police had them telling and re-telling what they thought was a highly dubious story. It was late in the night when they eventually let them go.

***

'So, Mani-hack found something, you were saying?' Bennett was probing for detail.

Stack had given an undertaking to answer Bennett's questions when it was over. A promised he'd keep – up to a point.

'The circuit board the hackers used for the sabotage, it gave them a private back door and some clever software to control the drill bit.' He reached into his pocket and brought the tiny board out as he said it.

Summer's eyebrow's rose in mock surprise when she saw it.

'You didn't think the police might want it?'

'They might do, Summer, if they knew about it. I might have a better use for it.'

Summer squinted a sceptical look at him.

'Just a little scheme I'm working on.'

They paused to drink more coffee in silence as they imagined the terrible consequences if the sabotage had succeeded in causing an earthquake.

Eventually, Summer asked the obvious question that no one had thought to mention yet.

'Aren't they going to have to start over, you know, drilling? They can't use that well again can they?'

Charlie followed through.

'That's right, Jimbo. We haven't actually made any progress have we?'

'I spoke to Harding about that while we waited for the police to arrive.'

My God James, you're merciless. The poor man had been shot.'

'Turns out they have a well-equipped first aid centre on the site. Nurses, bandages, morphine. That sort of thing.'

Charlie was less sympathetic.

'Yeah? And?'

'They're going to have to seal off the well but only from the point where the borehole starts heading north west, towards Mam Tor. Tomorrow they'll start drilling to the original plan and this time, as long as there's no sabotage or other hold-ups, they should have the well completed in two weeks or so.'

Charlie seemed disappointed.

'Does that mean I have to stick around roustabouting for another three weeks?'

Summer followed through.

'Yes, James. I don't want to spend any more time up at the protest camp. I won't be welcome anyhow.'

'Security is being increased both inside and out. I don't think we can add anything to that. They're going to be as nervous as hell after this cock-up. Nothing's going to get in the way this time.'

Bennett, keen to paint a full picture for his readers put his cup down and turned to Stack.

'Next question. What about this Russian guy? What's his name? Ulysses?'

'Ulyanin. Mikhail Ulyanin.'

'Are we going to let him get away with it?'

Stack noted the 'we' in his question.

'Not if I can help it.'

***

Gazpacho jelly and marjoram, followed by seared turbot, pea puree, spring vegetables, gem lettuce, potato crisp and hollandaise sauce - Sir Sebastian Winstanley hadn't tasted better in some of London's finest restaurants.

As the fight raged on up at Rebellion Hill, Mikhail Ulyanin's guest was just finishing dessert on board the Eba.

'The food was exquisite. Please pass my compliments to your chef, Mikhail.'

'We do our best. I'm glad it pleases you.'

Ulyanin had endured a long evening with the civil servant. All the while, keeping an eye on the progress of the frack. He was surprised and a little worried he hadn't heard anything by now. He had been unable to make contact with any of his operatives up in Hope Valley all evening. The last call, hours ago, came from Peter Kramar promising that whatever happened, he would ensure success.

He kept checking the news channels. An earthquake in this country, no matter how small, would certainly make the news.

'And this wine.' Winstanley lifted the empty bottle, turning it to discover its origin, 'Domaine Ramonet Montrachet Grand Cru. Rare and expensive. You have excelled yourself.'

'Not at all and not as rare as you might imagine.' Ulyanin could easily read the purpose of his guests devious enquiry, 'Would you like another?'

And so the evening continued until finally, only the entertainment remained. The Russian escorted Winstanley to a State Room on the deck below. He held the door open for the unsteady civil servant to enjoy the view inside. Two beautiful women waiting for him on the bed. One patted the fine Egyptian cotton sheets provocatively.

'You have two hours and then I'm afraid you must leave.'

Winstanley moaned that surely the entire night would be more appropriate. Ulyanin explained that sadly, on this occasion, it was not possible. The Eba will sail on the early morning tide.

The polite knock on the door came too soon. Winstanley had fallen asleep, but with the help of the girls, he dressed and reluctantly followed the man-servant to the complimentary limousine waiting on the quayside. As planned he was driven a discrete route back to his London apartment. Half an hour later, the girls were taken home less ceremoniously with the help of Uber.

The video file was logged and stored.

***

The Russian oligarch had heard nothing from Kramar, nor had anything been reported on the two main news channels, SKY and BBC. It was only later, while Winstanley was enjoying himself in the stateroom downstairs that a breaking news banner on the bottom of the TV screen gave the first hint of trouble. It was two a.m. when the first fuzzy pictures came through, recorded by one of the rig crew on their smart phone. Little white numbers at the bottom of the picture time-stamped it two hours earlier. Ulyanin wondered why the delay?

By four a.m. the tide had filled the river and the captain gave the order to prepare to depart. The Eba's engines turned over noisily. Their twin aluminium and steel alloy propellers driving a wash of muddy eddies out into the flowing stream.

It was as the hydraulic gangway was getting ready to be raised that three police cars arrived in a squeal of tyres and noisy sirens.

Half a dozen armed police officers rushed up the gangway, followed by a man and a woman detective.

The departure they insisted was to be delayed while Mr Ulyanin came with them to explain what his part may or may not have been in a serious crime. They couldn't reveal any more at this time. The Russian Ambassador had been advised of this development.

An indignant Ulyanin had no choice but to go with them, but merely as a courtesy. He was confident this would be a small but inconvenient delay. He warned them it was still his intention to depart on this tide.

***

In the event, such was the evidence against him, it took the Russian Ambassador's full panoply of political influence to get him released after two miserable days under house arrest in a suite of rooms at the Dorchester.

***

For a large vessel to navigate safely down the River Thames, a river pilot must be present on the bridge. They board in London and disembark several miles down-river at a small riverside port called Gravesend, just down-river from the Queen Elizabeth Bridge. The drab annex of a town had the curious distinction of being the place where in 1617, the Native American Indian, Pocahontas, lived and died.

On this occasion two men, a pilot and his assistant had boarded. By the time they'd begun the journey down river only the pilot remained on the bridge.

It was a pleasant afternoon and the oligarch chose to spend his time relaxing in the rear sun lounge, the one where he greeted his most important guests. He was surprised and more than a little irritated to find one of the river pilots sitting there as comfortable as a king. A butler had already supplied him with a drink. He would talk to him about that later.

'This is a private area. I'm sure you would be happier in the crew canteen on the lower deck.' He waved his arm in a large sweep towards the stairway. 'Follow the stairs all the way down.'

The man stood up, but instead of leaving, he removed his cap and took off his bright yellow hi viz life-jacket. He cast it casually on the sofa and sat down again.

The intruder's crude disrespect angered Ulyanin, but as he moved closer he noticed the man's face. It looked familiar.

'Not so good to see you again, Ulyanin,' Stack said raising his glass.

'The bar of gold.' Ulyanin searched for a name, snapping his thumb and finger as it came to him. 'Stack!'

He went over to a nearby phone to call one of his henchmen.

'I'll remind you, Ulyanin, you're still in British territorial waters. I wouldn't do anything criminal if I were you.' Stack deliberately chose a provocative word.

'What do you want, Stack? I thought I'd seen the last of you.' Ulyanin said menacingly.

'I wanted to look into the face of the man who sent a killer into my hotel room. A very close friend only just survived.'

'I'm sorry to hear that. Of course, it has nothing to do with me. Why don't you call the police?'

Stack ignored him.

'Sit down. We're going to talk.'

'I have nothing to say to you. What can you possibly say

that would interest me?' The Russian said as he sat in the white leather sofa opposite.

Stack took another sip from the glass, placed it gently down on the low table in front of him. He leaned back slowly into the soft leather seat, his hands folded on his lap. He gave the impression of a man with all the time in the world.

'I know everything about the sabotage conspiracy, Ulyanin. Everything.'

The Russian sat there listening. Not saying anything.

Stack told the whole story root and branch. He tried to keep it short, but didn't want to leave out key detail. When he'd finished, the oligarch sniffed a short mirthless laugh.

'And you can prove this, how?'

'Yes, proof. I did wonder how we could pin it on you. What evidence led directly to your door?' Stack began reaching into his pocket.

'It's extraordinary how young these brilliant computer geniuses are these days. I know of one. He's, what, 20 years old? I won't tell you his name because...' Stacked laughed at the realisation, 'I don't actually know it. But I do know his handle. They love nicknames. This young dude has a really clever one.'

He pulled the tiny card out of his pocket and held it up.

'See this? I'm sure you recognise it. One of your companies designed it. Would you like to know where we found it? But of course, you already know. Your fellow saboteurs designed it. It's what gave you the confidence to go ahead with the hack.'

Nothing from Ulyanin. His eyes were transfixed on the card.

'We found it in the analogue to digital converter. This is how you communicated between the Severgaz Postavka offices in St. Petersburg and the GeoPower's computers in Hope Valley. It was a backdoor into the directional drilling systems. What you didn't know was how complete the addresses were in the link from your end. Most hacks get to their cyber destinations via lots of innocent proxy addresses to hide their trail and point of origin. But to hack into the GeoPower computer and maintain control over a long period you needed a more hard-wired route. What's on this card is an invitation to walk right through your front door. A flashing neon welcome sign.'

Stack leaned forward and held it for Ulyanin to examine, so he could clearly see the Cyrillic markings of the Russian alphabet on both sides. It bore the trade mark of one of his companies in one corner, just as Stack had said. He gave him just enough time to verify it, then sat back in his seat again.

'What do you want?' Ulyanin seemed resigned.

'The question is. What do you want, Mr Ulyanin? Gravesend is only minutes away. When I leave, the card leaves with me. There are others who would be delighted to get their hands on it.' Stack reached for his phone and held his thumb over the green button, ready to dial a pre-set number.

'I press this button and police will be called to meet you at Gravesend. You and this circuit-board.'

Silence fell between them. Ulyanin stood up and walked over to the side of the yacht. He stood there watching a coaster being unloaded in the small port they were passing. Ahead he noticed, was the towering Queen Elizabeth II bridge that linked the north and south carriageways of the M25 motorway. They would pass under it shortly. Just beyond that was Gravesend. He turned around to face Stack.'How much do you want?'

Grand Cayman

Short List met them as they walked through customs at Owen Roberts International Airport, Grand Cayman. Stack was surprised how pleased he was to see him. Despite his small windfall he was still driving the same beaten up old Toyota taxi.

Hotel bills had been settled shortly after the sale of the gold bullion and they were welcomed back like long lost cousins. Different rooms this time, but the views were just as spectacular.

'Meet you at the Tiki Bar in five,' Charlie said enthusiastically.

'Might be just a bit longer, Hollywood. I have a call to make.'

A '*call this number*' message had come through on the way into George Town. For good reason, Stack chose not to ignore it this time. This should be news of the share price.

Summer was unpacking her bag as Stack punched in the number. He walked to the floor-to-ceiling windows and slid one side open to the balcony as the call went through. Three rings as always.

Humid Caribbean air wafted into the room as Blackstone answered.

'Stack,' he said, imperious as ever.

What was it about Blackstone's voice that set his teeth on edge?

'You have something to tell me, Blackstone? Good news I hope.'

'Very good news. The failed borehole has been tested and the shale layer looks like it will yield far more gas than previously expected.'

'But they won't be using that well. They've closed it down.'

'Yes, and drilling is proceeding quickly and without problems on the new borehole.'

'So how is this good news, Blackstone?'

'As a result of the early tests, the share price has already started to rise. When the new well is completed we are expecting shares to hit record values. Your '*investment*', and that of my clients, will return far more than the original outlay. Congratulations, Mr Stack. And may I thank you for your work.'

'I didn't have much option did I, Blackstone.'

'Nonetheless, please pass on my thanks to Summer and Dawson.'

Blackstone's shameless facade of innocence left Stack breathless.

'I understand you made a little extra money. Something on the side?' Blackstone probed.

Stack didn't see why he shouldn't tell Blackstone about the Ulyanin deal.

He told him about the circuit board and the sizable amount Ulyanin paid for it. A payment made directly into Stack's Cayman Island account while he was on board the Eba.

'Very clever,' Blackstone said. 'Very enterprising Stack. You have never failed to impress me. Perhaps we shall work together again in the future?'

'Not likely, Blackstone. We're done.'

This time Stack red-buttoned the phone, ending the call before Blackstone could. Childish, but a small victory that put a smile on his face.

***

What he didn't tell Blackstone was that after the money had been transferred, Stack handed Ulyanin an identical card supplied by Mani-hack. It was a risk, but it played out well because as soon as the Russian laid his hands on it, he snapped it in two and threw it over board, confident the trail to him had disappeared into the muddy waters with it.

***

Stack threw the phone onto the bed, glad to be rid of it. Summer had changed into beachwear and was ready to go. They headed down to the Tiki Bar.

Charlie and Short List's laughter rang out across the sand as they approached, the cheerful sound of it adding to their relief to be back. Nothing could spoil this moment as they took their drinks from the bar and joined them.

Looked like Charlie had found some female company. Charlie introduced her. Madelene. She said to call her Maddie. A British accent. Quite posh. An odd choice for Charlie but she seemed nice. Summer wondered what she was doing alone in that part of the world?

'Nothing really. Just taking some R&R from a stressful job.'

'What kind of job?' Stack asked.

'Oh, you know. Advertising. Marketing. PR.'

Stack's radar pinged. It was one of those 'nothing to see here' kind of replies. He tried to ignore it. Charlie was back in Labrador puppy mode, mooning over her, just like he was when he first met Summer.

Up in the hotel room, Stack's cell phone rang.

Fact and Fiction

This book was never intended to be 'Fracking for Dummies'. But when I set out to write this yarn I had no idea how complicated hydraulic fracturing was. I don't think many people do.

Two drilling supervisors guided me as consultants during the course of writing: Gary Taylor and Robert Chadwick. Gary mostly drew diagrams and Robert tended to go for the science. They both offered thorough and kindly given advice. My problem eventually became an overwhelming surfeit of information.

I was keen the story should have a bedrock of truth. What I hope I've ended up with is a believable depiction of rig life, but with some of the technical detail (and many of the personnel) thinned out.

Both Gary and Robert thought the sabotage idea was extremely plausible. However, in reality, the number of safeguards both on a technical and human level would make it hard to pull off – but not impossible.

The location in which my fictional rig is sited exists. I've been there. Mam Tor is known locally as Shivering Mountain. It's at the western end of Hope Valley in the Peak District. At the other end is Rebellion Knoll – renamed Hill. It's enormous and just doesn't look like a knoll to me.

Does a geological fault exist below Mam Tor? Something must make it shiver.

Finally, no sides are taken. It's just a story.

About the Author

During a lengthy broadcasting career, which included many happy years as a DJ on Radio Luxembourg, Mark Wesley also enjoyed success and critical acclaim as a song writer and record producer.

Jingle composition and copy-writing for radio commercials followed, but his early love of film making led him to launch the production company Mark Wesley Productions.

His first novel *BANGK!* is a direct companion to *FRACK!* It's a hugely entertaining action thriller with a truly original plot and a mind-boggling con.

Now you've read *FRACK!* buy yourself a copy of *BANGK!* and see how it all began.